Praise for Rick Boyer
and his Doc Adams mysteries

YELLOW BIRD
"There's a lot to like about Doc Adams. . . . [He] is
easygoing and unpretentious."
—*The Washington Post Book World*

GONE TO EARTH
"Rick Boyer has the knack. . . . The action doesn't
slow down until the tank is good and empty."
—*The New York Times Book Review*

THE WHALE'S FOOTPRINTS
"The plot, especially the snippets of whale lore,
holds our attention. . . . But the real pleasure here,
as in Boyer's previous novels, is in identifying with
Doc Adams."

—*Booklist*

BILLINGSGATE SHOAL
"Rick Boyer writes with verve. Freshness in both
plot and place will keep you hanging on for the violent and ironic conclusion."
—*The San Diego Union*

PIRATE TRADE

Rick Boyer

IVY BOOKS • NEW YORK

for my hunting-fishing-writing friend
BILL TAPPLY,
a genuine Keeper
*

The author wishes to thank the following people for their generous help in the preparation of this book: Jackie Geyer, artist extraordinaire and animal rights activist from Pittsburgh, whose ideas formed the basic premise of the story. John and Bruce Boyer and Deanne Smith, for their tireless help on the MS in all stages. Robert Buckner, DDS; Paul Tescione, DDS; and Robert Scully, DDS, MS; for their expertise and advice on the technical aspects of oral surgery. Major Bill Rawls and Jeanne Ye, for their help on the deadly arts. And these old-time S.F.'ers as well: Captain Tommy Daniels, Captain Pat McAfee, and SFC Isaac Welch, all of the 5th Group.

Ivy Books
Published by Ballantine Books
Copyright © 1995 by Richard L. Boyer

Library of Congress Catalog Card Number: 94-96289

ISBN 0-8041-0612-6

Manufactured in the United States of America

First Edition: February 1995

10 9 8 7 6 5 4 3 2 1

Lightship Purse

MOST PEOPLE MAY NOT HAVE HEARD OF THE FAMOUS NANtucket lightships, those red-hulled, twin-bowed, stubby vessels that were semipermanently moored over the treacherous Nantucket Shoals. They have two masts, each with a powerful signal light. In the old days the men who tended these ships were forced to spend weeks away from friends, family, and loved ones, often enduring sustained squalls, heavy seas, and the endless blasts of the overhead foghorns. Not fun.

To make this life somewhat more bearable, they engaged in various hobbies, such as board games, cards, crossword puzzles, shortwave radio, and the making of various objects such as ship models.

The most famous of their handcrafted items is an object of delicacy and grace, and the very last thing one would expect to emerge from the callused, gnarled hands of a deepsea sailor: a basket of woven reeds. These keepsakes were painstakingly made for sweethearts and wives waiting on the mainland. Of small to medium size and made with a special type of rattan, each basket is fashioned over a wooden mold, and each piece of reed is stretched and woven over this mold with all the strength a seaman's knotty forearms are capable of.

Sometime in the 1950s, a man named José Reyes made a handsome and functional variation of these baskets: he fitted a woven lid to them, put leather hinges on one side

1

and a leather latch on the other, and voilà: the lightship purse was born.

Traditionally, the most interesting feature of these purses was the medallion on the center of the lid: an ivory oval—generally a cross section of walrus tusk—engraved with sharp instruments and filled with ink, intaglio style, to represent a maritime scene or decoration. In short: scrimshaw.

These purses are expensive; Reyes's originals go for three grand and up. I know this because on a solo sail to Nantucket island last August, I found myself outside McQuaid's gift shop on Main Street, staring into the window at these beautiful purses, knowing Mary really wanted one. When I went inside, I was told that even with the international furor over the ivory trade, the original scrimshaw ivory oval decoration on the lid was still genuine ivory.

"But how can that be, when ivory's been banned in most of the world?" I asked.

"Because," said Ian McQuaid, the owner, "the ivory we sell is either fossilized ivory—ivory that's thousands of years old—or ivory that comes from stocks imported before the ban went into effect."

"So this is real ivory, and still legal?"

"Absolutely."

I pulled out the shiny gold card with the holograph in the corner.

"And this one is . . . how much?"

"Eighteen ninety-five."

"Uh, as in two figures, or four figures?"

He gave a merry laugh as he ran my card through the machine, and I took off in the light drizzle toward the harbor, and my little sloop-rigged catboat, the *Ella Hatton*. Expensive, to be sure, but then, it was for Mary, my wife of almost thirty years, and the mother of our two beloved sons. Why not?

I carried the treasure, wrapped in tissue, a box, and finally a waterproof plastic bag, close to my chest as I walked along the wet cobblestones of the old whaling port. When I got aboard the boat, I placed it in the mahogany shelf above Mary's bunk, waited out the bad weather, and departed early the next morning. The air was clear and bright; there was a stiff breeze that would carry me back to Cape Cod before nightfall.

If I'd had even the remotest inkling of all the trouble, danger, and heartache that damn purse would cause all of us in the following months, I would have flung it over the side and been done with it.

And cheap at the price!

1

A FEW WEEKS LATER, ON A CHILLY AFTERNOON IN SEPTEMBER, I was sitting in the sunporch of our house in Concord, Massachusetts, certainly the prettiest place to be in the fall. I had just turned on the NFL game to watch the Chicago Bears. As a born-and-bred midwesterner, I do like to watch the Bears and the Bulls every now and then when I have the chance. And today was extra special: the Bears were playing their oldest rivals, the Green Bay Packers. I settled back with a half-liter mug of German lager, lighted my pipe, and adjusted the volume.

Two minutes after kickoff Mary poked her head inside the door and said: "Charlie, there's a man here to see us."

I paused and eyed her wearily, warily. "On Sunday afternoon? Unannounced? Right at kickoff?"

"He's from the U.S. Department of Fish and Wildlife."

"So, what's he want? I buy hunting and fishing licenses. We give to the World Wildlife Fund, Nature Conservancy, Ducks Unlimited, Trout Unlimited—"

"It's not that. Remember the beautiful lightship purse

you gave me? Well, I never told you this, but to me, the ivory on the top looked genuine, but not old enough. Remember I was telling you about fossilized ivory?"

"Yeah ... the salesman mentioned it to me. He said that was the only legal kind nowadays, except for some that was imported before the ban ... or something like that. Hey, is this something you learned from that jewelry-making class you took?"

"That, and also my involvement in CapeWatch."

"You mean Bill and Sally's group?"

"Yep."

CapeWatch was a recently organized environmentalist group headquartered in Hyannis. Bill and Sally Bedford, who operated a marina, boat brokerage, and sportfishing charter service had founded it two years ago.

"The thing about the ivory was in some of the pamphlets Sally gave me last month, when I was down at her shop with Jackie," she continued.

"And?"

"Well, I read through the stuff pretty carefully, and the ivory on that purse—I mean it's beautiful, Charlie—but ... I don't think it's old enough. We studied ivory pretty closely in that class, and this looks too new to me."

"And so you sent this guy who's at the front door to check it out?"

"Well, sure. We don't want to participate in the illegal ivory trade, do we?"

"Of course we don't," I answered. But then I was thinking: What if this environmentalist cop nabs the purse? What then? But I held my tongue.

"You think the ivory on the purse isn't old enough? So maybe it's illegal?"

She nodded. "Sure doesn't look like it to me. I called Sally first, and she suggested I call the local office of the Fish and Wildlife—they're the ones chiefly involved in the enforcement of this kind of thing and ... and they said they'd send somebody around to see it. So he's here."

"Who's here?"

"A Mr. Brad Taylor. Here to see the purse."

I sat up in my chair, ignoring Al Michaels and Merlin

Olsen trying to work the TV audience into a frenzy during the pregame hype.

"Well, fine, but I sure hope he doesn't take it. I mean, it's not exactly something you get at the five-and-dime."

"No. I think he's just here to visit. He knows Joe; he seems like a nice guy."

"Well, let's see what he has to say," I said, getting out of the chair and flicking off the TV.

The man who came inside was medium height, dressed in khaki slacks and a brown corduroy sport jacket, blue work shirt, no tie. He had iron-gray hair, a tan face with no fat, and looked as if he spent most of his time outdoors. Seeing him on the street, I would have pegged him as a college coach.

"Dr. Adams? I am very sorry to bother both of you on a Sunday afternoon. I suppose you were about to watch the NFL game. . . ."

"Actually, yes."

"My name is Brad Taylor," he said, extending his hand, which I shook. Firm, dry, cool, callused. "Would you mind if I sat with you and your wife in front of the TV for, say, less than ten minutes and explained why I'm here? I promise I'll shut up during the plays."

"Deal," I said. "You want some beer?"

"That would hit the spot."

So, in a minute or so there we were on the sunporch, watching Al Michaels and Merlin Olsen hobnob during the pregame show. Brad Taylor took two large swallows of the Spatenbrau and registered his appreciation.

"You sure you should drink on duty?" Mary asked.

Taylor laughed, and almost choked on his beer. "This is my day off, just like normal people. I talked with your brother, Mrs. Adams, Friday afternoon about this business I'll mention. He seemed supportive, so I'm out here now to briefly tell you about this, and maybe ask for your help."

"You mean Charlie's help? He's the one who usually—"

"No, Mrs. Adams—"

"You can call me Mary."

"Uh, Mary . . . I think it's your help we need."

I settled the heavy mug on the table and leaned forward. This was getting interesting, whatever it was.

"Here it is. I work for the U.S. Fish and Wildlife Service. A twenty-year veteran. It might interest you to know that one of my close friends and working colleagues is a friend of yours—Larry Carpenter."

We both lit up. Who didn't love Larry Carpenter? An old school chum from Iowa, and friend for life, too. Mary beamed. "So how is he, the old stud? Gee, it would be nice to see him again, right Charlie?"

I nodded.

"He's been working for us in Seattle for the past several years, but I think you'll both get to see him again real soon . . . if you want."

"Hell, I didn't even know he was working for the government," I said, trying to get all the pieces of the past to fit together neatly. This, as we know, gets a tad harder as we age. "The last time I saw Larry he was still painting houses in Bucks County, PA."

Brad Taylor turned to us and grinned. "A lot's happened since then, but it is strange that we should come together this way, in between your brother Joe, a state detective, and your old friend Larry Carpenter. Mary, Joe tells me that lately you've been devoting some time to environmental causes. Endangered species, wildlife preservation funds . . . things like that."

"Now that the kids are gone and I'm only nursing one or two days a week, I was looking for something to take up the slack. Have you heard of CapeWatch?"

Brad Taylor nodded. "I know Bill and Sally Bedford. It's a small group, but it's a start. Joe says you've been volunteering at Drumlin Farm and the Children's Museum."

"Right. I'm giving them talks about ecology and the preservation of habitat. Stuff like that. But mostly, it's with CapeWatch and the Stellwagen Bank project. I guess I got the impetus from our oldest son, Jack, who's down at Woods Hole studying whale behavior."

"I see," said Taylor.

She paused, knitted her brows, and looked at Mr. Taylor out of the corner of her eye. "Hey, is this an antihunting crusade? Because if it is, then Charlie won't like it."

He shook his head. "Nope. I hunt myself. So do most of

the people in this line of work. No, I work to stop illegal hunting—poaching and trapping of endangered species."

"Then this ought to be interesting," she said. "So you heard from somebody that I made a telephone call about something Charlie bought for me in Nantucket, right?"

"Right. And yes, we're familiar with these lightship purses. The vast majority of them are legal. If it's not too much trouble, though, I'd like to see yours before I leave. Joe also thought I ought to show you some literature about the Fish and Wildlife Service, and what we do."

He took some brochures from his coat pocket and handed them to Mary, who sat on the couch flipping through them.

"Okay," said Al Michaels, "Green Bay wins the toss; they elect to receive. . . ."

Then a strange thought hit me: Why is he showing this stuff to Mary, instead of both of us? I glanced at Brad Taylor, who was sipping his beer, his eyes glued to the tube, his face impassive.

"Well, it looks interesting," Mary said. "I'm sure you and your bunch—including Larry—are doing the right kinds of things."

"We'd hoped you'd say that." Taylor grinned. "Because from what Joe says about you, you just might be the person we've been looking for."

"For what?" she asked.

"To work for us."

"It's a high, wobbly kick by Jensen," shouted Michaels from the tube. "Watch out; this could be trouble!"

2

I was still confused when Mary brought the purse downstairs and gave it to Taylor, who examined the ivory medallion on the lid carefully.

"Well, you have a hell of an eye, I'll say that, Mrs. Adams."

"Call me Mary. So I was right; that ivory on the lid is illegal."

"No, I didn't say that for sure. What I'd like to do, with your permission, is to take this back to the office and have the medallion removed carefully and sent to our lab in Ashland, Oregon."

"You've got a lab?"

"Yes, a very sophisticated one at that. They can determine if this is old enough to be legal. Frankly, I agree it looks like fresh ivory."

Taylor rubbed the piece with the tip of his finger and peered at it again with the aid of a lens he took from his pocket. "Offhand, I'd say this was taken from a live animal within a year. If so, we do indeed have illegal ivory, and we'll take steps to close in on McQuaid's shop."

"What would you do to them," I asked, "close them down?"

"No—we'd make a few more buys, and try to get the transaction on tape. Then we can use this evidence, and the threat of prosecution, to get them to tell us where they got these pieces."

"Well, what McQuaid told me was the ivory was legal because it was supposedly imported before the ivory ban. That make sense?"

"Uh-huh," murmured Taylor, idly watching two Goliaths in Bears' uniforms put the super kibosh on an unfortunate lad wearing the Packers' yellow and green. "That's the line all the shops give."

Two hours later, after the Bears had walloped Green Bay, Brad (I was calling him Brad now and he was calling me Doc) pushed himself away from the coffee table, on which lay the remnants of Mary's homemade lasagna and Greco-Romaine salad, and staggered to his feet.

"Jeez, that's the best meal I've had in ages. . . ."

"Brad, when will I get my purse back?"

"I'll try to get it back after the trial. Assuming, of course, there is a trial." He brushed the bread crumbs off khaki pants. "That's why I came here looking for your help."

"Just mine? Why not mine and Charlie's?"

I looked at Brad, anxious to know why I'd been excluded.

He turned to me. "Doc, you may not know this, but you've become a bit too well-known around here to be useful in undercover work. Talking with your brother-in-law for only a few minutes confirmed what I thought. Your past exploits have caught up with you."

"Well, I didn't plan on it. I'm just one of those poor jamokes who keep stepping into doo-doo. Did you say undercover work?"

"It's an idea I've got that I've mentioned to Joe, and Larry Carpenter as well. It's a bit involved, so I don't want to go into the details just yet. Why I came over today was to sort of feel you two out—see if there was a possibility of getting this plan off the ground. I must say that so far, everything seems perfect. That is, if Mary agrees to help."

"You want me to go undercover for you? To work as a secret agent for the Wildlife Service?"

"Well, I—"

"Oh boy!"

Brad held up a cautionary hand. "No, not as dangerous—or as glamorous—as that. But we would like to use you, on a voluntary basis, to make some buys at various places. Just think about it for now. Then tomorrow afternoon, or whenever it's convenient, I'd like both of you to come over to the Federal Building and watch a film, meet some of the staff, and tell me what you think. I'll arrange to have Joe there, too, if possible. Hey, thanks for the great meal Mary, Doc. Don't worry, I'll take good care of this little baby." He patted the lightship purse and tucked it under his arm, then headed for his car.

"Wow!" Mary sighed. "Undercover for the Fish and Wildlife Service. Can you believe it, Charlie?"

"I don't know if I do," I answered. "Or if I even want to."

3

THE NEXT DAY AT THREE, AFTER I WAS FINISHED WITH MY LAST patient, we went into Boston as scheduled and met Brad at his office at the Fish and Wildlife Service, New England Regional Headquarters. When we walked in, we got a surprise: Joe was there, too, showing his typical purplish-black five o'clock shadow. He lighted a Benson and Hedges and let the smoke trickle out his nose.

"Why aren't you out on a murder case," I asked, "or over at headquarters grilling somebody like you're supposed to?"

"Why aren't you pulling teeth, Doc? Listen, I came here as a favor to Mary. You've come to find out about this, I see. Hope it works out."

Mary and I sat down and looked at the two of them.

"You guys in cahoots or something?" Mary asked.

Joe dipped his ash and crossed his legs. "Here's what happened. Brad had some people over on Nantucket staking out that gift shop most of the summer. So when Mary called him, somehow during their conversation it came out that she's my sister. Since Brad and I have known each other for years, I let him in on your recent activities, Mary. You and that couple—what's his name down in Hyannis— the boat guy?"

"William Bedford," she said. "You know—Big Bill Bedford's Boatyard and Sea Charter Service?"

"Oh, yeah. I still think it's funny that a boat dealer is sponsoring so much environmental stuff. . . ."

"He didn't do it for lofty reasons, Joe," I said. "Bill's a realist. He makes his living from sportfishing. The way things are shaping up in our offshore waters, there just won't be any of it left in a decade unless somebody cleans it up. Bill joined the environmental movement because he wants to stay in business."

"Yeah, yeah, yeah. I know. Anyway, we were talking over lunch about how you're into all this stuff, and Brad happened to mention that for some time now he's been looking for people to do some buying. I told him you're a Brindelli, which means you've got the smarts, the guts, the looks, the—what's wrong, Doc?"

"Nothing."

"Nothing, eh? Then how come you're sitting there with your arms crossed, leaning back and looking at the ceiling? That's body language for 'I don't want any part of this.' "

"Well, maybe I'm not so keen on this idea of Mary going undercover."

There was a bit of a silence in the office, broken by Brad Taylor, who suggested that we all watch the wildlife film, then discuss the details. We adjourned from the office and went down the hall to a small auditorium, really a large room with folding chairs set up in three rows of four chairs each. We sat down, the lights went out, and the projector went on. Then we saw the title of the film flash on the screen:

PIRATE TRADE
The War Against Wildlife Poaching
A Presentation of the U.S. Fish and Wildlife Service

The film lasted about forty-five minutes. It began with a
brief history of the service and the various tasks performed
by the people in it. The role of the federal game wardens
seemed to be the most interesting, and dangerous as well,
especially when the agents went undercover, posing as tro-
phy collectors or international businessmen engaged in
smuggling. One story featured an agent in the mountains of
North Carolina buying and selling illegally acquired gall-
bladders from the black bear. He eventually gathered
enough evidence to put three men behind bars. I thought
this was dandy, but the film didn't mention what would
have happened to this government hero if the poachers had
discovered his true identity.

There were other stories, too. One covered the busting of
a fish-smuggling ring that shipped two tons of illegally
caught white perch a week from a lake in Louisiana to
cities like Chicago and St. Louis. There were all kinds of
poaching and smuggling operations that had been shut
down: elk, moose, black and brown bear, salmon, alligators,
beaver, seals of all kinds, and so on.

But the most grisly of all the rings was one operating out
of Alaska, in the Bering Sea.

The section opened with a shot of four Eskimos at sea in
a skin boat, approaching an ice shelf a half mile away. Affixed to the stern of this boat was an outboard motor. The
boat plowed through the frigid swells toward the ice. Soon
brown specks were visible on the ice: basking walrus, perhaps twenty of them. As the boat drew near, the animals
began to squirm and flop around . . . some managed to slip
off the ice and into the water, but most weren't that lucky.
Suddenly rifles appeared in the hands of the Eskimos. They
were automatic rifles; AK-47 assault rifles. The film
showed the men firing point-blank at the big, wrinkly
beasts. Bright brass shell casings flew everywhere as the
men emptied their magazines. The walruses died on the
spot. Some were severely wounded but managed to escape

to the water. I was certain, by the way they'd been hit, that they would die slowly later on.

"Oh God, Charlie! How could they? This is awful!" Mary held her hand up to her mouth and kept trying to turn her head away, but was riveted by the horror of it.

"We thought this part might get to you, Mare," said Joe, putting his big brown hand on her shoulder. "Hang on, kid; it gets worse."

The men rammed the boat up on the ice and three of them jumped out, leaving one behind to mind the motor. The three gunmen slaughtered the remaining walrus, then took out hatchets and knives. In less than a few minutes, they had beheaded the animals and tossed the bloody heads, complctc with tusks, into thc boat. Then they shoved as many of the huge corpses as possible into the sea, perhaps to cover up the deed. But five or six huge old bulls remained, headless and bloody, on the ice floe. The men in the boat shoved off, leaving the red-stained ice behind. The film ended.

"Don't tell me. . . ." Mary said. "Please don't tell me that the ivory on my lightship purse came from . . . from that!" She pointed a shaking finger at the dark screen.

"Could be," said Brad. "We'll know for sure when we hear from the lab in Ashland. And Joe and I had a hunch you might react this way. That's why we think you're a good bet to work for us. Don't worry; it won't be as dangerous as the adventures you just saw. I suppose most of this work will consist of simply walking into shops in major cities, buying things with government money."

"Do I get to keep the items?"

"Of course not, Mary," Joe growled. "Brad's doing it to gather evidence, for chrissakes. So we can put these sharpshooters out of business."

"I was just curious."

"You'll probably be wearing a wire during these buys. Does that bother you?"

"A wire? Wearing a wire?"

"A hidden microphone and recording device, concealed on your person," Brad explained. "I thought you would know what a wire is, hanging around Joe. . . ."

"Well, I don't use 'em. The guys in OC use them a lot."

"OC? What's that?" I asked.

"Organized Crime. Well, Mare, whadduyah think?"

"I think I'd probably like to give it a try."

"Hey, don't I get any say in this?"

They all looked at me. It was as if they'd forgotten I was even there.

"Well," she said, "I'd like your feelings on this, Charlie, but I think it's really my decision."

"Well," said Brad Taylor with a slight twinkle in his eye, "here's something that may help you make up your mind, Mary."

He went to a door on the other side of the room and opened it.

A man walked in, and Mary gasped. I confess that I, too, gasped, but perhaps for different reasons.

Larry Carpenter hadn't changed much in the twelve years since we'd seen him. Handsome, of course. The son of a bitch gets handsomer every year. We were the same age: early fifties. He looked maybe thirty-five, with no gray hair. Dark skin, bright turquoise eyes. Six four and a half, with the sinewy, wide-shouldered build of a great athlete, which he was.

"Hey, Mary!" Larry caught her in his arms and hugged her, lifting her off the floor. "Hey, Doc, shit, it's good to see you!" He came over and hugged me, too. I guess I hugged him back.

"Sure, Larry ... great ..."

"Well, whadduyah think, Mary Adams? We're the newest undercover team for the Fish and Wildlife Service!" said Larry with a wide grin. "Isn't that something!"

I looked at Mary. She was looking up into Larry Carpenter's clean-chiseled, movie-star face. She was beaming.

Beaming like I hadn't seen her beam in years.

4

I WALKED INTO DR. MORRIS ABRAMSON'S OFFICE THE NEXT afternoon. I was not in the best of moods and Moe—my closest friend and a professional reader of people's minds—knew it right away.

"So what's wrong wid you? I don't like the way you look today."

"Brilliant, Moe. Well, I don't like the way I feel today. So there."

"You wanna sit down and talk?"

"Yes."

"No chess? No complaints about my new fish?"

Moe Abramson is famous for a couple other things besides being an extraordinary psychiatrist who gives most of his money to charities and lives humbly on the banks of Walden Pond in his ancient Airstream trailer: a modern-day Thoreau. He is also a fantastic chess player, who can beat most folks blindfolded. Needless to say, he trounces me on a regular basis in this game. He is also notorious for keeping marine fish, and dotes on the ugliest of these, the cast-offs of the fishy world: bottom feeders, eels, loaches, skates, all those nasty, prehistoric-looking things with bulbous eyes, snaggly teeth, raspy tongues, gaping vents, and twitchy whiskers. For Moe, the more repulsive the creature, the more he's for it. Now he pointed to his newest acquisition: a swaying miniature palm tree in the middle of a twenty-gallon tank.

15

"Not too bad," I said. "Looks prettier than most of your friends."

"Watch," he said, giving the tank a sharp rap with his knuckles. Instantly, the top of the palm tree disappeared into the trunk, which writhed ominously. Then, slowly, one by one, the "branches" of the tree came slithering out again. Then I noticed that the "leaves" of each arm wriggled and twitched, and pulled back in little jerks and spasms. This was not a palm tree; this was some kind of horrid marine worm.

"Oh Jesus, spare me," I groaned, grabbing my midsection.

"It's called a Medusa worm," said Moe proudly.

"Well, you're sick, Moe. Sick, sick, sick."

"You don't look so good yourself, Doc. Have a bit too much to drink last night?"

"I suppose so. Mary and I are . . . having troubles."

"Uh-oh. Tell me about it. Here, sit down."

I sat down in one of Moe's belting leather Eames chairs and faced him. Fortunately, the tank was behind me. But the thought of that monstrous worm made me uneasy. Could it by chance crawl out of the tank and up the back of my neck?

"So, what's going on?" he demanded, poised in his own chair, notebook in hand.

"Ditch the notebook, Moe, and just listen."

"Fine. So go ahead."

The chair felt too comfortable. I realized I was exhausted.

"I want first of all to tell you the story of my old friend Larry Carpenter, who was born and raised on a hog farm just outside of Marshalltown, Iowa."

"What's he got to do with—"

"Shut up and listen. When I enrolled in the University of Iowa back in the late fifties, Larry was on my dorm floor, just down the hall. All the freshmen knew Larry because he played varsity football, as a freshman. He weighed around two-twenty then, and played halfback. But by his sophomore year he had moved up to quarterback. He was sickeningly handsome, too. We all liked to hang around Larry because whenever you went anywhere with this guy, there was always a flock of women following. Made you feel good."

"Sounds like quite a guy."

"Uh-huh, and nice as hell, too. The most good-natured, humble guy you'd ever meet. Didn't have a mean thing to say about anyone. He was nice to the geeks and the nerds on the floor, treating them the same as his friends. But the amazing thing was, he was also valedictorian of his high-school class. Turns out he was a National Merit Scholarship winner. He never paid a cent for tuition, room, or board; he had a double scholarship, one for academics, one for athletics. I found out later from his parents that several other schools, including Harvard, Dartmouth, and Johns Hopkins, had offered him similar deals. But he liked Iowa, and wanted to be near his family. He was one of six kids. Nice family. We became close friends because we joined the same fraternity, and on several occasions, during long weekends, I took Larry home with me to Chicago. He loved the museums and the lakefront. I entered the premed program, and Larry was in prelaw. We sort of fell out of touch after graduation, when I went to med school at Northwestern, and he went to law school at Yale."

I paused for a second to get my pipe out and began to fill it.

"Doc, no smoking in dis office. Don't you remember?"

"Well, I want to. I'm upset. Anyway, I lost track of Larry and didn't see him again until I was doing my residency at Mass General. By then he had joined some hotshot law firm in New York, and quit."

"Quit? Why?"

"Couldn't stand being a lawyer, said it was too adversarial. Too combative. I guess this happens to a lot of people, especially those who are naturally kind and idealistic."

"And this Larry is such a person?"

"Oh, yes. Very much so. He just hates to hurt people in any way, shape, or form. You know that after Iowa several pro football teams scouted him and offered him contracts. Now, you have to remember that back in those days, before the sixties, the money wasn't anything like it is nowadays. I doubt if he'd refuse a million-dollar contract now, but he turned these teams down. Said he was tired of hitting people."

"So what did he finally do?"

"He lived up to his family name; he became a carpenter."

"You're kidding."

"Well, a handyman, which is a painter, carpenter, gardener, right? After Wall Street he went back to the family farm and worked there awhile, helping his brothers and sisters. He liked it so much he decided then and there on a career that would allow him to work outdoors. I forgot to mention that Larry's passions, besides excelling in everything without apparent effort, are hunting and fishing."

"Wait," said Moe, holding up his hand. "I thought he didn't like to hurt anybody. Then why does he kill fish and animals?"

"I don't think it's the same thing."

"Why not?"

"Because people have hunted and fished for millennia. We are hunter-gatherers, Moe, like it or not."

"I don't like it."

"I know, and you're one of the few people I can respect for it because you don't eat meat of any kind. The people I can't stand are the ones who scold hunters, then go down to Star Market and buy two pounds of ground chuck or fresh rack of baby lamb."

"So, he liked to hunt and fish, and work outdoors. Then, I assume, he did these things?"

"Yep. He left the farm in the late sixties and became what we New Englanders call a handyman. Mary and I saw him pretty regularly here and there. He lived up in Vermont for a while. But what surprised us was, he always seemed to have plenty of money. He drove Volvos, went on several vacations a year, always owned a nice place with lots of land in the country—whether it was Vermont or Bucks County—he seemed pretty well-fixed."

"Well, maybe he didn't spend a lot of his money on silly things, like clothes and booze and women."

"Yeah . . . clothes are silly, aren't they? Anyway, something I wanted to mention first is about this guy's general health and constitution. You see, he was never sick, for one thing."

"Never? C'mon, Doc!"

"Okay, he did get sick once in the Iowa dorms, but that's because there was a serious case of food poisoning. I personally remember puking my guts out, and several of the kids on my hall were hospitalized. But he never had colds or the flu, never had the childhood diseases of mumps, chicken pox, measles—"

"He better be careful; they're no treat when you get them as an adult."

"He got vaccinated later, but his family always figured he had a natural immunity to these things. By the way, both his parents are still alive, and one grandfather—his mother's dad—who's over a hundred. Old man Zinghoffer—I only met him once, but he was pretty unforgettable."

"So you're saying he comes from healthy stock. That's nice. But so do you, Doc, if I recall."

"Uh-huh. But Larry was different. Way, way above the ordinary in health and vigor. He never wore glasses. Still doesn't, not even for reading."

"That's almost unheard of, when you're over forty your eyes—"

"Yeah, most of our eyes, but not Larry's. His teeth are amazing; has yet to get his first cavity. Once we went to give blood in college. Two weeks later Larry got a call from the local blood bank. They said they had a source who would pay him fifty bucks a pint for his blood . . . and that was thirty years ago!"

"What was so special about his blood?"

"Everything. I hadn't studied hematology then, but I would guess it is one of the rare and desirable bloods we read about in journals."

"Wow. And smart, too?"

"Brilliant. I found out later that he scored over a hundred and sixty on several standardized IQ tests."

Moe gave a low whistle. "Uh . . . truly exceptional."

There was a pause while I went over to the watercooler to get a glass of Moe's special springwater. The kind that tastes like rotten eggs and tin cans, and is supposed to be good for you. He lives on this stuff, and his blue milk. About three times a year he'll have a beer. Hey, live it up.

I went back to the chair. It felt cozy. Too cozy. That's when I realized I was in bad shape.

"Where was I?" I asked, lying down again. I could lie there all day. Early signs of depression.

"Talking about Larry's incredible genetics."

"That's exactly right, Moe. Genetics. When you think about it, every conception is a crapshoot. The fetus inherits roughly half its genes from each parent. But which ones, and in which paired combinations?"

"There are millions and millions of possibilities," he said.

"Right, sort of like a slot machine. You put in the coin and pull the lever. Those three wheels whirl 'round and 'round. Most of the time you lose the coin. Sometimes you get a few coins out the bottom. Big deal; that only makes up for some you've lost and allows you to play a bit longer, making you think your luck is changing. But every now and then—not too often—every now and then the wheels do the impossible and the machine comes up all gold bars."

"Jackpot."

"Exactly. Jackpot. And there is such a thing as the genetic jackpot. Mind you, the inputs must be good. That is, the parents, and the gene pool that you're dealing with should be generally good and free of defects. Like some of the obvious hereditary diseases and susceptibilities."

"Uh-huh, like diabetes, schizophrenia, hemophilia, heart disease—"

"Right."

"And you think your friend Larry hit the jackpot."

"No. His parents hit the jackpot, Moe. Larry *is* the jackpot."

"Gold bars . . . all gold bars . . ."

"Remember Walter Payton, played for the Bears? The greatest football player who ever lived. Period. A natural. And no dummy, either. You can't play today's pro ball the way he did and not be lightning-quick upstairs. Payton was another jackpot. So is Michael Jordan. Maybe Ted Williams, too. But let me tell you—there are precious few of them. Most of us, even us generally bright and healthy

specimens, have some flaws in our makeup which will
reveal themselves as we age. You, for example, are nuts,
Moe. And getting nuttier each day. Be that as it may, I like
you anyway."

He turned to stare at me.

"If I am crazy, then why am I a psychiatrist, trying to
help people from being crazy?"

"Simple. First—it takes one to know one. Second—life
is full of ironies."

He sighed. "Doc, I'm simply trying, in this brief life, to
do the next right thing."

"Well, the next right thing for you to do is to kill Larry
Carpenter. I'd do it myself, but they'd suspect me."

He stared at me again, shocked.

"What? I thought you liked this guy. Thought he was
perfect."

"He is. That's why I'm ... why I'm ..."

"Scared?"

It was several seconds before I nodded my head.

"Thought so. Aggression in any form is almost always a
sign of fear. Lorenz correctly identifies most mean behavior
as *Angst Beissen*."

"What?"

"German for 'fear biting.' Aggression is an outgrowth of
fear, or, on a deeper level, insecurity. Still, Doc, I don't see
why it's justified in your case."

"Oh, you don't, eh? Well then, let me finish my story.
My little tale about Larry the Wonderkid. Larry the Genetic
Jackpot. Remember I mentioned that despite his rather laid-
back lifestyle, he always seemed to have plenty of money?"

"I remember. I assume his parents are well-fixed."

"They are, but remember, there are six Carpenter kids.
No, Larry Carpenter was not only genetically blessed with
a flawless body and brilliant mind, he also has that rarest of
all commodities."

"Which is?"

"Common sense."

"Ahhhh, yes. How true. We often forget this."

"Larry instinctively knew that being a Wall Street lawyer, no matter the prestige and big bucks, was going to be
detrimental to him in the long run. What would have taken

most of us nitwits half a lifetime to figure out, he saw in
a twinkling."

"And so, he quit the high-pressure job. That makes
sense. But it still doesn't answer the question of his income,
which you seem to think is plentiful."

"I know. And I think that's the other thing that's bothering me."

5

"THERE WAS A RUMOR THAT CIRCULATED BRIEFLY AMONG LAR-
ry's friends just after we graduated from Iowa," I continued. "He got his girlfriend Nancy pregnant that summer.
Accidentally. He was willing to marry her. In fact, he told
me later, he really loved her, or thought so at the time. But
this woman had been around the block a few times—she
was basically less innocent than Larry was. While fond of
him, she was a pioneer in the new woman's alternative life-
styles thing. She said she wanted to have the baby, but not
marry. Fine, Larry said, and volunteered to help out financially, which he did. So, nine months later she gave birth to
a gorgeous daughter. Anyway, everything was working just
fine, when a friend of Nancy's noticed the baby and fell in
love with it."

Moe looked up at me, confused. "Where's this going?"

"Just wait. Well anyway, here's where the rumor came
in. This second woman was a lot like Nancy—she didn't
want marriage and a husband, just a wonderful baby. Well,
supposedly, the upshot was, she contacted Larry on the sly

and asked him if he was interested in providing her with a baby."

"And . . . ?"

"Well, the rumor went, Larry refused, saying that one kid was all he could support. But it seems this woman was rich. Apparently, she not only promised him in writing she would support the child on her own, but would reward Larry with a rather handsome stud fee to boot."

Moe snorted. "Sounds like bullshit to me, Doc."

"I guess I agree," I said, stretching my aching body in the easy chair. "But the rumor persisted. And I know a certain rich young woman who did have a baby boy at just about the right time, and remained single. Of course I asked Larry about it, and he denied it."

"So? I think he was telling the truth. I mean, nowadays there are sperm banks for women who want to get pregnant."

"Uh-huh, but this rumor . . . you know, I think it persisted for a while because Larry is basically so appealing. I mean, wouldn't a woman rather see, and meet, the man who would sire her child instead of simply reading a description of the donor on a label. Know what I mean?"

Moe stood up and paced the floor softly. "Hmmmph!"

"I agree entirely. It's probably just a bullshit rumor. But still . . . where does Larry get the money for his lifestyle? I doubt it comes from that farm in Marshalltown, Iowa. And I know it doesn't come from the Fish and Wildlife Service."

"He works for the Fish and Wildlife people? That sounds like a good job."

"It is, but it doesn't pay a lot."

Moe sat and rubbed his palms together reflectively. Then he stroked his chin. His high, straight forehead, made more pronounced by his thinning hair, glowed in the light.

"So why did you bring up this story, Doc? I don't get it. You come in here all upset, and then you tell me all about Larry Carpenter, who seems to be a great guy—on the surface, at least; we don't really know—and finish off with this rumor, which probably has no foundation in fact. So why are you so upset, and why did you say you wish I would murder him?"

"Because," I said, lacing my fingers together behind my neck and stretching my legs, "Larry Carpenter is going to be working closely, and alone, with Mary for the next few months."

"So?"

"*So?* Whadduyah mean, *so*? I don't want this. I don't want my wife working in other towns with Mr. Superhuman, is what."

"You mean you don't trust her?"

"I didn't say that; I just don't like it. You wouldn't like it either."

"And that's the element of insecurity, of fear on your part. You're afraid she'll fall in love with him."

"Or fall into bed with him."

"I don't think so."

"Well, I hope not, but I just don't like it, Moe. Admit it—you wouldn't like it either."

"Maybe this is a test of your maturity, Doc. Also, if I recall correctly, and I usually do, haven't you been guilty of a few . . . indiscretions in past years?"

"What? Absolutely not."

"How about going after Janice DeGroot?"

"I never 'went' after Janice DeGroot."

"How about that time in the phone booth at your Christmas party?"

"A simple misunderstanding."

"How about that time you were swimming naked with her down at Woods Hole? Mary herself told me about that."

"*She* was swimming naked, Moe. I was fully clothed. I finally jumped into Eel Pond to save her; I thought she was drowning."

"Well, what about the time down in South Carolina when you were hanging around with that young lady who worked at the snack shop?"

"She was helping me locate somebody, that's all."

"Mary said she found this young lady's beach bag in your motel room. It had all kinds of sexy woman's underwear in it. New underwear that you had bought."

"That was for Mary. I simply put that lingerie in Susan's beach bag for convenience sake. Mary knows this now—you can ask her."

There was a long silence then. I believe certain people refer to it as a "pregnant" silence. During this time Moe stared idly at the bookshelves. I looked up at him; his silence was unnerving me.

"What's the matter, don't you believe me? Your best friend?"

"Should I?"

"And why do you always answer a question with a question?"

"Do I?"

"Dammit, Moe, I'm in a tough spot here and you're not helping!"

"I think we're dealing with projection here, Doc. Often people see things, or fear possible things, in others that they have in themselves. For example, a person who is constantly preoccupied with fears of people stealing from him is likely to have more than a touch of larceny within himself. Now in your case, fearing that Mary will become intimately involved with this man Larry, who seems to embody everything attractive in a man, might reveal your own weaknesses of—"

"Oh, shut up!" I said, getting off the couch and leaving his office. I slammed the door, too.

I was almost to my office door when he opened the door and peeped his head around the doorframe at me.

"I wasn't accusing you, Doc. Just something to think about. And what are Mary and Larry going to be doing together, anyway? They building or painting a house together or something?"

"No. I mentioned that Larry's new career is with the Fish and Wildlife Service, which, in its infinite wisdom, has chosen Mary to be a temporary undercover agent for them. She and Larry will be making illegal buys and trapping informants with interviews, and so on. God knows where they'll be going together. Places like Sitka, Alaska, no doubt."

"Hmmmmm ... sounds exciting. I think that's going to be great for Mary. After all, she's been watching your exploits for years, sort of staying in the background. I hope she has fun."

"Hell with you, Moe," I said. Some friend.

"And you, Dr. Adams," he warned, wagging his hairy, bony finger at me, "had better grow up a little and accept this. Seems to me like the shoe is finally on the other foot."

"My shoe will be in your face if you don't shut up. I mean it."

I stormed inside my office and looked for my car keys. I was going to the track and running umpteen miles, then home to take several long sauna baths.

Life sure is funny, I thought, driving down to the Acton health club. One day everything's just fine. The next day your wife is going out of town with Mr. Perfect on undercover assignments, and your best friend scolds you for being jealous. Yep, life's funny. A regular goddamn RIOT.

6

I RAN TWELVE MILES, STARTING VERY SLOWLY AND WORKING up to medium speed, then slowing down gradually again at the end. I went home to find, guess who?

"Oh, hiya, Doc," said Larry Carpenter in his deep baritone voice. He had a voice like Elvis Presley, for chrissakes. "I hope you don't mind my moving this flower box for Mary. She was afraid you might strain yourself, so she asked me to do it."

He was carrying a window box full of gravel and dirt that was a foot wide and deep and maybe seven feet long. Weighed more than a defensive linebacker.

"Oh no. That's fine. Saves me the trouble."

I went on inside. Afraid I would strain myself, huh? I

knew it was time for Mary and me to have a little talk. That's what she calls these skirmishes: "little talks." Well, it was definitely time for one. Overdue.

But we couldn't have that little talk. Not right away, because I found Mary with Brad Taylor. They were in my study.

"Oh, hi, Charlie! Brad's here; he's going to explain a little more about this undercover operation. Brad, would you mind starting at the beginning again so he can catch up?"

"Not at all. Good to see you again, Doc. I'm giving Mary a little background on the situation in the Bering Sea. Glad you could join us."

"Oh, it's indeed a pleasure."

"Oh, Charlie, I forgot to tell you. Larry's here. He's moving that big flower box that's too heavy for you, I—"

"It's *not* too heavy for me," I growled, "and I already saw him."

"Well, maybe not too heavy, but Larry's so strong and all, I just thought—"

"Brad, let's hear this background, then—if it's okay with everybody here—I'm going to take a sauna bath before dinner."

They gave me a funny look; I suppose I was a little gruff.

Brad went over to my illuminated globe and pointed to a speck of land in the Bering Sea right smack between Alaska and Russia.

"This is Saint Lawrence Island," he said. "It's one of the main breeding grounds of the walrus. Over a hundred thousand of them gather here to mate during their annual migrations. That's significant, because the estimated remaining world population of these animals is thought to be only two hundred thousand. The film you saw of the slaughter of these creatures takes place here, and in and around little settlements like Dillingham and Savoonga, Round Island, Ekuk, and so on . . . all these little Eskimo settlements."

He traced his finger in a circular path around Alaska's northwest coast.

"But the real center of the illicit ivory trade is here—the city of Nome. The ivory comes into Nome through all these little towns and settlements. From there, it's sold to various criminal dealers, who then smuggle it into the famous carving ports."

"Carving ports?"

"Yep. Most are in Asia, but several are in the U.S. The most famous ivory-carving centers are Hong Kong, Singapore, Taiwan, Osaka, and Tokyo. The old whaling port of Lahaina, in Hawaii, is the most famous of all. But two are right here."

"Here? In America?"

"No, right here. Near us. Provincetown and Boston."

"Boston?"

"Right, especially Boston's Chinatown."

Mary gave a low whistle.

"The other cities of note in the continental U.S. are Bellingham, Washington, and the general area around San Francisco. In every case, the master carvers are Chinese, not Eskimos."

"Well, why can't you stop the slaughter, Brad?" Mary asked. "I mean, what we saw in this film was just awful."

"We can't stop it, Mary, because it's legal."

"Legal?"

Brad stood up and began pacing on my office rug.

"The Marine Mammal Protection Act, passed in 1972, was designed to protect animals like the fur seal, the walrus, polar bear, sea otter, and so on. But like so much well-intentioned federal legislation, the effect of this act has been just the opposite."

"How come?"

"Because, in addition to protecting the animals, the act was also designed to protect the native cultures of the region. In other words, it was designed to protect the Eskimo way of life, which is hunting. So the deal was this—nobody could hunt these endangered species except Eskimos. They could hunt as many of these animals— including even the polar bear—as they wished, so long as they didn't waste them. Also, they couldn't sell these animals, or their parts, such as fur, hides, teeth, tusks, and so on. Except—and here's the catch—except if the animal part had been worked by a Native American Eskimo into a work of art. Then it could be sold."

"Sounds pretty reasonable if you ask me," said Mary. "I

mean, look what's happened to most Native Americans who were deprived of their hunting way of life. What I hear is, a lot of them just sit around drunk."

Brad Taylor nodded, then held up his hand.

"You're right, Mary. And that's why this provision was put in. But here's the kicker—here's the way they get around the law—they make a few scratches on each tusk with a drill, that's all. Just a few rough carving marks, you know, nothing that will go deep into the raw ivory— nothing that will actually damage the tusk—just enough to say that an Eskimo—who cares terribly about preserving his native culture—has worked the piece into a form of Native American art."

There was a small silence. Then I spoke.

"So what you're saying is, they don't give a damn if all the game gets wiped out in another twenty years, they just want to make all the money they can right now."

"That's unfair. Not all the Eskimos think this way, by any means. But enough do to make bad things happen. Hey, how else can you make three or four thousand bucks in a single haul?"

Brad Taylor stopped pacing my study carpet and sank down into one of the leather chairs near the fireplace. He sighed.

"When I explain the markup, the immense profitability of this pirate trade, you'll understand the enormity of the problem. Here's how it works. These ivory smugglers— who aren't Eskimos; they're American crooks—are also dope dealers. They'll sneak, oh, say, three or four pounds of marijuana into Alaska. This three or four pounds of pot costs them less than a thousand a pound. The average street price here in the States is between two and three grand a pound, but they get it in Latin America much cheaper. The Anchorage price goes up to about five or six grand a pound, but that's not half the story. They take this good dope up to these villages and roll it into joints or just sell it by the ounce. They can sell these for a total of *ten or twelve* thousand a pound. Right there they've made a profit of over a thousand percent. And that's just the first step . . ."

"This whole thing is sounding a bit heavy," I said.

"Brad, I'm not sure Mary should be involved in any of this—even just store buying."

"I'm not sure it's up to you, Charlie," she said. There was frosting on those words.

"These Eskimos are so desperate for a high they'll sell the dealers raw ivory for ten to twenty bucks a pound, while they're buying the grass for twenty, twenty-five grand a pound. So already, just on the exchange of dope for ivory, the crooks are making an immense profit. Then they smuggle the ivory to the carvers—illegal Asian immigrants who work for peanuts—who transform the raw ivory into art pieces worth ten or twenty times the raw stuff. So you see, these pirates turn that initial investment of a thousand bucks into maybe a hundred grand. Now you see the problem?"

"Yes." Mary nodded solemnly.

"Now, what we have to do, we have to catch these people doing the illegal things, and put it on video- or audiotape as evidence. Mary, that's where we want you to come in. We want you to make illegal buys while you're wired for sound."

"I understand."

"Well, I don't," I said. "I mean, what about the danger involved? What if they discover she's wearing this gadget? Then what?"

"First of all, Doc, Mary won't be dealing with the actual pirates, the drug crooks, who are the dangerous element in the equation. She'll be dealing with the store and gift-shop owners who, usually knowingly and deliberately, buy illegal worked ivory and sell it. When we get these people in the net, we can charge them and hopefully get them to tell us who's selling it to them."

"Then you'll work your way up the ladder to the big guys at the top."

"Right."

"So what's Larry going to be doing?"

"He's on the more dangerous end. He'll try to go undercover in a variety of roles. Since he can fly a plane, he'll volunteer as a bush pilot who is willing to fly loads of contraband wherever he's asked."

"Gee," Mary said, "I didn't know he could fly a plane."

"He's done some work with timber in the Northwest, so

he can pose as a sort of out-of-work lumberjack. We're even thinking of putting him on a fishing boat out of Homer or Kodiak . . . see what information he can pick up."

"But how will the crooks trust him?" I asked. "How do they know he isn't the law?"

"We're giving him a false past. A legend, we call it. Larry's legend is that he's done time in Quentin. Been imprisoned for distributing cocaine. He's looking for a way to make a few big hauls, then get out before the heat closes in. He'll say he wants enough money to buy a hunting cabin in Montana or somewhere. See? The pirates will believe this kind of story."

"And meantime, Mary's just going to be visiting these stores, shopping for ivory?"

"Ivory, illicit fur . . . things like this."

"And there'll be no danger to Mary?"

"None we can see. Of course, she can't keep going back too often; after she's visited these shops, say, twice, we'll have to move her."

"Where?"

"Maybe to the West Coast for a few weeks."

"Oh, goody! I just love San Francisco!"

"Uh, where is she going to wear this 'wire,' Brad? Strapped to the inside of her thigh, or what?"

He laughed, and opened a briefcase that was sitting on the floor next to him. He took out several small electronic devices and spread them out on my desk.

"The latest in bugs?" I asked, turning over the tiny objects in my fingers. "Boy, are they small. Can these really work?"

"They sure do. We don't use recorders anymore; they're too big. Now we usually have the agent wear just a mike and transmitter, which send the signals to another agent in a nearby van, who's got a big recorder in the vehicle. See these?"

He held out three small tubes with wire screens on one end. They were scarcely bigger than cigarettes.

"Mary will have two or three of these on her person. In her pockets, right under her blouse, or"—he took some color photos from the case and flipped through them for me; they showed wrapped packages, an umbrella, a shop-

ping bag, and other paraphernalia of the serious shopper—
"hide them in objects that are left behind in the shop. We're
making more and more use of the planted bug, because
people talk more freely when the agent isn't in the shop."

"Planted bug?"

"Uh-huh. Say Mary goes into a fancy store and buys
some ivory, fine crystal, or whatever. After they put it in
the box, she takes the package, slips one of these tiny bugs
inside, and then, after a moment's thought, she asks if they
can gift wrap the items, and she'll be back later to get
them. She says she's going to look down the street at the
other stores. But she doesn't want to drag along this heavy
handbag, you follow?"

"So far."

"So she asks the salesclerk would she mind if she left
these heavy parcels in her shop, somewhere safe in the
back room or behind the counter, and she'll pick them all
up when she's done shopping. Right?"

"Exactly. So these wrapped packages and shopping bags,
with the bugs hidden inside, are sitting right there under the
noses of the shopkeepers. When the shop's empty, they
might talk a bit about the ivory Mary bought. We've had
lots of luck with this technique."

Just then Larry came in, looking like he just stepped off
a Marlboro billboard. Mary's eyes lit up when she saw him.

"Are we starting tomorrow?" he asked Brad.

"I'd like to. With you and Mary in Chinatown, and then
maybe sending you up alone to Gloucester, Larry, toward
the end of the week. See if you can't go undercover there
on the docks. Mary, do you think you're ready to visit Chinatown here in Boston, if it's okay with you?"

"Fine," she said.

"I'm going, too," I added.

"Charlie! No; you've got your practice."

"I can cancel the ones in the morning. I just want to
make sure you get off to a good start."

"I don't think that's necessary, Doc," said Brad.

Larry didn't say a word.

"It's what's going to happen," I said flatly, and headed
for the sauna.

7

Boston's Chinatown is probably the smallest Asian enclave in any major American city. Roughly speaking, it's about eight square blocks bordered by Kneeland, Harrison, and Essex streets on three sides. The fourth side boundary is the Southeast Expressway. Other streets within this microscopic neighborhood are Taylor, Oxford, and Edinboro. Certainly doesn't sound Chinese. The only street in Chinatown with a Chinese name is tiny Ping On Street, scarcely a block long.

Interspersed among the long-established Chinese businesses are new shops with names from Vietnam, Laos, Cambodia, and Thailand, evidence of the recent waves of immigration from that convulsed part of the world. Thus, this small neighborhood of Asian peoples is filled to brimming, with new arrivals each month.

As soon as I got out of my car and began walking around the neighborhood, I began noticing the underweight people, mostly elderly, in coughing fits, standing on corners or crossing busy streets with canes and giddy gaits. TB, on the rise alarmingly in the U.S., was visibly evident here. No doubt overcrowding was a major cause. Tuberculosis is very contagious—as close as the nearest cough or sneeze. Also, most people I saw on the streets and in the shops were smoking cigarettes, and the liquor stores were doing a booming business, even at ten-thirty in the morning.

It was sad, and I felt for these stressed-out people living

in this cluster of restaurants, apothecary shops, craft stores, laundries, and noodle factories located exactly between South Station and the Boston Common.

I looked in through the front window of the Golden Palace Restaurant, whose sign said the palace featured dim sum and cocktails. I thought I might try the place for lunch.

But then a big yellow truck pulled up in front of a Chinese grocery store and the driver and his helper went around back and slid up the corrugated metal door. Inside the truck were the fresh carcasses of ten or twelve hogs, freshly killed and gutted, but still whole. I don't think the truck had any refrigeration, and the faint whiff I got as I walked past confirmed this suspicion. The men grabbed a big hog, each guy taking a pair of feet, and they carried the dead piggy into the shop, staggering under the load.

Maybe better to go over to the North End for pasta at lunchtime, I thought. . . .

I lighted my pipe, assumed the jaunty but languid pose of the tourist, and walked slowly around Chinatown. Hell, you could do several laps of it in an hour. Finally I saw Mary come walking up Ping On Street with a big purse slung over her shoulder. She gave me a faint, quick smile as she paused outside a shop that said:

SAM HO
Gift Shop
Jade, Ivory, Precious Stones
hand-carved artifacts—porcelain

From where I lounged across the street, I could see handsome plates and vases in the window, along with China dolls in glass cases, ornate fans painted with floral designs, carved teak elephants, and ebony vase stands. But what caught my eye immediately was a huge elephant tusk sitting front and center on an ebony stand. It was horizontal and intricately carved. After Mary went into the shop I crossed the street for a closer look. The tusk was carved to represent a parade crossing an arched bridge, with scores of people, oxen carts, soldiers on horseback, and tradesmen bearing cargoes on their bent backs, all walking along the top of the carved ivory tusk. It was impressive, and incredibly intricate.

As I went back across the street the phone van pulled up next to me. Handsome, debonair Larry Carpenter, dressed in a New England telephone workman's uniform, smiled and winked at me as he left the driver's seat and went back into the truck. I knew what they had in that van: hidden mikes and recorders, and a video camera on a tripod right behind the small glass window in the side of the truck that no genuine telephone truck ever has.

The plan was this: Mary was to go into Sam Ho's, a reputed dealer—and perhaps carver—of illegal ivory, and try to make a deal. To gain Sam's confidence, she would buy a few other pricey items first, such as jade, cinnabar, or cloisonné. Then she would confess that her real love was ivory, particularly that which had been intricately carved, such as the tusk in the window. Would Sam Ho sell her some of this?

If he did, Mary would have his voice on her hidden mike, which would be transmitted outside to Larry in the truck, who would put it on tape. If possible, she would lure Sam outside the shop, perhaps to discuss the incredible tusk on display, so that Larry could get the two of them on his directional mike and the hidden camcorder. Supposedly, all this incriminating evidence against Sam Ho would be used later to "turn him over." This meant putting pressure on him to reveal his sources for the ivory, the "higher-ups" in the chain of pirates and thieves that the U.S. Fish and Wildlife people wanted to put behind bars. The best scenario of all would be to turn Sam Ho into an undercover agent, working for the government. This was how the big stings were made.

Within ten minutes Mary came outside the shop with a middle-aged Asian man. He wore a short-sleeved, blue seersucker shirt and had close cropped hair that stuck out straight in front and was graying at the temples, glowing, wrinkle-free skin on his pleasant face, a potbelly, and metal-framed, dark-tinted glasses. He talked earnestly with Mary, gesturing with his hands. I saw him point at the tusk and shake his head twice.

Then he turned. Before I realized it, he was staring at

me. Hard. I turned and pretended to look inside the window
of a shop renting Asian movies. It was a mistake, and I
knew it. I had drawn unnecessary attention to myself, and
my quick about-face probably confirmed any suspicions
Sam Ho might be harboring about the idle pedestrian across
the street who'd been staring at him. In the reflection of the
store window, I looked behind me across the street again.
Sam Ho—or whoever he was—was now looking at the
phone truck. I ambled on down to the corner of Taylor
Street and turned left. I stopped in front of a big store with
the name Sieu Thi Viet-Hoa above it. Apparently a Vietnamese store. Down the street was a shop called the Saigon
Market. Inside were all kinds of woks, rice cookers, bam-
boo steamers, skewers, and big huge tins of sesame oil and
peanut oil. Other names that stuck in my head were Pho
Bang, Thai Binh, and Banh Mi Ba Le—Chinh Cong. These
didn't seem like Chinese names to me, but rather Vietnamese, Cambodian, and Thai.

I couldn't help but wonder how the Chinese felt about
these newcomers taking up scarce living and commercial
space in their old and tiny community. To all appearances,
the Asian community seemed peaceful and united. But I
suspected that like most other neighborhoods, there was
some underlying friction and rivalry. How did they keep
this unrest and potential violence in check? I suspected it
was done the Asian way, with village elders calling some of
the shots, and perhaps some kind of ethnic enforcement
squads that operated mostly after dark. I decided to return
later and buy Mary some exotic kitchenware. Then I made
some more left turns, circling the block, and came up Ping
On Street again. Now the street in front of Sam Ho's was
vacant. I assumed Mary and the salesclerk had returned inside the shop.

But I made another mistake. As I passed Sam Ho's he
looked out through his window and spotted me. He did not
stare this time. Instead, he turned around to the wall behind
the counter and pulled twice on a red silk sash that hung
down like a bell rope. Almost immediately, I heard the rasp
and squeak of a window sash being raised. I looked up and
saw a face appear in a third-story window.

I won't ever forget that face. The man was very stout, his

face seemed a foot across. He wore thick glasses—so thick I saw a tunnel of refracting rings of light in them. He turned and bored those telescope eyeglasses right at me. He wore a wispy mustache that hung down around his mouth. A modern Fu Manchu. His face wasn't pleasant. I walked on, feeling increasingly uneasy.

Three hours later I was sitting out on the terrace behind our house, watching the leaves shake and rustle in the cool breeze. A lot of the bright red-and-gold tokens of fall were coming loose and spiraling down onto the grass. Danny, my yellow Lab, and Troubles, my Drahthar bitch, were nestled down on either side of my chair watching for squirrels. I was going over in my head what I was going to say to the Three Musketeers: Mary, Larry, and Brad.

I knew they were not going to be pleased with what had happened in Chinatown earlier in the day. After Mr. Big had leaned out that upper window to get a good view of Suspicious Person, I hightailed it around the corner and sat down on a bench that was near a quaint, Oriental-style phone booth with carved roof and red-and-gold trim. I wanted to leave the place and let the team do its work, but I was frankly worried about Mary in the shop. Would they think we were in cahoots, and the fat man above open a trapdoor and drop a cobra down on her head? Or maybe they would hustle her upstairs, tie her against the wall, and the fat man with the incredibly thick glasses would fasten a water bucket with a tiny hole in its bottom right over head, and transform her—in forty-eight hours or so—into a slobbering, sobbing, imbecile from the incredible water torture?

None of this was especially attractive, and so I waited around the corner for her to reappear before I was going to budge. I even began wishing I'd brought along my Browning Hi-Power in a shoulder rig. She finally came walking down the street, glanced at me and immediately away, and kept walking toward downtown. I got off the bench and followed her up to Chauncy Street, where she turned left on Bedford, then walked over to Tremont Street and turned left again. I kept following her. If she knew I was behind her, she gave no sign.

Question in my mind was, who was behind *me*?

A white van pulled up alongside me, keeping pace with my fast walking. A voice said. "You blew it, Doc. C'mon, get inside." I turned to see Larry talking to me from the driver's side window of the bogus phone truck. I went around and hopped inside.

"What happened? Who was that guy in the upper-story window anyway?" I asked.

"That guy, whoever he is, was peeking at us from what we're pretty sure is a carving parlor—a sweatshop that transforms illegal raw ivory into richly worked, incredibly expensive ivory, like the tusk in Sam Ho's window. Trouble is, your staking the place out was about as obvious as an elephant itself walking around Chinatown."

"Oh, c'mon, Larry; it was not."

"Unfortunately, it was. Now listen, Doc, we've been friends a long time. You don't have to shadow Mary so closely. You don't have to worry about anything, uh, personal, happening with us."

"Who said I was?" I said it defensively—I realized afterward. "And where the hell is she going, anyway?"

We were tailing Mary, who was now walking fast up Tremont Street toward Boylston. On the right side of Tremont was the Boston Common, which, unfortunately, seems to become more common each year. Now it was positively riddled with winos, some passed out on the grass, benches, or under shrubs, and others shaking Styrofoam coffee cups, begging for change. Up the walkway toward the center of this park—the nation's oldest—was a group of young black guys playing a portable radio so loud you could hear it down in Quincy. They were smoking, laughing, shoving each other, and making loud comments at each woman who walked past.

"Yeah, maybe I am worried about Mary," I said. "And a lot of it has to do with the fact that what you are doing is potentially dangerous. Just plain dangerous."

"Mary told me you love danger, Doc."

"That's not true. I hate boredom, but I don't like danger. The problem is, there never seems to be much in between the two. And anyway, I'm talking about Mary here, not me.

I don't like her in danger, Larry, can't you understand that?"

"I know. Only she wants to do this."

"Uh-huh, right. Right up until the time when the bad guys get wise to her and rough her up. And don't forget, they may do the same to you."

"Hey, what's that building she's going into?"

"I'll be damned; that's the Boylston Street Union, a health club I belong to. I've got a hunch she's going in there to see a friend of ours."

"Who is it?"

"She'll introduce you, Larry. I'm getting out here and walking back to the Haymarket Square parking deck. I'm going back to Concord. You're welcome to dinner, if Mary didn't already invite you."

"Am I . . . really?" he asked me, his turquoise eyes boring into mine. There was a moment of silence between us. It seemed like twenty minutes. "Ha! Anyway, I can't; Brad's sending me up to Gloucester this evening. I'm using my carpentry skills to try and find a job repairing draggers up on the docks."

"Why? What's going on in Gloucester?"

"Ivory smuggling. Lots of it, we think. See ya, Doc."

With that, I hopped out of the truck, went down to Haymarket Square, retrieved the XT6, and drove home.

So there I was, sitting on the terrace awaiting Mary's return. What I didn't expect was the party of four that showed up. Larry wasn't part of it, so I assumed that he was already headed up to the north shore. Mary, her brother Joe, Brad Taylor, and a short, hunched-up, gnarled man with a twisted gait. That would be Laitis Roantis, the most notorious denizen of the BYMCU health club. The guy who can kill you with his pinkie finger.

"Hey, Doc," said Joe. "I hear you messed things up this afternoon."

"Is the entire evening going to go this way?"

"Well, admit it, Charlie. Your hanging around Sam Ho's shop didn't help. I'm surprised you didn't blow my cover, too."

"Larry tell you that?"

"No. It's just the truth. In fact, Sam Ho himself asked me if I knew you. I said I'd never seen you before in my life. Then he said, 'He looks like he knows you.' "

"Well, big deal."

"How about a drink, Doc?" asked Roantis.

"Yeah, it's a big deal," Mary said. "He practically wouldn't talk to me after that. I was all set to buy some ivory—a really neat seated Buddha—when he suddenly said it wasn't for sale."

"Can I have a drink, Doc?" repeated Roantis. "You mind?"

I looked at Joe. "What are you doing here? You here to scold me, too?"

He took a mug shot out of his breast pocket and handed it to me. No Fu Manchu mustache and no thick glasses, but there was no mistaking that wide face and neck, and that menacing glower.

"Yeah, that's him," I said. "So he's a bad guy?"

"Certainly is. Can we go inside? The bar's in there."

"Thanks, Joe," said Roantis.

We trundled inside and sat in the sunporch with our drinks. Joe with his G and T, Mary with her glass of red, me with a mug of German lager, Brad with same, and Laitis with a tumbler of what appeared to be straight whiskey. Ah, well: *plus ça change, plus c'est la même chose,* I thought, and quaffed the beer. Joe came over and tapped the mug shot. Laitis came over and peered at the photo. He, too, pointed at it. "Johnny Ridge," he said. "Bad boy."

"Johnny Ridge? That's not a Chinese name, is it?" I asked.

"It's not," Joe said. "Ridge is a renegade Cherokee. Up until a few years ago he lived on the reservation down in Cherokee, North Carolina. Helped run the giant bingo game they've got there—biggest in the world, so I hear. Anyway, they caught him skimming the till and tried to banish him, but he came back and apparently killed a tribal brother in a fight. Then he left for good and made his way up to New York, where he fell in with the Westies, working as an enforcer."

"Westies?" asked Mary. "Who or what are the Westies?"

"An Irish mob on the West Side. They get their name

from there—or is it the west country of Ireland? I forget. Anyway, they're a mean bunch. As mean as the Sicilian mob, as mean as any of the black or Hispanic drug gangs. Things were cozy with this arrangement until Ridge tried to cross those lovely Sons of Erin. They didn't take kindly to this, as you may imagine. Word is, they beat him so badly that he still carries a limp and can't fully use his left arm. We hear he's still tough as nails anyway. He left New York for here. Now he's into smuggling and drugs as well as ivory. He's also an enforcer for the Chinese whose carving shop he operates."

"Sam Ho?"

"Maybe. Maybe somebody above Sam. Anyway, Johnny's been capitalizing on his Native American features to pass as Chinese. Works very well. But Laitis knows most of this story because of his close ties to the Asian community here." He turned to Brad. "In case you didn't get the picture from the walls in Mr. Roantis's office, he's heavily into the martial arts. Since Chinatown is only a few blocks from the BYMCU, and the Asians invented most of the stuff Roantis does, it's no surprise that he's in constant contact with these people. One of the main items of neighborhood gossip lately concerns Johnny Ridge. None of the neighborhood likes him much, except the bad part, of course."

"Mr. Roantis, would you know who he's linked up with in Chinatown?" asked Brad.

"I keep hearing two names—Sam Ho and Jason Steingretz."

"Who the hell is Steingretz?" I asked.

"Jason Steingretz, he used to own a pawnshop in Chinatown until he went bust a few years ago," said Roantis. "Some folks I know in Chinatown liked him. He was always good for a small loan without collateral. He trusted them and they trusted him. When his shop went under, he disappeared for a while, but then came back. He's been living there, right off Kneeland Street, in a big building he owns. The building is some kind of old warehouse. That's what they tell me, anyway."

"Well, Joey," said Mary, "can't you go and pick these guys up? Maybe search the building?"

"No, and no," her brother answered. "For one thing, we don't have probable cause. Also, this kind of thing's not our business. It's the business of the Fish and Wildlife, right, Brad?"

"Right, and even if we had a strong lead, we'd rather lie low and wait until a deal is coming down," said Brad, "then run in and catch all the parties in the act. But God knows when that'll be. This is a slick bunch, and mean."

"Do the New York cops have anything outstanding on Ridge?" I asked.

"Nope," said Joe. "A lot of allegations and rumors, but nothing that'll stick."

"One of the problems is that wildlife violations carry such rinky-dink penalties," said Brad. "I mean, it's really hard to scare the crooks into turning over or cutting a deal. What do they care? They're making hundreds of thousands of dollars on a minimal investment, with minimal punishment if they get caught."

"What kind of punishment?" I asked. "What would a guy like Sam Ho get if you brought him down?"

"A sentence of two to five years. After the defense gets done plea-bargaining, and you figure the crowding in the jails and prisons, with more serious violent offenders lined up in front of him, I doubt he'd get the better part of a year. Of course we'd fine him, too, for whatever he's worth . . . but I got a hunch his official worth isn't a fraction of what his hidden, illicit worth is—and we'd never touch that because we couldn't find it."

"And so the upshot is that the walrus and elephant are probably doomed," said Mary. There was genuine sadness in her voice.

"It seems that way—unless something changes radically. Like, for instance, we can get them on a serious charge like drug running . . . or murder."

"Murder? Who have they killed?"

"Four of our men in the past six years. Of course, we can't begin to prove it; our agents just disappeared. But what do you suppose happened to them?"

I looked over at Mary, watching her closely. I saw her shudder slightly. And well she might. "Larry tells me he's headed up to Gloucester to go undercover as a shipwright," I said. "Is he there now?"

"Yep. Just getting there," Brad said. "He'll probably call me tonight and tell me where he's staying."

"What are your plans for Mary?" I asked. I knew he didn't have to answer me, but I wanted to know.

"I thought, if it's okay with her, that we'd send her over to Nantucket again, back to that same shop where you bought the lightship purse," said Brad. "But I don't think we'll do that right away. Maybe wait a week or so and see what Larry comes up with in Gloucester. By the way, Doc, if you've got any time on your hands, you might want to help us out in P-town."

"What?" Was this really happening? They were actually going to include *me*? "Doing what? I have all of next weekend, starting Friday noon."

Brad pulled a notebook out of his breast pocket and opened it, running his finger down a list. "There are two gift shops there selling a lot of ivory. One is called the Whale's Tale, the other is Patsy's Sea Unicorn."

"You want me to make a buy, or what?"

"If you can, we want you to watch the shops closely to see who comes and goes. We want to see where these places get their ivory. Of course, the hard part is, they sell everything in these shops—T-shirts, carved wooden figures, prints, ship models, seashells, lamps, you know . . . the typical gift-shop gamut of things. Maybe it would be best to discover the residences of the owners, and watch the houses to see who comes and goes. We think it's unlikely that any illegal supplier is going to waltz into the shop like your typical wholesaler."

"You really want me to do this, after what happened in Chinatown this morning?"

"We're, uh, hoping you'll be more circumspect. We assume you will be, since you won't be worrying about your wife."

I did my best to ignore this barb, pretending to look out the porch windows at the falling leaves.

"Who says I'm worried about my wife?"

They all stared at me, saying nothing. Mary was staring at the floor.

8

On Friday afternoon, a week and a half later, I was over on the Cape, at the marina in Wellfleet, by a little after one. I climbed aboard our catboat, the *Ella Hatton*. The weather was cool and crisp, but the sun felt warm on my back as I bustled around the wide cockpit, getting everything shipshape for my solo sail up the bayside of the Cape's upper arm, toward Provincetown. P-town was about thirty miles distant, which meant that with a good breeze I should reach the inner harbor a little after sunset. A catboat has a wide, piepan-shaped hull that looks like a pumpkinseed. Its length-to-beam ratio is only two to one, which means she's half as wide as she is long, and her shallow hull is virtually flat-bottomed and draws less than two feet—perfect for sailing around the shallow estuaries, river mouths, and sandy beaches of a place like Cape Cod. These squat little boats can go like blazes, though, in a stiff wind, particularly when the wind is behind you. That shallow hull rides up on the water and scoots like a surfboard.

I had just finished cleaning out the small furnace heater below and stuffing it with newspaper and chunks of cannel coal. If it got chilly later on, I would light this little vertical fireplace and watch those coals glow through the isinglass door. Outside, the smoke would pour out the little chimney stack that projected through the cabin roof. I filled the gimballed brass lamps with kerosene and cleaned the wicks and the chimneys, loaded my groceries, beer, and tobacco

44

aboard, stowing all in the little net hammocks and the mahogany shelves that lined the cabin's interior. I was low on diesel fuel, but that didn't matter; I had enough left to get me twenty or thirty miles at least.

For more maneuverability, I decided to tow the dory behind. This flat-bottomed skiff carried a tiny outboard motor on its high, "shoe peg" transom, and allowed me to moor offshore and come in via the dory.

It was my plan—heartily endorsed by Brad Taylor—to anchor in Provincetown Harbor—the bay formed by the hook of Long Point. This shallow area is between the Coast Guard station dock and the two big piers that jut out from the center of the city: MacMillan Wharf and the Fisherman's Wharf.

Once inside this sheltered area, I dropped sail, and then the hook, and waited until it caught, swinging *Ella Hatton* around into a lazy stall. I trimmed the anchor cable and lounged on the cockpit cushions, smoking a cigar and glassing the shore with my binoculars. This was a great vantage point because I could keep a close watch on the backsides of all the shops, restaurants, bars, and hotels on Commercial Street—the main drag in P-town that is always swarming with sightseers and pedestrian shoppers. It was almost dark; the sky on the ocean side was flaming gold. I took the folded slip of paper from my windbreaker and examined the two names Brad had written on it:

THE WHALE'S TALE
256 Commercial Street

THE SEA UNICORN
314 Commercial Street

According to Brad, both of these shops sold a lot of ivory. I took the envelope with three hundred-dollar bills from my shirt pocket. I was going in there to make a few buys, then hand the ivory over to Brad, who would send it to the government lab in Ashland, where it would be dated. If it was fewer than twenty years old, it was illegal.

I kept swinging the marine glasses along the nearby shore. Past the beach was an unbroken row of wooden buildings, mostly painted gray with white trim, the standard Cape Cod color scheme. The sun's afterglow lit them up with copper brilliance. Many of the buildings were old and weathered. In the background rose the two-hundred-foot-tall granite tower the Pilgrim Monument. It, too, was bright gold in the sunset. It has a castlelike top, complete with crenellations and archer ports, and looks remarkably like the Medici Tower in Florence, Italy.

I kept looking at the backs of the hotels, shops, and taverns. How the hell could I know which ones were the shops? And did it matter? Then I remembered Brad's hunch that it was unlikely any illegal ivory would enter these shops directly. What guy smuggling illegal ivory would come in by boat and off-load it onto the beach? And then up the bank and the rickety wooden stairs into a gift shop? I thought not. In all probability he would arrange to meet the shopkeeper at some other rendezvous—far from the shop, and let the owner take his chances sneaking the contraband into the store. I decided to make a ham-and-cheese sandwich, then readied the dory for a trip into the beach.

I scooted over to the packed sand and drew the dory up high and dry, then walked up the beach, through a rickety gate in the slat snow fence, past a big gray building with a bunch of parked bicycles chained to its side, and found myself on Commercial Street. Many of the shops would soon be closing, but the street, as usual, was thronged with people and slow-moving vehicles. The tourists stopped often at the bars and restaurants, looking at menus tacked to the doorways and peering into bars, trying to decide where to stop for cocktail hour.

I went to the Whale's Tale first. It was in an ideal location, in the center of town near the two big piers. I fought my way to the back, where I was told the ivory was. The store was selling both carved ivory figures and scrimshaw. Scrimshaw is made from the teeth of sperm whales and killer whales. These teeth are enamel, not true ivory. Any dentist will tell you that tooth enamel—the scientific name is *Hydroxyapatite*—differs from true ivory. Exactly how, I wasn't sure, but I aimed to find out. Since Brad hadn't told me the status of scrimshaw, I ignored it and concentrated on the ivory carvings. Finally a young woman came up to wait on me.

"Hey, I thought it was illegal to deal in ivory nowadays," I said with feigned amazement. "What gives?"

"Oh, this is *legal* ivory," she answered, getting out a stack of certificates from under the counter. "See, each one of these pieces has been authenticated and numbered. You can even see the signatures. Now, if you'll tell me which one you'd like to look at . . ."

I pointed to a sizable carving of a polar bear. The piece was five or six inches tall and quite thick through the middle. I hefted it. It was heavy.

"How much for this? Number fifteen-oh-one."

"That piece is—let's see—six ninety-five."

"Uh . . . as in six ninety-five, or six hundred ninety-five?"

She looked at me, rolling her eyes a bit in exasperation. "Oh, come on, sir, hand-carved ivory *is* practically jewelry, you know. And this piece is exceptional."

"It sure is pretty," I remarked, sliding my AmEx gold card across the counter for her to ring up—the three hundred in cash certainly wasn't going to cover it. "But you sure it's legal? I'd hate to get picked up for illegal ivory."

"Oh, come on. . . ." She giggled as she ran my card through the roller machine. "None of us really worry too much about *that*."

"Well, is the owner around? I'd just like to make sure. I know you think I'm being overcautious, but if I could just speak with him briefly, maybe he could tell me where he buys this ivory, and—"

"Well, he's not here now. In fact. Mr. Harold rarely comes into the shop during the off-season, which is after Labor Day. He comes in a few times a week to check on stock, do inventory, check the books, make out our paychecks, you know, business stuff like that, but he rarely works the counter anymore."

"You say his name is Harold? Harold what?"

"Oh, no, that's his last name. His name is James Harold, and he lives over on Nickerson Street. It's not far from here . . . nothing is, really."

"Okay, maybe I'll give James Harold a call, just to make sure. Thanks a lot."

Leaving the place, my new treasure under my arm, I pondered what she had said. If her attitude was typical of those who dealt in ivory, was there indeed any hope at all of stemming this illegal trade, and the slaughter that it was based on? And here was I, a hypocrite to the core, ostensibly on an errand to stop this trade, yet secretly cherishing this wonderful sea gift that I hefted under my arm, hardly able to wait until I could see this handsome bear standing on my study desk back in Concord. I wandered farther down the street in search of the Sea Unicorn.

The Sea Unicorn's decor was a bit more subdued; there were fewer garish T-shirts and those multiformed, seminautical, entirely bogus souvenirs made in places like Haiti, Mexico, Macao, and Taiwan. The ivory was located in an elegant illuminated wooden shelf behind the counter. Both the scrimshaw teeth and the ivory carvings were plentiful and seemed of high quality. When I asked for prices, this was confirmed. I settled on a walrus tusk a full foot long. It was carved to represent an Eskimo hunter in a hunting kayak. The salesman—who was not the owner—told me that figure of the Eskimo was from a separate piece of ivory that was specially fashioned and added on. It was a handsome and interesting piece. The Eskimo, in traditional parka, held a paddle crosswise in front of him while a delicately carved harpoon lay fastened to the front deck of the small boat. Price: $1,100.

I pulled out the plastic and snapped it up, but not before getting the name of the store's owner. I went back outside, wondering what possessed Brad Taylor to think that three hundred bucks was going to even begin to cover these expenses.

I looked at my watch: almost seven, and fully dark for quite a while now. The stores were closing, the bars and restaurants gearing up for another hedonistic night in Provincetown. I checked a local telephone directory and found the names and addresses of the two store owners, then walked back up the street and turned right on Nickerson, the street where Jim Harold supposedly lived. This street was in the quiet, northwest end of town. The neighborhood was pleasant, and filled with moderate-to-fancy frame houses immaculately kept with manicured lawns and shrubs. Harold's house was a white frame residence with Victorian bay windows and a porch with fluted columns. Ivy grew along some of the walls, and a white picket fence surrounded the whole thing. A rose arbor trellis arched over the front gate. The porch light was dark, but there were lights on inside. I walked up the block, then doubled back and strolled along the back side.

The house was dark here, except for a dull glow coming through a translucent curtain covering a large window not far from the back door. A small, neat garage stood along the alleyway, which was not paved, but laid out in gravel and oyster shells. I studied the garage as I walked past. I couldn't see inside because it was dark, but there was a car parked at an angle near the garage, partially blocking the alley. This car seemed somewhat out of place—as if it were just visiting. Out of habit—one I picked up from Joe—I scribbled down the tag number and the make and model and walked on.

But before I'd gone two steps, I saw a brightness out of the corner of my eye. When I turned to face the window, I saw the curtain drop back down, and all was semidark in the back of the house again.

Somebody inside the house had been watching me check out the car in the alley. Great going, Adams, I said to myself as I ambled on. The person watching me wasn't upsetting. What was bothersome was that I could not now come to the front door and ask questions; I was certain Mr. Harold would think me a creep and refuse to speak to me. At least, if I were in his place, that's the way I would feel.

The other store owner, Patsy Wilkinson, lived on the other end of town, in an equally nice and established neighborhood. Her house was a very small Cape Cod cottage surrounded by a rustic rail fence. Same wonderfully kept lawn and gardens, same fresh paint job on the house. Nobody seemed to be home, and there was no car, either in front or back. I marked the location of the house and went back uptown for dinner.

I finally settled on a place on the waterfront that featured a nice dining porch with a magnificent view of the harbor. From my windowside table I enjoyed a huge bowl of clam chowder that was well made, with plenty of fresh clams, potatoes, bits of onion and celery, and best of all, no thickeners. I could look out and see the faint, darkened silhouette of *Ella Hatton*, riding out there on the water. Almost directly opposite me was the imposing MacMillan Wharf, with its big shedlike building at the far end. Fishing boats of all kinds were moored there. Many were lit up, and I could see the crews, clad in sweaters and oilskins, working on the decks. After the chowder and before the flounder I found a phone booth and dialed Joe's number on Beacon Hill. His wife, Marty, answered, explained that he was working late, and not at headquarters.

"Can you give him a license tag number to run down?" I asked. "And tell him I'll be back in Concord tomorrow by midafternoon?"

"I sure will. How are things on the Cape? Find anything out?"

"Nope, just that there's a lot of ivory for sale, and seemingly precious little control over it. Hey, what are you two doing for dinner tomorrow? Want to come out to Concord? Or should we come into town?"

"Well, I guess you heard that Mary's gone for the weekend."

"Gone for the weekend? Where?"

"I can't remember exactly. Something to do with this undercover work for Mr. Taylor."

"Well, I know they talked about her going out to Nantucket, probably back to McQuaid's—"

"No, Doc. I'm pretty sure she went to Gloucester."

"What?"

"To Gloucester, Doc. You know, that famous fishing port on Cape Anne where you got hit on the head once upon a time and dumped into the harbor to drown? Surely you remember this little incident."

"Oh . . . well, listen, Marty, have Joe call me tomorrow night at home, will you?"

She agreed and I walked back to the table. I was numb, with little buzzy, tingly sensations at the tips of my fingers and feet. I sat down at the table again and looked out at the darkening harbor. I watched it in a daze.

Gloucester was where Larry was working. If Mary went

there, especially without telling me, it meant they were up there together.

9

THE NEXT MORNING AT FIRST LIGHT I HAD *ELLA HATTON*'S AN-chor up and stowed, the diesel engine running, and the sails uncovered and ready to haul. I went out past the breakwater at full throttle, determined to reach Wellfleet before noon so I could be back in Concord by one o'clock. My head felt tight and achy, and my mouth was metallic. Too many scotches and pipefuls last night while lounging on the cockpit cushions in the dark, trying to make sense of it all. And then I thought of Larry. Handsome, brilliant, athletic Larry Carpenter, who assured me there was absolutely nothing "personal" going on between them.

I spit over the side, yanked the tiller around, and brought the boat on a southerly course.

Well, just maybe, a little voice in my head said, he was telling the truth. Maybe he latched onto something at the last minute and Taylor sent Mary up there to help out. It *could* happen. . . .

No way, the other, stronger voice answered. Brad made a point of not sending Mary in too deep, especially at first. In fact, it was a promise to me. Larry claimed to feel the same way. They certainly knew my feelings on the matter, as did Mary herself. Therefore, why was she in Gloucester? And even so, why hadn't she notified me? Why did I have to learn this from Marty?

Because, the other voice answered, there was no way to contact you except your ship-to-shore radio, and most of the time you weren't even aboard, so she couldn't tell you. So she did the next best thing, which was to leave word with Marty. So there.

I played this two-voices game all the way to Wellfleet. It just made things worse. And for the first time in an almost thirty-year marriage, I found myself disliking Mary—almost hating her. And something else that was strange: I found myself fearing her. Fearing the awesome power she had over me due to the enormous hurt she could inflict upon me.

I felt ten times vulnerable.

"Then where is she, Brad?"

"I don't know exactly; she's going to call me once she gets settled. I know that Larry's staying at the seaman's hostel called the Dory. Some kind of second-rate housekeeping motel out on Rocky Neck. I guess a lot of the shipyard help lives out there."

"I know the area. I think I'll drive up there and check it out."

"I'd rather you not; it might upset things."

"I'd rather I would, thank you. And why is Mary up there anyway, if you don't mind my asking? And maybe even if you do mind."

"Okay, now don't get huffy, Doc. Larry's working fast, is what set it off. Got a job right away at Yoder's Shipyard, repairing planking and trim on wooden trawlers. Did great work, and let it be known to his compadres in the sheds that this work was enjoyable, but a bit dull. Let it be further known that he had a much more exciting time running dope, and making ten, twenty times the money. In a few days we did the usual bit—sent around a shady-looking guy to call Larry off his job and have a talk with him. Then the guy leaves, and Larry tells his mates he's a guy from out of his past that he'd rather forget. This works like a charm. Soon several guys on Rocky Neck are buying Larry beers in the local bars, wanting to hear about his running days and his stretch in Quentin."

"And what, pray tell, does his employer, Mr. Yoder, have to say about all this? If it were me, I'd fire Larry."

"That's always a risk we take in these operations. But generally speaking, our Mr. Carpenter is so good in his work, and so likable in general, that this hardly ever happens. In four days Larry established himself as dependable and very competent on the job, and esteemed by his coworkers. The perfect plant."

"So where and how does Mary fit into this operation?"

"We're not sure yet. We do know there's a big warehousing operation near the docks that sells bulk frozen fish. Imported stuff from Greenland, Iceland, Alaska, and the Orient. Name of the place is Sea Feast. Larry thinks the place has possibilities."

"Possibilities for what?"

"Warehousing raw ivory . . . he's heard that rumor twice already. Maybe we can use Mary there in one role or another."

"How does Larry know all this so soon?"

"Talk on the docks. He says that several workers in this warehouse live down the street from the boatyard. These guys meet at night in the bars and talk. He hears interesting things. Plus, he's generally a fast worker—knows how to get inside things fast."

"Where exactly is Mary now?" I asked—thinking about this ability Larry had of getting inside things.

"I told you. I'm not sure. I think she's going to be staying at a Comfort Inn just outside Gloucester that Larry recommended. Going to pose as a tourist for the next several days. Apparently Sea Feast has a retail outlet in the front part of the warehouse . . . you know, kind of like a bakery? We'll send her in there, and then she'll put on her charm and ask if she can visit the plant. What do you think?"

"I think if it really *is* a warehouse for contraband, then it's a dumb idea."

"Suit yourself. If you want to go up there and talk her out of it, just please stay low; we don't want to blow the cover on this thing."

"I'll be careful, and I won't try to talk her out of it, either. I just want a better idea of the situation. If I do happen to run into Larry, is there anything you want me to tell him?"

"I would prefer that you didn't run into him, Doc."

I took a sauna, showered and changed, and later that day was cruising along Rocky Neck Avenue, which leads out onto the quaint little peninsula of the same name. Here are small cottages on piers, guest houses, bed-and-breakfasts, artsy shops, and small boatyards. It was midafternoon, and the sun was out. Pleasant along Rocky Neck, except for an occasional whiff of rotten-fish lobster bait that drifted over from across the inner harbor.

I finally found the Dory. It wasn't on Rocky Neck proper, but on East Main Street adjoining it. The body of water opposite East Main, and formed by the enclosure of Rocky Neck Peninsula, is called Smith's Cove. I think the Dory was once a middle-class motel, its gray composite shingle-sided form sprawled out along the road. The cars I could see parked outside the rooms were rather old and beat-up. A lot of them were pickup trucks, with various tools and tarpaulins stacked in their beds. A workingman's hostel, as Brad accurately described it. Larry sure did know where to go to fit into the local scene. When I came into town, I asked the first person I saw where the Comfort Inn was. He told me there was a new one out on Thatcher Road, which led to Rockport, the other famous fishing port on Cape Ann. I found Thatcher Road and followed it a few miles until I came to the new motel.

This was definitely upper middle-class, and claimed to have Jacuzzi baths in each room. Somehow, this advertisement disturbed me.

I circled the parking lot of the Comfort twice, looking for Mary's Audi. Nowhere around. So I drove back into the center of Gloucester, left the Subaru, and walked around to the inner harbor, that aromatic, hulk-lined place that was clogged with masts, radar domes, rigging, trawl nets, paravanes, Day-Glo orange net floats, and the like.

Yoder's Shipyard was over on Smith's Cove; I could see the sign painted on a shed roof from the main docks of the city, but it was not visible from East Main because it faced the water. I killed the better part of an hour walking around

PIRATE TRADE 55

looking at the boats. It was relaxing; I needed it. Then I went back to the car. The sun was getting low in the sky. In late September, the days get short quickly in New England.

Just past Plum Street on East Main, heading back toward Rocky Neck, I spotted a huge beige building with no windows. It had a giant circular logo with two fish swimming around as if biting each other's tails. Like the sign for Pisces. Mary's sign. Under the logo were the words SEA FEAST. So that was the warehouse. I drove up the drive to the parking lot, where I spotted about twenty cars. I parked and watched the cars for a while. No sign of Mary's Audi. And no sign of customers going in and coming out with packages of bargain-priced frozen fish, either. But that didn't mean there wasn't an outlet there. Then I wondered how the local fishermen would feel about a giant place that warehoused foreign fish right in their midst. Right in this famous fishing town that has the dramatic statue of the Grand Banks fisherman at the wheel, his sou'wester gear on, and underneath on the statue's plinth the words:

THOSE WHO GO DOWN TO THE SEA IN SHIPS

Each year in this town, at the beginning of the season, they have a ceremony in which the Catholic bishop blesses the fleet, and they sing hymns and sprinkle holy water over the boats as they sail past. It's a Catholic ceremony because the overwhelming majority of the fisherman are either Portuguese or Italian. But despite this holy entreaty, each year some fishermen don't make it back. Especially in the winter months, when a trawler can ice up in heavy seas so fast she becomes coated with ice on her topsides and cabin superstructure. When that happens the vessel becomes top-heavy. Sometimes, in a heavy swell, the boats coated with ice will just roll over and sink. Just like that.

In water that is just above freezing, a man won't live fifteen minutes.

So, at the end of the season, they have another ceremony, in which they sing hymns again, and toss wreaths into the harbor, to be carried out to sea by the tide, in honor of the men, and women, too, nowadays, who didn't make it back. That's why they erected that famous statue, too.

So I was wondering how the local residents felt about this Sea Feast outfit that was selling cut-rate imported fish right under their very noses.

I couldn't imagine they'd be very happy.

Well, no matter what Larry had heard in the bars, the Sea Feast warehouse didn't look that exciting. I drove on down East Main until I could pull off the road into a tiny gravel space between two old shacks. I got out of the car and walked along the road, approaching the Dory. I had no idea what kind of vehicle the Fish and Wildlife guys had provided Larry with, so I decided just to forget subtlety and ask which room was his.

A plump, redheaded woman wearing a navy-blue dress with white polka dots was in the office talking on the telephone. She looked about sixty and seemed to me to have seen a lot of the world; I had the feeling there was not much I could say or do that would surprise her. She held her speckled hand over the mouthpiece of the phone while she talked to me.

"He's in room one-eleven, but I don't think he's in now. You want to leave your name, deah?"

"I'm an old school friend of his—I heard he was in town is all; I guess I might come back later on tonight."

"Fine. If you cahn't find him here, try looking in at the Irish Fisherman, down on the shore road. Know where that is?"

"Didn't it used to be called the Schooner Race?"

"Yeah, that's right."

"I remember it; I almost got killed there one night."

"Oh, deah! Well, it's a better place now. And Gawd knows, Larry's big and strong enough to protect you. Whoooo, boy! Isn't he something?"

"Yes. I, uh, keep hearing that," I said, and left.

As I walked back to the road I passed within earshot of some of the rooms to let. A window slid open and a window shade zipped up and went *flump flump flump*. A deep male voice said: "Gawddammit, Denny! I'm gonna get bawmed tonight! Gonna get *snot-flyin' drunk*!"

Nice place.

* * *

I cruised back into the center of town and had dinner at the Captains Courageous. It's a decent harborside restaurant named after Kipling's classic sea tale about grand-banks fishing, which is appropriate for Gloucester. But besides the clam chowder and broiled scrod, I can't remember much about the meal, or the other people in the place, or anything else. I was thinking about Mary and Larry, and wondering if I was excessively paranoid, immaturely jealous, merely concerned, or God knows what. Probably all of the above. I lingered over coffee and watched the harbor grow dark purplish blue, then left the restaurant and drove back around the harbor, onto East Main, and up toward the Dory. I parked in the same place as before and walked toward the run-down motel. It was Saturday night, and the joint was jumping. Through various open windows came loud music: rock, heavy metal, and country. More than once, I heard an earsplitting "yeeeeee-haw!"

The infamous rebel yell. Why were these guys on the docks of New England shouting the rebel yell? Were they renegade drifters up here from the southern fishing towns of Beaufort, Charleston, Savannah, and Murrill's Inlet? Then I realized it was probably just television. You watch enough "Dallas," "Designing Women," "Dukes of Hazard" reruns, and "Hee Haw," and soon you're doing the rebel yell.

Room 111 was around on the other side of the building, on the ocean side. I wondered if Larry had to pay extra to get it. I stared at the room. Its window was covered with a drawn shade, and the light inside was on. Larry was in. But then I saw two shadows on the shade. One tall, one shorter. Larry had company. My stomach began to knot. I approached the door to knock on it when I heard voices coming from within.

One was Larry's voice; I recognized the deep, resonant, Elvis baritone in an instant. The other was a woman's voice. I was pretty sure I recognized it, too, and my heart skipped several beats in a row. Mary. Mary and Larry were in there together. I crept closer. Mary was speaking faintly, but I heard the words: ". . . he just won't understand. . . . I can't tell him . . ."

Then Larry answered in clear tones: "You've got to just tell the truth. Tell him the whole thing, before it's too late."

Then Mary again, almost sobbing, saying something like, "No, he's too jealous . . . it won't work."

I stumbled away from the window over to the edges of the parking lot. My head was swimming. I thought I might be sick.

I never, ever, imagined this could happen to me.

10

I STOOD AT THE EDGE OF THE REAR PARKING LOT, GAZING across the water at the town of Gloucester, frozen. I didn't see, hear, or feel anything. I was knocked out on my feet.

Maybe ten minutes went by. Or perhaps only five. Maybe it was an hour; I had no sense of time, only amazement, and pain. In cases like these, I had heard, as we all do, of the wronged person getting a gun and shooting one or both of the offending parties. I felt none of that now. Perhaps I would later. Now I only felt pain and emptiness. I felt the way a prizefighter must feel at the end of the eleventh round, when he's been carried back to his corner, where they sit him on the stool and his team is fanning him with towels and sprinkling cold water on him and trying to patch up his cuts with grease and bandages. He can barely see the bright lights of the ring and the flashing cameras through his swollen eyes, and his body is so pummeled and beaten he cannot even feel the pain. Just the numbing shock of defeat, while the winner dances in the ring before him with his arms raised above his head, the crowd cheering.

That's how I felt right then: knocked out.

Then I heard a door opening behind me.

Curiously, somehow I was ashamed and embarrassed at being there, and looked for a place to crawl away and hide.

The door to room 111 had opened. Yellow light oozed out from the room onto the asphalt of the parking lot.

Then Mary came out, walking straight and tall, her long hair flowing behind her.

I was torn between attacking Mary and hiding from her. I backed away, confused, like a fiddler crab in a tide pool, into the shadows.

Mary walked on into the parking lot. But when the faint glow of distant lights struck her, I saw that her hair was blonde. Bright, golden blonde. I looked closer at her as she turned and walked across the lot.

The woman wasn't Mary.

I eased down on the asphalt. My heart gave slow, steady, incredibly powerful thumps that rocked my head, neck, and body. I let my breath out slowly.

The blond woman, who had not seen me, walked purposefully to a white Mercedes sedan that stuck out against the other modest vehicles like a sterling-silver spoon in a pile of tin cans. As she was getting into her Mercedes I saw a flicker of motion out of the side of my eye. I saw a figure in what looked like a white sweater withdraw back through an open driver's side window of a car at the far end of the lot. The car was light tan. The man leaned out of the window again, holding something in his hands. I heard the clack of a mirror and shutter. No flash. The man was using high-speed film in a camera with a very fast lens. He was light-complexioned and had a very short haircut, almost a military crew cut. I also noticed, in the second or so he was visible, a wide neck and stout arms. Certainly this man was more than a hired photographer—he looked to me like a mean man in a fistfight. He was hired muscle. A spy?

But I didn't really give him much thought, I was so relieved. The Mercedes sped out of the lot and onto South Main. A few seconds later the other car followed.

I went up to the door of room 111 and knocked.

No answer. I knocked again, louder.

"Who's there?" said Larry. But the baritone was hushed, reluctant, perhaps even afraid.

"Larry, it's Doc. Let me in."

The door opened immediately, and there stood Mr. Carpenter, dressed in his working clothes: faded blue jeans and an old flannel shirt. Rags they might have been, but they sure looked good on him. Dammit.

"Doc, am I glad to see you! I'm in trouble, buddy."

"Women usually are," I said, trying to sound like Humphrey Bogart. Gee, I felt better all of a sudden.

"Let's go down the road and get a drink," he said.

"Sure thing. How about five or six? Or maybe ten or twelve?"

"So I take it you, uh, saw that woman leave here?"

"Yes, purely by chance, I did see a young and attractive lady depart from these premises a short time ago. The source of the problem?"

"Yes," he said, sinking down on the bed and putting his head in his hands.

"Well, what's the problem?"

"Her name's Margaret. I met her in Naples, Florida, two years ago. I was down there on some business for Fish and Wildlife, and doing some fishing, too. I met Margaret at the hotel where I was staying. She was there with a girlfriend of hers. Turns out she was recently separated from her husband. Well, we hit it off—"

"And so now she wants to get married."

"Nope. Not quite as easy as that. After the week and a half together in Florida, which was great—it's probably the happiest I've ever been in my life, Doc—we decided to stay in touch and to see each other as often as possible. Since she lives in New York City and I was working in Seattle, this wasn't easy."

"But you did keep seeing her."

"Oh, yeah. And before long she was putting some pressure on me to marry her. I thought about it. Hard. She's a great person, unemcumbered—"

"Meaning no kids?"

"Right . . . and she's very well-fixed financially. If we got married, we could do whatever we wanted—travel the world, buy a ranch in Montana, go on cruises ... you name it."

"Then marry her, dammit. Life is short."

He held up his hand. "Wait a minute. Two things happened that kind of blew that dream out of the water. First, about eight months ago she got tired of waiting for me. Her ex approached her for a reconcilliation. She decided to give it a try."

There was a pause. Larry looked like a sad old hound. I could feel his sadness.

"Well ... it happens. Maybe it's for the best. But then what's she doing up here, seeing you on the sly?"

"That's item number two. She didn't know it at the time, but when she went back to her hubby, she was pregnant."

"Hoo, boy. With yours?"

He nodded, looking down at his shoes. "It happened just before her ex came back to her with the offer. So she went back to him, only to discover her pregnancy the following month."

"Well, Larry, it'll be a healthy, good-looking baby. You've got the best genes I've ever seen, and she looked pretty regal herself, what I could see of her."

He held up his hand again. "Problem is, Doc, she convinced him that the baby was his. Even though it arrived a little early, he still believed it, not knowing anything about me, or our relationship. But the reason Margaret was childless when we met was not because she never wanted children, but because she was infertile. Or so she was led to believe."

"Aha! But she wasn't, of course. As you proved."

"Right. Turns out the reason she never conceived when married to ... married to her husband, was that he was sterile, not her."

"Ahhhhh. So somehow, Mr. Ex has since become slightly suspicious of the origins of his new child, and maybe went to the doctor."

"Exactly. And confirmed his suspicion—he is sterile. Therefore, the child is not his."

I sat down on the other bed and leaned back against the headboard. "Well, so what? They were separated at the time. Did this Margaret tell her hubby—what's his name?"

"Can't reveal it—" he said, waving me off. "Mr. Ex is an extremely rich and powerful businessman in Manhattan, with a lot of clout and political connections. He's thinking of running for national office. If I mentioned his name, you would know it."

"And may I assume he has an ego and sense of pride to match?"

"Exactly, Doc! You've hit it on the head. He's afraid somehow this secret of his son, and his infertility, will 'get out' to the public. For a man of his ego, with his public ambitions, this is intolerable. I tell you, he's a perfect son of a bitch."

"I was going to ask, did Margaret tell him about you?"

"No. She said she was artificially inseminated without telling him."

"But he's not buying."

"Hell no. And Margaret's scared. She's afraid maybe her ex is following her, trying to fit together the missing pieces."

"Well, Larry, I've got bad news—she's right."

I told him about the man in the car with the camera who left the parking lot right after Margaret did.

"Oh, *great*," Larry moaned, rising from the bed and pulling on a sweater. "C'mon, let's go have some drinks and food and figure out what the hell to do about this."

"Have you seen Mary?" I asked the question casually, so he would scarcely notice it. I watched him for any pause, hesitation, or other sign of furtiveness. There was none.

"No. I guess she's up the road in the Comfort Inn I told her about. I won't see her till tomorrow afternoon anyway, if at all. She's supposed to watch this warehouse. You want to call her?"

"Not now. Let's go up to the Irish Fisherman."

"How'd you know about that?"

"I know this town, Larry. I had some interesting adventures here about four years ago."

"Good, then we'll talk and then—"

The phone by his bed was ringing. We stared at it, as if it were a cobra rising out of a basket. Neither of us made a move to pick it up.

"Why don't you get it, Doc? Say you're a friend staying

here with me, and that I'm out to supper. Find out who it is."

I picked it up.

"Hello?"

"Larry Carpenter?"

"No, he's out right now. Who's calling please?"

"A friend. Joe Brindelli. Tell Larry I'm looking for a friend of his. A knucklehead named Doc Adams."

"Speaking."

"What?"

"It's me, Joe. What's up?"

"A lot's up. Most especially, the level of shit your standing in, pal."

"What do you mean?"

"You were over in P-town last night, right?"

"Yep. I was checking out some shops that sell ivory, as Brad Taylor instructed me to do."

"And then you called Marty and asked her to get me to run down a license plate number."

"Right. Did you do it?"

"Yes, I did. The car in the alley you saw belongs to its owner, James Harold."

"That's the guy who owns the store. So I guess everything's on the up-and-up. I thought the car was just pulled in there."

"No, that was Harold's car. That's where he usually parked it."

"Well, then?"

"Trouble is, Doc, they found James Harold this morning with a walrus tusk shoved through his chest. Extremely dead."

There was a few seconds' silence while I absorbed this jolt.

"Why?"

"Why what? You mean why is he dead? You're a surgeon; figure it out. Walrus tusk through chest—not a minor injury."

"No, I mean why was he killed?"

Another silence, this time on Joe's end. I heard him sigh, then take a long drag on his cigarette.

"Doc? You know how I, and countless others like me,

make my living. If you've forgotten, I'll remind you. It's figuring out why people are murdered. Then, when we figure out why, we can generally figure out *who* killed them. Follow?"

"This isn't funny, Joe."

"Who's saying it is? I was wrong on one thing. The weapon wasn't exactly a walrus tusk. It was a tusk carved in the shape of an Eskimo kayak, with an Eskimo hunter in it. The thing was shoved in bow first—isn't that correct, Doc, *bow* first?—into James Harold's heart."

I was getting a sinking feeling. . . .

"Now, it just so happens that in their preliminary inquiries, the Provincetown police have discovered that a person matching your description, with a name the same as yours, toting a bank card with your number on it, purchased a piece exactly like this yesterday."

"Well, yes. But not the same one."

"Well, they might think otherwise. That, and the fact that you were walking in that alley just exactly at the time the ME says Harold died, makes things a little sticky, if you get my drift."

"Well, you can vouch for me, can't you? They'll believe you, Joe." My heart was revving up again, skipping beats now and then like an idling race car with a hot cam in it.

"Thing is, before they even talked to me, they ran your name through all the official computer banks. Among other things, your file says you killed two men."

"Well, sure, Joe, but we all know these were bad guys. Hell, it was self-defense."

"Speaking of defense, I'm trying to get a lawyer of that persuasion for you right now. But you'd better get home, and pronto. The P-town cops want to see you, *toot sweet*."

He hung up the phone. I turned to Larry.

"Are we going drinking at the Irish Fisherman?" he asked.

"Uh-huh. And after that, guess what?"

"What?"

"I'm going to stow away on a tramp steamer to Papeete."

He opened the door and we stepped out.

"I don't think you can get a boat to Papeete from Gloucester, Doc. Farthest you can go from this port is probably someplace like Nova Scotia."

"Well, lead on, then. It'll have to do. It's better than nothing."

So we walked over to Larry's battered Ford pickup. When we were opening the doors, we heard an awful racket in the room up front. Yelling, cussing, and the breaking of furniture.

"Jesus," Larry said. "That's Brian Flynn again. Worst drunk I've seen in years."

"I heard him earlier. He vowed that tonight he was going to get snot-flying drunk."

"Well, looks like he kept his word."

I got into the truck, opened the window. Brian Flynn was still yelling.

"And them sons-a-bitches down at the yard can go *fuck* themselves, Denny! Am I right or *whut*?"

Two crashes followed.

"Well, at least with him things are going according to plan," I observed. "At least things are working out for *somebody*. . . ."

11

THE NEXT DAY WAS SUNDAY, WHICH I SPENT AT HOME—ALONE, of course—mostly recuperating from closing up the Irish Fisherman with Larry. I retrieved the dogs from my neighbors the Rutners, and played with them in the yard, then took them over to Great Meadows Wildlife Refuge to swim after the ducks. Then I ran and took several saunas. By dinnertime I felt fine, but had no appetite. I knew why: besides missing Mary and the boys, I was dreading the meeting the next day, Monday morning, with the Provincetown police.

When I went to bed, I was weary. But I scarcely slept.

By eight o'clock Monday morning Joe and I were driving up the neck of the Cape toward Provincetown.

"You look a little peaked today, Doc," he said, lighting a cigarette as he held the wheel of his police cruiser with his left hand. "Stay up late?"

"Not last night, but Saturday night Larry and I closed up the Irish Fisherman. Apparently, I was overserved."

Joe laughed. "Involuntary, eh?"

"I drank for two reasons—good news and bad news. Good news of not finding Mary in Larry's motel room, and bad news that you yourself gave me. I'm accused of murder."

"You are not accused of murder; you are a suspect in a murder."

"Great. I don't remember how much beer we drank; probably enough to float the *Nimitz*."

"Well, you better act respectable today, Doc. Be a pillar of your community, so to speak. I know it's hard for you to fake it, but do your best. I wasn't kidding when I told you that the cops in P-town aren't taking this thing lightly."

I opened the yellow paper bag with the Sea Unicorn's logo on it. I took out my kayak sculpture and held it up so he could see it. "Here's my proof I had nothing to do with Harold's murder."

He glanced at it quickly and then back to the road.

"Big deal. There are probably twenty or thirty of those things floating around Provincetown. Who's to say you didn't buy two of them and use one as the murder weapon?"

"For one thing, it's got a number on the bottom," I said, turning it upside down.

"Yeah, stuck on with a label. You could have switched labels."

"That's a pretty expensive dagger, wouldn't you say? Eleven hundred bucks?"

"Why do you think he was killed? Any theories?"

"None at all; I never laid eyes on the man. I would think that people who knew him would help out on that question."

"Well, a lot of people knew him, and liked him; he was one of the community's leading citizens. Assistant head of the chamber of commerce, on the board of the historical society . . . he served two terms as selectman a while back. It seems he had no enemies in the world."

"Well, he had one, and an extremely powerful one at that."

"How do you know this? How do you know the killer had connections?"

"I don't mean politically powerful. I don't even mean rich, though there's no telling about either of these. I'm speaking of physical strength. If the murder weapon was similar to this, you yourself can see the force required to drive this little ivory boat through the chest of the average man."

Joe took his hand off the wheel and felt the bow of the little boat. "Yeah, not very sharp . . . and it widens out fast. It would take a helluva strong guy to drive that into somebody's rib cage."

"There's something else you should know. I think the killer was in Harold's house when I went walking in the alley."

He turned to me quickly. "Why didn't you mention this earlier?"

"I was going to. I saw the dropping of a curtain when I was behind the house. Somebody was in there looking out the window at me, then dropped the curtain back into place when I turned to look. It was probably the killer."

"Or Harold, wanting to see who was trespassing."

"I was not trespassing, Joe; I was in the alley behind the house. That is not trespassing. I did nothing illegal."

He mused for a minute, then spoke.

"Well, if it was the killer, then he certainly got a look at you."

"It was nighttime."

"Was there an alley light? You know, one of those big powerful lights on a high pole at the end of the block?"

"Yes. In fact, I was facing it."

·"Then he could have caught an eyeful. And that isn't good."

"No, it isn't."

"Well, Dr. Adams," said Chief Lyle Henderson, "we certainly appreciate your past work with the Department of Public Safety. Paul Keegan even tells me you're a special policeman, in the capacity of medical examiner for Barnstable County."

"That was only for about a year; I was a temporary fill-in. But I still do work in forensic pathology for Joe and the guys over at headquarters."

"Teeth? That kind of thing?"

"Right. That kind of thing."

Chief Henderson, a big man with thinning light brown hair, a broad, puffy face, and wearing frameless glasses, leaned back in his swivel chair and stretched. Then he sighed and brought his arms down hard on his desk, leaning toward me.

"Still, it's strange," he mused, flipping the pages before him and running his big blocky finger down certain paragraphs and columns contained therein. "It's strange how trouble seems to follow you around."

I was going to do the Humphrey Bogart thing again and growl out of the side of my mouth: "Trouble is my business, pal."

But something made me hesitate. I think it was common sense. I wasn't certain it was common sense, however, because—as Mary points out—it so rarely comes my way.

"Lyle, Doc was on an investigative errand for the Fish and Wildlife Service. He's trying to help uncover a ring of ivory smugglers, who may also be in on the narcotics trade. Doc, tell the chief what you saw when you were in the alley behind the Harold residence."

I explained the dropping curtain.

"Well, maybe it was the killer, or maybe it was Harold. I mean, if somebody was after him and he knew it, he would be keeping a sharp lookout, wouldn't he?"

Joe and I nodded.

"What bothers me, gentlemen, is that he was killed with an ivory carving exactly like the one you purchased only an hour or so previous, Doctor. That, and the fact that by your own admission you were at the scene of the murder at exactly the right time. You have to admit the circumstantial evidence is compelling, even damning."

"If I had killed him, would I have made that phone call to Joe's wife telling where I was?"

"Probably not," answered the chief, "but the evidence is there, nonetheless."

"I assume you've interviewed Harold's close friends and associates," said Joe. "Anything come up from this?"

"Nope."

"Was he married?"

"No."

"Girlfriend? Boyfriend?"

"No, and no, to the best of our knowledge. Mr. James Harold, and everybody called him James, kept to himself, except for his devotion to civic and public issues. We've recently discovered he had a home in Key West, which I suppose might be considered the southern counterpart to this town. We've contacted the police there for any possible leads. Otherwise, there's no apparent motive."

"Was there a lot of ivory found in his house?" I asked.

"Some, but nothing out of the ordinary."

"Can we go look?"

"Dr. Adams, you are our official suspect as of this time. I hope you appreciate that. No, I don't think you killed him. But I'll tell you what I'm going to do. I'm going to book you and release you. He was a beloved man, and I want the community to know that we are following this thing."

"Come on, Lyle, you don't have to book him," said Joe.

"Well, I am, sort of. I'm going to take your prints, Doctor, and even a mug shot. We won't run it in the paper or anything, but it will be here, in this office."

So they did. They inked up a glass plate and rolled my thumbs and fingers over it, then rolled them onto a chart with ten squares, one for each print. But they could have saved their time; as a person licensed to carry concealed weapons in the Commonwealth of Massachusetts, my prints were already on file at the Concord Police Department and elsewhere.

After this, Joe asked if we could take a look at the inside of the late Mr. Harold's house. Obviously, Chief Henderson thought this was a bit strange, since I was an "official" suspect, but we went anyway. The house's interior matched its outside: immaculate and tastefully furnished with many prints, both nautical and otherwise. Nice Oriental rugs over varnished hardwood floors, and an impressive scrimshaw collection in the back parlor, where Henderson said the body was found. Careful not to touch anything—I didn't wish to leave my prints anywhere in this little house—I looked through a small slot between the curtains and found myself looking in the direction of the garage.

"This is the window," I said.

"Okay, thank you, Dr. Adams, and thanks, Joe. On second thought, I won't refer to you as our official suspect anymore. I hope you understand, it's just that, well, when somebody gets murdered, the townspeople put a helluva lot of pressure on us, wanting to know what we're doing to get the killer. You know. . . ."

"It's a bitch being a cop, Lyle," I said. "Especially nowadays. I've hung around Joe for long enough to know."

"Well, since you understand my position, Dr. Adams, I hope you and Joe will help out on this thing all you can."

"We will," said Joe. "All we ask is that you don't blow Doc's cover, if that's at all possible."

"I'll keep it as tight as I can."

"By the way, the young woman who waited on me at the shop said Harold rarely came into the shop in the off-season. So how was the death discovered so early?"

Henderson opened a pocket notebook and flipped through it. "Doug Mackie, assistant manager, was expecting him at the shop. They were to go out for lunch and go over some paperwork. When Harold didn't show, Mackie called. When he didn't answer, Mackie walked over to the house, saw him on the floor of the parlor from the front windows, and called us."

"Thanks," Joe said. "Maybe we'll talk to him."

"Chief, I appreciate being let off the hook," I said, "but there is one more thing you could do for me."

"What?"

"Let us look at the body. Is it in Boston yet, or still in the Hyannis clinic?"

"The clinic. You know where it is?"

"Oh, yeah," said Joe. "Doc worked there for almost a year. That's when they brought that floater in for him to work on. He resigned."

"I can see why," said Henderson, and we left for Hyannis.

Inside the small brick building, in the cool, tile-lined room that is way too silent, they pulled out the big drawer for us and drew back the sheet. A gray-haired man was in there. He looked pleasant enough. Better than a lot of deceased I had seen. But still, they don't look like they do in a casket at a "viewing" funeral. They haven't been worked on yet. That rosy-colored fluid hasn't been force-pumped into their blood vessels. The dark spots haven't been covered with makeup. And so on. Mr. James Harold's left eye was half-open. His mouth was open, too, as it is with almost all corpses. A major skill that all morticians learn is how to sew a mouth shut. I asked for a retractor and opened the mouth further, taking out my penlight.

"Jeez, Doc, I thought you hated this stuff."

"You're right; I can't stand it. But this is important. I want to know who was in that house. Because whoever it was, killed this guy. And he saw me, too."

"And you think he might . . ."

"Uh-huh, come to get me in the middle of the night."

"What's the mouth tell you? I swear, you can make a dead mouth talk."

"This mouth says, 'I belong to a sixty-some-year-old man who smoked a pipe, was born and raised in a well-to-do family in America's Southwest—I'd say west Texas or southern New Mexico—who was right-handed and enjoyed an excellent diet most of his life."

"How you get all that?"

"The age is determined by the gum line and general enamel attrition. People are like horses; you can pretty much tell their age by their teeth. Right-handed is simple— the wear on the gum line is more pronounced on the left side of the mouth. People always brush harder on the oppo-

site side, since they're drawing the brush back and forth
with more force. The most interesting thing about these
teeth, though, is their fine condition. I count only two fill-
ings. This guy was not a native New Englander, that's for
sure. See that purplish-brown discoloration? That's caused
by fluoride. Excess fluoride—maybe ten or twenty times
the normal prophylactic dose."

"Why'd he take so much fluoride?"

"Because he grew up in the southwestern desert, where
the water is loaded with the stuff. People from there hardly
ever get cavities, which is what clued dentists and health
professionals into fluoride in the first place."

Joe drew the sheet down further, revealing the gaping
dark hole in the center of his chest. It looked incongruous,
such a nasty murder wound in this distinguished-looking
gentleman who, according to Chief Lyle Henderson, hadn't
an enemy in the world. But obviously Chief Henderson
didn't know the whole story regarding the late Mr. Harold.

"Where's the weapon?" I asked.

"If I had to guess, I'd say it's been sent to our headquarters at Ten Ten."

"Would his personal effects be there as well?"

"Yeah, the stuff in his pockets and so on. Since Paul
Keegan's on this case for the state, why don't we talk to
him?"

"Good idea. I admit I feel better about this thing knowing he's on it. You know who I think did this?"

"Who?"

"Johnny Ridge, the big bad Indian."

"Why him?"

"Because of the strength needed to do this. Very few
people have that kind of brute strength."

"Umm. And this makes you uneasy, doesn't it? Because
Johnny Ridge saw you once before, in Chinatown outside
Sam Ho's shop. He might have thought something was
funny then. But if he's the killer, and looked out the window and saw you a second time . . ."

"Yeah, you got it. He wouldn't be pleased. And he
would know, beyond any doubt, that I was snooping after
him."

"You finished with this?"

"*This?* You mean Mr. Harold? Gee, when I die I sure hope nobody refers to me as 'this.' "

Joe pulled the cover back up over the late James Harold and slid the big drawer shut. We went out into the autumn sunshine, and I was glad to be alive. Nothing makes you appreciate life more than visiting those cool, tile-lined rooms that are way too quiet.

On the drive back to Boston Joe said, "I'm getting uneasy, too, Doc. It's about the murder weapon. I'm thinking that whoever did it was watching you earlier, when you bought that ivory Eskimo hunter in the kayak. Then he used the same thing as his murder weapon to implicate you."

"Right. Or maybe to warn me to stay away. Maybe he was saying, 'Listen, I know who you are and I've been watching you. I even know what you buy in stores.' "

"I wonder if he knows your name and where you live."

"Jesus, I hope not, Joe."

"Me, too. Hey, did that assistant manager, Doug what's-his-name, meet you or see you?"

"At the store? I didn't meet him. If he saw me, I wasn't aware of it."

"Think he could have done it?"

"How the hell do I know? There could be ten people in P-town who had reason to kill Harold that nobody knew about. But if you see Paul Keegan, you might mention it."

"Ah, he's probably already interviewed him. You want to stop off at headquarters and look at that ivory kayak?"

"Might as well, it's on the way home and I'm booked solid with patients all day tomorrow. Now's our chance."

Up on the top floor of the big building at Ten Ten Commonwealth Avenue, headquarters for the Department of Public Safety, Commonwealth of Massachusetts, lab director Karl Pirsch paced the shiny linoleum floor slowly, hands behind back, head lowered at the floor. His tall, angular body and beaky nose, the ruff of white hair around his bald head, and his intense blue eyes reminded me of an irate great white heron, stalking through the shallows, looking for fish to gobble up. He wasn't smiling. Karl Pirsch, fanatically devoted to his job—actually, fantatical in general—

seldom smiled. He was not an easy man to work for. But on the plus side, he was a lab chief extraordinaire, a brilliant chemist and logician.

I liked the guy. But then as Joe always reminds me, I only see him every two or three months.

Karl raised his head and stalked over to the marble-topped table in the middle of the huge room. Above it was a skylight and the grates for the exhaust fans, which worked constantly, ridding the place of the noxious fumes and dangerous gases that were a part of the daily operation of the state's biggest crime lab.

On the black marble lay the ivory carving, identical to mine, of the Eskimo hunter in his kayak. Next to the object was a small stack of eight-by-ten glossy photos showing James Harold's corpse with the murder weapon implanted in his chest. Some of the photos, taken at the scene in Provincetown, showed the corpse clothed. The others were taken in the Hyannis clinic, and were especially grisly. If you turned the picture upright, so that it looked like Mr. Harold was standing instead of reclining on the slab, it appeared as if this crazy Eskimo hunter was paddling his skin boat into the man's chest . . . and was halfway there.

Karl shook his head, peering at the carving through his wire spectacles. "No prints," he said in a clipped tone. "I am assuming the killer either wore gloves or was careful to wipe the carving off afterward."

"Would you say he's a pro, Karl?" asked Joe.

Pirsch shrugged. "I would say this much, he is an extremely powerful man."

Joe looked at me out of the corner of his eye. "That's what Doc says, too."

Pirsch shrugged again. "A rib cage is a rib cage, gentlemen, and you can see for yourselves how blunt the point of this boat is. It takes a big, strong person to drive it through bone."

I went close to the table and peered at the carving. It was identical to mine, even in size and color. The only differences would be minute variations in tool marks and the ivory grain.

"You know, Karl, I work with teeth every day. I know enamel isn't ivory, but I'm curious as to exactly how the two are different. I guess I'm amazed at why people are so fascinated with ivory."

"Ah, Doc, ivory . . . well, it is one of nature's truly precious commodities."

"But why? What makes it so special? I always assumed that ivory was just a variation of enamel. Aren't tusks simply the overdeveloped teeth of the elephant and walrus?"

"Yes, but over the epochs, the tooth enamel of certain mammals has evolved into something different . . . and wonderful."

"It's easy to work and durable, is that it?" I asked.

"That, and the color and warmth of good ivory. But the major differences lie in the internal structure, the grain, if you will, of the ivory itself. You know, I have a friend in town who is probably America's greatest expert on ivory. I could arrange for you to meet him if you like."

"Yes I would. I'd like that very much."

Karl wrote a name and an address on a card and handed it to me. Then Joe and I walked out to Joe's cruiser, which carried me home.

To my empty house.

12

I PARKED THE CAR IN THE BACK TURNAROUND AND WENT INSIDE the house. Empty. I walked through my study, back through the hall, and peeked inside Mary's ceramic workshop, which she calls her Atelier. Deserted and silent. I walked through our wide front hall. To say I was depressed would be an understatement. It was hard enough with the boys grown and gone, but Mary's absence struck me like a sharp knife. Slid right up under the ribs.

I walked into the kitchen, underneath the beams dripping with copper saucepans and pots. I looked over at the big blue enameled six-burner restaurant stove that Mary got from Sweden the year before . . . the white counters and French cabinetry. It was a great kitchen, and full of great memories, too. In the old days, before his recent marriage, Joe came out almost every weekend and helped cook those terrific meals. But now he was married and living in town almost full-time; he and Marty came out less and less frequently. Number-one son, Jack, now twenty-five, was still in Woods Hole working on his doctorate in the "ethology of marine cetaceans," or whale behavior. Number-two son, Tony, twenty-two, was working on a ranch just outside Livingston, Montana, rounding up horses, cattle, and stray young women. Emphasis on the latter, I believe.

And Mary, the erstwhile part-time R.N., was, of course, still up in Gloucester, reportedly staying at the Comfort Inn north of town, working with Larry Carpenter trying to bust the illicit ivory ring. I had not seen her or heard from her in almost three days.

Gee, the place sure was dark and silent. I went out the back and let the dogs in, and instantly felt a rush of relief as they sprang inside, licking my hands and wagging their tails. I had to remember to thank my neighbors the Rutners for feeding them in my absence. I ambled over to the sideboard and poured myself a Johnny Walker Red, topping it with warm soda water, no ice. I went into my study and opened the mail. Same old shit. I lighted my pipe and read through some medical journals.

Did I want to eat, or just drink? I didn't know. It sure would be good to have some company. I wasn't particular; Attila the Hun or Tamerlane would do. . . .

The phone rang, and I almost tripped over myself in my eagerness to answer it.

"Good evening," said a mechanical-sounding voice, "this is New England Credit Service, offering you a chance to save, save, save on your next loan! If you are using a Touch-Tone phone and are interested in a car loan, please press one now . . . if you would like information on a home or home equity loan, please press two now . . . one of our representatives will be with you shortly—"

I slammed the phone down and went back into the dining room to refill my glass. It's bad enough to get "telemarketing" sales calls. But the computerized versions, using a programmed fake voice, are inexcusable.

Somewhere in the middle of my third scotch I realized I wasn't really hungry—or didn't care. I stared at the phone, turned on the television, turned it off again almost immediately, and stared at the phone again. I wanted to call Mary but was somehow afraid. I didn't want to appear lonely or a little scared, I suppose. I once heard a song by Jimmy Buffett called "If the Phone Doesn't Ring, It's Me." Well, that's how I felt.

Finally I couldn't stand it any longer and dialed the Comfort Inn in Gloucester.

"I'm sorry, sir," said the young female voice on the other end. "I don't have a Mrs. Mary Adams registered here. Are you sure you have the right place?"

"I, uh, hell, ma'am, I don't know. I was told she was staying there, maybe for a week. Maybe she's not using her real, uh, that name—"

"I have a Mary Brindelli registered."

"That would be her. What room?"

"I'm sorry, sir, we do not give out room numbers over the phone. Would you like to leave a message?"

"Yes. Can you inform her that her husband called? She knows the number here—that is, she used to, back in the olden days. Perhaps she's forgotten it now, in her new life."

"Husband? Oh . . . see, she registered as *Miss* Mary Brindelli."

"Oh, she did, did she?" I felt my blood pressure go up a few notches. "Well, when she's free for a minute, if she can spare the time, would she mind calling home?"

"Yes. I'll make sure she gets the message."

Miss. Brindelli, eh? I thought as I dialed the Dory. I wonder whose idea that was?

"Thank you for calling the Dory, how can we help you?"

"May I speak with Larry Carpenter, please?"

"Just a second."

"Hello?" I recognized the Elvis baritone right away.

"Larry, this is Doc."

"Hey, how ya doing, Doc? Shake that hangover yet?"

"Sort of, I guess I'm building another one as we speak. I'm trying to find Mary; she's not at the Comfort Inn."

"Oh, she just left here. She ought to be back up there in a few minutes. We were just comparing notes on what we've observed here so far."

"Which is?"

"Which is, we can't see any sign of anything going on at the Sea Feast warehouse. At least not yet. Mary's initial story is that she wants fifty pounds of turbot for a big party she's throwing. They seem more than eager to oblige. Then, after she's bought this and established herself as a valued customer, she's going to offhandedly ask them that since they're in the import business, do they know any sources for fur and ivory."

"You think this will work?"

"Don't know; we hope it will."

"And there won't be any danger?"

"Naw."

"Did you know she's going by the name Miss Mary Brindelli?"

" 'Course. We told her to. If anybody on the other side of the fence gets suspicious, they could easily trace the Adams name to you, Doc, and put the pieces together. Then there might be a little danger. Who knows? This is pretty standard procedure. We gave her a new ID and a checking account in that name, too. When you think about it, it's not really a fake ID, since her birth certificate reads Mary Brindelli."

"Wonderful. Well, I guess she'll be calling me pretty soon."

"She ought to, unless she went out to eat first."

"Thanks, Larry. How are things going at your end?"

"Nothing much. Except I got the whole pier believing I did some time for smuggling, and that I'm a little restless and ready for more action. We're all hoping that somebody will approach me pretty soon to do some running, so I—hey! Guess what happened? You know that purse you bought Mary? Well, the results from the lab in Ashland came back. Brad called to tell me that the ivory medallion is definitely illegal. Mary's got a sharp eye, Doc."

"Yes, she does. Well, good luck, Larry. Be careful. Watch out for Mary."

"I will, Doc. Same to you."

Well, at least they didn't go out to dinner together, I thought. Of course, they wouldn't; that would blow their cover. Then I thought about the guy wearing the white sweater in the car outside Larry's room the night before. What if he saw them together? What then? If he really was tracking Larry's ex-girlfriend Margaret, probably nothing. On the other hand, maybe it would mean a lot. Maybe the rich so-and-so jealous husband would become enraged and go gunning for both of them.

No, that was unlikely.

I mixed yet another drink, waiting for Miss Mary Brindelli to call back.

I waited and waited, but she never called back. I fell asleep in front of the television watching some old Greer Garson movie.

Fell asleep in my clothes. Great evening. Absolutely terrific.

13

THE REST OF THE WEEK WAS NOT ANY BETTER. MONDAY I HAD three bad patients in a row, and one in the afternoon, a Mr. Hastie, whose clotting time was way above normal. He wasn't a hemophiliac, but pushing it. My assistant Susan

Petri and I couldn't figure out why we had no warning; the standard "office get-acquainted form" usually uncovers things like this. We learned later that he'd chugged half a dozen aspirin before coming in to get a "head start" on the pain. The result was he had almost no clotting capacity. If it's anything that an oral surgeon fears, it's Big Red, especially in the office, away from serious medical teamwork and a reserve supply of blood. As the name implies, Big Red is Mr. Hemorrhage. Severed blood vessels are always a problem, and the human head has more blood vessels per square inch than anywhere. On top of that, the patient's mouth is wet and funny-shaped. It's not "surgeon friendly." You can't even apply a pressure bandage most places in there. We were on the verge of calling an ambulance when I managed to put additional sutures in and pack him with gel foam.

It was a pretty close call, and I arrived home drained and edgy. I finally got Mary up at the Comfort Inn. Turned out she was drained and edgy, too, and before you know it, we were arguing. I sure wish I could say that none of it was my fault, but that wasn't the case.

Tuesday and Wednesday were not much better than Monday. And Thursday I was informed by the lawyer representing Mr. Edward Hastie—the aspirin chugger who'd put us under so much stress—that I was being sued for malpractice. Great.

So on Friday, when I finished washing up at a little past two, I turned to the lovely and patient (God knows she's patient!) Susan Petri and our new assistant, Diane Nakamura, and told them we were all finished for the day.

"But Dr. Adams," said Susan, "I do have some statements to get out. And then there's that, uh, legal matter. . . ."

"Hell with them. Let's get out of here; it's been a helluva week." I dried my hands and stalked into my inner sanctum.

"I wouldn't worry about it, Dr. Adams," said Susan in her low, sultry voice as she stood in the doorway of my office. She shook her mane of chestnut hair and looked at me through those big green eyes. "He told us about the aspirin.

I was a witness, and so was Diane. If need be, we'll tell that to the court."

"That's good to know. And anyway, he may cool down and drop the suit once he considers it."

Susan leaned against the doorframe molding. Her mouth folded into a half pout. I wondered what was wrong with her. I knew she'd broken up with her boyfriend of three years recently. Maybe that was it. Then she came in and sat down in the tufted leather Chippendale chair, facing me. She didn't say anything. Something was up.

"Something big is bothering you, right?" she finally said.

"Umm. No," I said, pretending to be busy by shuffling lab reports on my desk.

Silence. She sat there, gazing at me. Her hair hung down all over her shoulders.

"Are you having a fight with your wife?"

"How did you know?"

"Because I know you. There are not very many people you love enough to have them upset you. I know it's not Dr. Abramson; you were playing chess with him at noon, just before the two of you went running."

"We weren't playing chess. He always beats me in chess, and lately I don't need that. We were discussing my sanity, which, as you have correctly observed, Susan, is slightly tentative at the moment."

"Um. And how is Dr. Abramson's sanity?"

"Unfortunately, Dr. Abramson's sanity is quite beyond discussion. It is totally, irretrievably lost."

"Then why do you hang around him all the time? Why do you go to him for advice?"

I shrugged. "Somebody's got to humor him."

"Well, if you're really having trouble at home, you can always come stay at my place for a few days. My new town house has a spare bedroom."

I looked over the leather-topped desk at those green eyes again.

"That's really nice of you, Susan, but not necessary. Mary's not home right now; I have the whole, huge place to myself."

Her eyes widened. "Moved out? Gee, Dr. Adams, no wonder you're upset!"

"She hasn't moved out—she's up in Gloucester doing some work for the government. She's up there working with my former best friend."

The eyes widened again. Her chest rose and fell. Some chest. Actually, the sight of concerned Susan Petri was beginning to lift my spirits.

"So, are you going home now?"

"I was, but actually I just changed my mind," I said, pulling out the address Karl Pirsch had given me Monday evening in his lab. "I want to find out about ivory. What makes it so valuable. What makes people kill elephants, and themselves, over it."

"How come you're so anxious to find this out now?" she asked. Good question.

"Because this business Mary's working on. You know, for the government?"

She nodded slowly, her mouth half-open. Her face had a very soft look. There was a slight frown of worry over those eyes. "What kind of business?"

"She's tracking down illegal ivory. And from the start I've felt sort of . . . left out of the whole thing. So whenever I can, I try to get involved in it. Just around the edges, sort of . . ."

"Well," she said, rising from the chair, "I hope things work out for you; I hate to see you sad."

"Don't worry," I said, forcing a smile. "They will."

She paused at the doorway and turned and looked back at me, her face between a smile and a pout. She gave me a dainty good-luck wave. Be still my heart.

By three o'clock I was rolling along Atlantic Avenue in the heart of old downtown Boston, right under the shadow of the Customs House. When it was built in the middle of the last century, this peaked stone building was the tallest in town. Or rather, the only tall building in town. Then, somewhere around the middle of this century, Boston got its first real skyscraper: the Prudential Building. Now downtown is a forest of fifty-story monstrosities, and Good Old Boston looks a lot like all the other major cities. Too bad.

On a half-block lane called Newmarket, tucked away in the tiny, winding caverns of streets in this old section of the city, there's a little, room-wide emporium, one story tall, that huddles low under the big buildings. It's called the Olde Curiosity Shoppe. And in this place, I was talking to the man whose name Pirsch had scribbled on the paper: William Givens, old-time ivory broker, formerly of London and British East Africa.

"Hate the damned name, Dr. Adams. Dickens is turning over in his grave, no doubt. But it gets the tourists in. I need them to keep the place afloat."

"Why do it? From what Karl Pirsch tells me, you have no need to work."

Givens finished lighting his pipe—a vintage Charatan I guessed by squarish bevels on the stem—shook out the match, and made fragrant wreaths of smoke envelop his head, which was bald like Karl Pirsch's. And encircled on three-plus sides with a dramatic, fluffy, white main. But his nose and face, and body, were markedly different. Instead of having a vulturine face like Karl's, his nose and face were leonine: full, thick, strong, and compact. His body was heavy, but Givens carried the weight well, like Sidney Greenstreet or Jackie Gleason. His plumpness protruded out in a wide curve, it did not sag or sway. It gave the impression of power and resolve, rather than sloth or gluttony.

"Did Karl tell you where we met?" he said, turning to me and puffing.

I shook my head, sniffing.

"At the Society for Bald-headed Men."

"The what? You've got to be kidding."

"Absolutely not. Actually, the club is an offshoot of the local MENSA society. You've heard of them?"

"The club for geniuses? Yeah."

"*Yeah* . . . your reaction is typical. Certainly the organization has more than its share of conceited, boring, twerpy, adolescent, precious snobs. And worse. That's why Pirsch and I decided to drop out and form our own scion, as it were. We met a few times, over drinks, for conversation, when we met a third chap, who, as we suddenly noticed, was as bald as we were, which I suppose," he mused, stopping to tamp his bowl and relight it, "is not that unusual for men our age. However, we discovered that by calling ourselves the Society for Bald-headed Men, and imposing that arbitrary prerequisite for membership, we could considerably limit the applicants, or sycophants, or whatever foul vermin we wished to avoid. And I assure you, Dr. Adams, the human race is terribly full of foul vermin. If you don't believe that yet, just wait a few years."

"Don't worry," I said, recollecting the body of poor Mr. Harold with the carved ivory kayak through his heart, "I believe it now."

"Well, anyway, we decided it would be fun, and over these twelve years it has been great fun."

"How many members?"

"Thirteen. No more, no less. Plus I.A., an honorary member, or, uh, *was* an honorary member. We all miss I.A. very much."

"Who was I.A.?"

"Isaac Asimov."

"Ah, what a wonderful man!"

"He certainly was. Anyway, that's the story of the Society of Bald-headed Men."

"Sounds like a Sherlock Holmes case. How often do you meet, and where?"

"We meet every Sunday evening. We chose this time because it is, A) pagan, B) convenient, and C) it doesn't interfere with our careers in any way, and it allows us, all bachelors, to have some sort of family life on the weekends."

"What a splendid idea!"

"As to where we meet, it is almost always at one of the finer restaurants open on Sunday. We usually prefer the Ritz, meeting in the bar an hour before the meal."

"And what do you do at these functions? Talk?"

"Exactly. Talk about what we've read, seen, or heard, what's new—that sort of thing. I tell you, I learn more from my weekly Baldy meeting than—"

"Baldy?"

"Yes, we call ourselves the Baldies for short. Anyway, what brings you here? Karl phoned me earlier in the week and said you might stop by. You're an oral surgeon?"

"That's right."

"And a bit of a detective and adventurer, according to Karl. You want to buy some priceless artifact?"

"No. I want you to tell me everything you know about ivory."

He paused, puffed, and stared at me in disbelief.

"Hah! Have you got three weeks? If Karl told you the truth, he would have said that I know more about ivory than any man living—in America at least. There are a few old geezers in London, in 'the trade,' as we used to say, who can give me a run for my money."

"You still speak with a trace of English accent."

"I damn well ought to. Spent most of life there, when I wasn't in Africa or India."

"Why did you move here?" I asked.

"Because shortly after the war—you know which war I mean—the British soul lost its rigor. My countrymen decided—most unwisely—to put their future in the government, rather than in individual initiative. It's never been the same since, I'm afraid. And of course if you've got money nowadays, the British government will tax the life out of you."

"Taxes, eh? Then I'm surprised you've settled in Massachusetts."

"True!" He chuckled, turning and falling into a battered leather chair nestled up against an enormous bookcase. "But not half as bad as England . . . yet. And not as bad as New York, either. I know; I checked it out. And not half the city Boston is, either. Boston remains America's only European city. Now, I could have immigrated to Bermuda or Jamaica, or perhaps some other Brit holdout in the subtropics, but I don't like hot weather. I like four seasons, with lots of rain and chill. So, here I am. Like it or not."

He lighted his pipe again and puffed, looking at me out of the corner of his eye.

"So tell me about ivory," I said.

"Well, first of all, it's akin to tooth enamel. You do know teeth, Dr. Adams. Teeth are enamel: *Hydroxyapatite,* the hardest animal substance known. Even in cremation, the teeth remain."

"Exactly. Which is why teeth are so important for identification purposes after fires and plane crashes, and so on."

"Right . . . now, Dr. Adams, what do you think would

happen if an eight-ton elephant had tusks of enamel five or six feet long sticking out of his mouth?"

I shrugged. "I would think he'd be extremely well armed."

"Wrong. Dead wrong. He'd be disarmed in a day or so."

"How so?"

"Because the first time—the very first time—this huge animal would strike those long beams of enamel against a rock or tree, or against another set of enamel tusks, what do you think would happen?"

Immediately I knew the answer, and felt foolish.

"They would snap like icicles!"

"Yes, absolutely they would. Think of the enormous pressures and leverage forces existing here—tusks as much as eight or ten feet long, carried by an animal as heavy as three or four cars. So it's obvious that these weapons and tools must be flexible, else they would scarcely grow longer than a foot before they snapped at the slightest accident."

"How long do they get? Surely not ten feet."

Givens rose from his chair and led me over to a photograph framed on the wall between two antelope heads. The picture showed two Africans in Islamic garb—fezzes and big robes—each holding a giant elephant tusk. The tusks were a matched pair, and even the two natives seemed to be twins. The tusks rested on the ground, and their tops towered over the two men. The photo's caption read:

Heaviest tusks on record. Tusks from the Great Serengheti Elephant. Main tusk, 11 feet, 7 inches, 238 pounds. Secondary tusk: 10 feet, 9.5 inches, 214 pounds. Shown here in the Zanzibar Market, 1898.

"Wow. How many like that are left in Africa?"

"Probably none. But now and then a hunter takes a pair of one-fifties. No, all the huge tuskers are gone. Shot dead."

"Did you ever hunt elephant?" I asked.

"Once, and it was more than enough. I couldn't bear to kill those magnificent animals. Also, I couldn't bear the recoil of a Westley-Richards four-seventy double rifle. In almost all of the Dark Continent, elephants are now protected. And they should be. Still, I think their future is precarious in the extreme. There's no way to control the poaching."

"That's what's happening to our walrus now."

"Yes. I'm afraid it's same the world over. But the only true ivories are the elephant, walrus, and the narwhal. All the others, such as the teeth of whales, boar, and hippo, are really true teeth, or enamel. As such, they aren't nearly as good for carving because they're too hard and brittle."

"I still find it difficult to believe that ivory is so flexible."

"As flexible as a trout rod. Look here—"

He grabbed a pale riding crop and held it in front of him, each of his hands at the ends of the whip. He bent the crop in a deep U shape twice and whisked it through the air.

"Pure ivory. The British gentry used them a hundred years ago. It's the *grain*, a curious and unique arrangement of the cells and vessels within the tusks, that gives ivory its tremendous resilience and springy quality. Let me show you a cross section of tusk."

He led me into a back room to a table, on which rested a pale cylinder about six inches in diameter. He turned it over and held it under a the desk lamp. I looked closely and saw the grain he was speaking of, a series of intersecting arcs in the cross section of the tusk segment that resembled the engine turnings on a watchcase, or on the breechblocks of some double shotguns.

"That's amazing. You mean it wasn't carved that way?"

"No. It's the way ivory grows. There are three layers to true ivory—the bark, or outer covering, the body, and the inner dentine, which resembles the bark. Tusks grow from the outside, that is, the outer layers form first in the tooth socket, followed by the inner pulp. The whole structure is filled with millions of tiny tubes, like capillaries, that are in turn filled with a gelatinous substance. This is what gives even the thickest tusks their resilience and elasticity, and what produces ivory's unique luster and warm glow when it is cut and polished."

I noticed what looked like a walrus tusk at the far end of the same table and picked it up.

"Does this walrus ivory have the same unique grain and luster?"

"Not really. It is ivory, but a poor variation compared to elephant ivory. For one thing, the hollow in its center—the place where the nerve is, extends for two thirds the length of the walrus tusk, whereas it extends for only one third the length of the elephant tusk. Also, it is more brittle than elephant ivory and . . . just plain smaller; the work a carver can execute is limited in size and scope. Most of the oldest ivory carvings—pieces from the Cro-Magnon era of fifteen to twenty thousand B.C.—are walrus ivory. The animal was once much more widely distributed than now. The only other really true ivory comes from another arctic animal, the narwhal, or sea unicorn, but its tusk is hollow, twisted, and rough."

"Well, from what the Fish and Wildlife people say, the walrus won't be around at all in twenty years." I stood there in the back of the little, jam-packed shop, running my hands through my hair. I was trying to remember something. Then I got it.

"Hey, hasn't plastic pretty much replaced the need for ivory anyway?"

"Yes, for several important applications. The two most important are piano keys and billiard balls. Most pianos manufactured before the Second World War used ivory keys exclusively. Here, let me show you some old keys. . . ."

Givens opened the drawers of an ancient oaken desk. Inside were hundreds and hundreds of wafer-thin, yellowish piano-key tops. Many were cracked and chipped. He picked out a few and held them up.

"Each piano key top has two pieces," he said. "The thick part, the part the player's fingers rest on, is called the head. The thin part, the part that extends up between the black keys, is called the tail. As you can see, I am always on the lookout for old pianos, whose keys I salvage for their heads and tails."

"So what are these old keys worth?" I asked.

"Not much . . . yet." He shrugged. "But they're ivory, and most pianos now use high-grade phenolic plastic, which, though not as precious, maintains its color and doesn't crack or chip. But the billiard-ball industry was the premier use for high-quality ivory exported from Africa. This best-grade ivory, *live* ivory, not dead—"

"Wait a second; what do you mean, live and dead ivory? If you kill the elephant to get the tusks, then it must be dead, right?"

"Quite so, but only twenty percent of all ivory exports in the old days came from recently killed animals. All the rest was dead ivory—tusks found by natives and herdsmen from animals long dead in the bush. Only live ivory has the best concentrations of the gelatinous pores I talked about earlier."

"This is a bit much," I said, shaking my head. "I had no idea it was all so . . . involved and complicated."

"Of course it was, dear boy. The ivory trade was the principal reason for the exploration and development of the Dark Continent. Have you never heard of W.D.M. Bell, otherwise known as Karamojo Bell, the greatest elephant hunter of all time?"

"Can't say as I have."

"Well, he was the most amazing hunter and explorer in history, although what he did would be condemned nowadays. But as I was saying, this prime ivory would appear in huge stacks in the warehouses in London, near Mincing Lane on what was called the 'Ivory Floor' of the London Docks. Here was the greatest assemblage of ivory the world has ever seen. The auctions were held quarterly, and still are, but the scale has dropped to practically nothing."

"But even billiard balls are now made of plastic, aren't they?"

"Yes, a compound called bonzoline—I believe it's some sort of phenolic resin—and plastic is more durable and a hundred times cheaper. But it still lacks that wonderful grain and elasticity that true ivory has."

Givens led me back farther in the shop to a table stacked with square wooden cartons. I looked inside and saw that each contained a set of billiard balls. "There are two kinds of elephant ivory in Africa, Dr. Adams. The hard variety, found roughly in the western half of the Dark Continent, and soft, found in the eastern half. When the Belgians opened up the Congo Basin, and the Portuguese colonized

Angola, a lot of hard ivory began appearing in the markets of Europe. Still, the soft varieties found in Kenya, Tanzania, Abyssinia, southern Egypt, and so forth were and are the most prized. From each average-size tusk, one can extract three billiard balls of the first quality, one of the second, and a third with the bark still on."

"But wait—that's only five balls per tusk. It takes fifteen plus one—the cue ball—to make a set. So you're saying that it takes over three complete tusks to make a set of ivory billiard balls?"

"Exactly. And as you can imagine, Doctor, they're not cheap. And they must be seasoned for five years before being turned dead true on a special lathe. One manufacturer in London once had a stock of over thirty thousand ivory spheres in stock."

I did a quick mental calculation. At five balls per tusk, that meant that three thousand elephants had given up their lives for that one trove of billiard balls alone. I gave an inward groan and staggered back to the front of the shop.

"Are there any other cultures that prize ivory?" I asked.

"All cultures prize ivory, Dr. Adams, and have since the dawn of time, much as they all prize gold and silver, ebony, lapis lazuli, gems, and so on. But the Asians are prominent ivory carvers, and collectors. The Chinese have done excellent carving for centuries, which should come as no surprise. Lately, though, it's the Japanese who demand the stuff—at ridiculous prices—for two personal items most Japanese males deem essential—the *hanko,* or 'chop,' and the *netsuke.*"

"The chop. Is that the little carved cylinder of ivory they ink up and use like a rubber stamp to put their seal on documents?"

"Exactly. Now these aren't big—say, half the size of a cigarette lighter. But when twenty million Japanese businessmen want them, you see the problem."

"Then what are those other things you mentioned?"

"Netsuke. What they are really are huge buttons, from which hangs a silken cord. They wear these netsuke buttons—which are usually extraordinarily carved and of great value—on their waist sash when wearing the traditional kimono robe. Then the silken cord extends down from the netsuke and holds a small pouch called an *inro*. The *inro* is a small purse that holds pipes and tobacco, money, things like that."

I rose from my leather chair and thanked William Givens for his time and patience.

"Not at all," he said. "There's nothing I'd rather talk about than ivory. But one thing does disturb me. When Karl called to tell me your interest, I assumed you were a beginning collector. He said this wasn't true—that you were in fact helping to run down an ivory-smuggling ring. Worse yet, he told me that murder has already been done by this gang of pirates. This is true?"

I nodded.

"Then, Dr. Adams, I must now tell you the single most important thing about ivory you could ever know."

"You mean you left something out?"

"The most important thing. People kill for this stuff. They have already killed for it recently and . . . they could kill you. Be careful, my friend, and I hope to see you again."

When I returned home it was late. Too late to cook, and too late to get steamed up because nobody (read: Mary) had left a message on my answering machine. I was vaguely hungry, but noticeably thirsty. I downed a half-liter mug of Hacker Pschor lager, followed it with a JWR on the rocks with a splash, and was on the verge of going out to a local Greek restaurant to order a gyro sandwich when the front doorbell rang.

I almost didn't answer it because Mary and I don't use our front door except when company comes. Like so many people nowadays, we come and go through the back entrance, where our cars are parked. But the bell rang again and again, and I finally went down the front hall and turned on the front-door light.

There stood Susan Petri, wearing a handsome black sheath dress and holding some kind of foil-covered casserole dish. Her hair was done up in one of those French single braids, with little curls of her gorgeous chestnut hair wrapping around her pretty face in the evening breeze.

C'mon, Adams, be a sport: let the lady in.

She smiled at me slightly, saying nothing, and walked right past me down the long hall and directly to the kitchen. Boy, did she smell good. She walked with a grace and confidence that said, *This is my place, at least for tonight.*

"This is my special homemade chicken lasagna. I've got some fresh-baked French loaves in the car—I'll get them in a second."

"No, that's okay, Susan. I'll get them. And I've got some stuff here for salad. But tell me, how is it that you showed up at just the right time, with just the right stuff?"

"Don't you know? After all these years we've worked together? Don't you know that *I've got the right stuff?*"

"Well, yeah . . . but how come tonight? Is it because Mary's away?"

She walked toward me slowly, her eyes slightly narrowed, and soft. She was wearing heels—another thing I just hate—and was almost my height. She looked at me slowly, directly, without the slightest trace of fear or hesitation. It was that lioness-on-the-veldt look. That leopard-on-a-limb look.

A small voice in my head said: *Look out, Adams.*

"If you really want to know, my dear, I've been waiting for eight years for Mary to be gone."

"Uh, well, I'm not sure this is the time or place for—"

"If you go get the bread, I'll open the wine and start the salad."

So I did. But while I went outside to her car that small cautionary voice started up in my head again, telling me not to do anything foolish or impulsive, no matter how tempting.

I stifled it.

But then something happened to rather wreck the mood.

As I walked up our small stone stoop to the front door—the door I had not laid eyes on in at least a week—I noticed the object affixed to the door knocker with tape.

An ivory kayak, complete with Eskimo hunter, with the bow pointing directly at my chest.

At my heart.

14

SUSAN PUT THE MEAL TOGETHER WITH THAT INCREDIBLE COMBI-
nation of speed and efficiency that she displays in the office.
I had scarcely reappeared in the kitchen, somewhat somber
and sobered by the warning talisman on the front door,
when I noticed she had already set the table in the kitchen,
lighted the candles, turned on soft classical music—I think
it was a Beethoven piano sonata—on WBUR, poured the
wine, and was heating the lasagna in the oven while she put
the salad ingredients into our big teak bowl.

"This is lovely, Susan. You're very considerate."

"Feel any better?" she asked. Her voice sounded like a
soft silken waterfall. Her eyes were bright and happy.

"Well, yes and no," I said, and explained to her about the
ivory carving on the doorknocker.

"Hey, isn't that something? What a neat idea. Whatever
gave you the idea to do something that unusual and creative
on your front door?"

"I didn't put it there, Susan. Did you touch it?"

"Nope. I rang the bell."

"But you didn't touch it at all? Not even with your fin-
gertip?"

She shook her head, pouring dressing on the salad and
going over to the oven to retrieve the lasagna.

"Good. I think I better make a phone call. . . ."

She turned around quickly. "What's the big deal, anyway? It's just a guy in a canoe, right?"

93

"No. I think it's a warning meant for me. Or for me and Mary."

She flinched at Mary's name. I knew I had to call Joe about this. Trouble was, there was another woman, a woman twenty-two years my junior and heart-stoppingly pretty, in my house having dinner with me instead of Joe's sister. *Uno problemo* here. Maybe I could call Brad Taylor. Or even Larry Carpenter.

I winced at the thought of Larry Carpenter.

What the hell is this, I thought to myself, "Days of Our Lives"?

Then I noticed that Susan was setting the table all wrong. She was setting two places next to each other, on the same side of the table. What was this? Hadn't she read Amy Vanderbilt? Here I was thinking she was such a clever person, and here she goes, setting the table in this asymmetrical pattern.

"Why are you setting the table this way, Susan? I mean, aren't we supposed to be facing each other?"

"I think this will be fine. I think we'll both be comfortable this way. Okay?"

"Sure—"

I sat down, thinking are women dumb, or what?

Susan sat down next to me, and I smelled her. The room seemed to dim a little bit, the music became softer, more melodic. She scooted her chair over next to me. That's when I finally figured out that maybe she planned it that way.

Women can play dumb, but they're sneaky. Trust me on this. They're three laps ahead of us guys—every day of the week.

She bent her head over and whispered in my ear.

"How's this, fella?"

"Great," I said, giving her a peck on the cheek. That was all it was meant to be. But then she kissed me back.

I tucked into the lasagna, which was excellent. I realized I was very hungry, and finished the plate up in just a few minutes. I had three glasses of the red with dinner, and felt warm and mellow. Susan took the dishes over to the sink and sat down beside me again. Then she put her head down on my shoulder.

"I've wanted to do this for such a long time," she whispered. Her voice sounded husky. Before I knew what I was doing, I was kissing her cheek. And then her lips. I honestly, truly, couldn't realize what had come over me. For the second time in a week the impossible was happening.

"Why don't we go and watch TV?"

"Sounds good to me," I remember mumbling.

Of course, if she had said, Why don't we go outside and burn you at the stake? I would have answered, Sounds good to me. . . .

The thing I remember most about those few minutes was . . . feeling twenty-five again. And not believing it—but hoping it would last—pray to God—at least for a few precious hours.

Lord, what a tragedy is the mind-body dichotomy! The tragedy is not that we age and die, but that our minds, up to the end, recall our youth and fresh spirit, and we are young inside. And still full of the longings and desires of youth.

We were settled on the couch. I recall that there was actually a moving picture on the tube, with full color and sound, etc., etc.

Susan had snuggled up to me and put her legs over my thighs. *Ka-thunk, ka-thunk,* went her heels as she slipped them off. She took a deep swallow of her wine and placed the glass on the end table. Then she put her arms around my neck. God, she smelled great. She fidgeted on my lap, and I could see the dark tops of her stockings as her dress rode up.

Yep . . . feeling twenty-five again . . .

Then there came a sound that sent my blood cold.

The sound of the unlocking of our back door.

"Okay, Charlie—peace offering!" said Mary's voice, half shouting, from the back entry. "I've got some great seafood and . . . Charlie? Have you been cooking? I wanted to surprise you. Where are you anyway? And whose car is that in front? Charlie?"

Her footsteps were headed our way. Quick as a deer in a forest fire, Susan jumped off my lap, jumped into her heels, and stood at attention near the bookcase.

But it was too late, and we both knew it.

We were doomed.

15

"No, I haven't heard from her. And she hasn't called you or anything?" asked Joe.

"Nope. Wonder why?"

I had the phone cradled against my neck because my arms were busy with broom and dustpan. I was cleaning up part of the china fragments in the dining room. Three saucers, four coffee cups, eight plates. Haviland gold-leaf china. But the broken dishes and smashed windows weren't the real damage.

"Haven't heard a word. I tried to call Larry Carpenter up at his lodgings in Gloucester and guess what? He hasn't been seen either."

"But he hasn't checked out?" Joe asked.

"Nope. Still registered there. And the same's true at the Comfort Inn. Mary's officially still staying there . . . only she isn't."

"Aha. And so you think they've taken off together? Because she caught you with another woman? Yeah, that'd be just like her, to get revenge for something like that."

"Joe, listen. It was not another woman. It was my assistant Susan, who's known the family for eight years, for chrissakes. You've met her yourself."

"Yep. I have. And I know what she looks like, too. So when Mary's gone, Susan decides to come over and fix you dinner. Know what I think? Assistant or not, you asked for it, Doc."

"I did not ask for it; Susan showed up with the food. It was a nice thing to do. She knew I was down."

"Yeah, but see, you're holding some rather weak cards, you ask me. I mean, this isn't the first time. Who was that young thing down in South Carolina who left her bikini in your motel room?"

"Look, that was an accident, and it was her idea—"

"I know . . . you're always saying that. 'It was *her* idea.' Listen, as fond as I am of you, I think you bring a lot of this on yourself, Doc. And I know my sister when she gets mad. I'd rather face a wounded lioness. You're in deep shit, pal, and you're gonna stay in it for a while."

"Joe, level with me. Do you think they're together?"

"Wouldn't surprise me. But I don't think they're doing anything. Unless, of course, Mary is convinced you and Susan were—"

"No. We just had dinner—that evidence was there, and nothing more. And earlier in the day I was visiting a friend of Karl Pirsch's in town—an ivory expert—and he can vouch for me."

"Well, you know it doesn't take a lot to get Mary steamed—especially about this kind of stuff. My only advice to you is to lay low and wait to hear from her. She may call Jack and Tony soon—you might try them tonight. And, oh, you better fire Susan Petri."

"*Fire* her? No way, Joe; she's the best assistant there is. Just because she showed some personal concern for my emotional well being," I said, picking up the broken handle of a creamer, "is no reason to do that. What I think is, maybe you should convince Mary to give up this undercover stuff. Not only is it putting a strain on the two of us, but she could be in some real danger now. Which reminds me, there's something here at the house I want you to take a look at."

I told him about the carved ivory figure on our front door.

"You mean the same kind that killed James Harold in Provincetown?"

"Exactly. I think it's a warning, and not a very subtle one at that."

"But against you or Mary?"

"I think Mary; she's the one who's been doing all the buying and snooping."

"No. You've been doing your share of that, too. But tell you what, I'll come out tonight and have a look. Mind if I bring Marty?"

"No, that would be great. Nice to have some family in this big house again."

"And we'll all talk about what you can do, Doc, to make your home life a bit smoother."

I hesitated a bit; I had a pretty good idea what was coming.

"Does that mean Marty's going to lecture me, too?"

"Probably."

"How come I get all the lectures and Mary gets none?"

"Because, to our knowledge, she has not been in as many—shall we say 'compromising positions' as you have."

"I resent that."

"Resent it all you like. Just think about it. And buy some good stuff to cook tonight. *Arrivederla*."

After I hung up I thought about what Joe had said. He was right, as usual. Actually, I was amazed he wasn't more angry with me. But then, as Mary's kid brother, he had to put up with a lot from her. Like the time he was fourteen and hid her Bobby Rydell record and told her he broke it. Just for a joke, mind you. He told me that Mary had "beat the snot" out of him in front of his buddies. See what I mean? She can be difficult, and he's the first to realize it.

But then I recalled the previous evening with Susan. Certainly this was not just an innocent flirtation on our part; and I knew that if Mary hadn't returned when she did, there was no telling what would have happened between us. Actually, it didn't take much imagination to know: we'd have ended up in the sack. For sure.

So I wasn't feeling very good about myself. I went for a four-mile run and three visits to the sauna, showered, and called elder son Jack at the Marine Biological Laboratory at Woods Hole.

"No, I haven't seen Mom, or heard from her either, Dad. Why?"

"We had a fight, and she's still doing this undercover

work for the Fish and Wildlife people. I'm worried. If she's just hiding out because she's mad at me, I could understand it. But ... I think there is an element of danger here, and it's making me uneasy. Listen—I know she doesn't want to talk to me. But she will call you and Tony, so you guys won't worry. So when she does call, will you please call me right away?"

"Sure."

"And also, try to find out where the hell she is. It's important."

"What was the fight about?"

"Nothing that important."

"What's her name?"

"That's not funny."

"Well, all I know is that every time in the past—"

"How are your humpback whales doing?" I asked. Mention whales and Jack can go on for hours. Usually, this topic brightens him; it's what he lives for. But this time I heard a weary sigh from his end of the line.

"Bad news, Dad. The population on Stellwagen Bank is down again this year. Third year in a row."

"Why? The Japanese killing them again?"

"Nope. They haven't been hunted for some time now. That's why the news is so bad, I'm afraid. We think the populations are declining because whales breast-feed their young."

"So?"

"So what's happening is that in long-lived mammals which live off plankton and krill, the baleen whales, the pollutants in the seawater like PVCs and other toxins, build up in these small critters the whales eat. Then, the concentration of toxins builds up even more in the whale's tissues. Finally it reaches even higher concentrations in the mother's milk, which she passes on to her offspring. With each generation, the concentration of toxins increases. The increases might be three- or fourfold, or even higher. There's no way to stop it. It's ... it's hopeless."

He sounded near tears. Just what I needed. My wife trying to save the walrus, my son trying to save the whales, and all of it hopeless.

My marriage, the union going on thirty years that produced these great boys, perhaps hopeless. My throat started choking up, with that slow, sad ache, but I managed to talk.

"Well, I hope it's not as bad as you think, Jackie. I love you. God bless you, and be careful. Call me if you hear from Mom."

"Dad, you think she could really be in trouble?"

"I don't think so. Just keep me posted."

"Okay, Dad, I love you."

With my jaw clenched tight and my cheeks unexpectedly wet, I tried son number two, currently working on the ranch near Livingston, Montana. I looked at my watch as the phone in his bunkhouse rang. It was three-thirty in New England, which meant one-thirty Mountain Time. Maybe I would get lucky and catch Tony back at the ranch for lunch. The phone rang six times before I heard a young female voice answer it.

"Hello?"

"Hello, this is Dr. Charles Adams, Tony's father. Is he around?"

"Oh! Hi, Dr. Adams. Tony's told me so much about you! I can't wait to meet you! He's hoping maybe you and your wife can come out here for a visit before the first snow hits."

"Sounds good, we'll try and make it," I said, thinking: *If* we're still together . . .

"I'm sorry Tony's not here; he's out working with the horses now. He'll be back about six, at sundown."

"Are you a friend of his?"

"Oh, yeah. Big time. I'm Jenny Littlefeather; I work as a waitress in the main house."

"Well, it's nice to talk with you, Jenny. I'm just wondering if Tony's heard from his mother lately. Do you know if she's called him?"

"Not that I know of. Why? She missing?"

"Well, sort of. A lot of us are anxious about her whereabouts."

"Oh, this sounds bad, Dr. Adams. She didn't tell you where she went?"

"No."

"Do you think she's been kidnapped?"

"I, uh . . . don't know. And I don't want to alarm Tony

unnecessarily. Just please have him call me if he hears from his mother. Or even if he doesn't."

She promised she'd give him the message.

As I went out to the fish market I reflected that Jenny Littlefeather, a Native American of some sort, was probably living with Number Two Son in his bunkhouse. Anthony Hatton Adams was a caution, all right. Wherever he went or stayed—if even for a day or so—he always seemed to have a luscious young thing in tow.

It was then that the little, irritating voice in the back of my head started up again.

Well, Adams, it said, the seeds don't fall far from the tree, do they? Now, if you had listened to me last night when you went outside, instead of trying to hush me up, you would have been a good boy, an upstanding husband, and you wouldn't have lost your wife. Don't you think it's about time you—

"Oh, shut up!" I said out loud, and got into the car.

I cooked the meal for Joe and Marty, but my heart wasn't in it. I got a fresh half salmon, coated it with gobs of mayonnaise on both sides, and put it on a baking platter. On top I put on some paprika, a little of my own seasoning salt, cracked pepper, and dill, and some circles of very thinly sliced lemon. I baked the fish in a hot oven for about ten minutes. The mayonnaise, which looks so gross when you prepare it, melts into the fish and keeps it moist. I made a sauce with mayonnaise, cumin, curry powder, and capers to spread over it. Salmon done this way melts in your mouth, but my appetite just wasn't there.

When the meal was over and we had all cleared up the dishes, Marty made coffee, sat down in the sunporch with the two of us, and cleared her throat.

Here it comes, I thought.

"Doc, how mad is Mary at you? Can you guess?"

"Very."

"Then that's good news, I think, because it means that her absence is deliberate, not inflicted by somebody else, you follow?"

Her soft, contralto voice soothed me as much as her words.

"That's good, Marty," said Joe, lighting a cigarette, "but tell us what can we do now to get her back."

"Wait."

"I can't stand waiting," I said, jumping up. "I want a plan that we can follow. I need to keep busy at it or I'll go crazy."

Marty sat and sipped her steaming cup for a few seconds. "I think we should go up to Gloucester where she was staying and look at her room. If it's messy, or all her things appear to be there, then she was abducted. But if her luggage is missing, then she took off."

Joe and I sat in silence. I was trying which scenario was worse. It was a toss-up: both were terrible.

"Question is," mused Joe, "do we go up there tonight— it's now past nine—or wait until morning?"

"Wait until morning," said Marty.

But at the same time I had blurted, "Go now."

Joe looked at the two of us, back and forth, back and forth, as if watching an imaginary tennis game. He turned to me.

"Here's what I say—we spend the night here with you, and leave tomorrow at, say, six A.M."

"No," I said. "I think it should be now; I have to move on this."

Joe leaned over to me. "Doc, I can tell by your face you're exhausted. And frazzled. I think going tonight is a big mistake. Now we should watch a movie or something and relax as much as possible, then take off early when we're rested."

"I think he's right, Doc."

"Okay," I said, leaning back on the couch. I was tired, and I ached all over. "But tomorrow *early*."

16

"Doc? You awake?" Joe whispered as he stuck his big, dark head into my bedroom. For a big guy he can be awfully quiet and gentle when the situation calls for it.

"Yeah; I'm getting up." Truth was, I had been awake since about four. Awake with that dry-mouthed, tense feeling that comes with worry and two extra scotches. I got up and shaved quickly with the electric razor, brushed my teeth, and put on casual warm clothes. When I got down to the kitchen I met Marty, who had already made coffee. She saw me sitting dumb-eyed at the table and came over and put her dry, cool hand in mine. Thank God for family.

"I'm not very hungry," she admitted. "That feed last night was big, and we ate it late. What do you say we just get rolling?"

I agreed, and in a few minutes we were in Joe's unmarked cruiser, waiting for him.

"What's keeping him?" I asked.

"I have no idea, unless it's that box he's carrying."

Joe came lumbering up to the car and placed the cardboard box carefully between us on the front seat. Marty was riding in back, according to her preference.

"What's that?"

"The ivory kayak. What else?"

"Oh, you've got it in there? Is it that valuable?"

"Look, sport, it took me twenty minutes to get this damn

thing off your front door without leaving any prints. I want it as pristine as possible for Karl and the lab boys."

"Why didn't you wear gloves, dear?" asked Marty.

"They would erase any prints that were on it."

"Think you'll find any?"

"There's always hope. I think a guy this daring just might be careless. Now are we all set?"

We went into Concord Center, picked up 2A eastbound, hooked up with the 128 beltway, and were headed for Gloucester, on Cape Ann. Traveling on missions like this was great in Joe's car. He had his police radio as well as a cellular phone, which meant we could be in touch with anybody in a flash. Also slightly comforting, in an odd way, was the short, stumpy, Mossberg Model 500 twelve-gauge riot gun—the kind of gun Laitis Roantis refers to as a "streetcleaner"—tucked away out of sight on a horizontal rack fastened to the rear side of the front seat. I wasn't expecting any real trouble on this scouting mission, but you never know. The traffic was light on 128, and Joe maintained a speed almost fifteen miles over the limit. Police business, of course. We crossed over the Annisquam River and were in Gloucester by seven-fifteen. Then we went past the town center, found Thatcher Road, and rolled up to the Comfort Inn only a few minutes later. I asked the woman at the desk to ring Mary's room. She did, and got no answer. Then Joe nudged past me, flashed his badge, and asked for a room key. The woman hesitated, but Joe, in his official, but gentle way, persisted.

"If you like, you can come along with us—make sure we don't disturb anything."

"Well, I . . . I can't leave the desk here. In a few minutes I could maybe like send somebody along with you—" She looked at her watch. "Sandy should be here around eight."

"We need to see the room now," said Joe. His voice became slightly colder, more authoritarian.

"Um, can I ask you . . . what's this about?"

"Ms. Brindelli is missing," Joe said. "We're trying to find her. Have you seen her lately?"

"Nope. Not since . . . about two or three days ago. You might want to talk with some people on the night shift. I haven't seen her car in a while."

"Was she with anyone else?"

I asked this question as casually as possible, almost embarrassed to ask it in front of Joe and Marty, and was inwardly very relieved to see the clerk shake her head. She looked us over for another few seconds, then handed over the room key. "Please return this as soon as you can," she said.

Room 174 was in back, the door opening right onto the parking lot. The bed was made, with new towels neatly folded on the racks, the new soap still wrapped in paper, the tiny vials of shampoo, conditioner, and moisturizer in a little plastic basket. The maid had obviously been in to do her work. We checked the closet alcove and the dresser drawers. There was nothing personal left in the room, although she hadn't checked out. No clothes, shoes, luggage . . . nothing.

"Well, I think she left on her own." Marty sighed.

A pause, and then Joe said, "Looks that way."

Nobody said anything for a while. It was a long, lonely silence.

"Doc, you ready to go?" he finally asked.

It sounded as if he were far, far away. I wasn't looking at him. I was looking at the carefully made bed, as if it were an ancient Egyptian mystery.

"Yeah. Guess so," I muttered, and we filed out.

Nobody said anything again, for a long time. We were rolling along Thatcher Road toward Rocky Neck when I told Joe to go by the Dory. I was going to try to find Larry.

"Remember what Brad said, Doc, not make contact unless it's really—"

"I don't give a damn what Brad said. It's about a half mile up, on the left, the bay side. Just get there."

When we swung into the parking lot I immediately saw Larry's truck.

"Does that mean he's here?" asked Joe.

"I think so. Wait here and I'll check."

I hopped out of the cruiser and went to Larry's room. I knocked. No answer. Twice more. Same thing. Then I saw a woman come around the corner pushing the cart. She was the same chubby, red-haired lady who was at the desk before. She even had on that same navy-blue dress with the white polka dots.

"Wastin' your time. He's gone."

"To work?"

"Don't think so. Lady picked him up. Driving a fancy car. Hey, don't I remember you? Ain't you Larry's old friend from school?"

"Yep. What did the lady look like?"

"A real looker. Dark, with almost black hair. Fancy, you know?"

"Yeah," I mumbled, turning around, "I know."

"You mean you know her?"

The question rang in my ears as I began walking to Joe's car. It wouldn't go away. I turned around.

"I used to."

I walked over to the car. Marty was sitting in the backseat. I opened her door and asked if she minded riding in front with Joe. "No, of course not," she said, shaking her head, and then I got in the back, alone. I stretched out on the seat, resting my shoulders against the passenger-side door. I could scarcely move.

"They left together," I said softly.

Marty turned around and stared at me.

"Well, I'm sure it's not what you think, Doc. I'm sure it's strictly business."

When I didn't answer, or look in her direction, she finally turned around and looked straight out the windshield. Joe had the car spinning out of the lot and onto the road very fast. I suspected he shared my feelings—what was left of them—and to him, too, it was going to be a long, long ride back to Concord.

I took off my jacket and put it behind my neck for padding. Nobody said anything for about ten minutes, and finally Joe turned on the radio to kill the silence. It was WBUR—some classical thing that sounded good. Well, better than silence and road hum. After a while I pulled the collar of my windbreaker up over my head from behind and let it fall over my eyes, like a monk's hood. I thought I would try to sleep.

But really I was hiding. From Marty and Joe, and even from myself.

When they dropped me off at the house almost an hour later, I got right out, waved to them, and walked toward the front door. I was so weak I could scarcely move.

17

I COLLAPSED IN MY STUDY CHAIR AND STARED AT THE WALL. Then I stared at the globe in the corner. Where in the world was my wife? Where had she and Larry gone together, and not told me, or anyone else?

Why was all this happening to me? I closed my eyes, but sleep wouldn't come, even though I was terribly tired. I managed to get up and call the office. Susan Petri answered.

"Dr. Adams, where have you been? It's almost ten—"

"I, uh, had to go on an errand. Sorry."

"Dr. Adams, I want to . . . apologize for the other night—"

"No need to, Susan. You're the only bright spot I've got right now."

"Well, then, this is even harder to say. Doc, I'm leaving this job."

The words hit me like a pickax.

"What?"

"I just can't . . . stay here now. After the other night, when I told you everything about . . . how I feel about you.

And we were ... on the couch together I felt ... like maybe my dreams were coming true, and then—"

"Look, Susan, don't make anything more out of this than there is. I frankly had a great time. And you should know that Mary's gone now. Maybe for good."

There was silence on the other end of the line. Then Susan spoke in a low whisper. "Really? Oh my God!"

"So just stay put, okay? Listen, I won't be coming in today. I just ... can't make it. We have a third molar extraction set up for tomorrow morning with Mr. Soule?"

"Two of them. His at nine and another at two. What should I tell the patients who come in today?"

"Tell them I'm indisposed. Which is the truth. Call the others who are scheduled for later and reschedule them. I'll see you tomorrow morning for the procedure with Mr. Soule, okay?"

"Doc—this is all my fault!"

"No, it isn't. Trust me."

I hung up and went back to the chair. I wanted to go to bed but it would be too lonely up there in the bedroom all by myself. I sat in the chair trying to sleep for about half an hour before going through the kitchen to the sideboard, where I poured myself a very hefty whiskey and soda—so big it fit neatly into one of my German ceramic half-liter mugs—took it back into the study, and sipped it. Halfway through the drink, that crazy, frenetic, Chaplinesque bad dream in my head—the one that pictured Mary and Larry locked in lusty embrace in all sorts of romantic hideaways—started to fade away.

After the drink was drained, I settled back into the cushions and stared at my print of *Thermopylae Leaving Foochow.*

The glorious clipper ship was being towed out of the Chinese harbor by two paddle-steam tugs. Junks and sampans bobbed on the water on the foreground. The sun was setting behind the great ship and others like it, tucking itself in for the night behind the low hills of Foochow Harbor, silhouetting the ships' spars and sails against the glowing sky.

I wished, wished with all my heart, that I was aboard her, with Jack and Tony. In another place, another time.

"To hell with the twentieth century," I murmured. Then, mercifully, I feel asleep.

I woke up in early evening, edgy, and restless. Booze-induced sleep allows you a respite from reality, but it doesn't rest you because your body has been hard at work trying to rid itself of the poison. I got up, groggy and ill-tempered, and had a bowl of clam chowder. I flipped on the sauna bath, changed into my running clothes, and did a very slow and achy four miles along Old Stone Mill Road. The evening was pretty, pretty as only a fall evening in the heart of New England can be. But its beauty escaped me. I thumped along, still in ill humor, when a car horn sounded behind me. I moved over off the shoulder of the road, practically scraping my side against Dean McLeod's stone wall. I waited for the driver to pass me, but instead a white Peugeot wagon came rolling to crawl beside me. A bronzed, ruddy-faced man, wrinkled with age, warfare, and too much liquor and cigarettes, stuck his head out the window.

"What's up, Doc?"

It wasn't Bugs Bunny.

It was Laitis Roantis. He dragged off his Camel and let the smoke trickle out his nostrils, like an aging dragon, on the run from Saint George, the law, and society in general.

Somehow, I identified with him now more than ever.

I leaned against the car, panting, and asked him what the hell he was doing out here in Concord.

"I was sent here to find you."

Instantly, I thought of Mary.

"Who sent you? Mary?"

"Naw," he said, shaking his head. "You know Mary and me, Doc, we don't get along too good."

"Join the club."

"Know who it was called me? Moe Abramson, dat's who."

"Moe? What the hell does he want with me?"

"Worried about you, he says. Who's dat cute lil thing works for you?"

"Susan Petri?"

"Yeah. I guess she went to his office and talked to him about you."

"Oh, great . . ."

"And said it was her fault you and Mary broke up. Did you and Mary break up, Doc?"

"I . . . I don't know. I don't know what the hell's happening, Laitis. I'm just glad Moe's around, ready to help me."

"Well, he told me on the phone he's leaving for New Jersey later today to go see his mother. He'll be gone for a couple weeks."

"Damn . . . why does everything come unglued all at once? Like I said, I don't really know what's happening anymore."

"What's happening is this—you're gettin' inside this car and we're going to your house. Den you can clean up, change clothes, and take me to dinner."

"Who says?"

"I says. I come all the way from Jamaica Plain to find you, dummy. Now get in."

I didn't argue. There wasn't much fight left in me, and in any case, Laitis Roantis is a guy you don't fight with. Ever, ever.

"Jeez, Doc, you stink of old booze."

"How would you know?"

He gave a weary chuckle. "So c'mon, Doc. We been through a lot together. Tell me everyt'ing. What's goin on, hmm?"

I started to tell him, when suddenly I felt as if I might break down. My voice was shaking. My legs and body ached. My damn heart, what was left of it, ached. "Never mind. Later."

"Okay, home we go."

He helped me out of the car. I was all stiffened up, even from the short run. I felt as if I had aged ten years in the past couple of weeks. Laitis, now in his sixties, seemed strong as ever.

We sat in the sauna together and I filled him in on what had happened since we last talked. He listened to my tale with as much sympathy as he ever shows, which is not very much. Roantis doesn't have much room in his life for sympathy. He says, "Sympathy is right next to shit in the dictionary."

We left the sauna for brief showers, then went back in and baked some more. Did this routine four times, then went into the kitchen for two cold beers apiece. I felt almost human again.

"Let's go to the Colonial Inn for seafood," I said, and got no argument from Roantis. Since his diet—from what I've been able to observe over the years—seems to consist primarily of rare beef, alcohol, and Camel cigarettes, no doubt his body was in ecstasy over the mere mention of sensible cuisine.

There was a short wait when we got to the inn, so we sat in the parlor bar. I wanted booze, but stuck with beer, having made up my mind, while in the sauna, to level off alcohol and stop altogether for a few weeks at least, then pick up my running schedule. Running is the best antidote for worry and stress.

"So, what about this Larry guy?" asked Roantis, over his second bourbon on the rocks. "He on the level, or what?"

"Oh, he's on the level. Great guy, as a matter of fact. I think that's the problem. I think he's . . . well, a threat."

"You mean, along with Mary? She likes him?"

"Yeah, something like that, sort of."

"Well, if he gets to be a real problem, maybe there's something that we can do about it."

"Nah. Larry's also a friend, Laitis. We've been close since college."

"Den what's he doing messing with your wife? Huh?"

"Well, I don't know if he is messing with her. It's just that I feel . . . invaded."

"I think maybe it's time you and me went off somewhere together, Doc. Get away from all this bullshit. You wanna shoot doves in Mexico or Argentina?"

I brightened up immediately.

"Yes, I would. That sounds great."

"How about a safari? I was reading the other day they cost only about six grand. Dat's for only a week, but it would be fun, eh?"

"You bet. I wonder what the airfare is?"

"Twelve to fifteen hundred."

"Hmm," I mused, feeling my eyes growing bigger. "You want to try that?"

"Sure. If you loan me the money."

"You don't have seventy-five hundred?"

" 'Course not. But you do. So what I figure, I get rid of this Larry guy for you—that service is worth ten grand on today's market. But instead of paying me, you take me on safari, and maybe buy me a nice big-bore rifle. How's that sound?"

"It sounds like shit. The most painful thing about all this is that I always thought Larry was a friend. And he's a terrific guy in so many ways. I think that's what's adding to the pain. I guess I feel betrayed."

They called us into the dining room. I had flounder in herb butter and Roantis had a New York strip steak. We both had the salad with bleu cheese dressing. The food was okay, but nothing like the food Mary and I could fix at home. Then I got glum again, thinking that perhaps my days of cooking with Mary were over.

As we were leaving the inn Roantis rubbed his palms together, looking at the golden western sky.

"Nice night out, Doc. What say we take a ride?"

"Where?"

"Does it matter? Look how pretty it is out here. C'mon, give me the keys; I'll be pilot, you be the copilot."

"Fine—" I said vaguely. Roantis climbed into my little Subaru sport coupe with the big engine. The controls, dashboard, and especially the gearshift lever were all built to resemble the cockpit of a plane. Roantis started the engine and turned on the lights. Instantly, several score lights, gauges, and buttons glowed faint yellow. Roantis threw the XT6 into gear, revved the engine, watching the red needle flick up to the seven-g range and back down again, popped the clutch, and we screeched away from the parking lot and out onto Route 2A, west.

"Where are we going?" I asked as we left Acton behind us. We had merged back into Route 2, still heading west.

"Ayer," he answered.

"Ayer? What the hell's in Ayer that you want to see? Why, as far as I can remember, the only thing there is Fort Devens, and who the hell would—"

I looked out of the corner of my eye at Roantis, grinning behind the wheel. The gleam in his eyes intensified, and he pushed the pedal down further. The car leaped ahead, hugging the road in the tight curves.

"Oh no. Sweet Jesus, Laitis, are we really going *there*?"

"Could happen," he murmured between clenched teeth. "Could possibly happen—"

"Are we . . . going to see some of your old friends?"

"Hope so, sport. It's been a while. Gee, I hope Dottie and Laura are there."

"Dottie and Laura? Are they in the Tenth Group? I didn't know they took women."

"Naw. Not in S.F., Doc. At the Rotor Club, right across the road."

"Rotor Club? What, pray tell, is that like?"

"You'll see."

Roantis was true to his word: directly across Route 2 from the entrance to Fort Devens—home of the Tenth Special Forces Group—was a single-story, rambling building that looked prefab. There was a sign outside that featured helicopters and men falling to earth with parachutes. The place looked run-down, almost vacant, and no wonder: Fort Devens was due to close sometime in '95, and the Tenth Group was to merge with the Fifth, based in Okinawa. I knew all this because Roantis had told me, but I also knew that the area was still filled with old-timers and hangers-on from the Vietnam era. The guys, and their groupie fans and followers. I had a strong hunch that Laura and Dottie could be two of the same.

We pulled into the Rotor Club's big parking lot and walked across the dirt and gravel lot that was half-filled with old, beat-up cars and shiny, customized Harley-Davidsons. Uh-oh, I thought, a biker roadhouse. No thanks. I could hear the throbbing bass notes of dance music coming through the thin walls of the bar, but the beat wasn't rock and roll. They were playing country inside.

"C'mon, Doc; what are you waiting for?"

"Oh, I don't know, Laitis. I'm too old for this sort of thing. I really think we oughta be heading home. I'll just take the keys and—"

"Nah. I don't think so." He chuckled, pocketing my car

keys and winking his steely-gray eyes at me. "Not until you've bought me a couple drinks."

"I've already bought you four."

"Well, a couple more couldn't hurt. Let's go."

Since I realized that if I attempted to take the keys from him by force I would end up with a crushed spine, I followed him inside.

Oh, hell with it, I thought as we went through the door into the blaring music and blue haze of cigarette smoke, how bad can it be?

18

PLENTY BAD.

The place was dark and smoky, with cheap, laminated panel walls—some sections of which appeared to have been punched out by inebriated patrons—a dance floor that took up the far end and was topped by one of those thirties-style mirrored balls that turned slowly, sending sparks of light around the room. But these tidbits I noticed later. What got my attention right away was the assortment of people at the bar.

As far as I could tell, the patrons were about evenly divided between aging bikers and aging paratroopers. They seemed to be friends, and lounged at the bar and the near tables with ease. Some of the bikers had rags tied over their heads and fancy earrings. The military types had short hair, tans, grizzled faces, and bodies that showed their continuous physical regimen.

They seemed to recognize Roantis, but they eyed me suspiciously. They obviously weren't people to mess with. So as Roantis and I bellied up to the bar, I couldn't help thinking what a damn-fool idea this had turned out to be.

"Hiya, Warlock!" the woman behind the bar shouted, leaned over, and planted a nice kiss on his cheek. He almost blushed. But not quite.

"Hiya, Holly, this is my friend, Doc Adams. We want two double shooters of Cuervo Gold."

"Uh, no, I don't," I said, but apparently not loud enough.

"Two José Cuervo, comin' up," said Holly, who quickly poured the two big shot glasses to the brim with the golden tequila. "You want a lime, Warlock?"

"Why, of course," he answered. "What do you take me for, a barbarian?"

Watching Roantis closely, I copied his deft motions with the lime: wetting the web of my left hand between the thumb and forefinger with the slice of lime, then shaking salt over it. Next, he jammed his hand into his mouth, sucking in the raw salt, and immediately lifted the glass and emptied it in a slow gulp, slammed it down, and then bit into the lime. I did the same, but swallowed only a third of the glass.

"Great!" he said. "Hit us again, Holly."

"I don't think—" I began.

"Two Cuervo, comin' up!"

"What does Warlock mean, Laitis? Why is she calling you Warlock?"

"My nickname in the service. Warlock is a guy who can't be killed by another man. Dunno how I got it."

"Of course not."

We did another routine with the tequila, and then I went over to the nearest vacant table and sat down. If I stood at the bar with Roantis, I knew what would happen. The revolving lights were making me woozy enough as it was. I wasn't sitting there five minutes when a woman came over and sat down next to me. She was blonde, though I suspect, not a natural blonde, about forty, with a slim figure and a lot of miles on her. She wore too much makeup, but somehow, in the Rotor Club bar, across the road from Fort Devens in Ayer, Massachusetts, she seemed to fit right in, if you know what I mean. She had on a low-cut red sweater that revealed a lot of cleavage. She was nicely tan all over, probably an electric tan. She had also managed to pour herself into a very snug pair of faded blue jeans. And she was wearing what looked like cowboy boots with stiletto heels.

"Hi, hon. What's yer name? Never seen you in here before. Are you the new colonel they're all talking about? You're with the Tenth, aren't you?"

"Uh, no. Actually, I'm a civilian from Concord. I'm here as a guest of Mr. Roantis, that stumpy little guy at the bar with the accent."

"You with Warlock? What the hell you doing with him, mister?"

"A good question, ma'am. I've been trying to answer it for the longest time."

She half stood up, lifting her butt off the chair, scooted it over very close to mine, and put her cool hand on mine. I saw long nails and heavy bright polish on those hands, and smelled way too much perfume.

"Hon, my name's Dottie. What's yours again?"

"Doc."

"Hey, Doc and Dottie. That's cute, ain't it? What's your sign, anyway?"

"What?"

"You know—your sign. Mine's Cancer."

How fitting, I thought, and replied that I was a Libra.

"Heeey, great!"

Wondering how much of this inane stuff I was going to have to take, I looked up, searching for Roantis at the bar. I finally saw him half-wrapped around a brown-haired woman, who, by strange happenstance, was also wearing a pair of extremely snug faded blue jeans, low-cut sweater, tan, and heels. I saw Roantis's hand slide down her waist and grab an ample handful of her left bun. She leaned over appreciatively and stuck her tongue in his ear.

"Uh, that wouldn't happen to be Laura, would it?" I asked.

"Sure is. We're bosom buddies, me and Laura. Hey! That reminds me of a joke. What do you call twins?"

"Huh?"

"What do you call twins?"

"I don't know, Dottie; I've always called them twins."

"Nah, listen—they're womb mates, who later become bosom buddies! Get it? Ain't that cute?"

"Adorable."

"Hey! Let's do some boot scootin', pardner. C'mon, get up."

"Do what?"

"C'mon, we're gonna go out there and do the Texas two-step. Don't tell me you ain't hearda the Texas two-step, Doc. Why, it's the most fun thing there is. Except, uh ... *you know*."

"Well, I don't really feel like dancing now, Dottie. And you should also know that I'm married."

"Well, shit, we all make mistakes. I won't hold it against you, Doc. Hell, I done made that mistake four times. Laura, she's done made it five times."

"Where are you from, Dottie?"

"Waxahachie, Texas. Hey, it ain't no joke; it's a real place."

"I know it is; it's just south of Dallas. And it was where they made that movie with Sally Field—*Places in the Heart*."

Dottie sucked in a huge breath; her eyes went wide. She grabbed both my forearms so tightly that her long, butterscotch-colored nails dug into my flesh.

"Ohhhhhhhh! Wadn't that the *best* movie? Jes' thinkin' 'bout it makes me wanna cry."

She said cry like this: *crah*.

As if following some hidden cue, she took this moment to lay her head down on my shoulder and place her left hand on my thigh, which she began to stroke.

"Ooooooo, your legs is hard. You work out, don'tcha? That's why I thought you was in the service. As you can probably guess, I'm crazy over guys in uniform. All my exes are airborne."

"Is that what brings you here?" I asked.

"Why, sure, hon. You gotta go where the soldier boys are! Hey, Doc, you really a doctor?"

"Yes."

"Gee, I could go for a doctor." More thigh stroking. "Might be a nice change from all these airborne rangers. Hey! You hear that?"

"What?"

"That song."

A rather plaintive, bouncy-beat noise was coming over the worn speakers on the far wall. To me, it sounded not unlike most of the other pop-country stuff.

"I hear it."

"Well, dummy, it's the greatest song ever. It's 'Achy Breaky Heart'!"

"Really? Never heard of it."

"No! Never heard of 'Achy Breaky Heart'? Why, where you been, boy?"

"Don't know. Just unlucky, I guess, not to have come to the Rotor Club sooner."

"Well, you can say that again. C'mon, hon, we're gonna *daynce*."

"Oh no we're not."

She jumped up from the table, hand on hip, staring down at me. "Well, you're just no fun at all. I'm gonna go up and get me another drink. You want one?"

"No thanks."

"You need one, and that's the truth. Loosen you up a bit. That's the trouble with you people up north. You're always so damn tight-assed."

She stomped off to the bar. I had to admit she looked pretty good in those high heels and painted-on jeans. If I had a few more Cuervo Golds, I'm sure she would look positively delicious. Suddenly I caught myself and looked around the room. The crowd was growing more raucous by the minute. The music came up; the lights went down. Couples oozed onto the dance floor and began promenading in couples around in a big circle, turning and swishing as they went. I assumed this was the infamous Texas two-step. Frankly, as down-home charming as it looked, I could skip it. The only kind of dancing I enjoy, generally after about four or five drinks, is the up-close and personal kind to a slow beat. Meanwhile, at the tables and in the booths, couples who'd passed on the dance were making out. In the dim light I believe I witnessed a few instances of vertical near intercourse. In a corner booth two biker guys were arm wrestling, both wearing T-shirts with the arms cut off and rags tied around their heads. Between them they must have had eight tattoos. And those were the visible ones.

"What the hell am I doing here?" I whispered to myself. Hell, a month ago I was giving Mary, my wife and the mother of our two children, a handmade lightship purse from Nantucket. Simple as that. Now I'm sitting in an army-base bar, getting a load on with Laitis Roantis—a guy known not to travel in the highest of circles. Speaking of Laitis, where the hell was he, anyway?

I scanned the dark room, finally spotting him over in a dark corner with Laura. He had her pinned against the two walls, but she didn't seem to mind. Both pairs of hands were busy. I looked at my watch. Ten-thirty. Well, kiddies, time to go home . . .

I felt a hand on my shoulder, then the hand went up and stroked my hair, then my neck again.

"I'm sorry, Doc. I'm sorry I said those things about you. I just wanna dance one time, okay? Please?" She put her hands on my shoulders and began to rub them. It did feel good, I had to admit it. Then a real slow song came on, and the couples on the dance floor abandoned the two-step and clung together, like globules of oil floating on the water. Dottie leaned over and kissed me on the cheek. I turned to say something and she kissed me on the mouth. A lot of tongue in it. She half lifted me from the table and we went out onto the dance floor.

Her long, bright hair had a lot of spray on it, but hung in big curls all over her head. It's what Mary calls "big hair." It was the Dolly Parton look. Her chest, which she pressed into mine, was also definitely styled after Dolly. She reached around and grabbed my butt.

"Ooooo, what cute, hard buns you got."

I kept swaying to the music, what I could hear of it over the noise of the crowd, expecting her to remove her hands. She did not. Instead, she began kissing my neck, then moved over to my mouth. Then we were kissing heavily, and she took my forearms and pulled them down so that my hands were on her buns as well. We danced like this awhile, and she began pulling my hips in hard to hers.

"Oooooooo, babe, I could go for you, hon. I mean it," she

said. "After all these years I think this could be—you know—the *real thing. . . .*"

"Is that so?" I said, with all the sincerity I could muster. Still, why did I have the unshakable suspicion that this routine was carefully rehearsed, and oft-repeated? A set piece, as well choreographed as a ballet.

My thoughts were interrupted by a heavy paw on my shoulder. The hand, which was big, grabbed my deltoid in an iron grip and spun me around. Facing me was a man shorter than I, but very broad through the shoulders. He wore a white T-shirt with usmc on it, a Mohawk-style crew cut, and an extremely mean-looking face.

"Hey asshole, you're dancin' with my girl, 'case you didn't know."

"I didn't know," I said, feeling the adrenaline rising in me. The hair on the back of my neck stood up.

"Aw, get lost Randy," shouted Dottie. "And quit showing up here, okay? You heard what I said, okay? This guy's got twice the class you got, okay? So get lost, okay?"

He hit me on the side of the jaw, and I sank to my knees on the dance floor. I was losing consciousness, but vaguely remembered that my knees, hitting that hardwood floor, hurt more than my jaw. Randy's knee came forward and up, clipping me hard on the left side of my chest. The pain was awful. My vision went dim then, but enough light was left for me to see something that scared me so much I kept from passing out.

Randy was drawing his right leg back, far back, for a kick to my head, or throat.

A kick that could kill me.

With a speed and ferocity only those near death can muster, I grabbed his near leg right above the ankle, yanked it hard toward me as I got to the balls of my feet, and leaped upward. I butted him in the groin with the top of my head and, as he lost his balance, lifted the leg all the way up, spilling him backward.

Randy the marine was now on his back, looking up at this fifty-year-old man with surprise in his eyes.

Trouble was, he was not seriously injured, but simply humiliated, and in a lot of pain. In short, he was pissed off now, and doubly dangerous. And I was out of steam. He sprang to his feet and began going into a boxer's crouch, but I had anticipated this. Roantis had taught me a few basics, like anticipating what your opponent will do. I didn't have the power to knock him out with my fists. I have never had a strong punch or throwing arm.

But Roantis had taught me how to be nasty when the need arose. As soon as Randy was almost upright, but before he could throw a punch, I spread the two fingers of my right hand and drove them into his eyes, absolutely as hard as I could. I knew I'd hit pay dirt when I felt the wet goo and heard him scream. When he bent over, covering his eyes, I was the one who kicked. I jumped back and kicked him in the solar plexus, hard.

I knew then I could have killed him. But I didn't have time to consider this in depth, because I was then blindsided. Somebody had given me a hard forearm to the side of the head, and I was down for the count.

Whoever my assailant was, he grabbed me by the back of the shirt to pick me up, no doubt so he could pummel me. But his luck ran out then, because Roantis, busy smooching and feeling in the corner, had seen the commotion and now entered the scene. His mode of entry was interesting: he came flying in five feet above the floor like Baryshnikov. His left foot whipped out and hit the second man in the neck, knocking him down and almost out.

But Roantis had not finished with him. He reached down and grabbed the man hard in the crotch, and squeezed. He squeezed so hard the veins on his arms stuck out like spaghetti. Then, still squeezing ever harder, he began to twist his hand back and forth, back and forth, like the agitator in a washing machine.

The talk at the Rotor Club later on was that a bunch of guys in their barracks across the road could hear him screaming.

I felt hands under my armpits and drew back my arm for a swing.

"No honey, it's me," said Dottie's voice. "Boy, hon, I guess you showed him! Why, you're such a tough hunk! I just cain't wait to get you back to my place and take care of you."

She led me outside as the crowd parted before us. It took

me a second or two to realize they were cheering. Then I realized they were cheering for me. I felt slaps on the back and guys grabbing my arms.

"Hey, way to go, dude!"

"Shows you what the marines are really made of . . . *haw, haw, haw!*"

"Yeah, man . . . *semper fi,* my ass!"

"Hey, anytime you come back here, man, I'll buy you a drink!"

"Thanks, guys," I murmured. But I didn't think I'd be coming back soon. Not if I could help it.

Next thing I remembered we were standing in the parking lot. The air was wonderfully, refreshingly cold and without the continual blue haze of cigarette smoke. I saw Roantis and Laura standing there looking at me. Dottie was holding me up with my arm around her neck. My side hurt awfully. I felt tentatively at my jaw. Not broken. Good. But a hell of a bruise would follow. I wasn't drunk, but the fight had taken it out of me. Now that my adrenaline was wearing off, I felt weak and tired. Dottie was rubbing my tummy, kissing me all wet and saying, "I've got to get you home, babe. Take care of you."

"Uh, I don't think so, Dottie. I've got to get home. . . ."

My voice trailed off. I felt woozy again.

She turned me toward her, put her arms around me—put her face in mine. I realized then that she was drunk. "Now you lissen a me; you're going to my place for tonight, ain't he, Laura?"

"You betcher ass, sweetheart!" answered Laura, then turned to Roantis. "Same goes for you, Warlock. I know you cain't drive worth a shit, fucked up as you are—"

Roantis weaved on his feet, trying to focus his eyes on his date. "I resennn that," he slurred. He got out his Camels and tried to shake one out of the pack. Instead, the whole pack came tumbling out onto the asphalt. Roantis stared at the tiny white cylinders for a few seconds, unable to comprehend what had happened. Then he bent over to reach for them and fell on his face. Great, Laitis. How he was able to pull that Bruce Lee move only a few minutes ago was beyond me. Must have been running on pure instinct and hate juice. Now he couldn't stand up.

"Thanks for saving my life, Laitis. Again. But Laura's right; you're dead drunk."

"I resennn that, Doc."

Dottie walked me around the parking lot a few times, like a slavered horse that's just run the Derby, while I caught my breath. I felt my side again, and suspected at least one broken rib. Then somebody came running out the bar, shouting. It was Holly, the bartender. She jumped in the middle of us, fussing and fuming.

"Jesus Fucking Christ! I'm tryna run a nice place here, and look what the fuck happens! You believe this bullshit? Those goddamn marines. I swear, they're nothin' but *animals*!"

Then she heard somebody calling her from the club. She turned to see one of the help making a strange motion.

"Holy Jesus! Just what we need—the cops are coming! C'mon y'all, you better split before they get here. We'll cover for you—don't worry."

Dottie was positively yanking me somewhere, so hard and fast it hurt.

"C'mon, Doc, quick! We gotta haul ass, the cops are comin'!"

She half carried, half dragged me to my car, feeling around near my pockets for the keys. She felt a few other nearby places as well, giving my sport section a little rub and a squeeze.

"Just wanna make sure you're okay, hon. . . ."

But she couldn't find the keys. Roantis had them. I hoped. A night in the pokey was all I needed. She put me in the passenger seat and went to retrieve them. Then she came back, keys jingling, and got in to drive.

I didn't realize at first that this was a big mistake. We squealed out of the lot and onto Route 2 so fast I almost got a whiplash. She had revved up the little sport coupe's six cylinders and then popped the clutch.

"Hey! This lil bugger's fun!" She giggled. "Hold on, naow!"

I don't know who taught Dottie to drive. Must have been Richard Petty or Dale Ernhardt or another one of those

NASCAR guys. I opened the window and let the cool air wash over me.

"Where's Roantis?" I asked.

"You mean Warlock?"

"No, I mean Shit-for-Brains. That's what we should call him."

"They're behine us ... in Laura's car. We'll be home soon. Uh-oh ..."

She was looking in the rearview mirror. I turned my head painfully and could barely see the distant pulsing of bright blue lights near the bend in the road.

We whizzed along, the cool air blowing hard on my face. I breathed deep, and soon realized that I was sober. I had not had that much to drink; my temporary dizziness was due to the bar fight. Now I felt fine, while Dottie was truly bombed. Sure, she handled the car well—she would do any North Carolina "ridgerunner" proud. But she'd had enough booze so that her reflexes were way off, and at the speed we were going, it spelled trouble. When she went off the road in a turn, the tires spitting gravel and the rear end sliding around, I ordered her to stop.

"Whass wrong, sugar?"

"Let's switch places; I can drive better than you."

She started to argue, but I could see that the little fish-tailing of the car had shaken her a bit. We both got out and passed each other coming around the back of the coupe, and I could see she was weaving on her feet. Suddenly I wanted nothing more than to be back home, even if it was cold and lonely there.

"Just tell me the way, Dottie, and I'll get us there."

Her inability to give clear directions notwithstanding, we finally made it. Dottie's place, which she shared with Laura, was a trailer set half a mile up a dirt road, in a clump of big New England pines that smelled good.

"Is this the place?" I asked.

"Huh? Oh, yeah ... you gonna love it. ..."

She looked almost out on her feet. I went around and helped her out of the car and led her up the little wooden stairs and under the deck roof to the trailer's door. She fumbled for her keys, but couldn't find the right one. Then she couldn't insert it into the lock, so I did it. We stumbled inside and I found the light switch. I remember laminated paneling, gaudy curtains, a big new television, two purple love seats, and an Elvis painting on black velvet. I helped her down a hallway two feet wide, where she found a sliding door and opened it. I found the switch, turned on a light, and lowered her onto the bed, which had a pink velveteen spread.

"Whatcha thinka this, hon?"

I was about to say not much, but stopped when I saw her lift the sweater up over her head and hold her foot up.

"Take off mah boots, big boy. . . ."

She said boy like this: *bo*way.

I pulled her boots off, and then she squiggled out of her jeans.

"C'mon, Doc—take yer clothes off . . . why ya think I brung ya here . . . hmm?"

When her jeans were off she tried to jump off the bed, but almost fell back.

"Forgot sumpin'," she mumbled, then got up, weaved over to the wall—a distance of about four feet, and snapped off the big overhead light, then turned on a small lamp near the bed. It had as much illumination as a night-light, and made the room dark and cozy.

"This is mah love light, babe. Ain't it better?"

I nodded and heard a squeak, squeak, squeak as she cranked open the jalousie glass window. The sound of the wind in the pines came into the little room.

Outside in the hallway, Roantis and Laura bumped and slid their way toward what I supposed was Laura's bedroom. "C'mon, dummy," said Laura. "Jeez, sweetie, I wish you hadn'ta drunk so much. . . ."

Dottie now staggered over to a built-in dresser and opened the bottom drawer. I had to admit that she looked tempting as she leaned over in her panties. She straigthened up, still weaving slightly, holding a negligee so sheer it could fly, and said, "Now you stay right cheer, Doc. Don'tcha go away . . . I'll be right back and show you things you ain't *never* gonna forget—"

She made her way down the little hall to what I assumed was the bathroom. Next door, through the paneled walls that were at least a millimeter thick, I could hear Laura cussing out Roantis. Then I heard another sound: poor Dottie retching her guts out in the john. It didn't take long for me to realize this was the perfect moment—the break in the action I needed for a quick exit, stage left.

I was out the room and down the hallway in a wink, stopping only a second to open the refrigerator. I saw a few cans of Coke in there and snagged one. Outside, I started the car, turned in a tight circle, and went back down the gravel road to the highway, letting the cold Coke slide down my parched throat.

I swept by the Rotor Club; it was all dark and the parking lot deserted. A crude logic convinced me that the two marine-corps rowdy boys had survived. Otherwise, the police would surely have questioned Holly and others and found out where Dottie and Laura lived, and we would have had a visit from the law, toting warrants.

But we had not, and I assumed we were in the clear, at least for the present.

Then I remembered that I had to be at the office by seven-thirty, for the surgery at nine. My watch read ten to two. I wouldn't be in bed before three or three-thirty, and should be up at six, looking sharp. Oh my God. Surgery is tense enough under ideal conditions, but with lack of sleep, a rib cage that might be broken in spots, a sore jaw and terrible headache, it was going to be a real son of a bitch.

As I entered Concord, just a few minutes from home, I couldn't help thinking that just a few weeks ago my life was normal. Now it was all coming apart.

"Dear God," I whispered to myself, "what the hell is happening to me?"

19

WHEN I WOKE UP—IT SEEMED I'D BEEN ASLEEP ALL OF TEN
minutes—I was edgy, groggy, and in a lot of pain. The mirror in the bedroom revealed several bruises beginning to
color. The smaller one was along my left jawline. By mid-
day it would be purple, and no doubt instill a lot of faith in
my clientele. Nothing like an oral surgeon with a busted-up
jaw. The other, an especially big one, was along the right
side of my rib cage. The area was still very tender to the
touch. Broken rib? Maybe. Perhaps two. I took some adhe-
sive tape and did the best I could shoring up that side of
my torso. It helped a lot. If it still bothered me in a day or
so, I would get an X ray. My head was killing me, from
Randy's first punch to the jaw and his buddy's forearm to
the side of my head. I gobbled aspirin, put as much talcum
powder over my jaw as possible, and staggered downstairs.

I managed to gulp down some fresh fruit and a mug of
coffee. Dizzy, dry-mouthed, exhausted, in pain, and slightly
nauseous, I drove to the office. Goody; I couldn't wait.

"What's wrong with you this morning?" said Susan Petri,
looking up from the instrument tray.

"Oh . . . late night," I said, going in to the washroom to
scrub.

"What happened to the side of your face? And why are
you walking funny?"

"Uh, long story. Are the syringes ready?"

"Yes . . . *Doctor.*"

Susan obviously knew something was up. Well, it could wait. I had to concentrate on what was going to happen in the next hour. Ted Soule, like so many people who finally become my patients, chose to ignore the discomfort in his lower jaw caused by the impacted wisdom tooth, hoping it would go away, until it turned to pain. He then ignored even the pain until infection and swelling set in. When I had finally examined him, I put him on Keflex, a broad-spectrum antibiotic, for a week prior to this visit. This would also help fight infection after the procedure, which was to commence in a few minutes.

It was now necessary to incise the surrounding swollen soft tissue and drain it, section the impacted molar with a bur or chisel, remove the pieces, and finally drill and chisel out that portion of mandibular bone that the infection had rotted away.

All in all, it was at least a forty-minute operation, and could have complications.

Great, and on a day in which I felt like hell. Physically, mentally, and even spiritually. I put on my mask and began the systematic scrubbing of my hands and forearms, then coated them with a dermicidal antiseptic solution.

"Well, Mr. Soule is due in only a few minutes," Susan continued, pulling on her surgeon's gloves. "Diane is already waiting for us," she said, covering the sterile instruments with a white cloth and wheeling the tray into the small OR.

I finished scrubbing, put on the greens and cap she held for me, and went into the OR, where Diane Nakamura placed the light harness on my head and fed the cord of the tiny quartz-halogen spotlight over my shoulder and back to the power pack. The little spotlight, clamped to the head harness, rested on my lower forehead right between my eyes. Then Diane unwrapped a pair of surgeon's latex gloves, expertly slipping them on my outstretched hands.

Thank God I had good help . . .

Susan Petri came in, a stern look in her gorgeous green eyes.

"You just got a phone call, Dr. Adams," she said in an icy voice. "She said her name was Dottie."

"Dottie? Gee, I don't believe I know any Dottie," I said,

trying to appear calm as I flipped on the X-ray view box. Affixed on it was a buccal-view shot of Soule's lower jaw, or mandible. It showed a classic horizontal impaction: the crown of the third molar, or wisdom tooth, wedged underneath the crown of the second molar in front of it. The dark, shadowy mass at the junction of the ramus and the mandible, called the angle of the jaw, was big. This was the infection site, and it was going to be a doozy of a procedure, and today of all days.

"She says she knows, you, Doc."

Susan said it matter-of-factly. But I noticed that for the first time in our long acquaintance, she called me Doc in the office. Diane Nakamura, ever reserved and polite, showed no response.

"That so?" I replied nonchalantly.

"Yes. That is so. In fact, she referred to you as her *'hunky man with the cute buns.'*"

"Jeeez!" I exclaimed, faking a laugh, "Oh wow! Hey, it sure takes all kinds of nuts to make a world, eh?"

Hearing nothing in response, I turned to look at her. Over her white gauze mask, Susan's green, feline eyes were boring right into mine. Uh-oh. Susan took a sterile wipe from the tray and wiped my brow. I suppose I was sweating a little. . . . She came close to me, looking in Diane's direction out of the corner of her eye.

"We're going to talk after this is over," she whispered.

With no comment in return, I proceeded to undrape the tray, exposing the five syringes of Xylocaine that Diane had prepared. All this dope was to deaden the inferior alveolar, lingual, and long buccal nerves in the mandibular nerve division of Ted Soule's lower left face. From what I knew so far, he was going to need it all. Every bit. I checked the swab, coated with topical anesthetic that I would rub on the surface of Soule's mucosa before beginning the injections. The other instruments were arranged precisely on the tray: elevators, gouges, drill bits, bone burs, retractors, scalpels, Bard Parker blades, chisels, and the hefty Myerding stainless-steel mallet. They were all clean and shiny . . . but still, to the uninitiated, they probably resembled torturer's tools.

Now where was the patient?

Ted Soule was almost twenty minutes late. I guess I couldn't blame him for not rushing right over to be cut, gouged, hit with a chisel, and sewn up. Not everybody's favorite way to begin a day. But when you're ready for a procedure, you're ready. I knew the reason for the delay: Ted Soule was scared to death. Of needles, of pain, of blood, of operations in general. And he had some reason not to look forward to this one; there was going to be lots of the aforementioned. But only because he waited way, way too long to have his third molar, or wisdom tooth, extracted.

"Did you eat anything this morning?" Susan asked from the anteroom.

"No, nothing. Nothing except the Valium tablets Dr. Adams prescribed for me. *They're not working!*"

"You'll be fine, Mr. Soule, as soon as we numb you up."

"I hate needles! Scared to death of them!" He stood in the doorway with a look of a man about to be led before the firing squad. I covered the tray again, but not before he saw the five syringes and all the other interesting tools.

"Five? You need *five*?"

"Yes, but don't worry," said Susan in her best soothing voice. "These will just—"

But she didn't have time to finish, because Ted Soule bolted the scene and was halfway out the office door when I snagged him by the shoulder and turned him around.

"Ted, how does your mouth feel?"

"Better," he lied.

"Hell it does; I can see the swelling from the outside." I touched the back of my hand to his jaw. It was hot, and I knew he was in terrible pain.

"Look, this won't be a picnic, but it won't be agony, either. If you want, I can put you to sleep."

"No!" he yelled, cringing against the wall.

"C'mon ... the more you put it off, the worse it'll get. Now, you've got to have faith that we know what we're doing."

But he was in a full-blown panic attack, so I led him back to the anteroom and sat him in a chair and made him watch a loud television—put there especially for this purpose—while Susan deftly inserted an IV into the top of his left hand. He never knew she did it until afterward.

Then I pumped one cc of Versed into the tube, and within a minute Soule's face softened, as did his white-knuckle grip on the arms of the chair. His gaze assumed a languid, faraway look, and Susan spoke to him softly and led him into the OR without a whimper. Great stuff, Versed. Loaded up with it, you could face the rack or the guillotine without a flinch. We sat him down in the chair, where I opened his mouth and swabbed his gums generously with the topical ointment. At my signal, Susan placed the earphones over his head, and I could hear the faint strains of a Haydn string quartet coming from them. Then I deliberately rubbed his gums with a lot of pressure, syringe in hand. Twice he squirmed, but I told him I had not done anything yet. I managed to slip in the first needle partway with not even a twitch from him. Then I removed the syringe and massaged the gum, letting the Xylocaine spread. I did this in all locations. A few minutes later I put the needle in all the way each time and pumped him full of the drug. By waiting for the effect of each injection to start, I did all the others without so much as whimper from Ted Soule.

The fact is, pain in the dental office is bad because it is *anticipated* pain. The patient is waiting for it, expecting it, and his imagination gets the best of him, whereas stubbing your toe in the dark actually hurts much more. But since the pain is sudden and unexpected, the injury already over with, we pay it little mind.

Ten minutes later Soule could not feel a damn thing on the left side of his lower face. Not his lips, tongue, or anything in his mouth. I began the procedure by lancing the swollen mass in posterior portion of the buccal fold. A great quantity of pus and blood came forth, along with the putrid odor of trapped gases being released. Susan and I turned our heads, but got a whiff anyway. Just what I needed today of all days. I let it drain and bleed freely while Diane kept the suction hose at the mouth of the incision. With light pressure, I massaged the outside cheek to gently milk out as much of the corruption as possible. If I pushed too hard, it might force the infection into surrounding tissues.

With the swelling down and the pressure relieved, I could now work. I took the Bard Parker scalpel and made a vertical incision down the ascending ramus to the back surface of the second molar, around the front of it, and two teeth farther forward to the first molar. Then I pulled back the large flap of gum tissue, and Susan held it out of the way with a retractor, thus exposing the heart of the infection and laying open to view the crown of the third molar. I tried the elevator first, but, as expected, the tooth did not budge because it had grown crookedly into the tooth in front of it. And the roots and tooth were bent, and even "hooked" from this crooked growing.

"How you doing, Ted?" I asked.

"Unnnnh, unnnnnh," he said.

He was bleeding like a stuck pig, but he didn't know it. Thank God for that suction hose. The impacted tooth was lying almost horizontally in the back of the jaw. I took a drill and cut about three quarters of the way through the root at the point where it joined the crown of the tooth and inserted a broad-bladed elevator—which I could use as a chisel—into the groove I'd made. I twisted it and heard a distinct *snap* as the tooth broke in two. Ted's eyes widened. He seemed anxious again. Perhaps the Versed was wearing off. . . .

I switched to a narrow elevator and tried to pry out the root half of the severed tooth. No go: the hook on one of the roots wouldn't let it rotate out. Hoping Ted wouldn't notice what I was about, I placed the chisel on the root portion, took the Myerding stainless-steel mallet, and gave the chisel a sharp rap.

"Unnnnnhhhh!" said Ted, half sitting up, his eyes wide. I smiled, gently pushing him back down. I teased out the top root with a small elevator. With it out of the way, I could rotate out the hooked portion with ease. Whew!

Then, with the pressure gone, taking out the impacted crown was like picking a cherry. I lifted one side of the earphones and said: "Toughest part's over," and gave him the thumbs-up and a wink. He almost smiled.

And I almost gagged and collapsed. God, I felt awful! The pain and damage and lack of sleep were suddenly *very* evident. If I could only hold on another half hour . . . then I could take a *nap.* . . .

Now there remained the task of removing all the diseased tissue with my spoon excavator, which is a scooplike curette, and suture him up. There was plenty of it, and Ted would be in what we physicians euphemistically call "discomfort" for a few days.

After I had scooped out all the infected soft tissue, I put down the curette and picked up the drill with the bone bur attached. This tool would ream out the rotten bone in the mandible that had spread from the socket. It would do this fast, but it was tricky, the tool could cut tissue like blazes. I had just started with the drill when we all heard a voice from the outer office.

"Where's that hunka mine? Doc, you in there? You better come out here and see your lover girl, hon, or I'm comin' in there after yah!"

Susan looked at me, frowning. Diane, distracted, let the suction hose and her tissue retractor slip. I slipped with the drill, hitting a small artery in the mucosal lining of Ted's cheek. Blood spurted on the floor and all over Ted Soule's smock.

"Yahhhhhhhh!" yelled Soule, sitting bolt upright in the chair.

"Yoooo-hooooo!" shouted Waxahatchie Dottie, pounding on the door. "Hey Doc, I gotta see you, babe! And I'll tell you raht naow, we're a-havin' our first *faht*! I don't like men who sweet-talk a gal and then run out, *ya hear*?"

"We're having that talk *now*!" Susan hissed through gritted teeth.

"Yahhhhhhhh!" yelled Soule again, struggling to get out of the chair.

There was blood everywhere now. We had Big Red in the OR.

Dear God, I thought, why me?

20

Two hours later Susan Petri and I were in the Concord Professional Building's parking lot. She still had her green smock and her OR cap on. She was standing there, hands on hips, shouting at me.

"And of all the things, Doc, that you could do to hurt me ... shacking up with that cowgirl whore is the *worst*—"

"Shhhhhhh! Not so loud, Susan, okay? Some of these people are my patients. And I didn't shack up with her; I think that's why she was mad at me."

Passersby were staring at us. A little girl stopped to stare, and her mom, with a disgusted look on her face, took her by the arm and yanked her away.

Susan yanked off her OR cap, one of those disposable deals made out of paper and elastic, and flung it down on the asphalt, then kicked it.

"I don't give a shit if the whole world's watching! I finally tell you how I feel about you and look what happens! And I suppose you now think I'm mad because you wouldn't go to bed with me. Is that it?"

"Of course not. I thought what you did was sweet ... and I really liked our time together." I opened the car door and got half inside. "I'm sorry, Susan. My world seems to be coming apart. I don't know what I did to deserve it—but it's happening anyway."

She just stood there, her hair blowing all around her head, arms crossed over her chest, tears down her face.

"Are you still going to take off after I close the office?" she asked.

"Yes. I'm not sure where, but I'm going. I've got to get away from this place—especially my house. It's so . . . empty."

"Can I go with you?"

The request took me by surprise.

"Uh, no, Susan. I have to be alone."

"It's my fault, isn't it? If I hadn't come over to cook for you, then—"

"No; it was nobody's fault. It was just bad luck and bad timing. And the fact that Mary's . . . gone now . . . leaves me vulnerable to make stupid mistakes."

"Like me?" she said, her eyes flashing anger.

"No. Like Waxahachie Dottie."

She wiped her eyes and took two deep breaths. "What I think is, you should quit hanging around with Mr. Roantis. Every time you're with him, you get into trouble."

"Yeah, but lately I've been getting into trouble without his help."

"Do you like me?"

Again, I was surprised at her remark.

"Very much. Professionally, and personally. I would think you would know that without a doubt."

"If Mary doesn't come back, will you see me?"

"Yes, absolutely," I said without hesitation.

She leaned into the car, put her arms around my neck, and gave me a long, wet kiss on the mouth. Then she moved her head down and gave me a strong kiss and a wet bite on my throat that hurt so much I almost yelled. And then finally another humdinger on the mouth. Her breathing picked up. I gently pushed her away, saying she was the best friend I had right now.

I knew if I let her inside the car, we would drive to Vegas and tie the knot.

Is life crazy, or what?

"I'm closing the office now for a week, right?"

I nodded. "Might as well; I'm in no shape to do much. And Moe's up seeing his mother in New Jersey. Damn! Why does he have to go away now, when I need him the most?"

She shrugged her shoulders. "But I'm here. Remember that."

She leaned inside and kissed me again, all over my face. I pulled out of the lot and headed for home. But I looked back at her. She blew me a kiss and mouthed the unmistakable words: *I Love You!*

By the time I walked into the house, I was actually feeling almost human again—I think the kisses and nice words from Susan really helped—when four big slugs caught me in the chest, one right after another.

Slug Number One:

Roantis called from Laura and Dottie's trailer, cussing me out for not giving him a ride home. And also to inform me that Dottie had decided to file charges against me.

"For what?"

"Rape. She claims you got her drunk, took her back to her place, and raped her."

"For chrissakes, Laitis, you know that's a lie."

"How would I know? I was kinda under the weather."

"You and I, and Laura, know it wasn't rape."

"Well, she says she's going to the police and charge you anyway."

I thought a second about what he'd told me. "Laitis, I think I know why she's doing this. She came barging into my office this morning in the middle of a procedure, yelling at me. I guess she was hurt more than I imagined by my leaving the trailer. But anyway, she almost blew the operation, and I lost my temper and yelled at her—told her to get the hell out of my office and leave me alone. When she left, she was crying. So I owe her an apology. She's a sweet person—just a little too desperate, maybe."

"You think she'll drop the charges?"

"I sure hope so. It's the last thing I need right now. I'm already being sued by a patient."

"Will you come out here and apologize to her?"

"I'm a little . . . hesitant to do that. She might get riled up again. Maybe over the phone."

"Well, how about coming out here and getting me? I'm stuck here."

"No way. I never want to see Ayer, Mass., again. Good-bye."

I hung up on him. The jerk. If I hadn't taken him out to dinner, this whole thing would never have happened.

Slug Number Two:

Holly Hickman, co-owner of the Rotor Club, called to tell me that one Randall Hartrey, USMC, was charging me with aggravated assault.

"Hell, Doc, you really did a number on that sumbitch. You cracked his, uh, uh, watchamacallit. . . ."

"What?"

"Steroid? Somethin' like that. The place in the middle of your chest . . ."

"Sternum?"

"Yeah, that's it; you smashed his sternum, and now he's in the hospital, and he's AWOL anyway, and he's mad."

"So what? He attacked me first; it wasn't my fault."

"Well, him and his buddy Mike Emmett are saying you and Warlock beat them up—"

"Listen, Holly, I'm over fifty. Roantis is sixty-three. How old are those two clowns? Twenty-eight?"

"Somethin' like that."

"Well, they ought to be ashamed, getting their asses whipped by a couple of old guys."

"I know, and I spoke up for you, but you should know they're tryin' to make these charges stick."

Slugs Three and Four:

Joe called and dropped the last two salvos on me before I could begin to recover from the first two.

"Hate to say this, Doc, but that murder up in P-town. They say you still look good for it."

"C'mon, Joe, you and I know I didn't kill James Harold. You can vouch for me. For crying out loud, I was the ME for Barnstable County!"

"We know this. Chief Lyle Henderson and the P-town Police Department, they know this, too. Trouble is, Doc, they can find absolutely no other lead. You are the only guy who was in the right place at the right time. You asked how to get to his house. You bought an ivory kayak just like the one that—"

"Yeah, yeah, yeah. So what are you telling me?"

"I'm telling you that you're still the number-one suspect, like it or not. I want to help get you off the hook; so please help me in any way you can to solve this thing. You know anybody at all who would want Mr. Harold dead?"

"Yes. I don't know the person, but I know what he does. He's the person who's smuggling in that illegal ivory. Or running the carving shop, or whatever. It could be Johnny Ridge. He's not only involved with thugs, but has a record of violence and is very big and strong. Or it could be this shadowy guy Jason Steingretz, or even Sam Ho."

"Or . . ." said Joe slowly and deliberately, "it could even be Larry Carpenter."

There was a silence lasting several seconds. Why had Joe said this? Was he playing games? Didn't he know already how screwed up I was over this superman squiring my erstwhile wife around?

"What do you mean by that?" I asked.

"What I mean is, new information shows that Mr. Carpenter is not exactly what he appears to be."

"What do you mean by that?" I repeated.

"We have some evidence—it's not admissible evidence, but it's there—that Larry might have stolen some securities from a firm he worked for."

"What? I find that hard to believe, Joe. How did you come up with this stuff anyway?"

"We got onto it by accident. We knew that Brad Taylor wanted a legend for Larry—you know—a fake record of his being incarcerated at San Quentin. Well, when we were working up the fake scenario, we found out something interesting. This wasn't on the usual data tracks, either, but a little-known one called JUDAS."

"Judas? As in the guy who betrayed Jesus?"

"Yes, and that's the way the acronym is spelled, but really it refers to the letters *J-U-D-H-I-S*. This is an abbreviation for 'judicial histories.' "

"What the hell are judicial histories?"

"They're records of court cases, hearings, prosecutions, etcetera."

"Well, isn't this info on the standard crime files?"

"Nope. Only convictions are on that. But JUDAS tells us if a person's been to court, been sued, been the subject, or even a key witness, in a trial or hearing."

"Isn't that kind of unconstitutional?"

"Probably. And none of it is admissible. But I think it's indicative. Anyway, your friend Larry was accused of embezzling forty-four thousand dollars' worth of securities from the brokerage firm he worked for in New York back in the early seventies."

"What? He was never a broker, Joe; he was a lawyer. You've got the wrong Larry Carpenter. It's a pretty common name, you know."

"Nope. Got the right guy. Anyway, it didn't stick. They settled it out of court, but the upshot was that Larry left the firm and lost his brokerage license."

"What about the law firm? I know it was one of the better ones. Strandburg, Carlson—"

"Carlson, Haffner, and Stafford. Very well respected. And nothing on the JUDAS file."

"Well, maybe the thing at the trading house was a quirk."

"So we called the law firm. Turns out he was asked to leave there as well."

"*Really?* No shit! Reason?"

"Would not discuss it. Never want to even hear Larry's name again."

I thought for a moment. Then the fog lifted, and it all made sense. Fit together like the floating pieces of a jigsaw puzzle that come together in your head.

"Hey, Joe, this explains something important. It explains why Larry suddenly became a handyman. He always claimed he just couldn't take the bullshit of the big city— that he wanted to get back to nature, do all the things he really liked, like saw wood, pound nails, paint porches ... but don't you see?"

"Yeah, I see. The truth was, he was forced into becoming a handyman. If he stayed in the world of law and finance, any prospective employer would want references. He would see two dismissals and possible criminality. Bad news ..."

"Wow ..." And then a very unpleasant thought struck

me. "Joe? You realize that right now Larry is God-knows-where with your sister?"

"And your wife."

"I don't think she's my wife anymore, Joe."

"C'mon, buck up. You always make things out to be worse than they are. But infidelity, bad as is, isn't what I'm most worried about. Suppose you're right. Suppose they are together somewhere, maybe intimately. That news is bad enough for us, but what if Larry Carpenter, in addition to being a thief and a liar—"

"—is a killer?"

"Yeah," Joe said, with a definite edge to his voice. "What then?"

"Joe—we've got to find them. And fast."

"Okay, tell you what. I'll be over in Concord tomorrow before four."

"No. I've pretty much made up my mind to get out of Dodge. I'm going down to the Breakers tomorrow. Want to join me there?"

"Sure. I'll tell Marty you and I are worried about finding Mary and I'll come down solo in the evening. Okay?"

"Sounds great, buddy. That's what I need. A little support."

"No problem. One other thing. Brad Taylor and the Fish and Wildlife people don't know any of this new information about Larry. We want to keep it that way. We want to run this investigation on our own, okay?"

"Why the secrecy?"

"Well, for one thing, it may turn out that Larry is now entirely on the up-and-up, and having told his superiors about these allegations would look bad for us. Make us appear as if we were trying to smear him. I don't think Taylor and company would appreciate it."

"I understand."

"On the other hand, if there is something there, we'd like to pursue it with as few people knowing about it as possible."

"Well, I won't say anything to anybody. How's that?"

"Good."

"Uh, speaking of investigations, Joe, what are the three most serious crimes?"

"You mean the three most serious felonies?"

"Yes."

"Well, there's murder, of course. Second worst, well, it's a toss-up, I think, between aggravated assault and forcible rape."

There was a pause while I digested this.

"That's what I was afraid of. I am now accused of *all three* of these. I could go to trial for all three of these felonies within a month!"

"What do you mean, all three? I thought you were only accused of murder. You mean you're facing rape and assault as well?"

I then briefly explained the episode at the Rotor Club, describing the barroom fight and the interlude with Dottie.

"Jesus, Doc. How do you do it? How the hell do you *do* it?"

"Gifted, I guess . . ."

"Listen—you've heard about treading water? Well, it seems you're treading shit. Just keep treading shit until I see you."

I sighed. "It doesn't sound like much fun. God bless you, Joe."

"Arrivederla."

I went to bed feeling a lot better. As bad as everything was, I had bared my soul to another person, and he had understood. More importantly, he was going to stand by me.

I went into my study and had two beers. No booze for a while, anyway. The two beers, and the phone call to Joe, had lifted enough of my nervous frenzy so that I was left exhausted. Also, the effects of last night still lingered. My head, jaw, and side still ached. And I was exhausted from lack of sleep, the mishap in the OR, the argument with Susan, and . . . well, everything. I went upstairs and collapsed into bed.

I dreamed something so ridiculous that, even asleep and dreaming, I knew it was a dream: *Ms.* magazine had voted me "Man of the Year."

21

I SLEPT BETTER THAN I THOUGHT I WOULD, BUT WHEN I WOKE up, the old depressing events of past, present, and future loomed in front of me. Collectively, they were formidable enough to make me want to go into a fetal position (what Roantis and other soldiers refer to as the "whine" position, which is what you assume, as close to Mother Earth as possible, when enemy artillery starts hammering you), and stay that way for maybe two years.

Or, I could be a woodchuck. Since it was now almost October, I could dig a deep hole, eat heartily for two weeks, then go down in there and sleep for four months. And with luck, when I emerged in the bright of spring, all these cares would have vanished.

But they wouldn't. As I was shaving and looking at myself in the mirror, I realized I had to face them. I also had to face the purplish oblong mark on my lower neck where the passionate Susan Petri had kissed and bitten me the previous afternoon. Quite a girl, that Susan.

I was looking forward to going down to the Cape for a week and recharging my batteries. I would run on the beach, sit in the sun while there was still some remaining, swim, collect clams, surf-cast for fish, and eat this fresh food with lots of salads and green vegetables. No red meat. No booze. Beer maybe, but not much. I would regain my physical, mental, and spiritual strength.

I hoped.

And I would begin to make plans for accepting the fact that perhaps Mary wasn't coming back.

What would I do then?

I had an idea.

First, I would retire. I had enough money to do this, and had been looking forward to it for the past six or seven years. Then Mary and I would sell the house. This was a must, since we each owned half of it. Either we would sell it and split the proceeds, or I would take half the value from her and let her stay there.

With this money as a base, I would then shop around until I found the deepwater sailboat of my dreams. Something roughly between thirty-five and fifty-five feet, beamy, with a deep keel hull, round chines, and a lot of sheer to the hull, which meant a high, well-sheltered bow for big rough water, and a high, wide transom aft for the master stateroom. It would be a two-master, probably a ketch or a yawl, but perhaps a schooner. The cockpit would be midships, and there would be two companionways: one forward, into the main living and cooking areas of the vessel, and another aft, which would lead to the engine room and the master stateroom. Power would be a big diesel, the prop self-feathering.

The crew would be from four to eight people. I hoped Jack and Tony would be my mates on at least several of the longer trips. Ultimately, there was a chance I would sail south through the Caribbean, down the coast of Central America, through the big ditch at Panama, and into the Pacific, where I would work my way up to La Paz, and ever northward, stopping at San Diego, Los Angeles, San Luis Obisbo, Morro Bay, San Francisco, Bodega Bay, Mendocino, the Oregon coast, and on up until I got to Puget Sound and Vancouver.

Who knows? I might settle down for the rest of my life on the Oregon coast. . . .

Or, I might go up to Alaska for a summer.

I was excited about this, and raced downstairs for a breakfast of coffee and oat bran—Moe Abramson's insidious influence—and packed the car. Then there were the dogs. The Rutners were out of town, so I arranged for another neighbor's kid to feed, water, and exercise them.

Then I tore out of there, heading down 128 for the Cape. But as I drove down to the ocean I couldn't hide a lingering fact that was the saddest of all: on my dream boat, even with my friends and two sons as crew, there would still be somebody missing: my FIRST MATE.

All during the trip I puffed nervously on my pipe, running the events of the past several weeks through my head like a fast rewind on a videotape. I found myself tapping fast on the steering column. I was wound up; I needed to run, run, run.

Where was she? Why hadn't she at least called the boys? Was she ever coming back? Had she and Larry hightailed it to Paris?

As I saw the exit sign for Hyannis I had a sudden idea, and a glimmer of hope, however faint. I exited Route 6 and made my way into the town of Hyannis to Bill Bedford's marina and charter service. If Mary had confided her whereabouts to anyone other than her close friends and family, she would have told Sally or Bill Bedford. After all, the mission she was on was one that had sprung from her association with CapeWatch. And if I could casually approach these people and ask if they'd seen her lately, they just might give me some idea of where to start looking.

The main shop and headquarters of Bedford's operation was a handsome two-story house done in the weathered gray cedar shakes and white trim so common on Cape Cod. Mary told me the Bedfords lived in a spacious apartment above the shop—she'd been to several meetings there. I parked the Subaru and walked down to the marina docks, which were equally divided for sailboats and power craft. Snugged against the nearest dock was a big Bertram sportfisherman, the *Bim Bam Boo,* one of the two charter sportfishing boats Bill owned. The other one, *Dream Days,* wasn't to be seen, so I assumed Bill had a party of clients out for a day's fishing for stripers. A lot of the boats in the marina had For Sale signs on them. The recession, which seemed to hit us particularly hard in the Northeast, was taking its toll.

I made my way up to the office, which doubled as a bait-and-tackle shop, and showroom for small runabouts like the

Boston whalers. Over the front door, underneath the big marina sign, was a smaller one of carved wood, painted green, turquoise, and gold that showed a pod of dolphins leaping out of the waves. Underneath this bas-relief in wood were the words:

HEADQUARTERS: CAPEWATCH

I went inside and wandered through the store, looking at the big "fighting" rods, as thick as my thumb with roller guides for the heavy wire line. The big brass Penn and Fin-Nor reels that cost hundreds of bucks apiece. I envisioned Brady Coyne and me doing some heavy fishing someday, either up here in New England or perhaps in the Bahamas. That and an African safari were perhaps the only Papa Hemingway things we hadn't done together. As I walked on to see the giant spoons, bucktail jigs, rubber squids, and other baits, I realized that Brady was a prime contender for crewman on my blue-water cruiser. The one I was dreaming of. I already had the name picked out: *Star Rover*, after the title of one of Jack London's last books.

I stopped in front of a large display rack filled with pamphlets and literature from the Sierra Club, Greenpeace, the NRDC—National Resources Defense Council—the Audubon Society, and several other groups devoted to cleaning up the air and water and saving what wildlife remained on the planet.

"May I help you, sir?" said a pretty blond woman with short hair and a deep tan. She had a leggy body and good muscle tone. Mary had mentioned to me that Sally Bedford ran road races and swam. She did aerobics and jazz dancing, too. She looked it. At maybe fifty years old, she had a bouncy step and a bright smile. Very attractive person, was Sally Bedford. I took off my dark glasses and turned to face her.

"Hello, Sally."

"Doc! Well, how are you? We haven't seen you or Mary in some time."

This was disappointing news, and I told her so.

"You mean she just . . . disappeared?" Sally asked. The concern showed on her face.

"Not exactly. We ... had a fight and she took off. I thought if there was one place she might check into, it would be here."

Just then Bill Bedford came in through the front door. Though I had only met him once, there was no forgetting him. He was six four, about two hundred seventy pounds. It certainly wasn't all muscle, but enough of it was to make him a first-rate big-game fisherman. When those eight-hundred-pound tunas and big mako sharks come into the boat, you've got to be big and strong to handle them and not get your client's leg chewed off. From the look on his face, I surmised he was not in the best of moods. I was correct.

"Shit!" he thundered as he approached us, then managed a temporary smile when he saw me. "Oh, hiya, Doc. Good to see you again."

"What's the matter?" asked Sally.

"Come over to the window and I'll show you."

He led the way, and soon the three of us were looking out into the big marina parking lot. Bill pointed to a huge white van, a Chevy Suburban, I think, white, that looked new. Thing was, there was an ugly scrape and dent along the right rear side, and the end of the bumper was pulled out and bent.

"Oh, honey. How'd that happen?" Sally moaned.

"That's what I'd like to know; when we left this morning, it was fine. Some joker backed out too fast and scraped me as he pulled out. You didn't hear anything?"

"Nope. But it's pretty far away, and we've had the windows closed."

Bedford shook his head in disgust. I noticed a new bumper sticker on what was left of same:

SAVE STELLWAGEN BANK

This referred to the famous "bank," or shallows, rich in krill, thirty miles out of Gloucester where the humpback whales feed and mate during the summer season. If Stellwagen Bank continued to become polluted and over-fished, the whales would leave, perhaps even starve.

"Where can I get one of those stickers for Jack?" I asked.

"Ha!" said Bill. "He beat you to it. Came in with his mother and got several."

"You've seen Mary?" I asked.

"Not recently, Doc. Hell, this was last May, I think, when we first had them printed."

"You haven't seen her recently?"

Bedford stroked his big chin. "When was our last meeting, hon? July or August?"

"August twentieth."

"And neither of you has seen her since?" I asked.

"Don't think so. Is she missing?"

"Sort of," said Sally. "Doc says they had a spat and she left. How long ago was that, Doc?"

"Let's see . . . three nights ago."

"Well, hell . . ." Bill mused. "That's not so bad. She have any relatives she could've gone to to cool off?"

"Her mother in Schenectady. I haven't tried her. But I would think she'd at least call the boys, and she hasn't."

"I'm sure you'll hear from her soon," said Sally.

"The thing is, she's become involved in something that's . . . a little out of the ordinary."

"What the hell is it, Doc, some kind of Taoist cult or something?" Bill chuckled.

"Wish it were that simple. I can't tell you much except that it stems from her involvement with you and your group. Let's just say you'd be proud of her. I am, too, I guess. But I also worry."

"What the hell is she doing, anyway?" Bill asked. "Is she on one of those Greenpeace boats? Christ, they're always blowing them up. If that's where she is, I'd be worried, too."

"No, not nearly that dramatic."

"Well, we'll let you know if she shows up," said Sally. She was smiling her best smile, trying to cheer me up. "And of course we'll tell her to call you—"

"No! No, that wouldn't be the best idea. What you can do is call me if you see her, but I'd really appreciate it if you don't mention we had this talk. To Mary, or anyone else."

"Aw, don't worry about that; you've got our word," Bill said. "I just hope she isn't in over her head."

"Me, too. Listen—I'll be at our cottage in North Eastham. Let me leave you the number."

"I've already got it," said Sally. "I have the numbers of all the members."

I left the shop with Bill, and we walked out onto the parking lot. I looked out at the docks and saw that *Dream Days* was riding quietly in her berth. I asked him how the fishing was.

"Well, some days are better than others, Doc. But it isn't like it used to be twenty years ago when I first started chartering. And not all of it is pollution, either. It's just plain human encroachment. See, I didn't start CapeWatch just out of the goodness of my heart. I mean, my business, my livelihood, depends on sportfishing. When the game fish disappear, so do my clients. My boat and tackle sales plummet. In short, I'm outta business. And what business I got left is shrinking."

"Well, at least you've made a distinction between the conservationist groups like Sierra Club, Audubon Society, NRDC, and so on as opposed to the 'don't touch the animals' nuts."

"Oh, for sure. Hell, right now there are groups trying to ban rodeos, circuses, horse-drawn buggy rides."

"Not to mention hunting," I added.

"Right, and even *fishing*. I admit, we had a few of these wackos in our group early on, but they left when they found out I'm a professional fisherman. And you know what's weird?" He turned his big blond head at me. "A lot of these animal-rights activists are cat lovers. Don't know why, but often it seems to be the case. Know what cats eat?"

"Cat food."

"Know where cat food comes from?"

"The ocean, mainly, I guess."

"Well, that's not entirely true. To be fair to the pet-food companies, much of it comes from leftovers from the meat-processing industry. But a lot of it does come from fish. Even some tuna. Even *netted* tuna. Foreign, not U.S. But does that make it right? And when you net tuna, you also entangle porpoises in the nets, and they drown. Ironic, isn't it?"

"Well, I do hope you stop those Japanese long-liners. They're slurping up everything along both coasts."

"That's our number-one battle plan right now," he said softly, squatting down beside his van, running his big red hand along the injured skin of his van.

"Looks new," I said.

He turned around and said, "Three months old. What do you think it will cost to fix it?"

"I would guess a couple hundred dollars, but nowadays I multiply everything times three. So figure about six hundred."

"I agree. Dammit, dealing with the public is such a pain in the ass at times. You get some jerk—hell, he coulda been one of my clients—catches a few big fish on the boat, starts in on the beer or gin, and gets so bombed he trashes your car leaving the parking lot."

"Well, good luck against the long-liners, Bill. You know where to reach me—"

"Wait a second, Doc. What's this about Mary? She doing something with the cops, or what?"

"Sort of. Nothing dangerous, supposedly. But you never know what could happen."

He squatted down near the van again, shaking his head. "Well, if I were you, I'd persuade her to try something a little less dramatic. She's been a big help to us—we'd hate to have anything happen to her."

"Do me a favor, Bill. When and if you see her, you tell her that. She won't listen to me."

"I promise."

"Oh, one more thing. I know you deal mostly in power-boats, but if you happen to know of any blue-water cruising sailboats on the block, let me know."

"Sure. How big?"

"Something like the Morgan forty-one Out Island."

"Hey, I'll give you a buzz if I hear of one. See ya, Doc. Hope everything works out."

I rolled out of the lot, watching poor Bill Bedford scowling at his damaged truck. I looked at my watch. It was past two. I wanted to be settled into the cabin, unpacked, and beginning a long slow beach run by three, three-thirty.

I drove on up to North Eastham, past the famous Cape Cod windmill, then headed on the smaller road off Route 6 to the bay side and Sunken Meadow beach.

There was our little cozy cottage, the Breakers.

But what caught my eye was the car parked in the driveway.

There, big as life, was Mary's Audi.

22

I SAT THERE STUNNED, NOT KNOWING WHAT TO DO. I WAS pretty sure she was in there with Larry. The question was, how to approach them? Or should I? Maybe I had just better back off. . . .

No. No matter how painful and embarrassing this might be for everyone, I decided to square my shoulders, walk up to the door, and go right in.

But what a stupid place to have a love tryst. Right in our own cottage!

Wait a minute, wiseass, a voice said to me, wasn't that the same arrangement you and Susan were enjoying for dinner the night that Mary walked in? I had to admit it was. People are sure stupid.

I opened the front door.

"Mary! Mary, are you here?"

No answer.

Maybe they took Larry's pickup and went out to eat or

something. I walked all around the house, upstairs and down. No Mary. Then I went out on the deck. Far, far up the beach, I saw a woman in khaki shorts wading in the incoming tide.

It was Mary. Alone.

My heart beat so hard and fast I thought it would explode. I ran to the brass bell affixed to the doorframe and rang it four or five times.

She looked up at me, then looked away. She walked slowly along in the shallow water, trailing her hands now and then in the small waves, never looking back. Pout.

I went down to the beach, walking fast, and caught up with her.

She turned around when she heard me in the water behind her. She was crying.

"We've all been worried sick about you," I began as calmly as I could. "The least you could have done was to call the boys, even if you didn't want to call me."

There. Well said, old chap. Good opening move.

"And just *why* must I keep you informed of my every move?" she said, crossing her arms in front of her chest. Fighting stance.

"Because you're my wife, and their mother, that's why. And also because there a lot of people who are very fond of you—admittedly, they're growing fewer as each day passes—that would like to know where you are and if you're all right."

"Well then," she said, half turning, "you know where I am. And I'm all right."

"Where the hell is Larry?"

"How the hell should I know? I haven't seen him in a week. I think he's up in Gloucester again, or maybe over to Nantucket. I haven't been hanging around with him . . . the way you've been hanging around with Susan."

"I was not hanging around with her. She showed up at our door with dinner when she found out you had run off."

"How sweet of her; the little bitch. And I didn't run off. I was on an assignment. And also, buddy boy, I'm not blind. I saw what she was wearing."

"Really? It totally escaped my notice," I lied.

"Don't you lie to me—" she hissed. Sounded just like the cobra in the movie *The Jungle Book*.

"Look," she continued, "all I ever wanted out of this thing was a chance to be ... to be somebody on my own. With my own responsibilities and my own accomplishments or failures. And I also just wanted it for a little while. Not forever."

She began walking slowly toward me. Perhaps there was hope we would survive as a couple.

"I understand," I said. "You wanted some autonomy. Some individual recognition ..."

"That's exactly right. And I never planned on going on assignment with Larry."

"That's the part that's, uh, very difficult for me."

"Well, he's totally aboveboard. No shenanigans. At all. So I resent you creeping around spying on me. Larry's very forthright. Unlike You-Know-Who in the miniskirt."

"Okay, Mary, I'm sorry. But you should remember how mad you got when I'd disappear for several days. Well, I feel the same way. And so do Jack and Tony."

Her eyes softened a bit. We were coming together again; I could feel it.

"There's one thing you could do to make things better."

"Name it."

"Fire Susan Petri."

I had to think a minute before replying.

"If she were the cause of all this trouble between us, and if we were having sex together, then your request would not only be reasonable, but just. And yes, I would fire her in a minute, even though my practice, and our income, would suffer. But the fact is, Mary, that she is not the cause of this trouble, and her appearance at the house was meant to help, no matter how it seemed to you at the time."

"Somehow, Charlie, that's just not enough," she said, arms crossing her chest again.

"Okay, tell you what. I'll fire Susan if you quit this job with Larry.

"No way. We're close to finding the people who are smuggling in this ivory, and we've got to finish it. Dammit! I want to do something *on my own* for a change!"

We were walking back to the cottage now. The only

sound was the water: the soft curl of the waves and the sound of our legs moving through the knee-deep tide. Suddenly she turned and hugged me around the waist, tight. Felt like a million bucks. Better than Susan Petri and definitely better than Waxahachie Dottie.

"We can make a deal, Charlie. I'll finish up this thing in a few weeks, whether we succeed or not, okay?" She looked up at me, from only inches away. I knew I was going to kiss her. "And then we can go somewhere together, or maybe with the boys, and—"

She stopped in midsentence, staring at my neck as if there were a scorpion on it.

"What the hell is *that*?" she screamed.

"What?"

"That's a *bite mark* on your neck!"

"What? Impossible, there's no—"

WHACK!

I stumbled back into the surf. The water was cold and the side of my injured chest hurt terribly as I tried to get up. Also, the sting on the side of my face wasn't pleasant either. Mary had seen the remnants of Susan's love bite and walloped me.

I stood up in the rolling water, trying to regain my balance. Mary was walking fast, already at the foot of the stairway leading up to the back deck of the cottage. I decided not to confront her then. Our tempers were both too hot, and we could get into a battle that would permanently scar, or destroy, the relationship. So I walked up the beach, past the Breakers, and on and on over the packed wet sand of the water's edge for perhaps another mile. I was wet and freezing.

Just my luck that Susan would do that to me. Mary and I had almost made it. We'd almost come to the point of making up and reaching some kind of compromise, when this happens.

Luck sure wasn't running my way.

I knew this was true when I finally turned around and headed back toward the cottage. I was thinking that perhaps she'd had time to cool down and we could talk again. But I was wrong.

Because when I returned, her car was gone.

I went inside. There was no note. Nor could I find any of her clothes or other personal belongings.

She had disappeared again.

I was back to square one.

23

WELL, I JUST SAT THERE ON THE DECK FOR AN HOUR OR TWO, watching the sun sink lower in the western sky over the water. The temptation, of course, was to have a few cocktails and then head out to a nice restaurant and treat myself to a lobster dinner and try to forget about what had happened. But I remembered my promise to myself, and wanted to keep it. I turned on the sauna bath so it would be nice and hot when I returned, and changed into my running clothes.

The tide was far enough out now so that I could run on the wet, packed sand flats practically forever in either direction. I ran south, going slowly at first, relaxed, letting the stringy muscles in my legs get warm and supple. In my hand I carried one of those bicyclist's plastic water bottles, filled with crushed ice and Poland Spring water. I shifted the bottle from hand to hand now and then, but was glad I had taken it with me. I ran my usual eight-to-ten minute miles, probably closer to ten, so after forty minutes I turned around and headed back. When I finally saw the tiny gray cube that was the Breakers in the distance, I hoped against hope that Mary had changed her mind and was waiting there for me.

But her car wasn't there.

I went into the sauna and baked for twenty minutes, went under the cold shower on the deck, back into the sauna, shower, sauna, etc., back and forth for over an hour. I heard the gravel on the driveway crunch. Excited, I went into the living room and looked out the window, expecting to see Mary's Audi again. No such luck. Instead there was a pale, cream-colored Mercedes. Ancient vintage. Strange, I thought. The only person I knew who owned a car like that was Karl Pirsch, the director of the state police lab at Ten Ten Commonwealth Avenue, where Joe worked. Sure enough, the driver's door opened and the gaunt, storklike German emerged from the well-kept car. Another surprise: the passenger-side door opened and another bald, white-haired man emerged. This one plumper than his companion. It was my new acquaintance Mr. William Givens, proprietor of the Olde Curiosity Shoppe and perhaps the world's greatest expert on ivory.

"Do come in, gentlemen," I said, swinging open the door. "The arrival of two of the 'Baldies' lifts my spirits. They've been rather down."

"Well," said Givens, entering the cottage and looking around, "I must say you look fit, Dr. Adams. With a body so well kept, surely your mind can't be too far gone."

"Yeah? Well, don't bet on it. What brings you here? I thought nobody knew where I was hiding."

"We came down because we have some information for you. Joe told us you were down here for a few days. Tell me, is your lovely wife here, too?"

"Uh . . . afraid not, Karl. In fact, that's rather the source of my depression."

"Oh, I see. Well, perhaps it would be better if we left you alone, then."

"No. Trust me; it wouldn't."

"Then it's perhaps a good thing that we brought along something that might cheer you up. We have on ice in the boot of the car a good supply of Pilsner Urquell and Dinkel Acker."

"Sounds good to me; bring it in."

As they brought in the beer another car rolled into the drive. Joe's cruiser. The big man hopped out of the car with a speed and grace that always amazes me. He swiftly opened the car's back door and grabbed two huge shopping bags. He joined us in the kitchen. Setting down the bags, he announced, "Lobsters, shrimp, oysters, potatoes, and corn. We're gonna have a shrimp boil and steamed lobsters, Doc. Also French loaves, Brie, Chardonnay, and cheesecake for dessert. Anything I forgot?"

"Yeah," I said. *"Pâté de foie gras."*

"Oh, yeah." He dug deeper into one of the bags and drew out an ominous-looking oblong tin with a red-and-white label on it. "Thanks for reminding me. The little tin can is easy to lose with all the other stuff." He handed me the coronary in a can. "With truffles ∴."

"Listen, dummy, I'm supposed to be on a health kick."

"If you persist in something so foolish, that's your problem. Personally, I'm going to enjoy myself tonight."

He fetched one of my half-liter beer mugs from the freezer, threw in a handful of ice cubes, and filled it with a hefty gin and tonic, which he half drained in a gulp, then lit a cigarette.

"Le chaiim!" he shouted, and ambled out onto the deck.

I filled a mug with some German beer and followed him out there, where Karl and Bill Givens were admiring the sunset, the crying gulls, and the incoming tide. It never fails. The beach at sunset is soothing to everyone who visits the Breakers. We exchanged pleasantries for about twenty minutes before Karl, as if taking some secret cue from Joe, turned in his chair and faced me solemnly. Not that Karl is a jovial person, but he does have his light moments. But I could see that this was not one of them, and I realized then that perhaps this somewhat explained his visit.

"Doc, we have some . . . interesting news about the ivory kayaks. Some disturbing news. Tell him, Bill."

Givens leaned forward in his chair.

"The kayak you purchased in Provincetown is true walrus ivory. It is less than seven years old, to my reckoning. But since it could be claimed that it was carved by a Native American, it is probably legal ivory, at least as far as the Marine Mammal Protection Act is concerned, even though we know what a joke that has become."

There was a pause as he lighted his pipe and sipped his beer.

"The problem, Doc, is with the other two kayaks. The one used as the murder weapon in Provincetown and the one fastened to your front door. These are ivory, too. Elephant ivory."

I sat for a second in shock.

"You're kidding! They look so much like mine!"

"To any but the best-trained eyes, they certainly do. But remember what we talked about in my shop. The color, texture, the feel of ivory. How this same substance varies in hardness, luster, and so forth, not simply in different species, but in the same species, due to differences in location, the mineral content of the soil, and so on. Even the peculiar cross-hatching of the grain differs."

"You're saying, then, that these two kayaks, carved by Eskimos or impostors, are definitely illegal."

"Without a doubt. Tragically illegal, too, because I am positive these were carved from the best ivory on earth—the soft ivory of the East African elephant."

"Killed by poachers . . ."

"Most definitely killed by poachers and smuggled, God knows how, to wherever they were carved, and then to the shop in Provincetown."

"The shop owned by the late James Harold," said Joe. "Which, when we consider what Mr. Givens has just told us, might help explain why he was murdered."

"He was dealing with crooks—pirates," I said, "and they turned on him."

"I think you are right, Doc," said Karl, pointing his long bony finger at me. "And what worries us is that those who killed him think you know too much. And maybe they want you dead, too."

"At the very least," Joe said, flicking his ash over the deck railing onto the beach sand twelve feet below, "they're giving you a warning. Stop snooping around."

The four of us sat there for maybe half a minute, listening to the far-off cries of the gulls, and the approaching crump and hiss of the waves as the tide crept in.

"The thing is," said Joe softly, "a lot of things seem to be coming together here. Intertwined, if you will. And they seem to be centering on two people close to me—you and Mary."

"I saw her today."

"What! Why the hell didn't you—"

"I was going to. But we had another fight, even before we could talk, and she took off again."

Joe rubbed his face in his big brown hands.

"Holy shit."

I then told all of them what happened. I told them all everything.

"Well, maybe it's a good thing we have this out in the open," said Karl. "By the way, Doc, Joe has told me everything about Larry Carpenter."

"But," Joe cautioned, "we're sticking with our plan of not telling Brad and the Fish and Wildlife people. I think we can uncover more working on our own, and leaving them as is."

"Why do you say that?" I asked.

"Because directly or indirectly, Brad and company would tip Larry off. He's savvy; he would pick up some signals that we were all onto him. If we keep it to ourselves, we can watch him better."

"Not if you don't know where he is," I said.

"We can persuade Brad to tell us where he's working. Particularly if my sister's working with him. I think this is the best way to handle it. And we are officially involved in this thing now anyway, since it includes murder."

"Any way you look at it, Joe," I said, "Mary should get out. Get out before Johnny Ridge and company link me with her. They haven't done so yet because Mary's using the name Brindelli."

"Yeah, but that also happens to be my name. So I think you're right. Next time either of us runs into her, we're going to yank her."

"Easier said than done. You know how she is. You know the hold she has on you, Joe."

"On many things, yes. Maybe even on most things. But not when it comes to her safety. Then we'll take control. Hell, I'll put her into protective custody if I have to. Protecting people is my job. I'm good at it, and I intend to keep doing it. Especially for my sister."

And then he added, "No matter how much of a pain in the ass she can be."

A little while later we opened the oysters and ate them with the beer. We put nothing on them except fresh lemon juice, ground pepper, and a dash of pepper sauce, then sucked them right out of their shells. Joe put a huge stockpot on the outdoor burner and, when it was at a rolling boil, put in small russet potatoes along with a few onions. He added some Old Bay seasoning, too, but not much. Later he added the ears of corn and set the steamer rack over the top of the stockpot and put the lobsters in it. While these cooked he melted a big saucepan full of butter, adding the juice of six lemons to it and stirring. Well, I thought, there goes my health kick.

When the lobsters had turned red he took off the rack and dumped the two pounds of shrimp into the pot. A few minutes later everything was perfectly ready, and we were in an orgy of eating.

I was too full for the cheesecake, and am not a dessert person anyway. But the others lit in, and I made strong French-roast coffee to go with it. We spent the rest of the evening relaxing and talking on the deck, with the tide full in and the waves breaking only a few yards away. There was a faint golden glow to the west, and a cool, strong sea breeze. I lighted a Honduran Corona. It was a great cigar; I achieved cardiac arrhythmia after only four puffs.

At around eleven, we stumbled happily into bed, each in his own private room, listening to the surf crash outside and the wind howl through the windows.

For the first time in a month I was almost happy. Mostly because of Joe's rallying 'round. God bless him. And because we had made up our minds to get Mary out of this mess before it was too late.

24

I SPENT THE REST OF THE WEEK RUNNING AND READING. I RAN over ten miles each day, on the hard beach sand at the water's edge. My diet was vegetables, fruit, fish, bread, and pasta. I drank only mineral water, coffee, and tea. When the water was warm enough, I swam in the heavy surf, getting into the sauna afterward. In the shallow pools of the receding tide I watched for little squirts and depressions in the wet sand, and collected razor clams and quahogs for chowder. By week's end I had dropped seven pounds, tipping the scales at one seventy-two.

I felt great in a way, and miserable, too.

The day after Joe, Karl, and Bill Givens went back to Boston, both Jack and Tony called to say that Mary had talked to them, but could not say where she was or what she was doing. I did my best to explain the reasons for this ... but I knew the real reason: she wanted to assure them of her well-being, but didn't want me to reach her. Well, at least she was calling them, and at least she was all right. But still, she was in more danger than she suspected. I called Joe and we agreed for him to tell Brad it was imperative she speak with her brother. When she did, Joe would explain the peril in no uncertain terms.

Every night, as I sat on the deck watching the sunset, I had the strong urge to call Susan Petri and invite her down to spend the night. No, spend several nights ...

But I didn't. This was mainly because, convinced though

I was earlier that Mary and Larry were intimate, I now had my doubts. Her being alone at the cottage was the main evidence of this. Of course, she could be lying, but since all love must ultimately be based on trust, I assumed she wasn't.

But what about me? What about my behavior? Not the best, any way I looked at it. But hell, I was just doing the best I could under the circumstances. When you think about it, that's really all you can do about any situation. My job now was to keep myself together—keep myself strong enough to make it through these difficult times—and hope for the best. Above all, I couldn't dwell on the past. This seems to be one of the worst mistakes people make—in all of life's endeavors. If and when Mary got sick of adventuring and came back, I could not, *must* not, press her for details.

Gee, I wish Moe were in town. I mused on the irony of his absence when I most needed him.

At week's end, after seven days of exercise, abstinence, and a super-healthy diet, I felt lean, strong, bronzed, and determined. But there was an uncertain note as well: after Mary's initial call to her two sons, they heard no more from her. Since she told them she would call again soon, this was disturbing.

I arrived back in Concord late Sunday afternoon. It was the second week in October, and no place on earth is lovelier than New England in the second week of October. The maples out in front of the house were brilliant yellow gold in the cool, clear air. The oaks were deep crimson with tinges of gold. The grass was still green, the sky bright blue. It was between fifty and sixty degrees outside, which bioclimatologists—people who study the interrelationships between climate and living things—will tell you is the optimal temperature for human achievement.

Still, despite the gorgeous surroundings, my nice, big, clean house, my dogs jumping all over me as I brought them inside, I had never felt more lonely.

Just as it was getting dark, as I was preparing to go out to the Stop & Shop for groceries, two cars pulled into the drive. The second one was Joe's cruiser; the first one was familiar, but I couldn't place it. It was only after Brad Taylor stepped out, looking rather glum, and came up the front walk followed by Joe, that I became worried.

"It's been four days since we've heard from either of them, Doc," said a very sober Brad Taylor as he settled himself into one of the leather chairs in my study, "and frankly, I'm quite concerned."

"They've never gone this long without reporting in?" I asked.

"Never. Mary would call less frequently than Larry; that's the way we arranged it. Larry is very experienced, and knows how to report in without attracting undue attention."

"Where was Larry working week before last?" I asked. I wanted to check out Mary's story.

"Nantucket. He was building the case against McQuaid's gift shop. You remember McQuaid's, Doc, the place where all this started."

"Yes, I do," I said, wishing like hell I'd never set foot in the place. "And where was he supposed to be going next?"

"Back to Gloucester. We had Mary scheduled for New Bedford. But to our knowledge, neither one is in place, and neither has called in."

I looked down at the carpet. "What do you think's happened?"

"Can't say. We just hope it's nothing . . . serious."

"Well, Brad, it better not be—" I was leaning forward, into his face, talking low and slow. There was menace in my voice, and he sensed it.

"C'mon, Doc," said Joe. "Brad's not responsible for this mess. I think our beloved relative is primarily responsible. Question is, where the hell is she, and how do we find her?"

"What leads do you have so far?" I asked Brad.

"We're putting a lot of pressure on McQuaid's to reveal their sources. I think they'll cooperate. I would be curious to know if it's the same source that James Harold used. Unfortunately, since he's dead, we can't ask him. The other leads are the ones you know about. Sam Ho's gift shop in Chinatown, Johnny Ridge's carving parlor one floor above,

Jason Steingretz's warehouse—or whatever it is—in Chinatown, and the Sea Feast warehouse up in Gloucester."

"Sea Feast? I never understood why Larry was so anxious to check that place out. Who put him onto it anyway?
When I saw the place, it looked perfectly normal. Absolutely boring, in fact."

"It was a couple of his buddies at Yoder's boatyard. He
never gave me their names. Apparently, he thinks they're
tied in with the smuggling part of the operation—bringing
illegal ivory into the country."

"Did he ever get inside the place?" Joe asked.

Taylor shook his head. "Not to our knowledge. I know
he was trying to get employment there before he left for
Nantucket."

I looked at Joe.

"What can we do, Joe? What can the law do at this
point?"

"You mean to find them? Nothing, except ask a bunch of
questions. Interview people. But that would blow their
cover."

"I'm not sure it would," Brad mused, rubbing his chin.
"Remember, we've got this bogus story about Larry's doing
time and being involved in illegal running. If some cops
went around flashing his mug shot, asking people if they'd
seen him, it would fit perfectly with this legend."

As Brad was talking I shot a questioning glance at Joe.
He shook his head quickly, which meant that he had not
told Brad or any of the Fish and Wildlife people about what
he'd found on Larry from the JUDAS computer bank.

After another twenty minutes of rough planning, Brad
left for an appointment. Joe and I were free to sit out on the
porch under the ceiling fan and make our own plans.

"Okay," I said, "now tell me what the cops can *really*
do."

"Legally, nothing but what we talked about earlier. Of
course, since it's my sister who's involved, I think we can
plan on a bit more support from my colleagues."

"That's good. How much can we bend the rules?"

"A lot. We can even break the rules as long as nobody
finds out."

"Can we break into these places we talked about?"

He thought for a while before shaking his head. "Nah. If we got caught it would look bad."

"What if I did it?"

He raised his eyebrows. "It wouldn't look so bad, as far as the police are concerned. Of course, if caught, you'd be facing a B and E. That's not good."

"Hey, I'm facing the three worst felony charges, remember? After murder, aggravated assault, and rape, what the hell's a B and E charge?"

He stroked his chin stubble. "You may have a point. . . ."

"Somebody's got to do something."

"You're assuming they've been taken. Kidnapped?"

"I guess. Unless this time they really are shacking up somewhere."

"I know. I was thinking of that possibility myself."

There was a bit of silence as we each considered this. I think we were both silently wincing.

"But," Joe continued, "for the nonce, we'll figure they're either doing something very secret, or have been . . . somehow intercepted." He looked up with a smile on his face, but I realized from his eyes it was fake. He was trying to keep his courage up.

"Now," he said, leaning over the coffee table with a pad and pen ready, "let's make some rough plans."

I was on the phone, trying to woo Roantis back into the fold.

"All right, dammit, I'll even pay you."

"Lucky me."

"C'mon, Laitis."

"How much?"

"Several hundred dollars."

"Make it a thousand."

"C'mon, Laitis."

"Hey, just how much do you love your wife?"

"Okay, a thousand."

"Plus expenses."

"What expenses could you have? I'll be with you."

"I'll think of some. Don't worry."

"What if we disagree on the expenses?"

"Do the words *Rotor Club* and *Dottie* ring a bell?"

"Okay. A thousand plus expenses."

"See how easy we can work these things out?"

25

MONDAY MORNING I GOT UP AND WENT IN TO WORK. SUSAN was there, looking unusually terrific. She seemed in a good mood and glad to see me. I told her I was glad to be back with her. She smiled and blushed. We had a very busy day with a lot of catch-up work, which was perfect; it gave us no time to think or talk. I went home feeling pretty good, about the professional side of my life, anyhow.

In the turnaround at the end of the driveway behind my house sat Roantis's battered Peugeot. I looked around for the owner; he couldn't be far away. I found him sitting in one of the terrace chairs, petting my dogs and demanding liquor. Before we had a chance to go inside, Joe pulled up in his cruiser. He got out, carrying a black leather briefcase. He keeps this in his trunk right near the enormous metal toolbox that unfolds to reveal rows and rows of locksmithing tools. I knew what was in that briefcase: catalogs from lock manufacturers and alarm companies.

"You remember Herbie Sams, our ace photographer?"

"I sure do," I said. "He do anything for us?"

"Yep. A whole roll of film, taken at the Sea Feast warehouse. We've got shots of the building from all sides, shots of the nearest roads, trees and bushes for covered approaches, interior shots of the place's layout so you'll know what to expect. I'll have them ready tomorrow afternoon, early."

"I trust you didn't, uh, tell Herb what the pictures were really for, did you?"

"I told him we were investigating the place, that's all. That's as far as it went. That's as far as it's ever going. *Capisce?*"

We went inside; Joe sat at the kitchen table, sifting through the catalogs in the open case. "I'll bring you the prints tomorrow when they're printed. Just keep it confidential." Finally he had two catalogs out on the table.

Roantis leaned over, inspecting the booklets.

"How about a booze, Doc?" said Joe. "I've spent an afternoon's hard work in your behalf."

"Took the words right outta my mouth," said Roantis.

"You guys get your own; I'm not drinking."

A minute later, glass in hand, Joe shoved the first catalog in our direction. It said SCHLAGE on the front and showed a variety of brass and bronze locks that looked extremely well made and tough. I was intimidated. How the hell were we supposed to defeat locks like these?

"There's no metal fence around this warehouse—that's the best news," Joe began. "It means you guys won't have to cut your way inside the grounds. It also means you're less likely to get trapped inside the property by a man-eating rottweiler."

"Amen," I said.

"Okay, no real surprises here. Sea Feast buys top-of-the-line equipment, but nothing truly state-of-the-art or weird, which means either that they have nothing to hide, or are just practical."

"Who'd want to break into a fish warehouse anyway?" said Roantis. "Phew!"

"That's the question you and Doc are trying to answer," Joe said, opening the catalog to a two-page spread that showed a big bronze lock inside and out. "The lock on the rear door—not those big corrugated doors on the truck bays, I mean the brown metal door with the wire-glass window—is this Schlage Model 460, Series F. A popular twenty-pin-key tumbler lock that is great protection against common crooks, but pretty easy to defeat if you have the right tools and the know-how."

"We have neither," I said.

"You'll have both by tomorrow night. I'll show you how to defeat this lock using two different methods. So the lock's no problem. You just better be thankful the lock isn't a Greenleaf."

"Greenleaf?" asked Laitis. "I never heard of it."

"Not used that often. The military uses them a lot, when security is vital. Believe me, you could not defeat a Greenleaf. But a Schlage is possible, if I show you how."

"You don't feel the slightest bit strange? A cop showing two guys how to break into a warehouse?"

"My sister is missing. If I could do this myself I would. As it is, I will deny everything if you're caught in there with your pants down. So you better listen up, and do it right."

"We're all ears," said Roantis.

"The alarm system is more difficult, but not insurmountable," said Joe, opening the second catalog. He rapped his finger on a big photo of a cream-colored rectangular box. It had a display window on the front with digital readout like a pocket calculator, and two rows of black plastic buttons, numbered 1 to 10, underneath it. Below the buttons was a metal turn switch that received a key, just like the key switches in elevators for private floors.

"This is the Honeywell Pro-Alert. The picture's a little bigger than actual size. This alarm senses motion, sound, structural vibrations, and even body heat. It's pretty sophisticated. In fact, without our special equipment and some coaching, there's no way you guys could get inside the building without setting it off."

"Does it just make a noise," I asked, "or does it send a signal to the cops or a security agency?"

"All of the above. When this little sucker senses you, all the big exterior lights go on, a bell goes off, and signals go out on phone lines to the alarm people, the company owners, and the local cops. You're *history*."

A vague, queasy feeling rose in my stomach. I looked at Laitis. He sipped his whiskey, lighted a cigarette, and appeared impassive. Some things never change.

"When the alarm is switched on at the day's close, it is activated. It is deactivated when the person entering the premises inserts the correct key, turns the switch, then punches in the correct sequence of numbers. This way, even somebody who knocks the guard or janitor on the head and steals his key cannot deactivate the alarm after entering the building."

"After entering? You mean the alarm is inside?"

"Yeah. This one is where ninety percent of them are located—right inside the door on the wall. Shoulder height."

"So it doesn't go off when you open the door?" I asked.

"Nope. It senses the intrusion, but these alarms are always set with a delay, which allows the guard to come inside, maybe set down a package, unzip his coat, take out the key . . . you know. The delay is usually thirty to ninety seconds."

"How long is the delay for this particular alarm?" asked Roantis. Good question, I thought.

"Don't know. I guess you guys will find out."

"Great."

"So I'm going to coach you on picking the lock, then deactivating the alarm once you're inside." He held up the photo of the alarm control panel again. "Now, what this photo does not show are the two tiny pin-jack ports underneath the box. These are a half inch apart. Nobody but the Honeywell technicians, the expert thieves, and, of course, upholders of law and order such as yours truly, know about these ports. . . ."

"What's so special about them?" asked Roantis.

"You insert two jacks from a special instrument called a decoder. This unit is used by technicians to install and test the systems once they're installed. I'll lend you my decoder—you had best not lose it—so you can plug it in, activate the alarm's memory, deactivate the alarm system without using the key switch, and can look around the premises without setting off the alarm. *We hope.*"

"Sounds simple enough to me," said Roantis.

"Joe? What if they actually do have guard dogs inside?" He looked at me with dead eyes.

"Then you're shit out of luck, pal. You're hamburg."

"I was afraid you'd say that."

Twenty-four hours later Joe arrived back at my place with a whole bunch of toys. First was a device that resembled an electric toothbrush, except there was no brush at the business end, but something that looked like a narrow saw blade with longish but blunt teeth. Joe said it was an electric lock pick. I saw the name Fedcorp: COBRA on its side. Roantis picked it up and switched it on. It hummed.

"A girlfriend of mine had something like this," he mused, "but it had a different tip."

Joe snatched it away from him and, holding it in his right hand, inserted the blade into a lock that was implanted into a two foot high "dummy door" that was sitting on the porch table. Joe flicked the switch, the battery-operated gizmo hummed, and then Joe rotated the apparatus in his hand. The lock opened with a soft clack, exactly as if he had used a key.

"That's neat," said Laitis. "In Special Forces, we had a course called DAMES and DASES. DAMES stood for Defense Against Mechanized Entry Systems. DASES stood for Defense Against Surreptitious Electronic Surveillance."

"Clarify," Joe demanded.

"Well, DAMES was essentially lock picking, and how to guard against it. Actually, it was more a course on how to do it than how to guard against it. They taught us how to break into places. DASES was how to detect bugs, and how to set them. We had a bug so small it was disguised as a thumbtack. Stick it on a wall or under a wooden table, bingo! You had the place bugged."

"That was twenty years ago, Laitis," warned Joe. "We got stuff now ten times that small. But I'd like to see you use this set of lock picks I brought. Let's see how much you remember from your training. Electric lock picks can damage the lock, which is bad."

"You mean they could tell someone broke in?" I asked.

Joe nodded. "The old-fashioned burglar's way is slower, and takes a skilled hand, but it leaves no evidence. You need a tension bar and a pick. Laitis, for this Yale Protector 5-14, use this number-four pick—" Joe withdrew the pick from its case. It looked like a small file with a narrow, pointed fore section that ended in a slight hook, like a bent crochet hook. Roantis took the tool in his right hand and the tension bar in his left. The tension bar was also a bent bar, but very small, like a tiny Allen wrench. Laitis put the tension bar into the bottom edge of the tiny keyhole. He then inserted the pick, hook end up, and shoved it all the way in. He then worked the pick in upward motions, much the same way I use the elevator bar to pry out teeth. Joe looked on with admiration, which was strange for a cop, I thought.

"Haven't lost your touch, Laitis," he said, smiling. Then he turned to me. "Pin tumbler locks work on the principal of a thick rod, or trunion, turning inside a mortis. Teeth, or pins, from the mortise, are spring-loaded or gravity-based, and fall into a groove in the trunion, which blocks its rotation. Follow?"

"Sort of . . ."

"Anyway, the key, which is inserted teeth up, slips inside the trunion and each tooth on the key forces a corresponding pin in the lock up and out of the way, so the trunion can rotate—"

"And the lock can unlock—"

"Right. But any key will tell you that the teeth inside the lock are arranged at various heights. It's this variance of height and distance along the key shank that makes all locks different. What Laitis did first was insert the tension bar and give it a slight twist, which forces the trunion against the lock casing. This pressure will keep the teeth he pushes up in place so they won't fall back down again when he moves the pick. Most experts move the pick from rear to front—beginning with the innermost teeth first. A lot of beginners, and thieves who are rushed, simply rake the pick back and forth, keeping upward pressure on it. This is called 'raking,' and it's a fast way to defeat a cheap lock. But it won't usually work on a good lock like a Yale or a Schlage—"

Clack.

Laitis looked at us triumphantly. The bolt of the lock had rotated, and Laitis now drew the small dummy door open.

"Well, it looks like you've got that part of the program

down well enough," Joe said. He handed Roantis the Cobra electric pick. "My advice would be to try the manual pick first. If that fails, you can use this one, but remember—you may tip them off you've been visiting."

Roantis took the burglary equipment and stuffed it in his pants pockets. Then Joe took out another array that looked more sophisticated. I recognized the alarm system's keyboard from the catalog picture he'd shown us the previous evening. He hooked this up to a low-voltage transformer, then plugged it into a wall outlet. He set the alarm by inserting a special key and turning the switch. The display window on the control box lit up. I saw the word *activated* in the window. It stayed there for a few seconds, then the tiny screen went dark again.

"The alarm is in active mode now. You won't have this," he said, holding up the key, "and you also don't know the deactivating code. But, you will have *this*—"

He produced from his bag an electronic device with a series of buttons and switches on the body and two wires protruding from its side. It looked similar to those used by mechanics tuning cars and by television repairmen checking tubes and circuits. In short, to my untrained eye, it was an electronic device . . . of some sort.

Joe had me hold up the alarm control, as if it were fastened to an imaginary wall. He then inserted the two wires into the jack ports on the underside of the alarm control and turned on the battery-operated gizmo in his hand. Instantly the alarm-box display window lit up again with the word *activated*.

"Now watch closely," Joe instructed, and turned a switch labeled *codes* to "seeking code" command. The alarm box display changed to *seeking code*. Then Joe turned another switch that said "deactivate." The display changed to *deactivate*. After a pause there was a beep, and the number "2" appeared in the window. Joe pushed the button on the alarm face that corresponded to the number 2. Next, "4" flashed in the window; Joe pushed 4. Then 7, 6, 3, and back to 2. Then the window said *deactivated*.

"There it is. Simple, eh?"

"Piece of cake," echoed Laitis.

"Then all you do when it's time to leave is reinsert these

little jacks—make sure the red one goes in the red hole and the white into the white, and switch to activate, and it will return to active mode. Most importantly, nobody the following day will even have a clue you've entered."

"Piece of cake," Laitis repeated.

"Watch it," I said. "Every time you say that, something goes wrong and we wind up neck-deep in shit."

26

LAITIS AND I SLEPT UNTIL TWO IN THE MORNING, THEN GOT IN my car and headed north on 128 toward Gloucester.

We'd spent so much time with the lock picks and the decoder that we had pretty much ignored Herbie's photos of the layout. I glanced through them briefly before we began the hour's drive to Gloucester from Concord. Shots of the parking lot and the customers' vehicles. Shots of the building from all sides. Shots of the doorways. I studied the back entrance. Brown metal door with a small square window with wire glass, just the way Joe had described it. The building was that corrugated aluminum that covers so many big industrial buildings these days. The building was windowless, as one would expect for a freezer warehouse. It seemed from the photos and what we had been told that the owners did not expect anyone to break in. But as Roantis had observed: who would want to steal fish?

We were especially lucky in one respect: the back door and the little set of metal stairs leading up to it were partially hidden by several pine trees. They weren't big or full enough to completely hide us, but in the dark of night they would be a big help.

At three-thirty in the A.M. we were cruising around Rocky Neck, looking for a place to park that wasn't too close to Sea Feast, but within a reasonable walking distance. We also wanted a place that wasn't conspicuous, which meant we wanted a parking spot with other cars around. People notice an isolated parked car late at night; this isn't generally true with a bunch of parked vehicles. We passed the Dory, and I considered parking there. After all, as a workingman's hostel, the Dory's parking lot saw cars coming and going at all hours. On the other hand, the tenants were a tight-knit group that would notice strangers, especially late at night. We finally settled on a spot halfway up a little side street that went off East Main. It had little houses and six or seven other cars parked along it.

Roantis and I got out of the car, locked it, and walked down our little street past the tiny houses, then out onto East Main, which was the road the warehouse was on.

We walked right alongside the road, taking full strides, not slinking or skulking about. For one thing, nothing attracts suspicion like furtiveness. Secondly, Joe had come up with an excellent cover for us: we each carried a tackle box and a fishing rod. A pair of 7×50 marine binoculars was slung around my shoulder. Laitis had put his lock-picking set and the Cobra electric picker in the bottom of his tackle box, along with a vast assortment of hooks, wire leaders, bright lures, and so on. I doubted a cop would ask us to open the tackle boxes if he saw us; we could simply say we were returning from a late night of fishing aboard a friend's boat. In my tackle box was the Honeywell decoder. But it looked enough like one of those electronic fish locators that I wasn't too worried. Hell, the average American now has so many electronic gizmos that nobody can figure them out. Joe, an excellent locksmith, would be able to identify the decoder for what it was, but a local cop on a beat, no way.

At least that's what he'd reassuringly told us before we left. . . .

We took the shore road, and it wasn't long before we saw the Sea Feast warehouse up on our right. We walked past the front of the building first, and I looked hard into the glass front door, trying to see light or life within. There was a faint glow coming from ceiling lights in the big room in front—I saw a sales counter in there—but there was no evidence that anybody was in the offices.

A hundred yards beyond the building, and having seen no cars on East Main, we left the road and climbed up a gradual sandy bluff into a copse of New England pines. Once in the grove, we chose a big tree that we could find quickly and ditched the bogus fishing equipment. We put the tools we needed in our pockets. We were both wearing dark, unfaded blue jeans and navy sweatshirts. These had hoods, which are popular with Gloucester fishermen all year round. If we drew up the hoods, we were practically invisible. Roantis, an expert at doing nasty things in the dark, had selected the attire.

We crept through the trees, slanting back toward where Laitis reckoned the building to be. He was right on the button; we came to the edge of the forest and were looking right down on it. With our tools and flashlights, we scurried down the sandy slope to the three trees that were partially hiding the back door. Toward the road from us was a wide asphalt lot for the big trucks that brought the frozen blocks of foreign fish. They would turn in the big lot and back their rigs up to one of the three big bays on the building's rear.

"I keep thinking about *beams*," Roantis whispered as we slipped, crouched over, up the metal stairs to the brown metal door. He was talking about electronic beams that large buildings use to activate their alarms. The beams are effective over long ranges, such as warehouse aisles. If anything interrupts the photo electric beam, the alarm goes off.

"Joe said he didn't see any beams," I whispered back at him. "He saw a closed-circuit TV, but that's used during the day so the office can check the loaders on the back dock. Joe said they probably can't use beams in this place because of the cats."

"Did he say he saw cats in here?"

"No. But they love fish. They can smell the fish, Joe says, and sneak inside through cracks in the wall or foundation. Once inside at night, they climb and leap, and could set off the beam."

"But he didn't see cats. So there could be a beam."

"Odds against it. I just don't want to meet a watchdog."

We waited there on the stoop for a few minutes, watching the empty road. My eyes had grown accustomed to the darkness by now and I could see more than I expected. Laitis stood up and took the pick and tension bar from his pocket. I shone the small Maglite on the lock. He stuck the tools inside it and began ticking and rasping at that lock. Minutes went by. The ticking and rasping grew louder, more frantic. Finally I saw his hand slip, and the small metal glint of the pick as it dropped from his hand and fell through the steel grating of the stoop onto the ground five feet below.

Ping.

"Fuck!" said Roantis. It was officially a whisper, but you could hear it a football field away.

"Shut up!" I hissed. I saw him fling down the tension bar.

Ping!

He took out the COBRA, stuck it into the keyhole where my small light still shone, and flipped the machine on. I heard a faint hum, and within seconds he had rotated the Schlage's bolt and opened the door. Upon advice from Joe, we had brought along a roll of strong "gaffer" tape—the kind with the metallic finish that can hold two buildings together. I took a tongue depressor from my pocket and broke it along the door edge. Then Laitis taped it over the protruding latches of the lock. Just in case. We didn't want to get locked inside.

Then we were standing in the narrow, tiled hallway. I got the now familiar adrenaline rush that comes when you're someplace you are not supposed to be, doing something forbidden. I held the small metal light in my mouth, shining it on the decoder, while Roantis held his flashlight steady on the alarm's control box. I had some time . . . but how much? I inserted the two jacks in the appropriate ports underneath the box: the white wire in the white port and the red in the red. I turned the code switch to "seeking code." Sure enough, the display window on the alarm box read *seeking code*. I switched the second dial to "deactivate," and the alarm responded. After a second or two, there was a beep, and the number "6" appeared in the window. I pushed the 6 button on the alarm. Then 4, 5, and 8. The window read *deactivated*. With a piece of the gaffer tape, I fastened the decoder, jacks still inserted, to the wall next to the alarm so it would be ready when we left, and we went down the hallway with Laitis shining the beam in front of us.

"I told you, Doc. Piece of cake."

"Piece of cake," I echoed.

The hallway terminated in another metal door, but it wasn't locked. Once through this door, it was cold. We drew up our hoods again and put on the gloves we'd brought. Turning left, we followed the flashlight beam to the dock area. Here was the wide concrete space where the trucks were unloaded as they backed into the bays. We saw two wheel carts, forklift trucks, and roller racks used to unload the cartons of frozen fish. But the cartons were obviously elsewhere. Laitis located another door and we went inside, checking first to make sure it didn't have any kind of locking latch on it. Freezing to death in a fish warehouse is not the way I want to go out.

It was cold as hell in the freezer. Must have been zero degrees in there. Laitis turned the lights on.

"I mean, hell, Doc, there are no windows. Might as well see what we're looking for."

What we saw were piles and piles of long crates, most wooden, some cardboard. Most had foreign words stenciled on them, and many were done in Chinese and possibly Indian and Arabic script. Some fish came from Chile and Costa Rica. There were crates from Singapore, Hong Kong, Yokohama, Kobe, and Kodiak Island.

There were even a few from exotic places like Seattle. Even though the fish inside the crates was frozen in solid blocks, the odor of fish still permeated the freezer. We walked around the stacks of cartons, each measuring about a foot and a half square on the ends and perhaps six feet long. They weighed plenty, and were securely fastened by staples and bands of metal strapping.

"You want to pry one of these open, Doc?" said Laitis, in a breath full of steam.

"Don't think so; it would only tip them off. And I wonder how many we'd have to open before we found anything. Assuming there's anything to find. Frankly, it seems like fish to me."

"Smells like fish."

"Let's leave this locker for a few minutes and look around the rest of the building. It'll give us a chance to warm up, if nothing else."

Outside the freezer room, we wandered down aisles stacked with more boxes and crates. The fishy smell was much stronger here, presumably because the fish weren't frozen.

"This must be where they thaw out the fish they sell up in front," Laitis said. I agreed. We got to the far wall and another door. Locked. Laitis took out the Cobra lock pick, but I grabbed his hand. "Hold it. We don't know if there's another alarm on the other side of that door. And if there is, maybe it's not the same kind as the other one. See what I mean?"

He shrugged, and I shone the flashlight through the wire glass window of the door. On the other side was a linoleum hallway and a series of office doors opening off it. Nothing special.

"I think we can learn more about the front end of this place by coming back during the day and buying some fish," I said. "What do you think?"

"I think we should look for a hiding place."

"What?"

"If there's something illegal here, wouldn't the guy want to hide it?"

"Okay, where would that be?"

"Someplace the workers don't go very often. Let's look around."

We found it on the other side of the loading dock, the end opposite the freezer. It was a room about twenty feet square. The only door covering was made of hanging clear plastic strips so lift trucks could drive through it. I suppose the plastic strips kept the cold in. Anyway, the place stank like hell. Rotten fish. Lobster bait.

"Laitis, do you think this is reject fish, or are they letting it rot on purpose for bait?"

"I have no idea. In Vietnam they'd let fish rot in giant stone jars, then use it as a sauce. It's called *nuc bam*."

"You tried it?"

"Oh yeah. Actually, it was pretty good once you got past the stink. Maybe this room is what we're after, Doc. I mean, would you want to spend time in here?"

"Hell no!"

"Then I say we look in here."

In the middle of the room was a stack of thirty long crates, six wide and five high. The crates said SNOW CRAB, from Homer, Alaska. Others were in Japanese or Chinese, and other than the fact that they probably arrived from somewhere in the Orient, we hadn't a clue as to what was inside. The aroma was high, though.

While I held the flashlight Laitis found a small crowbar and pried one end off the nearest crate. He had to step back at first whiff, then went grimly to work, poking around inside.

"Hold the light over here where I can use it," he instructed.

Then he grabbed something inside the crate, gave a yank, and pulled out what I thought at first was a skinny, frozen, bent fish. He turned it around in his hands.

"This what you're looking for?"

It was a walrus tusk. Raw ivory. We poked around in the box again and saw several more. We let them be and opened one of the Asian cases. This time Laitis brought out a monster tusk. African elephant. I looked in the crate and saw the sockets and points of another half-dozen elephant teeth. I gave a low whistle.

"What do we do now?" he asked.

"Let's take one of each and get the hell out of here. We need evidence, and I doubt they'll miss two. We'll refasten the crates so they won't suspect."

So, each holding a stinky, slimy animal tusk, we left the small room, went back through the loading-dock area, and headed back to our narrow hallway, and outside.

"Just a second, Doc, I forgot to turn the light off in the freezer room. Be right back."

"Be careful."

"Don't worry. Piece of cake."

While he was gone I turned on the decoder, holding the little Maglite flashlight in my mouth like a cigar, shining it on the instrument. I entered "seeking code," and the alarm control answered me. Then I turned the master knob to "activate." The alarm flashed back a series of numbers, which I entered by pushing the buttons on the face. Then the alarm displayed *activated*, and I got nervous. How much time did I have to wait there for Roantis before the damn thing went off?

But I hardly had time to consider this question, because as I drew out the tiny jacks underneath the alarm box and pulled off the gaffer tape from the cinder-block wall, the lights in the hallway went on.

Not only that, but a loud alarm bell outside the building started ringing.

Not only that, but a piercing klaxon horn inside the building began blaring.

Roantis appeared, coming through the far doorway at light speed.

"Hurry up," he said as he passed me, trying to catch his breath. "I think I hit a light beam."

I followed him outside in a flash, and we were scooting up the hill as fast as we could go. Christ, the alarm bell was loud. And the exterior lights were on as well. The parking lot, the back loading dock, the front and sides of the big building were all lit up. Just our luck.

"I told you not to say 'piece of cake'!" I hissed at him as we dove and crawled our way through the thick woods at the top of the slope.

"Did you get the decoder?" he asked.

"Yeah. How about the lock pick?" He pulled it from his pocket, and we fought our way forward through the woods in the dark. When we finally found our big tree where we'd hidden the fishing gear—I don't have any earthly idea how Laitis was able to locate it—we sat down and caught our breath. Sirens in the distance became louder. Soon a caravan of winking blue strobe lights came up East Main, stopping in the parking lot of Sea Feast. We couldn't see much of the place through the trees, even with the aid of my binoculars. But I spied several bluecoats running around the building. One looked as if he had his sidearm drawn. The squawk of two-way radios filtered up to us, and the opening and slamming of doors.

"What do we do now?" I asked Roantis. After all, he was the expert in clandestine operations.

"Let's bury the lock stuff and the tusks under these loose leaves. We'll take only the fishing equipment and head back down the road past the cops."

"Are you out of your mind?"

"Nope. The fact that we want to take a closer look will show them we couldn't have done it. Let's go."

"But it's almost five in the morning!"

"Perfect time to go fishing."

"But the car's up past the warehouse. We'll be walking in the wrong direction."

"We can say we walked the wrong way."

"No. Let's make our way through the trees on the top of this ridge until we come out near the car. Then we won't be as suspicious."

He finally agreed to this, but cautioned me that if we were caught up in the trees we would definitely be suspects. Trying to walk through the dark woods with fishing tackle was a real pain in the ass. We slipped and stumbled countless times, but finally came out onto the road where the car was. Once there, stowing our fishing gear inside, I felt much more legitimate and much safer. We drove down the road back out to East Main, up around Rocky Neck, then down past the warehouse again. By now it was six-thirty and getting light. We could see nobody at Sea Feast, but there was a car in the parking lot in front of the office, a silver Ford Taurus wagon. We assumed it was the owner's who had been notified by the alarm or by the cops, or both. I drove inside the lot, pretending to simply turn around, but came close enough to the car for Laitis to read the tag number and jot it down. Then we headed for the harbor docks, where we parked the Subaru close by and ambled out onto one of the piers and began fishing. By eight o'clock we were hungry, so we headed into town and stopped at a Dunkin' Donuts in the center of town. The place was crowded, but we heard nobody talking about the break-in at Sea Feast. Maybe the cops thought it was a false alarm. After all, we didn't leave anything behind, and we didn't take anything immediately noticeable.

After breakfast we drove back toward Rocky Neck, found a nice little pier, and sat down on it and pretended to fish. Both of us dozed in the fall sunshine. But by noon we were antsy.

"How the hell are we gonna get the tools and those damn stinky tusks back to Joe?" Roantis asked, leaning up against a piling and stretching his legs out on the warm wood of the dock.

"I'm thinking we'll drive past the warehouse again. If things look normal, let's try and find a road on top of the ridge above our hiding place. I'll park on the side of this road and pretend to fiddle with the car, as if something's wrong with it. Then you can slide down the hill into the woods and retrieve the stuff. All you have to do is wait undercover while I watch the road. When I give you the all clear, just bring the stuff up to the car and hop in. What do you think?"

"I think it sounds great, Doc. I think it'll work. In fact, it's a piece—"

"DON'T SAY IT!"

27

IT DID WORK, TOO, JUST LIKE DOWNTOWN. IT TOOK US A WHILE driving around and exploring, but soon we found a small gravel drive off Mount Pleasant Road that Laitis was pretty sure was directly above our stash. I pulled over and raised the hood while he scurried down the slope. In less than ten minutes I heard him hiss at me from the woods, and I gave him the thumbs-up. He brought up the tusks and the burglary tools and popped them in the trunk, joined me in the car, and off we went.

We got home just before three, dead tired. Roantis went straight to sleep on the couch on the sunporch. He likes to sleep there; the room gives him a clear view of the approaches to the house and the distant tree line of the woods on the far side of Dean MacLeod's orchard across Old Stone Mill Road.

Once, one winter morning after he'd spent the night on that couch, we walked out onto the frozen road into an ambush, and Laitis was shot by a sniper. But he survived, God knows how. He always does.

Before I turned in I called Joe and told him what happened. He wasn't happy that we'd somehow tripped the alarm, but was relieved that we didn't lose his prized decoder and the Cobra lock pick. Then I told him about the tusks.

"Damn! Then Larry was correct in his lead. Maybe we're misjudging the guy."

"Nobody ever said he wasn't good at his job, Joe. It's just the, uh, other stuff. . . ."

"Yeah. Well, I guess I should call Brad Taylor. You have the tusks with you?"

"Hosed them down and put them under your bed in the guest room. But I wouldn't call Brad and company yet. It will just irritate him that we went in behind his back. And you'll be forced to admit aiding and abetting. For now, you could just run down a tag number we saw on a Ford Taurus wagon. It could be the owner's, or somebody else that's key in the operation."

I read off the number to Joe.

"What makes you think he's the owner?"

"Because that's the car that arrived on the scene first, right after the cops."

"It will be interesting to keep a low-level eye on this character," Joe said. "I bet he doesn't think this was a routine break-in attempt. If he's involved, he'll double-check

those crates full of rotten fish and contraband. My guess is
that he'll then attempt to move it out of his warehouse, and
fast."

"Can you put a bumper beeper on the car?"

"We could try. But who knows? He could be hundreds of
miles away by now, or not even involved. For all we know,
he could be the security man, not the owner."

"I know. But it's probably worth a check. I'm going to
sleep now for a couple hours, then Laitis and I are going
out to eat."

"Maybe I'll stop by later. Any word from Mary?"

"Nope."

"Nothing on the phone machine from her or the boys?"

"Nothing. I'm all alone."

"Then I'll definitely come over. And I'll bring food. If
you're asleep I'll let myself in and start cooking. How's
that?"

"Joe, I don't know what I'd do without you."

"Ah, hell with ya. See you in about three hours—"

A little after six I awoke to the strains of opera and the
aroma of onions and garlic sautéing in olive oil. One of my
favorite smells on earth. I went downstairs to find Joe and
Laitis in the kitchen. Joe was enjoying a gin and tonic and
a Benson & Hedges, Laitis a half tumbler of scotch and a
Camel. Same old same old.

"What's that on the radio?" I asked.

"La Traviata," Joe answered, tipping up the wide copper
pan on the stove so the hot oil reached all the onions.

"What's on the menu?"

He pointed to a mixing bowl full of round, whitish disks
sitting in a sauce. *"Cappe saltate al rosmario e limone.*
Sautéed scallops with rosemary and lemon. Be ready
shortly. And in the oven is one of your favorites—eggplant
parmigiana."

"Can't you fix something decent for once?"

"The eggplant would be more decent if you and Mary
would let me make it with veal like I used to."

I sat down at the bar table that adjoins the stove. Joe
could see the sadness in my eyes. I was thinking about
Mary's sudden and passionate banning of all veal from our

kitchen. This decision was based on the terrible conditions under which the meat is produced. The little calf is taken away from its mother while still nursing, placed in a cramped, filthy cage that is kept totally dark, and fed milk and special chemicals until it is slaughtered. Somehow this cruel process is supposed to produce better veal. It is an outrage. We now substitute turkey breast for veal. Thinking about Mary hit me suddenly. Her absence weighed down on me unbearably.

"C'mon, Doc. Keep your spirits up. She'll be back. Have a drink or glass of red. That'll cheer you up."

"I'm not drinking anything until this thing is resolved. You don't think she's in danger?"

I saw a slight frown crease his big forehead. He was trying to hide it, but it was there. "I think she may be in . . . difficulty, but not real danger. These are smugglers and counterfeiters, not murderers."

"How about Johnny Ridge? Is he dangerous?"

"Very," said Roantis. We both turned and looked at him. "I told you guys earlier. That's the word in Chinatown. And Joe, you told us that he was in trouble with that Irish gang down in New York. What's their name?"

"The Westies. Yeah, Ridge is a bad guy. But I don't think he's in charge of this thing Mary and Larry are working on; I think he's just an enforcer."

"*Just* an enforcer? Great."

"Hey, Doc," said Laitis, "I think that may be our next project."

"What?"

"Breaking into Jason Steingretz's warehouse on Ping On Street. See if we can make any connection. We're pretty good at it by now."

Joe rolled his eyes heavenward, as if in silent prayer.

"*Good* at it? Jesus. I'd hate to see you *bad* at it, then. How can you say you're good at it when you tripped the alarm on the way out?"

"Bad intelligence," said Roantis, taking a drag off his Camel and letting its smoke seep out his nostrils. "You said there were no electronic beams in there. Well, guess what. There was at least one."

"The owner of the Taurus wagon is Willard Hastings. No priors."

"Is he the owner of Sea Feast?"

"I didn't ask that, yet. I was waiting to talk with you two. I had an idea. In my law-enforcement capacity, I could call the Gloucester police and say that there's been a rash of similar break-ins around here, and we're wondering if there's any connection. Then I'd pump them for details about the break-in, ask about the owner's response to it, and so on. This information would be helpful, especially, I think, the owner's reaction."

"What would that tell us?" I asked.

"Well, if he's on the up-and-up, then he'd want all the help he can get, even though nothing was apparently taken. If he claims a lot of valuable fish were taken, at least we know he's lying, perhaps for the insurance money—but maybe for another reason. If he's closemouthed about the whole thing and shoos the police away, I think that would be a clue that he doesn't want the law involved, which means he's probably hiding something."

"Hell, we *know* he's hiding something—smuggled ivory," said Roantis.

"Hey, maybe it's an employee doing it, not the owner."

I thought about Joe's idea for a while. It made sense. "Are you going to call Brad?"

"Depends on what we find out," he said, banging the spoon on the skillet and turning off the gas. "Back in a minute. I'll use your study phone and take notes."

While he was gone I poured myself some Poland Spring water and cracked open the oven door. Great smells. I was hungry, even though I thought I hadn't any appetite. Joe's Italian cuisine could do that. In a few minutes he reappeared, checked the food, and sat down on a stool.

"Willard Hastings—he calls himself Will—is the owner of the warehouse. He claims nothing was taken and is anxious for the police to investigate fully."

"That either means he knows nothing of the ivory in the crates," I said, "or else he's already disposed of the incriminating evidence. Frankly, I believe the latter. If he's the owner of the warehouse, how could he not know about those crates of rotten fish in his building?"

"I agree. Laitis?"

"I think Doc's right. So this Hastings doesn't know that we know about the tusks."

"He probably doesn't."

"But wait, Joe. If he's in on the ring, and maybe helped abduct Mary, or knew about the killing of Harold up in P-town, then he knows that somebody is snooping around his operation."

"That's right. But as you said, if he's cleared out the illicit ivory and invites the cops in full-scale, he's obviously trying to clear himself."

I felt a sudden, deep anger rise in me.

"What we should do—Laitis and I—is take Hastings to some quiet spot and make him talk."

"There ya go!" said Roantis, brightening. He seemed to like the idea so much he went to the sideboard and poured himself another whopper belt of single malt. "I like the direct approach."

"Well, you're not as good at the direct approach as you think, guys. The Gloucester cops have a clear thumbprint of one of the burglars."

"That's not possible," I said. "We wore cotton gloves the whole time, just the way you told us to."

"Even when you unwrapped the gaffer tape from the roll?" Joe asked. He was smirking.

"Well, no. You know how hard it is to get tape off a roll, Joe. You need your fingernails. It's like opening a jackknife. I started the roll with my hands, then put the gloves on again."

"He's right," Laitis said. "I saw him do it."

"And the tape that you used. You took it all with you?"
"Every bit."

"Every bit except that piece on the door edge, holding the broken tongue depressor in place over the latch," Joe said, swiveling on the stool, his arms crossed over his chest. Smug as hell.

"Oh, shit!"

"Careless of you, Doc," said Roantis in a scolding tone.

I turned on him. "Listen, bozo, who was it who set off the alarm?"

"Hold on," Joe said, holding up his arms. "There's no

sense blaming each other over it. It's too late. What worries me is this—if the police do a print search, you could be at risk, Doc. Remember the P-town police fingerprinting you recently?"

I sank down into a chair. "Great. I could be arrested and tried for burglary. That's all I need."

"Look on the bright side," said Joe. "While a felony, it's not as serious as the other charges facing you—murder, aggravated assault, and rape."

"Aw, shut up."

"I mean, that only means a sentence of, say, three consecutive life terms."

I buried my face in my hands. What had I done to deserve all this? All I did was buy a present for my wife. And look what happens. "*Bright side?* What bright side? This is about as bright as the dark side of the moon, for chrissakes."

"Look—with the state of our judicial system, you'll plea-bargain, appeal, get counseling, and be out of the slam in six months. And I'm serious, dammit. That's the *worst* part." He rolled his eyes again as he reignited the gas. "Jesus H. Christ. Why the hell am I a cop anyway? I ought to have my fucking head examined."

"When do we eat?" demanded Roantis.

"Soon. And I'm gonna do you two crooks a favor. I'm going to try and interview Hastings personally. See what he says. See if he drops any hints. Who knows? I might just lose it and grab him and make him tell me where Mary is."

"If he does know where she is, he knows her name is Brindelli, and he won't let you near him," I reminded him.

"Hmm . . . good point. Didn't think of that. Well, I'll use an alias. But the main thing is, if I can get near him, I'll have Kevin or Herbie go with me, and when we're off talking about the break-in, my helper will find the station wagon and put a beeper on it. *Capisce?*"

"*Capisce!* Then the car can lead us to Mary."

"Let's hope so. Now set the table, you guys. Dinner is only seconds away."

We all dug in, and it was terrific. I missed the wine, but the mineral water tasted good, and the cappuccino afterward topped it off. Joe declined our invitation to stay, saying he should get back to Marty. Who could blame him? I sure wished I had a wife to snuggle up to.

To get my mind off Mary after Joe left, Laitis and I watched a movie on TV. It was about a team of thieves who break into a currency-holding facility for an armored carrier. It passed the time. Roantis was mesmerized by it.

"Remind you of the old days, Laitis?"

"Uh-huh."

"Well, forget it. Joe took the decoder with him, and the Cobra lock pick."

"Uh-huh. But he forgot to take the lock-pick set he loaned me."

"Really? Well, you dropped one of the picks and the tension bar through the grating at the warehouse. Remember?"

"There are a lot more picks in the set, Doc. And I know how to make the tension bars."

I leaned forward in the easy chair and turned to look at him.

"What are you getting at?"

"Jason Steingretz's warehouse. On Ping On Street, just two doors down from Sam Ho's gift shop. You remember, the place where you saw Johnny Ridge stick out his big ugly head?"

"You're serious? I thought you were joking before."

Then he turned and faced me, the humor all gone from his bright blue eyes. They had taken on that flinty coldness, crinkled up around the edges like Charles Bronson's. Look out.

"Hey. I thought you wanted to find your wife."

"You know I do."

"Then listen to me. This owner of the warehouse isn't in charge. He's not the head of this operation, whatever it is. And Sam Ho isn't. Johnny Ridge isn't either; he's the muscle. Joe was right about that."

"So you're saying Steingretz *isn't* the head?"

He shook his head. "Nope. I know enough about him to know he's greedy, but he's not mean and strong enough. Listen—I was head of our recon team that became known, and feared, as the Daisy Ducks. I was head of it because I was strong. And mean when I had to be. Steingretz is neither. Ridge is strong in muscle, and mean, but he's not strong enough in mind. His kind are never in charge."

"Okay, so solve the puzzle. Who's in charge?"

He shook his head, stabbing out a Camel butt in my ashtray. Smelled terrific. But I wasn't about to complain to this battered soldier of fortune. I was all ears.

"Whoever it is, we haven't seen him yet. Or, if you maybe have seen him, you don't realize he's in charge."

I sat for a minute watching a commercial on television. I don't remember what it was about. I was thumbing mentally through my recollections of the painful past month or so, trying to remember all the faces, voices. . . .

"Doc?"

"Ummm—"

"You thinking?"

"Yeah . . ."

"Shall I leave you alone?"

"You know how to work the stereo; put on *Finlandia*."

He was up and out of his chair in a twinkling. Roantis loves Sibelius. It's no surprise; the Lithuanians and the Finns have many common bonds. In a few minutes I heard the haunting opening strains of that great musical work that has since become Finland's national anthem. My God, it's a pretty anthem. The only one to rival it is France's "La Marsellaise." Roantis came back in with a beer and settled down. I looked over at him.

"Speaking of Finns, Laitis, how's your pal Timo Pekkalla?"

He shrugged. "Out of the country somewhere. I think maybe somewhere off the Dalmation coast."

"We have SF guys in Bosnia already?"

He glared at me. "*Already?* Hell, Doc, they been there a year setting things up."

I thought again, but what I was thinking disturbed me.

"I'm going up to hit the hay, Laitis. Maybe tomorrow morning I'll have a better idea of who the leader could be. Good night. Don't drink all my booze."

"Ha! I'll try my best."

28

NEXT MORNING I LOOKED AT ROANTIS ACROSS THE TABLE AS he stuffed egg and English muffin into his mouth.

"I have an idea who it could be, Laitis."

"Huh? Who could be what?"

"Who could be the leader of this smuggling ring."

"Who?"

"Larry Carpenter."

He almost dropped his fork. *"What?"*

"You heard me. Just think about it. He's strong, smart, and has all the qualities of leadership to run an organization like this. Plus, he's traveled a lot—been all over this country and many others. You said yourself that I might see this leader, but not recognize him as such."

"But he's your friend, Doc. Your best buddy from a long time ago."

"I know. But a long time ago is a long time. A lot can happen to change a person over thirty years. Remember your best friend in SF? Ramon Vilarde?"

"Okay. It can happen. Never would I guess that Ramon would try to kill me. On the other hand, maybe you're just sore that he and Mary are working together."

"I realize this; I admit it. But still, he's had a lot of experience playing the crook. Then one time, when the stakes are big enough, and maybe the risk is thrilling enough, all he'd have to do is just act it out for real. See?"

He chewed thoughtfully and finally gave me a slight nod.

"Yeah, I see what you mean. But why suspect Larry over everybody else?"

Then I told him about the two jobs in New York that Larry had blown. Roantis seemed more convinced now. "Why didn't you tell me this earlier?"

I explained Joe's and my position vis-à-vis Brad Taylor. He understood the rationale, but was irritated he'd been left out.

"Well, okay, bright boy," I said, "what do you think we should do now?"

"Break into Steingretz's warehouse and see what we find in there. Or don't find. I think I said this before—"

"You really think you can get us inside there?"

He nodded, smiling.

"*Without* getting us hurt or killed? That's the tricky part, you know."

He was still grinning like a kid on Christmas Day. "It's also the fun part."

"You're nuts, Laitis," I said as we cruised the narrow, twisted streets of Chinatown in Roantis's old Peugeot. The neighborhood sure was lit up at night. The only place I'd seen more flashy neon was the Chinatown in San Francisco. I hear Vegas also has spectacular neon signs, but who cares?

"Know what our problem's gonna be?" he asked.

"Waiting until it gets dark and quiet."

"Right. Thing is, Doc, I spent a lot of time in Asia, and it still amazes me how similar American Asian communities are to the ones in Vietnam, Thailand, Japan, and Hong Kong. Hell, you walk down the streets of some of these American cities and you'd swear you're in Kowloon, or Okinawa."

"And . . . ?"

"And, those places just don't shut down. They get going around ten at night, and don't shut down until dawn."

I looked at my watch. "It's one-thirty already. So how much longer will we have to wait?"

"Don't know. At least till three."

"Great. So what do we do to kill time?"

"I say we park the car, go to a bar, and sip drinks until it's time."

"I don't know, Laitis. This will be hairy enough without you getting bombed beforehand. The last time we went to sip drinks we wound up at that goddamned Rotor Club."

"I sure miss that place."

"Yeah? Well, I don't. Listen—to hell with waiting. Let's just park the car and slide on over there. You said there was a door to the place off the alley."

"That's the door we should try first, anyway. Here it is, up on the right."

We drove slowly by the buildings on Ping On Street. The three-story one with no windows built of dun-colored brick—and looking so run-down you could buy it for ten bucks—was the Stiengretz warehouse. The building next to it was in about the same shape, not as tall, and had more windows. It looked unoccupied, maybe condemned. It was the building that abutted this second one that I was most familiar with. On the street level was the gift-and-curio shop of Sam Ho. The floor above it was windowless, but the third floor had plenty of windows. It was through one of these windows that Johnny Ridge had stuck his wide, ugly head out and glared at me. Just remembering this gave me the chills.

"You carrying?"

"No," he said. "Remember, I told you I was on probation again. I get caught with a piece on me and it's the slam for sure. How about you?"

"No, I'm following your advice."

"Swell. Let's just hope we don't bump into anybody once we get inside."

"Think they have a watchdog in there?"

Roantis laughed. "Not a chance! I can fuckin' guarantee it."

"How come you're so sure about this?"

"Watchdog? In this neighborhood? Tell me, Doc, how many dogs you see around here?"

"None, but I'm talking about a watchdog."

"Know what you call a Korean with a dog?"

"What?"

"A vegetarian. Know what you call a Korean with two dogs?"

"No. What?"

"A rancher. Thing is, Doc, Asians love dogs even more than you do. But they love them as the main dish. A watchdog's a dog, right? Well, it wouldn't last here. Somebody would kill it and eat it within two days."

"You're kidding, of course."

"Hell I am. Kill and eat every one they can find. Why do you think the Chinese named their dog the chow? Seem strange that it means dog *and* food?"

"So, no guard dogs."

"No guard dogs."

"Then this place ought to be simple. I bet the lock's not sophisticated. And I doubt they have an alarm system."

"Piece of cake, Doc."

"I told you not to say that."

"Piece of cake! Piece of cake! Piece of cake!"

He sounded like Long John Silver's parrot.

"There you go, you son of a bitch. A *triple jinx.*"

We parked about two blocks from our destination, managing to squeeze the big Peugeot into a curb slot just past Essex Street. Laitis still wanted to go to a bar—surprise, surprise—but I nixed the idea. Two Caucasian men going into a bar in Chinatown at two in the morning on a weeknight—at a time when we were almost certain to be the only Westerners in the place—was asking for it. I wanted as few residents to see or remember us as possible, so I suggested we simply wander the streets, backtracking the same ones as little as possible. That way, people who might notice us would assume that we were simply passing through on our way to Boston's infamous Combat Zone, the tenderloin district in the heart of Boston set aside for the flourishing of sin. This enclave of several square blocks abuts Chinatown and is notorious for its prostitution, porno houses, and assorted illicit trades.

The streets were still crawling with foot traffic. Though mostly Asians, there was enough of a general mix so we didn't stand out. More than one young Chinese or Korean kid acknowledged Roantis with a short bow and the words *sifu* or *sabom*, which he told me meant master, or teacher.

"Kids in my daytime classes at the Union," he explained. "Nice kids. I think they're worth keeping out of the gangs and the drug trade."

"You mean they think you're legit?"

"Why, of course. What reason would I give them for thinking otherwise?"

"The fact that you're about to pull a B and E in their neighborhood."

"Well, except for that—"

At quarter to three we both felt it was time to make or break it. We were tired, strung out, and close to collapse. So we ducked into the narrow, grimy alley that smelled of garbage, cat spray, and faint wafting odors of deep-fry fat and sesame oil, and Laitis unrolled his little cloth packet of lock picks. I held the tiny flashlight upon the door. The lock was a Yale, model unknown. He inserted the tension bar, holding it expertly to the side with the edge of his left hand so it exerted a rotational force on the side of the cylinder, which would hold the pins up in place as he pushed them upward with his pick. With his right hand he inserted one of the picks and began at the lock's rear, pushing up the pin tumblers one at a time. It took him three passes, but on the last one, the mortise gave way to the pressure of the bar and the trunion cylinder rotated counterclockwise with a soft clack. Roantis looked my way and grinned, and replaced the picks in the canvas roll-up case, which he stuffed between the brick wall and a downspout.

"Don't want to get caught with this on me," he whispered. "If something happens, play drunk as hell. We'll just say we got so shit-faced we came in here by accident because somebody told us there was a hot card game inside, savay-voos?"

"Right—" I whispered, with a mouth dry as Death Valley.

Roantis shoved at the door. It opened easily, which meant, to me anyway, that it was used with some frequency. I shined the light inside to reveal a concrete floor and the beginning of a gray wooden stairway. I saw two fifty-five gallon drums of trash just inside the doorway. Apparently, this door opened onto an interior stairway, nothing else. The only way to go was up. Just before we were all the way inside we heard loud voices and laughter in the alley, coming in our direction. Roantis yanked me inside, and we peered out through the crack in the doorway as two young men came staggering down the dark lane swilling from a bottle of something they were passing back and forth.

"Chinese kids," he said. "They're speaking Mandarin. I think I know the one on the left."

When the kids passed, I asked if it was safe to shut the door behind us. He said it was, and we pushed it closed and turned the latch, locking us inside.

"No guard dogs," I said.

"No guard dogs."

We started up the stairs. After the first flight we turned and found ourselves in a big room.

It was littered with more drums and waste containers. They gave off a strange, organic smell not unlike singed hair. I felt my stomach rock slightly as my nose picked it up.

"What is it?" I asked Roantis.

"Something burnt. Maybe burnt bone?"

By the faint light of the flashlight, we went over to some of the drums and peered inside. I was almost afraid to look. All we saw was old crumpled newspaper and gray-tan dust. Roantis lifted some of the sawdust-looking stuff and held it under his nose.

"I think this might be ivory dust. From carving."

"Then we're in the right place."

"Let's go on up."

I followed Roantis up the next flight of stairs. Although we were certain the building was deserted, we crept up the stairs as softly as possible.

At the second-floor landing we shined the little light around again. This time we saw something more interesting. Cardboard boxes full of raw ivory. Walrus tusks mostly, some that were long and spiralite, which I assumed were narwhal, and a big stack of crescent tusks, yellowish white, in a far corner. The teeth of *Africanus loxidonta,* the fast-disappearing African elephant.

And then we heard something.

"Laitis! What was that?"

"A woman's scream, I think."

"From where?"

"Above us. Next floor up."

"Should we go and call somebody?"

"Why? Let's go up and see."

"But what if there are a bunch of bad people up there? We're not carrying—"

"I'm going to have a look. Come on if you want."

He said it in a flat, dead voice. I didn't especially want to go on up, but I didn't want to stay behind, either. We crept up the last set of stairs, extra slow and quiet. There was another sound now. It came to our ears clear and sad. There was no mistaking it.

It was a woman crying. Sobbing as if her heart would break.

29

WE CROUCHED THERE, BEHIND THE DOOR AT THE TOP OF THE grimy stairs, listening to the girl being beaten.

It was always the same: rough words in a drunken man's voice, then a whimpering plea from the woman, who sounded young. Then a slap or smacking sound, and more tears. I felt my anger rising; I imagined at first it might have been Mary, but I knew from the voice, even behind the thick door, that it was a much younger woman. Perhaps a child.

I looked at Roantis. We had switched off the small flashlight and I could see his face from the light that seeped beneath the door. Besides the voices, the sound of rock music came from the background. I leaned over and whispered to Roantis.

"What do we do?"

"Wait."

"Why wait? That girl is—"

"See how many others are there. If it's just the two of them, we can go in. Assuming the door isn't locked."

Then Roantis jumped, almost knocking me over. When I recovered, I saw him holding a cat. It was a small calico cat, gray, white, and brown. Between a kitten and a cat. Cute. Why the hell was he holding it?

"Thing came up against me," he said in a low voice. We could talk above a whisper; there didn't seem to be any danger of our being heard, not with the violence and the loud music coming from the other side of the door.

"Well, put it down."

"It won't leave me alone."

He continued to hold and stroke the cat, who began purring so loud I was certain it would give us away. Roantis is a strange man. . . .

The girl's sobs became a series of slow, desperate moans. I tugged at Roantis's sleeve. He continued to hold the kitten. Then he leaned over and said, "Push on the door."

I did. No go. He rose and turned the knob. I pushed. No go. The sounds continued from within; nobody had heard us.

"What now?"

"Try knocking."

"Seriously, Laitis."

"Let's go back down and try the front. At least if we try there, he may leave her alone for a while."

So we crept back down the dingy stair flights back out into the alley. Laitis locked the door open so we wouldn't have to pick the lock again, and walked around to Ping On Street and came to the front door of the building. He let the cat down, but it wouldn't leave—it kept doing figure eights around Roantis's legs the way cats do. There was just a door in the wall. No window, just a doorknob. I tried the door. Locked.

"There's no doorbell," I said.

Laitis cuddled the kitty up into his neck with his left hand and knocked loudly on the door with his right fist. We looked up. There were two dusky windows two flights up. But nothing moved behind them that we could see. Laitis began kicking at the wooden door. It made a lot of noise, and I suspected at least some of the sound wafted upward via the inside stairwell, because shortly afterward one of the windows above us slid up.

"Who the fuck is it?" said a deep voice. I could see the silhouette of a large and heavy man half out the open window. Johnny Ridge, without a doubt. And he didn't sound any better than he had looked earlier.

"I got business with you," said Roantis.

"What the fuck kind of business?"

"Private. Let me in and we'll talk."

"Go fuck yourself." The window slammed down.

"Rather limited vocabulary, wouldn't you say?" I said. "Let's go back around."

Back in the alley, Laitis retrieved the lock-pick set from behind the downspout and we climbed back up that dark, grisly stairway to the top floor, leaving the door at the bottom partly open for a fast exit should the need arise. This time he was noticeably quieter at the top of the stairs. We sat there for a minute or two, heads against the door, listening.

"Just the two of them, I think," he said finally, and inserted the tension bar into the lock face while I held the Maglite. He then raked the lock as softly as possible. Once, we heard footsteps approach. They were heavy but moved fast, passing the door. We froze for the moment, then Roantis went back to work. We were relieved to hear the music grow noticeably louder. We could no longer hear the girl.

"Maybe he's finished with her and is just listening to that crap," I said in the lowest voice I could utter. Roantis nodded back. He continued to work, making clicking and scraping noises with the small tools. It certainly seemed to our advantage that loud music was on the other side of the door.

Finally I heard the telltale clack of the mortise turning in the lock. Roantis looked at me in the faint light. Then he leaned over and whispered. "I'm going to open this very slowly and take a peek. I think he's a room or two away. Once I get inside, follow me. Stay close to the walls and be ready to duck. Watch my hands for signals, okay?"

I nodded.

"If I yell 'hit it,' drop to the floor."

I nodded again, my heart going like a trip-hammer. I could hear my pulse in my neck.

"If there's more than one, we may have to leave fast. Head for the door—I'll keep them busy so you can get moving."

He then went into a low crouch, turning the doorknob. Then he pushed at the door. It stayed closed. He pushed harder and, in a series of creaks and thumps, pushed it open four inches. I saw dirty, oil-stained wooden floors in dim light, and a wall about six feet away painted bile green. I smelled Chinese food and marijuana. The rock music used up all my hearing. We seemed to be along a hallway between rooms.

In the next second something strange happened: the kitten scooted between us and entered the hall. Somehow it had followed us back up the stairs through the open door below.

"Shit!" whispered Laitis. There it was, the curse: he should never have said "you-know-what . . ."

Roantis watched horrified as the kitten sauntered across the boards to the wall opposite, then pressed itself against the wall and scrunched up against it in an ecstasy of rubbing.

Roantis extended his head carefully into the hallway, looked both ways, then back at me. He pushed the door open further, extended his upper body, and looked around. Then, as if suddenly making up his mind this was the time to enter, he slid into the hallway in a low crouch, motioning me on.

I followed, wishing that at least one of us was armed.

Then we were crouching in the dim hallway, looking around.

To one side, the left as one came in the door, was a distant room at the end of the hallway that looked like a crude kitchen. I could only see into the room by the tiny hallway light, but I could make out a table and chairs, and some table appliances. I saw the silvery-gray crescent shape of a wok. That's where the odor of Chinese food had come from. The kitchen was dark and vacant; it therefore seemed that whatever business we had to transact was at the other end of the long hallway. I saw an open door at the end of the hall, which led into a dark room. The bedroom? But there was another room that opened off the hall just before the dark room at the end. The room was lit up, but we could not see inside it. It seemed the music came from this room.

Question: was Ridge in the living room listening to the music, or was he in the bedroom with the girl? Assuming, of course, she was still there, still alive, and so on. . . .

What to do? Even Laitis Roantis, mercenary soldier, didn't seem to know.

But we didn't have time to decide. Because just as Laitis started to creep down the hallway toward the lighted room, a deep, gravelly voice spoke to us from behind. It was not Asian in the least. It was American as it could be. With a Southern drawl.

"Don't move, and don't turn around," it said.

We froze.

I heard big, heavy footsteps come up behind me. Then I felt a ring of cold steel, like a hollow quarter, rest on the back of my neck.

"Twelve-gauge here. Number-one buck. It'll cut your neck in half. Got it?"

I nodded, and felt my knees beginning a horrid electric vibration I was powerless to stop.

Roantis was frozen in a half crouch ahead of me. The cat was doing figure eights between his feet, rubbing himself along his pant legs and purring.

I saw a faint shadow behind me, a flicker of motion that some deep, atavistic receptor in my brain told me was danger. I tried to move my head but not in time. There was a

sharp clip on the back of my head, and I fell forward onto
the floor.

30

I WASN'T OUT, BUT I WAS WEAK AND WOOZY. I HALF ROLLED
over on the floor and was able to look back down the hall,
where the big man stood, towering massive and dark in the
dim hallway, clad in a pair of Hawaiian shorts. Johnny
Ridge did not have his thick glasses on. Gone also was the
Fu Manchu goatee. He had done away with his Chinese
disguise. But the big Cherokee looked Hawaiian, Samoan
. . . he looked like a sumo wrestler. His hairless, heavy
body blocked out the hallway, and although it was liberally
hung with folds and mounds of fat, there was no mistaking
the giant frame and the swathes of huge muscle underneath.

He wasn't dumb, either. Though my head hurt and
reeled, I realized several things in a hurry as I lay on that
filthy floor and saw Roantis cowering in the arc of that
twelve-gauge barrel.

First, he'd gotten the drop on us perfectly. After seeing
us in the street below his window, he had appeared to slam
the window and forget about us. But he obviously did not.
No, he had sat inside listening carefully, and paid special
attention to the backstairs, where he'd heard us picking the
lock. Then he had cleverly turned up the music to lull us
into thinking we couldn't be heard.

Finally he'd hidden himself in the dark kitchen, at the
vacant end of the hallway, the one we were sure he wasn't

in, and waited there with a twelve-gauge—the best short-range weapon known to man—until we'd started down the hall after him.

And then he came up behind us and clipped me so there was one less to worry about.

We were in bad trouble, and what scared me most was Roantis. He looked scared indeed.

"Walk," he told Roantis, waving him on with the shotgun. I saw Roantis walk down the hall. I have never seen him look more fragile and frightened.

"Sit over there," he said, and before Roantis even turned to enter the dim room, he had reached back and fastened a giant iron grip on my upper arm, dragging me along the floor and flinging me on a couch next to Roantis as if I weighed as much as a four-year-old.

We didn't see the girl until we were sitting on the couch. She was cowering in the corner against the wall, naked, swollen, and bruised, her eyes tight with crying and her tears all used up. She looked Chinese, and was at most thirteen or fourteen. I saw her ribs gaunt at her sides as she heaved dry sobs. She was clearly scared to death.

She wasn't alone.

Ridge sat in a straight chair opposite us. He sat far away from us—about twelve feet. Far enough away so neither of us could jump him without taking a full charge of buckshot. He was smart even in that. Johnny Ridge certainly lived up to his rep as a dangerous character. Out of the corner of his eye, he seemed to notice the girl at the last instant. Without taking his eyes, or the gun, off us, he rose from the chair and backhanded the girl on the side of her head, sending her sprawling toward the bedroom door, through which she crawled, still trembling. I don't know what my face looked like; I would like to think there was at least a slight frown on it. Roantis was impassive, shrunken and old, looking totally scared and helpless. But I knew that he did this deliberately in tight places. He is not a big man—around five nine, maybe a hundred sixty-five pounds. He can appear absolutely frail, and startle people when their guard is down. At least I hoped so. I noticed one good sign: while seated nervously on the couch, never taking his eyes from Ridge or the shotgun muzzle, he had managed to turn his wristwatch inside out so that the face was to his wrist, and the mirror-smooth metal of the back of the watch was facing out. This enabled him to see behind himself. But I could scarcely see what good it would do us now.

I began to pray.

"I know you," Ridge said, staring at me. The black eyes were cold, flat.

"Where's my wife?" I asked. I was surprised at how loud and urgent my voice was.

He jerked his thick head back, laughing. "You'll never see her again!"

I was in the air, leaping for him, when Roantis caught me in the chest with a hard backward fist and sent me back again onto the couch.

I can never remember feeling so miserable, because at that instant, I really believed him.

"Look, he just wants to find his wife," Roantis said. His tone was soft, apologetic. "If you can help us with that, we'd just like to leave."

"Maybe. Maybe not. Why was your friend so interested in hanging around our street?" he asked, looking at me again.

"He made a mistake. His wife was shopping at Sam Ho's and he wanted to follow her."

The cat jumped up on the couch and went onto Roantis's lap. He stroked the kitty. It half closed its eyes, snapped the end of its tail, and purred.

"We know why she was shopping there. That's why she's in trouble."

"Where is she?" I asked. It was a plea.

"Up north. You may see her again, Dr. Adams. Maybe. Maybe both of you will die here. Soon."

My body took on that liquid, electric, all-encompassing fear that left me paralyzed. I tried to fight it, but it was no use. Mary, Jack, Tony, I thought.

I thought I saw the Indian's hands tense slightly on the gun stock. That faint muscle twitch that told me he was about to shoot.

A muffled squall came from Roantis's lap. He was rubbing the kitten's stomach. He must have been as nervous as

I was; his hands were moving fast over the animal, whose eyes were open wide.

For an eye blink, Johnny Ridge looked down at the kitten just as Roantis raised his hands four inches and flung the animal in a basketball chest pass at the big man's head.

Any cat flying through the air—leaping or thrown, a leopard or a kitty—travels the same way: with all four legs windmilling in frantic circles, claws extended, searching desperately for a foothold in the void.

The animal hit Ridge's face like a buzz saw. Blinded, he brought the muzzle up toward Roantis. But Laitis was already on his feet, and did a sweep kick to the gun, knocking it to the floor. The big man flung the cat from his face and turned toward Roantis, breathing fast and heavy. His face oozed lines of bright blood; his sumo wrestler's body was now bathed in a sheen of sweat.

And it was at that second that the tired, stooped old man who was my protean companion came violently to life. He dropped his torso and shoulders into a half stoop, then began a spin on the ball of his left foot, much like a figure skater winding up a routine. After a full spin, which was a blur, his right foot shot out and up in a flying reverse kick.

Groggy as I was, I could not see his right leg as it went through the air. But I heard it.

It swooshed like a swallow's wing.

And the side of his foot caught Johnny Ridge right on the side of his neck where it joins the jaw. There was a big thump, but the man did not drop. He staggered backward into the wall, his eyes rolling up, showing a lot of white underneath. But the wall held him up. His eyes were glazed, but then they came back into focus and glowered at Roantis with a fearful intensity.

Ridge came off the wall, growling with rage and hurt, the way a wrestler bounces off the ring ropes and flies toward his opponent. He came at Roantis, but he couldn't catch him, because my friend, suddenly looking terribly old and afraid again, was running down the short hall, away from the angry giant who was right on his heels.

I leaped on the shotgun, rolled upright into a sitting position, pointing it at the center of Ridge's wide back, and pulled the trigger. Nothing. I pumped the forearm, thinking the shell hadn't been chambered, and pulled the trigger again. Nothing. The gun wasn't loaded; Ridge had bluffed us with an empty gun.

I got up and rushed after the two men as fast as I could, raising the shotgun up in both hands so I could bash it into the back of Johnny Ridge's head.

And then I saw the most amazing thing. Roantis, having reached the end of the short hallway, chose not to enter the dark kitchen. Instead he veered to the right, which meant he was going to run directly into the wall. The big man was right behind him now—beginning to reach his huge right hand out to grab Roantis by the shirt collar or neck—

I now held the twelve-gauge like a spear, the butt end forward, hoping to jam it with all my strength into the nape of the neck that towered over me.

Then Roantis hit the wall, running.

And climbed right up it with his legs.

He jumped high just before the wall, his forward momentum carrying him up the vertical face with powerful pumping strokes of his legs.

For a tenth of a second he hung there, seven feet off the floor, like some giant jumping spider. He was turned around now, facing Ridge, who stopped in amazement. That was his mistake, because then Roantis sprang from his high perch, sweeping his left leg around in a perfect crescent kick as he came sailing off the wall.

The toe of his shoe caught the big man on the side of the head right behind the eye, along that thin, concave portion of the skull called the sphenoid bone. Most people call this region the temple—perhaps a corruption of the term temporal bone—which lies nearby. It is the most vulnerable part of the skull, and Roantis scored a bull's-eye. I heard a dull click as the bone broke, and Ridge sank to the floor in his tracks without a sound.

Laitis quickly regained his feet, warily watching the fallen man and huffing and puffing as if he were at death's door. Poor Roantis, never in the best of shape, had extended himself to the max during the previous ten or twelve seconds. He now paced around his fallen foe like an enraged and triumphant gladiator, hungrily drawing air into his lungs. How they still functioned—even minimally—after decades of sixty Camel cigarettes a day remains a mystery to me.

Finally catching his breath enough to look down at Ridge, he went to the side of the man, who was lying motionless facedown. With a sudden recurrence of rage, Roantis jumped into the air, grabbing his right foot in his hand, thus making a wide, blunt spear of his right knee. He then fell onto the man, aiming the point of his bent knee into the man's lower back, just to one side of the spine.

Knee drop to the kidney. A dirty, nasty thing to do, and incredibly painful. Ridge would piss blood for a week or more before losing the burst organ.

But Johnny Ridge apparently did not feel this horrendous trauma. He didn't move. Didn't even twitch.

I staggered over and looked down.

"Maybe you kicked him a little too hard, Laitis."

"Nah," he panted. "I kicked the bastard just perfect."

I felt the wide brown neck for a pulse. Nothing. I checked the eyes, then finally took Roantis's wristwatch from him and held the polished stainless-steel back directly under the mouth, searching for a faint cloud of breath vapor. Nothing.

I straightened up and looked around the apartment. "He's dead."

Roantis looked up at me with those pit-bulldog eyes. He took out his flattened pack of Camels and shook one out, lit it.

"Like I said, Doc, I kicked him perfect."

31

"NOW WHAT THE HELL DO WE DO?" I SAID, PACING UP AND down the tiny hallway, glancing out the windows. "Every time we go do something, it ends in disaster."

"Nope," Roantis said in a voice husky with fatigue, "this thing we did just right."

"Yeah, right. But what do we do now?"

"Go to the girl. See if she's okay."

He went into the bedroom. From the doorway, I heard him ask something in a strange language I assumed was Chinese. Getting no response, he tried another tongue, and I heard the girl's faint and shaking voice answer. He then gave her some instructions, and soon the delicate thing appeared in the bedroom doorway in a T-shirt and jeans. She was still shaking. Laitis went over and gathered her in his arms, stroking her head and talking softly to her.

This tender side of Laitis Roantis didn't surprise me. Most people don't know that Roantis has a step-daughter. Danielle Cournot was a child of three when Roantis's best friend in the French Foreign Legion, René Cournot, was killed at Dien Bien Phu, in what is now Vietnam. But way back then, in 1954, it was French Indochina. Anyway, Roantis promised the dying paratrooper he'd raise little Danielle if he got out alive.

He did, of course, just barely, and took the girl, half-French and half-Vietnamese, back with him to his new home in America. He nicknamed her Daisy, and taught her everything he knew about the martial arts as she was growing up. When Roantis returned to Vietnam eleven years later, he was working for Uncle Sam in Special Forces. Daisy, home in the States, missed her dad terribly, so when she became eighteen, she joined him in the land of her birth. Still fluent in Vietnamese and all the other exotic languages her dad taught her, and extremely capable not only of defending herself, but killing most men in hand-to-hand combat, she proved invaluable to Roantis and his team of secret saboteurs and assassins. So grateful were these men for what Daisy had done for them that they named themselves the Daisy Ducks in her honor.

So when I saw Roantis holding the terrified girl—an Asian one at that—I knew he was right at home.

"What now?" I asked. "She was here; she knows we killed him."

"So? What should I do? Kill her? Then we can walk out of here with no witnesses. How would that be?"

"C'mon Laitis—"

Laitis bent down and whispered in her ear. The girl spun around and around, her eyes wide. Finally she saw the man lying in the dark end of the hall. Then she flung herself into my friend's arms, crying again. But I sensed it was from relief.

"I just told her he's dead. As you can see, Doc, she's glad."

"Does she have any parents? Any family?"

Again he whispered to her; the girl pointed to a door. I then recognized it as the front door, which led to the stairwell in the front of the building. The girl spoke to Roantis for perhaps half a minute. Her words were animated and intense.

"She says she wants to take us to meet her mother and father. They're staying in the next building over."

"And they know she's *here*?" I was shocked.

"They know; Ridge has been using her for almost two weeks now. There's not much they can do about it; he's the head boss of the ivory-carving shop, and they're illegal aliens."

There was a pause as the two stared at me.

"Well? You coming?"

"But what about . . . ?" I gestured to the fallen man. Roantis waved me off.

"We'll take care of that. Now follow us, and no noise. . . ."

We went through the front door and down the stairs. We had turned down the rock music on the radio, but left it on to mask our footsteps. On the second landing the girl opened a door and led us through a long room with no windows. Then we went into what seemed to be another building, this one with windows on one side. We felt our way between benches and worktables in the dark. I smelled the odor of burnt hair. Then I realized that we were making our way through the ivory shop. The burnt smell was the result of sawing, grinding, sanding, and drilling raw ivory. My eyes became accustomed to the faint light from the streetlights that came in through the windows, and I could see that the tables were littered with pieces of ivory. I saw bow saws, jeweler's saws, and grinders and drills on flexible shafts that were evidently powered by foot treadles, like the old sewing machines. The shop also stank of old sweat. Hence the expression, I thought.

At the far end of this big room was another door, and through it we came into a small hallway that was empty except for some old rugs and clothing strewn on the floor. The girl went to the door at the far end of this hall and slowly opened it. Immediately I heard faint snoring and smelled strong odors: Asian sesame oil, pepper sauce, more sweat, and stale urine. The girl went on into this room while Roantis and I waited out in the hall, looking into the dark sleeping quarters through the partially open door.

People were sleeping on the floor. I saw no beds or mattresses, just people wrapped in blankets or robes, lying in rows, like the old drawings of the slaves in ships bound for America and the Indies. I had no idea if there was a washroom or toilet in there, but even if there was, it was obviously way overused or broken. Faint stirrings in the room were followed by the return of the girl, leading an older man and woman, who I assumed were her parents. When the couple saw us, they panicked—the look of fear in their eyes was obvious and unmistakable.

Then Roantis spoke to them in a whisper, and they

looked at him in awe. Finally we began to walk back to the
apartment with the three of them following behind. I heard
the girl whispering excitedly to her parents.

"She's telling them the big bad man is dead," Roantis
told me in a low voice.

"Great. Soon the whole community is going to know."

"I don't think so; I have a plan."

Once back in the apartment, the couple—who were perhaps in their late thirties, looked in horror at the body of the
Indian. Roantis sat them down and talked to them, then
turned to me.

"They're worried, but very glad Ridge is dead. He's been
raping the young girls here for two months. There's not a
damn thing these people can do because they're illegals. If
caught, they'll be sent back to China or put in a camp with
no way to make a living. The girl's name is Beng. I guess
she thinks we're really something, Doc."

I could tell this by the way the girl was looking at us,
particularly Roantis, who could speak to her and comfort
her. Then Roantis began an intense discussion with the
adults, asking them question upon question. Finally the man
rose and left, leaving the mother and daughter together on
the couch, holding each other and talking softly. Often they
looked at us and smiled.

"Where'd he go?"

"Off to get some friends. We're going to have a little
meeting here—decide what to do about the late Johnny
Ridge."

"Don't you think it would be wiser to call the police and
just tell them what happened?" I said. "After all, everybody
knows he was a bad guy. Certainly these people can testify
about what—"

"C'mon, Doc! Use your head! What would happen to
these people, then?"

"Oh. You mean deported or interned?"

"Sure. That's why they're living like slaves in here. They
hardly ever go outdoors, for chrissakes. No; we're gonna
make old Johnny Ridge"—he turned and stared at the man
on the floor—"*disappear.*"

"I'm not sure I like that idea."

"I'm not sure I care."

"Listen, Laitis—"

"No, you listen—I've been around these people most of my working life. I've killed them; I've had my ass saved by them. What you don't see is how tight these people are. They hated this man; he fucked their babies. They're glad as hell he's dead. Now the best thing for them to do is to help us hide the evidence. And that's what's gonna happen. Just you watch. But first, why don't you examine the girl. See if she needs to go to the hospital."

As I approached the couch Roantis spoke to them, I suppose telling them that I was a doctor. I examined Beng's injuries, all of which were bruises. They were ugly, but would heal in a few days. I wish the same were true of her emotional damage. Then I heard noise on the back stairway.

Beng's father returned with three other men. One was quite old, and was seated in a chair while the others sat cross-legged on the floor around him. But then the old man rose and motioned for Roantis to seat himself there, and he joined his companions on the floor. Apparently they forgot about me, which was just as well; I wanted no part of this scheme.

They chatted in Chinese—some form of it, anyway—for several minutes. Roantis ran the discussion. Finally there was a general nodding of heads, and one of the men went to find a phone. He returned shortly, and then there was silence until the doorbell rang.

I almost jumped out of my chair, but the others rose expectantly and received the caller. I looked at my watch; it was almost four-thirty in the morning.

Through the door came a middle-aged Chinese man—I assumed he was Chinese, but he could have been any of four or five other nationalities—carrying a duffel bag. Now, what the hell's in there? I thought.

He was introduced to Roantis, and they both bowed. Then the man went up and shook his hand, beaming at him and saying something that was obviously complimentary.

Then the men went over to the prone Ridge, took off his grimy shorts, and hauled him into the bathroom and laid him in the tub.

Just before the men closed the door, I saw the visitor open the bag and take out two big knives and a hacksaw.

"We can go now, Doc," Laitis said, leading me over to the back door. Then he stopped and turned to the girl. She was cuddled up next to her mother, holding the cat, which purred in her lap. He went over and hugged her, and she hugged him back. The mother cried again and looked up at Roantis with tears of gratitude in her eyes. We waved good-bye and went down the grimy backstairs, around the corner, over three blocks in the now deserted streets, and found the battered old Peugeot.

We were heading west on Storrow Drive before he said anything.

"Cute kid."

"Who, Beng?"

"Yeah."

"Aren't you afraid they'll tell?"

"Nope. More chance of an earthquake in Boston than any of them saying a word."

"Who was that guy who came in with the bag?"

"I think you know. He runs a local butcher shop."

"Oh my God." I thought back to that first day in Chinatown when I'd seen the whole pigs being unloaded outside the shop.

"So, after they cut him up, what then?"

"Well, I think they'll be a lot of toilets flushed tonight. Maybe some garbage bags thrown into local Dumpsters. Who knows, they might grind a lot of him up in the shop. . . ."

"You don't really think they'd . . ."

"Let's put it this way—I'm not going to any of those restaurants for at least a month."

We drove on in silence. Then I thought of something. "When Ridge turns up missing, what then?"

"Got it covered. Sam Ho runs the operation. He's the boss, but not as mean as Ridge was. The workers can tolerate him. We've got a nice story cooked up for Sam. It seems that sometime in late evening, after Sam went home, a big white Cadillac with New York plates drove up to the shop. Some big white men got out and went up to Johnny's apartment. Later they came out with him, laughing. They might have been drunk. They all got into the big white car and drove away. . . ."

"That's it? Make it look like the Mob?"

"Not the Mob. Remember the story about Ridge in New York? I made sure they all added a detail about the car. On the back window was a decal of a flag with three broad stripes—green, white, and orange."

"The flag of Ireland!"

"Yeah. The Westies strike again."

A few minutes went by. We made great time on the empty roads. At Fresh Pond I said, "I just thought of something. I wish Ridge were still alive."

"What? How the hell can you say that?"

"Because he knew where Mary is. He could have told us. Now . . . maybe it'll be too late."

He reached over and gripped my shoulder.

"Nah—we'll find her, Doc. I promise. He said she was alive."

"Yeah, alive and in trouble. He said she was in trouble."

"Not as much trouble as he wound up in. Don't worry, Doc. We'll find her and get her back. I promise."

32

I DIDN'T WAKE UP UNTIL NOON. I WENT TO CHECK ON LAITIS IN the next room and he was still zonked out. Kicking the big Indian to death took it out of him, I guess.

I went downstairs and made coffee, then took a steaming mug out to the sunporch. God, I was down. I missed Mary terribly. Was she still alive? If so, where was she, and could she get away? Should I tell the boys, or would it only upset them? I debated calling them for almost forty minutes, finally deciding against it. If Mary could get to a phone, she could and would call them. Hopefully, she would also call me. Surely she wasn't still so angry with me that she wouldn't call and let me know she was okay.

But then, Mary has a lot of pride, and a temper to match. When wronged, or simply feeling wronged, she can pull out all the stops.

I needed to talk to somebody close. Moe was still out of town. That left Joe. I was holding the receiver in my hand and pushing the buttons on the kitchen wall phone when Laitis came slouching through the doorway.

"Who you calling?"

"Just Joe."

In a twinkling, the old, slouched man became a panther and was at my side, forcibly replacing the receiver back on the hook.

"Maybe we talk first, huh?"

He poured himself a mug, went over to the sideboard in the hallway, added a double dollop of Courvoisier, and settled back at the kitchen table.

"You don't want me to call Joe."

"No. Not for a day or so."

"Why?"

"I think the business of last night should settle into the background a bit before you talk to him. Joe's smart, and alert; he could sense something in your voice and ask you a bunch of questions real fast. You might tell him something we don't want him to hear."

"You mean Ridge?"

"Who the hell else? The Easter bunny?"

"I was thinking of maybe telling him anyway. He'd understand."

I'll never forget the look he gave me. He oozed over real close, getting "into my face," as the expression goes. The downsloped, squinty, ice-blue Mongol eyes bored into me. His gravel voice was low and menacing.

"Well, if you were thinking that, don't think it anymore. Forget it."

"Why? It was self-defense."

With a weary sigh he seated himself at the table and took a sip of java.

"Sometimes you are so fucking dumb I can't believe it."

I sat down across from him. I figured with the table between us, at least he couldn't kick me. There was some comfort in that.

"Mary's told me the same thing a few times."

"Listen—Joe's our friend, but he's also a cop; he'd have to report it. There would be a trial. I'm in enough shit as it is. Leave it alone; our friends in the neighborhood will take care of everything. When Joe finally tells you that the Westies took Johnny Ridge for his last car ride, go along with it."

"But I want to tell Joe I heard that Mary's 'up north.' Maybe he could help out . . . get the law-enforcement agencies to cooperate."

"Wait on that, just for a day or two. Meanwhile I want you to think of what happened over the past two weeks, before Mary and this Carpenter guy got missing. Anything stick out in your mind?"

"No," I said, shuffling through the stack of Herbie Sams photos that were left on the kitchen table. "I've been through it all a hundred times in my head. I think what happened is that Mary or Larry slipped. Made some minor mistake that the pirates picked up on. Of course, there are other possibilities. One is that I'm at fault."

"How?"

"Well, you remember that day in Chinatown when Sam Ho saw me on the street and Ridge opened the window and looked down at me. I'm sure they fixed me in their minds, and maybe connected me to Mary. I think this because I'm pretty sure it was Ridge who killed James Harold down in P-town and then left an identical kayak carving on my door as a warning."

"We've sort of thought that all along. Which means, maybe we start with Sam Ho tomorrow. If he was Johnny's boss, then he would know even more about this. Maybe we'll take Sam Ho for a ride in the country and ask him some . . . intense questions."

"That's a good idea. And since the strongman is now gone, he'll be scared; he might figure he's next."

"Yeah. So let's go pay a visit to Sam Ho tomorrow, after our friends tell him about Ridge and the Westies. But you said there might be another possibility."

"I don't think I mentioned Larry Carpenter's girlfriend to you, did I?"

"Nope. What the hell's that got to do with anything?"

I told Laitis about the incident in the parking lot of the Dory, and the mysterious man in the sedan with the camera who was tailing the woman.

"He told you she was married to a big shot? What kind of big shot?"

"Don't know—Larry wouldn't tell me. Wouldn't even tell me her name, either. The guy could be a millionaire businessman, a politician, even a kingpin in Cosa Nostra."

"So, what are you saying?"

"I'm saying that there's a possibility that Mary and Larry aren't in trouble over the pirate trade in ivory. Maybe this jealous husband has tracked Larry down and snagged him . . . and Mary just got in the way."

"So, you think she was with him?"

"Maybe. Intimately or maybe not intimately, but she's been with him, yes. And if the New York hotshot wanted Larry out of the way, and she was there, too . . ."

I stared down at the table, lost in a dark sea of depression. Laitis sensed it.

"I don't think so. One—if the guy's a prominent person, and proud, he wouldn't harm somebody next to his target. If he wanted revenge, he'd isolate Larry and do it right. There's just no sense worrying about it. What are those pictures?"

"The ones Herbie Sams and Joe took of the Sea Feast warehouse before we went in. So, do you think our Chinese friends will tell Sam tomorrow?"

He nodded. "When it's time to open, Sam will be up there to check with Johnny. No Johnny, so he'll ask the workers if they've seen him. That's when the story comes in. He'll figure the Westies got Ridge, and maybe he's next. By the time we show up on his doorstep, he'll be scared shitless."

I was staring at one of the photos of the parking lot of

Sea Feast. I stared at it a long, long time, trying to remember something. . . .

"Didn't you just ask me to go over the events of the past couple weeks?"

"Uh-huh."

"Well, there's something in this photograph that Herbie Sams took that has me wondering."

Roantis rose and came around to my side of the table. He peered over my shoulder at the warehouse and the parking lot.

"Don't see many cars. Not many customers. Is that it? You think they made so much money off the ivory that the fish business was fake?"

"Nope. I'm asking you—*What's wrong with this picture?*'"

He stared at it awhile. "Nothing I can see."

"Okay, look at the vehicles in the lot. Do you see any that are damaged?"

"Ha! This is Massachusetts. The way the insurance is set up, everybody's driving damaged cars. So that's—"

"Look carefully and tell me. A new vehicle . . ."

He scanned the photo for almost half a minute. Then he said, "Okay, that white van has a twisted bumper and a scrape along the side."

"Yes, it certainly does."

"So?"

"I believe I know who owns that vehicle. And he is in the fish business. Or at least that's what he told me."

33

WE SPENT THE NEXT THIRTY MINUTES PACKING. INCLUDED IN my stuff was a Berretta 9mm automatic and a scoped rifle in 30-06.

That was from my house. Then we stopped at Roantis's place in Jamaica Plain. He packed some cold-weather gear in case the chase led us outside for any length of time, then packed up his Colt AR-15 and three spare magazines, his government model Colt .45, and the infamous "Street-cleaner" shotgun, an old and battered Remington 870 Wingmaster with extended magazine and stock wrapped with black electrician's tape, and two Randall knives he had left over from Vietnam.

"Need a rocket launcher?"

"You have one?"

"Sure, that old Soviet RPG-7, remember?"

"Well, I don't know. . . ."

"It'll sink a boat. Even a very big boat."

"If Mary's on the boat, I don't want it to sink. Besides, don't you keep telling me that you're on probation?"

"Oh yeah . . . forgot, I guess."

He brought out the duffel bags and dumped them in the backseat. His long-suffering and sweet wife, Suzanne, came out onto the front porch of their modest bungalow.

"Where are you going, dear?" she managed to ask. I suppose she's gotten some interesting answers to this question over the years.

"Hunting."

By two-thirty that afternoon we were headed down to Cape Cod. For Hyannis.

"Are you sure it's the same truck?" asked Roantis. "You don't have a tag number or anything definite."

"We've got something very definite. I stood there in Bill Bedford's marina parking lot while he examined the damage. The odds of another new white Chevy van having the same scrape and bent-up bumper are nil. For a while I thought, well, maybe he was up there at Sea Feast buying bait fish for his party boats. But then I wondered; why would a guy who needs bait fish every day go all the way from Hyannis to Gloucester for it? Hell, that's half a day's drive."

"But I still don't think it proves anything."

"That's because I haven't filled you in completely yet. Remember I told you he and his wife founded an organization called CapeWatch? It's a group of volunteers who keep tabs on pollution, fishing violations, industrial effluents, stuff like that. Mary joined it last year; that's how she got to be close to them. Well, just before I left the marina a couple weeks ago, I told them something I shouldn't have."

"Ahhh! You told them Mary had gone undercover."

"Not that specific, but it was enough. I crept around the corner of it, saying that she was working for their cause, and that they'd be proud of what she was doing, and so on."

"And what did they say?"

"Nothing much, except now I remember Bill tried nonchalantly to press for more information just as I was leaving. I never thought any more about it, even after Mary disappeared, because, hell, they'd be the least likely to suspect for something like that."

"That's always the way it is."

"But once I saw that van in the photo, far, far away from where it was supposed to be, and in the very place that was involved in the smuggling . . . then one thought led to another, and the whole thing came into focus."

"Why would he do it?"

"Why? Same old reason—money. I know the marina business is not doing well these days. Slow hardly describes it. In this economy—and especially up here in New England—owning a twelve-foot runabout is a luxury. And think of this—Bill Bedford has two big sportfishing boats. Both are capable of extended cruising and have big holds."

"You think that's how the ivory got to Sea Feast?"

"No. I think most of it comes in airfreight, hidden in those blocks of frozen fish. As we all agreed, what inspector's going to unpack and go through a crate of stinky fish? But those boats of Bedford's could come in handy for the occasional errand. And I wouldn't be surprised if he uses that new van of his to take the raw ivory from the fish warehouse to Sam Ho's carving shop in Chinatown."

Roantis half squinted his eyes, picturing it in his mind. "Yeah, his partner at the warehouse defrosts the crates, takes out the raw ivory, washes it down . . . and before daylight the van pulls up to the loading docks and hauls it into Boston."

"Yep. Just like that."

"You say this Bedford has a wife?"

"Uh-huh. Sally's a real nice woman. At least she came across that way."

"Think she's in on this? Think she knows?"

I watched the highway unfolding before us for a while before answering. "That's a good question. Now that I recall what Mary told me early on, when she was just getting into this stuff, Sally was the prime mover on it. Bill fought it at first, thinking it would threaten his business. Later something changed his mind, and he jumped into it, too, with both feet."

"What changed his mind was, he was in the smuggling business—of endangered species to boot—and this could be the perfect cover-up."

"Yep. Perfect enough so that the only people I told about Mary's work was the Bedfords—" I smacked the dashboard hard. "*Damn!* Why was I so dumb?"

"You weren't dumb; you were just trying to find your wife."

* * *

We pulled into the parking lot at Bedford's marina and
looked around. The new white van with the crumpled
bumper wasn't there. *Dream Days* was at her mooring, but
the bigger of the two boats, the *Bim Bam Boo*, was gone.
Whether by land or by sea, it was a pretty safe bet that Bill
Bedford was not around.

"So what do we do? Go in there and make her talk?"

"No," I said. "There's a chance she doesn't know about
this thing. In fact, if I had to bet either way, I'd say she
doesn't. Put yourself in his place. You're going broke and
need some cash to stay afloat. You somehow hear of a
chance to get into this illegal trade for big bucks. You not
only have boats to help you, but you have a built-in excuse
for long absences. Would you tell your wife?"

"Nope," he said, lowering the passenger-side window
and lighting a Camel, "I wouldn't tell her. And I would get
all excited about this CapeWatch thing to keep her happy
and to cover my ass."

"So let's assume she doesn't know. What now?"

"How about I go in there alone, posing as a cop? Ask
her where her husband is. Say we'd like to question him
about some illegal ivory."

"That might work. Her reaction alone might tell you
something. Let me hide this car; it's conspicuous, and she
knows it. Go in there and see what she says and does."

"Wish I had a badge to make it more official."

"Can do," I said, opening the compartment behind the
shift lever. I took out the worn leather wallet with the "Special Police" badge inside. It looked exactly like Joe's, except it had the words *Special Police* instead of *Detective
Lieutenant* on it. Everything else, including the state seal of
the commonwealth, was the same.

"This looks real."

"It is. It's what they gave me for being medical examiner
for Barnstable County. It'll work—in fact, it's perfect. Now,
what are you going to say?"

"That we need to talk to her husband about contraband
ivory."

"Be sure to ask where he is."

"Stay out of sight and wait till I get back," he said, taking the badge with him. He didn't look much like a cop,

with his old khaki pants and faded windbreaker, but he had presence; he could always act authoritatively when he had to. I saw him go into the door to the shop, and I pulled the sports coupe around outside the lot behind a copse of birch trees. I put on a canvas fishing hat, pulled it down low, put on sunglasses, and ambled back into the lot, pretending to look at boats.

Laitis wasn't in there fifteen minutes before he came back outside, leading Sally by the hand. She was still the lovely, blond athlete I knew, but now she was holding a handkerchief up to her eyes with her free hand. It didn't take a rocket scientist to figure out the situation. They looked around the lot for a few seconds until Roantis spotted me, waving me over.

As I approached, Sally broke free from Roantis's grip and came over to me, hugging me and crying. I was amazed at how hard she was hugging me. A lot of upper-body strength.

"Tell me, Doc, what the hell's going on? I knew something was wrong . . . I could just tell . . . the way Bill's been acting. But I thought . . . I thought it was nothing like this . . . that it would pass. So I didn't ask him . . . didn't say anything."

I patted her back. She held on to me, crying, for a minute or so, then I suggested we go inside for some coffee. In an hour's conversation, the pieces began to fall into place: the near bankruptcy, Bill's depression and drinking over it. The attempt to sell the business, to no avail. And finally, at the darkest hour, Bill's coming up with enough money to keep the business going.

"He said it was a sudden upsurge in business," Sally said, staring into her coffee mug, "but the charter-boat traffic looked the same to me. He said he'd managed to attract wealthier clients, who wanted to stay out several days on the big boat. It didn't take very long for us to pay the bills and get things going again."

"How many nights a month was he gone, on average?" I asked.

"Eight to ten. And like I said, some of these were two- or three-night trips—way out on the banks where the big fish are."

"And you never thought he might be somewhere else?"

She thought a minute before answering. "Well . . . for a while I thought he might be seeing another woman. I suppose that enters every wife's head at some time or another. In a way, I'm relieved to hear this might be something else."

"But, Sally, if it's true, then Bill's in big trouble with the federal government."

She lowered her head, staring at the coffee again. I saw a change in the pretty face. I saw the sadness and fear turn to slow, burning anger. Her eyes hardened. Her jaw came out a little bit in defiance. Her strong hands clutched at the coffee mug so tightly that the tendons stood out on her tan skin.

"What if I help you? Will that help the situation?"

"A whole lot," Roantis interjected. I supposed he was still playing cop. I didn't ask; I wanted Sally on our side in the worst way.

"Assuming he's not really out fishing right now, do you have any idea where your husband could be?" I asked.

"Oh, but he *is* out fishing; the big boat's gone."

"We know," said Roantis. "But tell us, did you actually see him leave on the boat?"

"Oh no. They leave about four in the morning."

"Where's the Chevy van?"

"Why, it should be outside in the lot."

"We didn't see it."

She went and looked out the window. "That's strange. Maybe Pete took it."

"Who's Pete?"

"Pete O'Mara. He works with Bill."

"For how long?"

"About four months. Other than that, I don't know much about him, but he seems to be Bill's right-hand man now. He goes out with him on the boats and helps book party cruises, too."

"Sally, we have reason to think that maybe Bill has taken Mary and her coworker."

"Taken her? What do you mean, taken her?"

"Kidnapped her. Taken her hostage. Abducted her."

Sally Bedford folded her arms across her chest. "No, he

wouldn't do that, Doc. He may be into something crooked, but he's not mean."

"Sometimes, Sally, when you mix with the wrong people, you do things you wouldn't usually do," said Roantis. "We've been told that Mary is in trouble. This person did not say what kind of trouble, but added that she might be 'up north.' Do you have any idea what this person meant by this?"

"Up north? Well, we have a fishing cabin on a lake in Maine. It's been in Bill's family for a long time. That's the only place I can think of offhand."

"Could he get there by boat?" I asked.

"It's inland, up near Farmington. A little lake called Crescent Lake."

"So he would drive there?"

"A few times he's taken the boat and put in at Kittery or other harbors on the Maine coast, then rented a car and driven the rest of the way up. But driving's the quickest. Except for flying in."

"Can you draw us a map of exactly where this cabin is?" I asked.

"Why don't I just go with you? I'll feel better and so will you."

"How so?" I asked.

"Because how do you know I won't call and warn him once you're started?" Her blue eyes flashed. Was it in defiance, anger, fear? I didn't know. But there was a strength behind those eyes—a strength and ferocity that could be frightening.

Roantis and I looked at each other.

"And how do I know you two won't hurt Bill?" she said.

"We won't hurt Bill or any of his buddies if he hasn't hurt Mary or Larry."

"Then I think one issue is settled," Sally said, rapping the table with her fingers impatiently. "I'm coming along. That okay with you?"

We found ourselves nodding.

"The cabin's about a six-hour drive from here. But there's a charter service at the Hyannis airport that can have us up there in ninety minutes—if he's not booked."

"Call him," I said.

She went to the back of the store and came back shortly, with that bouncy, athletic walk, looking at her watch. "It's now almost five. Arnie says he can have the Beechcraft fueled and ready by the time we get there. That's about fifteen minutes."

"Let's do it," I said. But Roantis grabbed my arm.

"Be sure now, Doc. After all, he could be on the boat."

"Johnny Ridge said 'up north.' Sally says there's a cabin in Maine. That's the best guess we have. If he's got Mary and Larry with him, how can he get them off and on the boat without anybody noticing? In a closed van, he could take them anywhere. I think they're at the cabin and the boat's absence is a diversion to cover their tracks. Sally, can this Pete O'Mara operate the boat?"

"As well as Bill can."

"Then I bet he's out on the *Bim Bam Boo,* and Bill's headed up to Maine with Mary. Or else, she's already up there."

"It's a small lake, Doc, and a tight community," Sally warned. "You guys will need some cover. I can stay in the background and tell you the layout. The best way to approach the cabin is by the lake. Otherwise, everyone is going to wonder what you're doing sneaking around in the woods. I figure the best thing is to go as fishermen."

"Good thinking," I said. "I guess it's a good thing we left that equipment in the trunk of the car; right, Laitis?"

He nodded, and Sally told us we could take anything else we needed from the store. So in under ten minutes the three of us were headed to the Hyannis airfield in the Subaru, its small trunk brimming with fishing rods, nets, and tackle boxes. Roantis and I were careful not to mention the firearms.

"There's a small fishing lodge at the opposite end of Crescent Lake," Sally explained. "If we get rooms there, they won't recognize me. I'm hoping we can stay there and rent a boat. That way, you can go up close to the opposite shore where the cabin is, trolling and casting, and maybe see what's going on. I might want to go with you."

"If you don't mind the question," said Roantis, in a deadpan tone. "Why are you so anxious to help out? That's your husband involved, you know."

She turned to him and her eyes grew icy again. It was a look that made me uneasy. This woman could be capable of violence if pushed too far.

"Some strange things have been going on lately. Every time something out of place happened, I would try to ignore it, focusing on the increased money that was keeping us afloat. So there I was, stuck in the store all day, and almost all night, while Bill and his buddies were out there fishing, or doing God knows what. Now that you've told me this—especially about the ivory thing—well, I've *had* it! Something inside me just snapped."

"So you want to be in on the whole thing? It may be dangerous. If Doc senses his wife is in danger, he could get mean." Roantis sounded like a cop. I wondered if or when he was going to tell Sally his real identity.

"If there's another woman involved in this—besides Mary—then Doc's going to be the second meanest person in on this thing, if you get my meaning."

We said no more. The Hyannis Municipal Airport, located just north of town, was a small, three-runway facility, mostly for private planes and some commercial flights to the Cape and the islands of Nantucket and Martha's Vineyard. Almost directly under the red wind sock stood Arnie. He was wearing a dark blue jumpsuit and had iron-gray hair cut short, a mustache, and aviator glasses. The perfect image of a charter pilot. Behind him on the tarmac sat a white twin-engine turboprop plane with small round windows.

"Beech King Air," said Roantis under his breath. "Nice equipment."

"How do you know?" I asked.

"I been in them. The army version is called the U-21. They're comfortable and fast."

"Hey, Arnie!" said Sally between clenched teeth. She went over and threw her arm around him, drawing him close. "How's business?"

"Slow, Sally. Slow."

"Well, we're here to help out. How long to Farmington?"

"In this ship, under an hour."

"Well let's go. This is Doc Adams and Lieutenant what's-his-name. Can't pronounce it."

"Smith," said Roantis, smiling as he boarded the plane. I followed. Inside was nice, with six plush seats for passengers. The interior was dark and elegant, and so quiet you could scarcely hear the big jet engines rev up. In a few minutes we were airborne, heading north. Roantis lighted a cigarette and looked out the window at the ocean, then the coast of Maine. Sally scarcely said anything. She sat in the copilot's seat, her jaw set tight. I could tell she was as troubled as I was.

34

"THERE IT IS. SEE THE CRESCENT SHAPE?" SALLY POINTED OUT the window, and Arnie banked the plane in the fading light so we could get a better view. "Our cabin's on the upper end—look, see the dock? You can barely see it sticking out into the water. See it?"

We nodded, and looked closely at all that lay below us.

"Arnie, would you mind making another pass?" asked Roantis, his eyes scanning everything rapidly and intently. We flew on then returned, this time flying over the lake from the north.

"Get ready, Doc—I thought I saw something in the trees about fifty yards from shore, behind where the cabin might be—there! See it?"

"A flash of white—"

"It's the van. I'm sure of it."

"You're right," Sally said. "Good guess, Doc. They're here. Okay, Arnie, put us down."

We banked away toward the airfield. I heard Sally say under her breath, "That son of a bitch . . . that sneaky son of a bitch . . ."

The airfield was so small there was no car-rental place, so we got a ride into town and picked up a Ford Taurus wagon. We piled the gear in back. Sally didn't even blink at the two long gun cases. Perhaps that was from a lifetime of being in the sportsman business. We called the fishing lodge from the car-rental office and reserved two rooms, a double and a single, then headed out of Farmington for Spooner's Crescent Lake Lodge. I wished Brady was with me—he'd just love this. And he'd know the best places to fish, too, even though he'd never seen this lake before.

We followed Highway 156 northwest out of Farmington for two or three miles, then turned left on a gravel road, which we followed for the same distance until it ended in a T at the lake. It was a pretty lake, about a mile across, but extending in long arms in each sideways direction. A long, narrow crescent-shaped lake, like a sliver of moon.

"Turn left here," Sally said. "The lodge is less than a mile up, on the right, smack on the shore, facing the sunset. If you turn right, it'll take us to the cabin."

"How many cabins on this lake?" asked Roantis, scanning the opposite shoreline through his binoculars. "I don't see many."

"There aren't many. I'd say maybe thirty or forty, and they're spread out."

"Any cabins near yours?" he asked.

"Nope. The nearest neighbor is more than a mile away."

Spooner's Lodge was a rustic log building. The logs were peeled and varnished, expertly joined, notched, and mortared, and the roof was dark green rolled shingle. The ends of the logs, where they stuck out the corners, were painted alternating white and green. I've seen a lot of northern fishing lodges; ninety percent of them look like this. I love them, and wished I were simply here to fish. The electric feeling in the pit of my stomach told me otherwise. The adrenaline rush that was hopefully going to carry me through the next day or two was beginning.

Hell, who was I kidding? It had started days and days

ago, when Mary disappeared, and never really left. The queasy, quaky feeling simply ebbed and flowed, like a sick tide.

Mr. Spooner, a kindly gentleman in his sixties wearing a blue shirt, bow tie, and a plaid vest and granny glasses, greeted us warmly. I signed in while Sally and Laitis each took a key and went to find the rooms.

"Fine, Dr. Adams. Now, I assume you'll want a boat for tomorrow?"

"Yes. With a motor."

"They all come with motors. I'll reserve number eight for you. It's the Peterborough boat with the Johnson motor at the far end of the dock."

"Great. Thanks."

"Will you be needing licenses?"

"Oh yeah. Forgot. We'll take three."

I paid for the licenses and picked up my bags.

"Dinner's being served until seven-thirty. That's not long. If you want, I'll have them hold three dinners for you even after they close."

I thanked him and went to find our room. I had a hunch Roantis wouldn't be there—he'd be at the bar. I had a key numbered 21. At the far end of the hall were two rooms: 21 and 22. I pushed the key into 21 and opened the door.

Sally Bedford was standing there. At the foot of the big double bed.

In her undies.

"Oh, hiya, Doc. Gee, isn't this a neat place?" She made no move to put on the robe that was lying on the bed. She just smoothed out the bedspread, smiling at me. She was tan all over, and in fantastic shape. A blonde with a deep tan is one of nature's wonders. And seeing one smoothing out a big double bed in her bra and panties was, well, something. . . .

"Sorry, wrong room," I said, and backed out. She stood upright fast, stamping her bare feet. She jiggled a little in exactly the right places, then hopped over to the door, grabbing my arm and pulling me inside.

"Hold on a sec, Doc. Uh . . . you didn't get the wrong room. See, I thought it would look better if they thought you and I were married. Don't you think?"

I could smell her. I put my hand down on her silky forearm. Felt the firm muscles underneath.

"No," I said. "And not because I'm not attracted to the idea. It's just that I've been through too much lately and I'm just . . . worn-out."

I turned about-face, ready to leave the room, but she held on tight to me, turning me around and putting her arms around my neck.

"Doc, please don't go! I'm so scared and alone! Please stay and just hold me? Please? Just hold me a little. . . ."

"I wouldn't just hold you, Sally, and we both know it."

She hugged me then, kissing me on the neck and rubbing my back. "Well then, whatever. Whatever happens, happens. . . ."

"Oh no. Too much has happened lately, Sally. Sorry . . ." I went out the door and down the hall, knocking on the door of number 22. Roantis opened it. He, too, was in his undies. In his hand he held a pint of whiskey. I took the bottle and took a swig. It felt good. I took another.

"Thought you weren't going to drink until you found Mary."

"I'm assuming she's up here. That's close enough." I shut the door and sat down on the bed.

"You're on my bed," he said. I looked around the room. The small, single bed was the only one in the room.

"No, Laitis. This is my bed. Why don't you go in there and stay with her?"

"Fine. Suits me." He put on his pants and shirt and left, taking the bottle with him. I stretched out on the bed, pondering women. Why was Sally so cozy all of a sudden? There were several explanations. One was that she'd discovered her husband was doing things secret and illegal behind her back. That would make her want to get back at him. Secondly, she probably was telling the truth about one thing anyway: she was lonely and scared, and it would feel good to have somebody warm holding you in the dark. I knew about this, too.

Hell, all it meant was that Sally was wounded and afraid, and vulnerable. And lonely. I couldn't get the vision of that gorgeous tan body out of my head. The smell of her.

A knock came at my door. I went and opened it. It was

Sally. She had gotten dressed—changed her clothes. Now she was wearing a wool skirt and sweater. Still looked great. But she was not in a good mood. I could tell this by the way she folded her arms over her chest and glared at me.

"For your information, *Doctor* Adams ... I am *not* a tramp!"

Now, what the hell brought this on?

"I don't recall ever saying you were—"

"Oh yeah? Well, then why did you send your gorilla friend to take your place, huh? So I'm not good enough for you? Is that it? So you think I'm just a horny slut who wants a guy? *Is that it?*"

Her bright blue eyes bored into me. All I wanted was a good meal and a good night's sleep. Why was this happening?

"Look, Sally. I didn't mean to insult you. I just thought that Laitis and I would stay in the double and you would stay in the single, that's all."

"So you'd rather stay with him?" She sounded hurt. I did not understand this at all.

"Yes, I would. To avoid ... complications."

"I mean, do you want to stay in the same bed with him?"

"Hell no. Oh, that's right—there's only one bed in there—"

"Wouldn't you rather stay in there ... with me?"

"Yes, but that's not the point."

She folded the arms again. Somehow, without moving her feet, she was closer to me now. I don't know how they do that. Women move like cats. I remember those *National Geographic* films. They had one showing a female leopard. Killing machine if there ever was one. The first shot, she's in the tree. Fine. Next thing you know, she'd be on the ground with an antelope in her jaws. She's got the poor thing by the neck. Shakes the animal twice and it goes limp. It's sad and brutal but, what the hell, that's the way it is in the wild. Fine. Then, next thing you know, she's back in the tree with the dead antelope. And you never saw her move. What the hell is this? How do they do that?

Whatever it is: *look out!*

"Well, what's it going to be?" she said.

"I don't know; I just want to get to sleep."

"Fine." She took me by the hand and we went over to room 21. Sally peeked her delicate little head into the dark room.

"Hey, Lieutenant Smith, or whatever your name really is, listen up. Doc and I are staying in here. You go back to your room, okay?"

"No."

It was a gruff reply, full of menace.

Sally turned to me. "Make him leave."

"I can't."

"Why not?"

"Because he'll kick us to death."

"Oh, come on! He's a little guy—"

Inwardly trembling, I grabbed Sally and led her down the hall.

"Can we talk?"

"What's the matter?"

"You could get us killed, is what's the matter. Laitis Roantis is a dangerous man. Listen—I'm just going to sleep in the lobby. There's a nice couch there, and I'm going to sleep there after we eat."

"I'm not hungry. I'm ... sleepy...." She laid her head on my shoulder, put her arms around me, and began a slow waltz.

Who needs this? I thought. I unhinged her and went into the dining room. She followed me there, and we ate two of the three dinners they had saved for us. The reheated pork chops, baked potato, and iceberg-lettuce salad with bottled dressing was—shall we say—sufficient. But I wouldn't push it beyond that.

Sally had three Manhattans with her dinner. Oh-oh—

"Doc, you do whatever you want. I'll be in there, waiting for you."

"Sally? Are you being this way because you're mad at Bill? And maybe hurt?"

She sat there for half a minute before her eyes crinkled up and poured. "That son of a bitch! Oh, what a fool I've been. All this time I thought things were getting better—"

I walked her to her room—number 22—and told her to get into bed alone. Sleep would come.

"I'll still be waiting, Doc. The door will be unlocked. I won't tell Mary—I wouldn't in a million years."

Great, I thought, and went to the front desk again and asked for another single.

"Why, certainly we have one available. Is there . . . some problem with the rooms you have?"

"Yes. One shy, it seems."

I took the key and went into the bar, which luckily was still open. There was a TV in there, showing some Canadian football game. I couldn't have cared less, but I pretended to watch it anyway so I wouldn't have to talk with the other three patrons. I ordered a scotch and soda. Tasted great. I ambled down the other hall to my new room, number 12, and opened the window wide, letting in the chilly fall air of Maine that smelled of pine. Hell, in interior Maine, everything smells of pine. I put three heavy wool blankets on the bed, crawled between the cold sheets, and began to drift off.

Peace . . .

No, wait a minute! There wasn't any peace. I was thinking about women. *Women!* God, I prayed, if I ever get out of this one, I'm going to check into the nearest monastery.

This must have been the correct vow to make, because soon I was asleep.

35

I WOKE UP IN THE DARK AND GOT OUT OF BED. I PACED AROUND the small room nervously after I got dressed; I knew I couldn't sleep anymore. It was almost five. I went down the hall and knocked on room 22. Was Laitis in there, or Sally? Or were they in one of the rooms together? Who knew? Who cared? All I knew was I wanted to get moving. Real fishermen get out on the water at dawn, and I wanted to give all appearances of real fishermen.

Laitis answered the door. He, too, was dressed, which didn't surprise me. Old soldiers, in my experience, always get up early.

"How do you feel?"

"Fine," he said. "All ready to go. I feel great. Let's get some coffee."

"First, let's put the long guns into the boat they've reserved for us. We should do it while it's still dark out, and cover them with ponchos. They're going to wonder why fishermen are packing artillery."

We went out to the car and toted our gear to the boat, placing the long guns, my 30-06 and Roantis's M-16, in the very bottom of the boat, under the thwarts, and put the waterproof fishing ponchos over them. The rods and tackle boxes came next. I went inside to see if there was anything to eat. The restaurant was open, as one would expect at a fishing lodge. I could smell bacon and eggs. Roantis went to wake Sally, who soon joined us in a big breakfast.

"Stoke up," I said. "It'll be cool out on that lake."

"What I thought was, I'll go with you guys now and show you where everything is," Sally said. "But I don't really want to sit in a boat all day."

"That's fine; you can stay here during the afternoon run and read a book if you want." I shoved a white-paper place mat in her direction. "Can you draw us a rough map of the cabin and the road leading to it? Where the doors and windows are?"

She drew the map and we studied it. Roantis pointed to the spot that corresponded to where we'd seen the white van from the air. "Is there some cover between the van and the cabin? I mean, if we get to the van and wait there, can we be easily seen from the house?"

Sally thought for a second. "It would be very hard to see you. There's a grove of pine and hemlock here, at the bend in the driveway."

"Good. That may be our best bet—sneak up on the van and wait in those trees until somebody comes out to the vehicle. Then we can jump him, take the keys, and drive off with him in the back."

"What good will that do?" I asked. "We're after Mary and Larry, not the van."

"If we get one of them in the van and drive off with him, he won't be missed. The people inside will assume he's off running an errand. We can drive to a deserted place and make him talk."

"How will you make him talk?" Sally asked. Her face showed worry.

"I can do it. We'll find out exactly what the layout is, and the routine. Find out how many there are inside, and if they're armed. That way, we'll know the best way to get inside."

"Do you . . . think anybody could get hurt?"

"A possibility," Roantis said. "A distinct possibility. But I got a hunch it's not going to be us."

Sally couldn't hide her fear.

"I . . . didn't think it was going to be this rough. I mean, shouldn't we maybe just call the police?"

Roantis shook his head. "That could make them panic and do something bad to Doc's wife, or his friend. If we do it my way, it'll be clean and quick. And if anyone gets hurt, it's likely to be them, not us."

She squirmed in her chair, playing with pieces of scrambled egg with her fork. Her hand was shaking ever so slightly. "I don't want Bill to get hurt or killed. You have to understand that."

"Neither do we, Sally," I said. "We don't want anybody hurt. Therefore, rather than stand outside with a bullhorn the way the cops do, we're going to do it the way Laitis says. Quick and clean. Catch them off guard before they know what's up."

"I don't know. . . ."

"Well, we never thought you'd go with us," said Roantis. "It's best if you stay here."

"And you won't shoot anybody."

"Highly unlikely. And it's unlikely they'll shoot. They haven't committed murder."

"None that we know about, anyway," added Roantis. "Does Bill have a gun?"

"Several."

"Does he carry one usually?"

"No. He's got some hunting rifles and shotguns. He has a couple on the boat. I think he has a handgun in the van, but he doesn't wear one in a holster, if that's what you mean."

"You think this Pete O'Mara might be with him up here?" I asked.

"No. The *Bim Bam Boo* is gone, and somebody's got to be skipper. It's most likely Pete."

"Any chance that Bill is aboard?"

"Sure, but my guess is he's up here."

"This Pete fellow dangerous? Does he know how to fight?" Laitis knew just the questions to ask to get a feel for the mission; I could see his years of experience in action. "Military background?"

She shrugged. "He's not big like Bill. But he's strong. He's short and wiry."

Roantis nodded slowly. "Yeah. That's the kind to worry about. Big guys usually aren't mean. Does he have a temper?"

"Probably, but not like a firecracker. Hell, you guys, I don't know!"

"Take it easy," I said, grabbing her hand. "Let's all go to the john and get out of here. We'll get down to the far end of the lake and pretend we're trolling."

Sally stood up. She brushed the bread crumbs off her sweater and jeans. "Do we have to take the guns? I just hate them. Scared to death of them . . ."

As she walked back to her room Laitis said, "She's lying, Doc. At least about one thing."

"What?"

"The guns. Last night when you were fighting with her and I was supposed to sleep in her room, I got a peek inside her big leather purse. There was an automatic in there. Berretta three-eighty, and the bluing a bit worn. Somebody's used the gun a lot. If it's her, then she isn't at all afraid of guns."

I stared down at the breakfast table, trying to fit the pieces together. This was not a good development.

"Don't you think she was a little eager to come up here with us?" he continued. I nodded.

"So question one," he said in a low voice, "who's the gun for? Is she really mad at Bill? Or is the gun maybe for us? Did she make the fuss about our guns so we maybe wouldn't take them? That way, she'd have the gun and we wouldn't."

"Which would tip the scales heavily."

"Yep. And she could be up here to warn Bedford. Maybe he already knows, and they're all waiting for us. Then we'd have the enemy at our front and back."

"You mean she's in on it?"

"Maybe."

"Then why didn't she just call him from Hyannis and tell him we're coming?"

"Does the cabin have a phone?"

"Don't know. I'll ask."

"Don't—she could lie again. Let's find a phone book."

We went to the front desk where the phone was. Spooner's Lodge had phones only at the desk; the cabins and guest rooms didn't have them. We found no local listing for

Bedford. Still, that didn't tell us much; the number could be unlisted.

"Damn, Laitis. This is going to be trickier than I thought. Should we disarm her?"

He thought for a minute before answering. "Not yet, anyway. If I sense danger, I'll mention 'live bait.' Something about live bait. That will be the signal I'm going to rush her and get the gun, or for you to do it."

"Okay. Good idea."

Sally came back wearing a windbreaker and a big felt hat. The wide hat was a good idea; it would hide her face. Her leather purse hung from a shoulder strap.

"You won't need the purse," said Roantis casually.

"I'll feel better with it; I don't want to leave it in the room."

"Ha! Maniacs don't steal!" I teased.

"Maniac?" asked Roantis, bewildered.

"Yeah, that's a person from Maine. Call them Maniacs. They don't steal."

"Some do; we had our cabin burgled three years ago. C'mon, guys, let's go fishing."

Roantis and I glanced at each other, and we all went down to the dock.

36

We were up at the far end of the lake in short order. The sun was coming up, and the lone cabin at the lake's northern shore was more and more distinct with each passing minute. It was a single-story building made with real peeled and varnished logs, just like Spooner's Lodge. There was a screened porch on one end, a front door in the middle, two sets of windows on each side, and a high sloped roof to keep the thick Maine snow from staying up on top and collapsing the structure. From the front door, a path led down to a wooden dock that jutted out over the water about thirty feet. There was an aluminum runabout boat with an outboard motor hitched there. I wondered if the people inside, whoever they were, were going fishing or if the boat was there merely to provide cover.

Sally pointed her finger at the cabin. "The living room and dining area is to the right, and the two bedrooms to the left," she said, sweeping her hand.

"Don't point, Sally, just tell us," Laitis instructed, "and look at the place only now and then, okay?"

"All right. The kitchen projects off the rear end of the house, and the back door, which we use when coming from the car, is there, too."

"Those are the only two doors?"

"Yep."

"Is there a basement?"

"Uh-huh. See those small wide windows under the logs? It's barely tall enough to stand in, but it helps in the winter. And we put in a furnace eight years ago. It's down there, too."

"If you had to keep two prisoners in there, would the basement be the best place?"

"There, or maybe in the crawlspace attic. There's a trapdoor that leads up to it from the master bedroom."

"Is there a phone in there?" Roantis added this last question casually, as if it were a mere afterthought.

And Sally gave herself away then. She didn't answer, but looked down at the tackle in the boat, scratching her head. Finally she raised her head and said, "You know what's weird? I really can't tell you? I mean, Bill said he was putting a phone in last May. He usually comes up here to fly-fish in May, you know, when the hatches are out? He told me he was planning on putting a phone in, but he never mentioned it when he got back."

"Well, wouldn't you have used the phone in the meantime?" I asked.

"Why? Who would we call when we're both in Massachusetts?"

I squinted at the cabin furtively. Roantis was right: to stare at the place openly invited suspicion if anyone inside saw us. And then, if they had binoculars, they could recognize Sally, and perhaps me as well. Speaking of binoculars, I wished I had a pair so I could look for a phone line.

Then I realized her answer was perfect. If she'd admitted the place had a phone, she would be holding back nothing. If she denied the phone, however, and our subsequent reconnaissance confirmed it, then she would be caught in a lie. Nope, Sally Bedford was a clever gal; the answer she gave us was absolutely indecipherable. I suspected her even more now.

And I had little belief left that she was on our side. I stared at the leather purse resting on the thwart next to her. The big brass zipper was pulled tight; there was no peeking inside. Yet it was next to her on the seat, where she could get the concealed pistol in an instant.

I didn't like it. I didn't like it at all. Roantis held the throttle of the small outboard as we cruised around the end of the lake, trolling two lines. We didn't catch any fish. Not even a nibble. I thought it might be that we had the wrong kind of lures. But Sally said that the landlocked salmon the lake was famous for were up in the rivers spawning—that's why we hadn't gotten a bite.

"You guys forget I'm in the fish business," she said.

We headed back to Spooner's around nine-thirty, still having seen nobody in or around the cabin. From the lake, we couldn't even see if the van was in the driveway. But somebody was inside: light blue smoke rose out of the chimney.

"I'm going back to bed and take a nap, unless there's something you want me to do," she said, climbing up to the lodge dock. We followed her up to the main building. It was getting warm out.

"Can you tell us how to drive to the cabin?" asked Roantis.

"Are you going to . . . go into action?"

"Nope. We just want to check it out from the land side."

"Just follow the road we came in on, only don't turn at the intersection, just go straight."

Laitis and I got into the rental car. Sally poked her head in. "When are you coming back to get me?"

"Don't know. Probably around one or two."

"Fine. I'll either be in my room, or out on the porch if the weather stays warm and sunny."

"What do you think?" he asked me as we drove along.

"I'm stumped, Laitis. From all appearances, she's a straight shooter."

"I like that woman."

"I can tell. But what if she's a traitor?"

"You mean against us, or her husband?" he said. "One way or the other, she's got to betray somebody."

"Which way do you think she'll go?"

"There's no telling. The first thing I want to check out is the phone situation at the cabin."

"Let's do it."

We parked the car on the side of the road and walked toward the cabin in the woods. The leaves had mostly fallen from the hardwood trees, but fortunately, the Maine woods are ninety percent conifers. We had plenty of cover as we sneaked up for a once-over of the cabin's rear side. The van was there. We crept up to it and tried the doors. Locked. But then Laitis went around to the rear and tried the big doors in back. They'd left these open.

"Good," he muttered, and we went on into the little copse of trees and scanned the house.

"Phone line, big as life," he said, pointing to a cable coming out of the trees and connecting to a corner of the log building just under the eaves.

"Isn't that a power line?"

"No; the power line is down further. See it?"

He was right; two big cables came into the side of the cabin farther to the front. "So where does that leave us?"

"Vulnerable. She could be calling them right now. What I'm going to do, I'm going to get inside that van and hide behind the front seat and wait. I bet somebody will want to run an errand before noon. When they come out and get in the van, I'll be waiting."

"You're not going to kill them—"

"Nah. I'll immobilize them. Then you come up fast and get in the driver's seat and drive us away from here. When we get to a deserted place, we'll make them talk."

"I don't know if I like the sound of that."

"You like the sound of seeing Mary again?"

"Well, yeah—"

"Then let's do this my way. I'm pretty good at it. It's my thing. That's why you're paying me three grand."

"Two grand."

"Whatever . . ."

Laitis stuffed his .45 into his belt, took a big strong bandanna out of his hip pocket, oozed over to the van, climbed inside the back, and shut the door with no sound by holding the latch back until the door closed. I had to hand it to him: he seemed to know how to do everything. I stationed myself, at his direction, in the grove of trees that overlooked the cabin. I was to watch the rear of the place, and stand up and wave my arms at the van when I saw anybody come out the back door. When Roantis, who would be watching from the driver's window, waved back, I was to hold up a finger for each person I saw approaching. If it was two or more, I was to draw my gun and be ready in an instant to leap out of the trees behind the men, backing him up. The black nylon holster on my belt held the Smith & Wesson model 66 stainless revolver, loaded with six cartridges topped with 125 grain, jacketed hollow-point bullets, the ultimate manstopper load. Hit a man anywhere except the extremities with this load and he's down. Down for good. I didn't want to shoot, but I was damn-sure ready.

Yes, we'd lied to Sally. Had to.

At eleven-thirty the back door opened and a tall, middle-aged man stepped outside. He had sandy hair and pale skin. He zipped up his light poplin jacket. I saw a ring of keys that he rattled in his hand. I moved to the far end of the copse and waved at the van. I saw a hand in the driver's window flash back. I held up a finger and went back into the trees to watch.

The man, who seemed tired and nervous, his eyes downcast, walked to the van, unlocked the door, and got in. I saw him lean over slightly, putting the ignition key in.

Instantly, the thick bandanna whipped down over his head and around his neck. It pulled back hard and to the side. The man's head disappeared toward the passenger side of the car, and I was running up to the truck. I got inside, grabbing the man's flailing legs and shoving them over. As I turned the key Roantis pulled him over the seat back and into the rear of the van. I could hear the thumping of arms and legs against the floor of the truck, but nothing else.

I backed up, turned around, and headed out of the drive onto the road. We turned left on the road and drove about ten minutes until there was nothing as far as the eye could see in any direction but pine trees and muskeg.

"Look for any way to get off the road a ways," said Roantis through gritted teeth. I could no longer hear the thumping of the man's arms and legs.

I pulled the van off the road where I saw a faint logging road, barely visible, to the right. We went down it a hundred yards to where it curved gently so the white vehicle was invisible from the road. I shut the engine off, put on the brake, and joined Roantis behind the van as he dragged the man out. The bandanna was in the guy's mouth like a bridle bit and fastened around the back of his head. Roantis had fastened the man's arms and legs with his "Ty-tons," those half-inch strips of tough red nylon. They work by inserting the free end into a molded ratchet. When you pull it tight, it doesn't reverse. It's on there; I don't care if you're Superman. And believe me, this guy wasn't. We dragged him over to a big tree and stood him against it.

"Can you hear me?" Roantis asked.

The man nodded, panic shooting out of his wide eyes.

"If you answer all my questions immediately, without hesitating even a second, and if you do exactly as we tell you, we *might* let you live."

The eyes grew wider. Roantis was talking in that low, menacing whisper—the stuff that dreams are made on . . . bad dreams. He took the .45 from his belt and held the muzzle under the man's chin. "If you make any noise when I remove the gag, the top of your head is going to fly off. Clear?"

The man nodded quickly, and Roantis removed the gag.

"What's your name?"

"Steingretz. J-Jason Steingretz."

"Is Mary Adams in there?"

"Yes. She's okay. I swear to God she's okay."

"Who else?"

"B-B-Bill B-Bedford and Pete . . . Pete . . . somebody."

"O'Mara?"

Steingretz nodded quickly again.

"Anybody else?"

"A guy named Carpenter. I think he's a cop."

"Is he okay?"

Another nod.

"Where are these two? Tell me exactly where they are and how they're being kept. Don't stop talking or I'll blow your head off."

"The woman is in the attic with a sleeping bag and some food and a light. She's handcuffed to a rafter beam. The man is in the cellar, handcuffed to a column. They're both fine."

"If Pete's there, too," I asked, "who's skippering the big boat?"

"We . . . we took the boat up to Chatham and berthed her. Pete met us there with the truck."

"Why did you take the boat just twenty miles away?"

"So that Mrs. Bedford would think that Bill was at sea."

"What does she know about this?" asked Roantis.

"Nothing."

"You sure?"

"I, uh, no. But I don't think—"

"Is there a phone in the cabin?"

Nod.

"Has it rung since you've been there?"

"No. Not that I'm aware of."

"Have you been there the whole time?"

"No. I'm the one to run errands."

"Where are you going now?"

"Get food and booze in town."

"Has Bedford made any phone calls from the cabin?"

"Yeah. Lots."

"Where to?"

Steingretz hesitated, looking down at the forest floor. Roantis took the .45 and clipped him a good one on the chin with the muzzle end. The man's knees gave way and he slumped to the ground.

"Don't fuck with us, Steingretz. We'll kill you and dump you in that lake. They'll never even find you."

It was then that Jason Steingretz began to babble and whimper, and peed his pants. Roantis yanked him up by his jacket front and slammed him against the tree.

"This is Dr. Adams. If you can't guess, dipshit, he is Mary's husband. He is not pleased that you took his wife. It's all I can do to keep him from slitting your miserable throat. . . ."

I thought poor Steingretz was going to die of fright. Clearly, though involved in this pirate ring, he was not the leader.

"Dr. Adams is going to ask you a few questions. And you're going to answer them, aren't you?"

Quick nods, and near fainting.

"What's the plan? What does Bedford want with Mary and Larry?"

"Just to . . . just keep them until the deal comes down, then release them. We had . . . had to keep them quiet so the deal would come through. The last deal. Bedford knows . . . it's over with. He's going to . . . going to take the boat down to the Caymans . . . maybe Costa Rica with the money when it happens. . . ."

"How's he planning to release them?"

"He's got a letter to the people who run this fishing lodge on the lake. When we get back to Chatham, he'll drop it in the mail and the people from the lodge will know where to find them. Where . . . the key is "

"The key to the cabin? Where is it?"

"Bedford has it on him."

"The keys to the handcuffs, too?"

"Yes. On him at all times."

"Do they have guns?" Roantis asked.

"Bedford does. We don't."

"Only Bedford has a gun?"

Nod.

"Pistol?"

"Yeah. An automatic."

"On his person?"

"Not usually. Like, on a table near the couch."

I wanted to ask a question. "How did Bedford plan on keeping my wife alive while the three of you sail to Costa Rica?"

"He's got food and water, a chemical toilet, a lamp, and warm blankets for each of them."

"What if the letter he wrote gets lost? Did he think about that?"

"He was . . . going to follow the local news, I think. . . ."

"You *think*. . . ." Suddenly. I wanted to hit the man. But I had a few more questions.

"Who killed James Harold?"

"Who?"

"James Harold, he ran a gift shop down in P-town."

"Never heard of him."

I looked at Roantis. As if taking a cue, Laitis bent over, swung his hand in a wide arc and swatted Steingretz on his kneecap with the .45. He fell down, crying, and we hoisted him up again."

"Refresh your memory?" I asked.

"There's a guy, a big guy . . . Johnny Ridge . . . he did it."

"How?"

"Stabbed him with an ivory carving. Bedford was mad as hell about it, but there was nothing he could do. Harold took a load of our stuff and didn't pay . . . threatened to tell the police where he'd gotten it."

"Will you say this in court? That is, if we don't dump you in the lake?"

"Please don't dump me in the lake. Please. I'm not really a mean person. I've done illegal things to make money, sure. But I've never hurt anyone."

"And this Johnny guy . . . he hurts people?" asked Roantis.

"Yeah . . . he's a big mean guy. The reason I didn't tell you at first is because of what he would do to me . . . you know?"

"Not as bad as what we'll do to you . . . that's a promise," hissed Roantis.

"But I'm thinking, maybe he's gone now. Run out."

"Why you think that?"

"Because Bedford's been trying to get a hold of him, and he can't find him."

There was silence for a few minutes. Then Roantis began to speak.

"Here's what's gonna happen, if you want to save your hide. We're going to drive you back to the cabin, where you will pull up and honk the horn until somebody comes out. Whoever it is, wave him over to the truck, saying something's wrong with the transmission. Say you want him to get inside and take a drive with you. How's that sound?"

Steingretz looked sick. "What's going to happen to me afterward? You're going to kill me, aren't you?"

"No. We have no reason to kill you, especially if you help us get Mary and her friend out safely. You follow?"

"What about Bedford?"

"Depends on him. Entirely. I'll tell you what: you don't help us just the way we say . . . or if you try to warn them, or try anything funny, know what? You're going into that lake."

Steingretz looked down at his feet and tried to spit. But he couldn't; his mouth was too dry. He knew Roantis wasn't kidding.

37

We drove back to Bedford's cabin. I drove while Laitis kept Steingretz company in the back.

The plan was this: As soon as I pulled into the parking spot, Laitis and I would hoist him into the driver's seat, where he could honk the horn and call for help. Of course, we would have to cut the Ty-ton ties around his wrists first. But we felt it was a risk we could take. Steingretz did not impress either of us as the fighting type, and we would keep his legs bound. After he fulfilled his function as bait, we would put him in back again until we could haul him to the cops.

Laitis said it would work like downtown.

But based on our recent escapades, I had my doubts.

We got to the cabin road and I turned off. Seconds later I was guiding the big van into the parking spot on the rough gravel drive. Roantis and I hauled Steingretz into the driver's seat, lowered the window, and got behind him with our pistols pointed at the back of his head: Roantis with a .45, me with a .357 Magnum. Just for added incentive . . .

From where we were, we still couldn't see the cabin. Then Roantis got out and hid in the copse of trees, his gun drawn. Steingretz beeped the horn with shaking arms and hands.

We waited.

He blasted the horn again. We waited. Then a short, wiry man with a balding head appeared, coming toward the truck. He looked up at the driver's window. He couldn't see me because I was in the deep dark of the windowless interior of the truck.

"Pete, something's wrong with this thing; I can't go far or fast. I think the transmission—"

"I better get Bill."

"No, just come over and listen to it."

Pete O'Mara waltzed over to the truck, innocent as a puppy. He bent his head, listening for wrong noises.

Roantis, deadly as a leopard, oozed out of the trees behind him and smacked him on the side of the noggin with his pistol. Pete fell in a heap and Roantis tied him up with those nylon wonder strips. Then he opened the driver's door, refastened Steingretz, and put him in the back, along with O'Mara.

Hey, it was working like downtown. Roantis really knew his stuff. We were just about home free. . . .

Roantis stuck the muzzle of his .45 into O'Mara's mouth. "Want to see the sunrise tomorrow?"

O'Mara stared at him wide-eyed and promptly wet his pants.

"Who belongs to the strange car?" he asked, and withdrew the pistol so O'Mara could talk.

"Bill Bedford's girlfriend."

"What car?" I asked. "I didn't see any car."

"What's her name?"

"Cassie McNally."

"How long have they been . . . friendly?"

"Hey . . . I, uh, don't think I should—*ahhhhhhhhh!*"

Roantis had clipped him on the knee with a big swing of the Colt government model. It got his attention. The van rocked as he writhed around in pain.

"Did you understand the question?"

"About half a year, I think. They were seeing each other when I started working for Bill."

"Well, what about Mrs. Bedford? How does she fit into this picture?"

"I don't think she knows."

"Is there anyone inside besides the two of them?" Roantis asked. I knew he wanted to see what O'Mara would say. He said nothing, just kept glancing over at Steingretz.

"I'm not sure—"

There was another whap. The other knee this time, and O'Mara really began to make noise. Roantis turned him over and pressed his mouth down against the van carpet with all his weight. O'Mara couldn't scream then. Also, he couldn't breathe, but this appeared to be a minor point. Finally, when he was a nice shade of purple, Roantis flipped him over.

"Do you want to answer the questions or will I have to kill you?"

Then O'Mara told us everything. His story jibed precisely with Steingretz's. Roantis then patted Steingretz down and retrieved a key from his jeans. Steingretz confirmed it was the key to the cabin. We got out of the van and shut the doors. The two would keep in there.

"Draw your gun and go around to the front."

I turned, starting to walk through the trees.

"Doc?"

"Yeah?"

"I know you're pissed off right now. Try to hold it in. We can do this thing quickly, without blood. I think it's best that way."

"I agree. What should I do?"

"I'm going to knock on the back door and show my badge, saying I'm a wildlife officer, then barge in. I'm hoping Bedford will answer the door. You come in the front when you hear voices. If it's locked, use this." He handed me the key and I went around to the front of the cabin, ducking under the windows. I waited in the bushes near the front door until I heard Laitis shout, *"Don't move!"*

Then I put the key in the door and went inside.

Roantis was covering Bill Bedford, who was saying something to the effect that this was all some "monstrous mistake." Then he saw me, and his face went ashen.

"Take the keys to the handcuffs out of your pocket. Slowly," Roantis commanded.

Bedford complied right away, like a sheep. Turned out that Big Bill Bedford wasn't so tough inside. Roantis threw me the keys. We made Bedford lie down on his stomach and fastened the Ty-tons on his hands and feet.

"Where's your girlfriend?"

"Upstairs, taking a nap. How did you find us?"

We didn't answer, just went upstairs and opened doors until we found her. She sat up in the bed with a start, wearing only a nightie. She had shoulder-length straight blonde hair that flipped around when she moved her head. She was pretty. And shapely. And young. It was easy to see how Bill Bedford had been taken with her.

"What? What is it? Who are you guys?"

"The cops," said Roantis, yanking her from the bed and leading her downstairs. The nightie, I noticed, was *quite* short. . . .

But I was here to get my wife. . . .

Directly over my head was an elongated door in the ceiling with a rope hanging from it. I pulled the rope, and the door swung down on spring-loaded hinges. A ladder was fastened to the door, which I unfolded. There was a dark, yawning space up there.

"Mary? . . . Mary?"

No answer. I got scared and dashed up the ladder. As soon as my head and shoulders were inside the dark space, a set of big claws raked my face and neck; a woman's fingernails. I ducked back.

"Charlie! Oh my God! *Charlie!*"

I went all the way up the stairs. I could see the dim outline of her face. We stared at each other for a few seconds, not knowing what to say or do.

"You okay, babe?"

She threw an arm around my neck, crying, saying she was sorry for everything. I hugged her for a bit, but she couldn't stop shaking. I had to get her out of that hellhole first. I took the key and unfastened the handcuffs, slipping them in my pocket.

She was so weak and giddy and shaky that she could scarcely make it down the ladder, which was steep, like a stepladder. I had to go first, letting her lean on me. We got to the floor and I held her.

"Oh shit . . . you're bleeding, Charlie," she said in a

hoarse voice. I wiped my face; there was some blood on the handkerchief. "I thought it was that asshole, O'Mara."

"What did he do to you?" I was ready to go out to the truck and beat him to death.

"Nothing. But it sure wasn't from lack of trying. Ohhhhhh, God! And I trusted Bill Bedford . . . you believe it?"

"Yeah, I can believe most anything nowadays. Tell me, does Sally know anything about all this?"

"If she does, it's a mystery to me." She grabbed me around the waist and we went to the stairway. "Have you seen Bill's little honey?"

"Yep. She was just taking a nap in here."

"Well, I don't think Sally knows about her . . . *yet*."

"I've got to go get Larry."

"Where is he? He's not here, is he?"

"They say he's down in the cellar."

"Oh God. They never told me. I thought maybe they killed him. Oh Christ, Charlie, it's been hell!"

I put Mary in an easy chair in the living room, just opposite where Bill and Cassie sat bound on the couch. Roantis was sitting in a chair holding his automatic on them, sipping a cold beer he had snagged from the refrigerator. I went to the cellar door. It was open. I went downstairs and saw a door in the paneling. I opened it and stuck my head in.

"Larry? It's Doc—"

"Doc! Hey, guy! Am I glad to see *you*!"

He tried to come over to me but was stopped. His right arm was shackled to a big water pipe. He yanked at it, and the whole pipe and water heater rocked and swayed. Larry still had the strength of an ox. I saw his face was bruised.

"Yeah, they clubbed me every time I tried to pull loose. The sumbitches—"

I unhitched him, and he rubbed his right wrist, which was raw and bleeding.

"Is Mary okay?"

"Not totally. Not yet. She will be soon, though. How long have they had you shackled like this?"

"This is the twelfth day. Whew! Do I stink!"

"Let's go on up." I wanted very much to see Mary's expression when Larry came into the room. When he did, she looked up, beaming through her tears.

Then I saw she wasn't even looking at Larry. She was looking at me.

"Well, well," said Roantis with a grin. "Are we all here? Is everybody ready to go home now?"

"Have you called the police?" I asked.

"Nah. Just getting ready to. Now that everybody's present and accounted for, I can do it. If anybody had been hurt, I wouldn't call the police, Doc. I would probably have put all of them in the lake. Except maybe for cutie-pie over there. . . ."

He was looking, of course, at Cassie, who grew red in the face as she tried to pull her nightie down around her thighs.

Roantis walked over to the phone and lifted the receiver. He turned to me.

"It's dead."

We all looked at each other. "How long has the line been dead?" I directed the question at Bill.

"Far as I know it's working."

"Was it working this morning?"

"Yes. We called a store in town."

"Well, maybe we just better get this crew into the van. Doc, why don't you take your bunch in what's-her-name's car? I'll drive the van to the police station and meet you at the lodge."

This sounded practical. Cassie told me her keys were upstairs in her blue jeans. Could she go upstairs and get them?

"Not on your life," I said. "Mr. Roantis and I have had enough trouble to last us for the next ten years. I'll go up and get them for you."

I was just starting up the stairs when I saw something out on the lake out of the corner of my eye.

It was a motorboat, heading right for our dock. I squinted and recognized the person in the boat. I turned to face the people in the room.

"Speaking of trouble," I said, "guess who's coming for lunch?"

38

Sally Bedford brought the boat up to the dock slick as a whistle. She obviously knew boats. She obviously didn't know what was about to greet her eyes when she opened the door to her cabin.

Mary came over to my side and put her arm around my waist. Felt like a million bucks. Then she saw Sally walking up the dock in her red parka.

"Uh-oh. Looks like the shit's gonna hit the fan," she said.

"Here comes your wife, Bill," said Roantis. He, too, was looking out the window.

"Oh, God! Get her out of here!" he said, staring terrified at Cassie and trying to wriggle off the couch.

"Thanks a lot!" piped Cassie. "That's all the gratitude I get?"

"This is going to serve you right, Bill." Mary was talking at him through clenched teeth.

"You're lucky, Bill; at least she doesn't have her handbag with her," I observed, opening the door for Sally.

"Hey! Where the hell have you guys been? I thought you were coming back to get me."

"We were. We just had to wrap up some loose ends first. Like this one—"

I drew Mary toward the door. She and Sally stared at each other for a second, then embraced. Sally kept murmuring, "I'm so sorry . . . so damn sorry. . . ."

She was hugging Mary, but her eyes could see past her into the room. They fastened on Cassie, who was desperately trying her damnedest to look respectable. But that's rather difficult to do when you're wearing nothing but a semi-transparent baby-doll nightie.

"What the hell is *that*?" she spat.

"You better ask your husband, dear," Mary whispered. Her voice was full of sympathy, and it seemed to inflame Sally even more. She walked across the room toward Bedford, her eyes slits, her mouth turned down in a sour look, her breath coming in little fast jerks. Bedford was transfixed; he didn't, couldn't, move.

"I'm sorry," he managed to say.

"Sorry? You're . . . *sorry*? That's all you can fucking say after all you've done? *Sorry?*"

She dropped her right hand into the deep pocket of the parka. When Roantis saw this he lunged for her.

But he was too late. The little auto came out in her hand, and then instantly Sally had it up in both hands, spitting flame and lead at the big man frozen on the couch. She had practiced with that pistol; it was obvious. Roantis and Larry knocked her arms down and the gun clattered to the varnished floor. Sally collapsed on top of it, sobbing.

Bedford was jerking and gurgling on the couch. His eyes were open, but he wasn't seeing anything. There were three red holes in the middle of his chest, so close together you could cover all three with the lid of a coffee can. He jerked a second or two longer, then sank down limp. He leaned over on his side, spilling blood on Cassie and her nightie, then rolled off the couch onto the floor. As he rolled over I saw that a lot of his back was gone. Hollow-point bullets do that.

Roantis and Larry carried Sally upstairs. Cassie jumped off the couch, hysterical. She screamed and moaned, covering her face with her bound hands and doing a crazy jig-step dance around the room. I went over and grabbed her. Then I cut off her Ty-tons with my pocketknife and took her into the kitchen.

Mary followed me in, looking down at the trembling girl. Her face changed from anger to pity.

"Charlie, I think one hysterical woman in here is enough.

What do you think if I go up and get her clothes and keys and let her leave?"

"Don't think so. For one thing, she shouldn't try to drive in this condition. Also, she may be needed as a witness."

"Well, I'm going up and get her things anyway. She's a dope, but she's not a criminal."

When Mary came back with Cassie's clothes and car keys, I asked her how Sally was doing.

"Still crying. She should cry herself out before we leave. That's what I think. Have you looked at Bill?"

"Don't need to."

She leaned close to me. "Will it be murder, then?"

"Not first degree. I'll testify to that."

Mary handed Cassie her car keys.

"Get in your car and get out of here," she said.

I sat down at the kitchen table and brought Mary over to sit on my lap. I didn't mind that we were letting Cassie get away. I had the feeling that if we needed her, she wouldn't be that hard to find. Mary put her arms around my neck and we just sat there. Boy, did it feel good, just having her there.

"Thanks for rescuing me."

"Aw, it was nothing."

"Should we call the police?"

"Good idea." I went over to the phone. Still no dial tone. I told Mary to wait in the kitchen while I went outside and checked the lines.

I went out the back door and around the corner, almost bumping into Cassie's generous chest. She had a stout forearm around her throat. Behind her was a blondish man with a thick neck and a crew cut. I had seen him before, not too long ago, but could not remember where. The man's other hand held a revolver, which was pressed to Cassie's head.

"Bring the pretty boy out here," the man said.

"You mean Larry?"

"Yeah. Bring him out here or the girl gets it. You can't call for help; I took care of that."

Then it was this man who'd cut the phone line. Behind and above him, I could see the cut wire hanging down from the cabin eaves, swinging in the wind. Where was it I had seen him before?

"Get going," he said, jerking his arm tighter around Cassie's neck.

I went back inside. Mary, Laitis, Larry, and Sally were all in the main room, looking down at Bill Bedford's body. I explained what had happened.

"Who is he, and why does he want Larry?" Mary asked. And it was then that I remembered where I'd seen the stocky man with the short blond crew cut: in the parking lot outside the Dory, where Larry was staying. He was the guy who had leaned out of the white car, perhaps to take a picture, and followed the woman as she drove away in her Mercedes. But somehow I didn't want Mary and the others to know this. I took Larry aside and told him who the man was. He nodded, stroking his chin in thought.

"Well, I guess I better go," he said finally.

"Why? He could kill you."

"No. Not after all of you have seen him. I think he wants to put some kind of pressure on me, or on . . . her."

"You mean the wife?"

"Yeah. Make her quit coming around. Which would make me happier anyway."

"You don't think he'll hurt you?"

"Why? He didn't the time before, did he? No, he won't hurt me, especially if you all look out the window and get a good look at him, and he knows you've seen him."

When we told this to Laitis, he wasn't pleased.

"I say we rush him. Larry, with Sally's gun that makes three armed men against one. We'll take him out easy."

But Larry wouldn't agree to this, saying that the girl might get hurt or killed. "There's been too much violence already, and this is something, uh, from my past that I have to straighten out. I'm sure I'll be right back."

And he went outside. We all gathered in front of the window. Larry turned and the man with the gun on Cassie turned, too, seeing us watching him. They walked to the dock and stopped, and the man made Larry turn around while he fastened his hands with handcuffs behind his back. I didn't like this development, and neither did Laitis.

"Get ready to move out, Doc. Sally, did you touch anything in the bottom of the boat?" He turned to face Sally, who was sitting in a cane rocker, staring at her late husband

and shaking her head slowly, big tears rolling down her tan cheeks. "Sally?"

But there was nothing from her.

"Well, let's hope he takes the nearest boat, then. There are rifles in ours."

The three of them got into Bedford's runabout, started the engine, and headed across the lake. When the boat was about a hundred yards offshore, we saw the man pitch Cassie overboard, and Roantis and I sprinted for the dock. I heard Mary screaming at me; I yelled over my shoulder for her to watch after Sally, and we ran for the boat.

It started with two yanks of the cord, and I throttled up while Laitis hunched in the bow. Poor Cassie, obviously scared to death and freezing, was thrashing her arms and screaming. When we got close I eased off on the throttle and Roantis steered me by hand signals, then reached down and grabbed her arm and flung her into the bottom of the boat like a big halibut. Then he put one of the wool coats on her and sat her down low. She went into a fetal position, crying, spitting, and shaking.

When we rounded the wide bend in Crescent Lake, we could see the boat ahead of us. It seemed we were the only two boats on the entire lake this late in the year. We couldn't gain on them, even with the outboard cranked up all the way. But we weren't falling behind, either. I knew the man could see us now, and no doubt he wished he had towed our boat out a ways, then let it drift. But he hadn't, and we were on his tail.

Laitis took my scoped 30-06 and jacked a round into the chamber.

"Careful," I yelled at him over the whine of the engine and the slap of the waves, "don't hit Larry!"

Laitis leaned forward from the bow thwart and rested his forearms on the boat's bow. I ducked down, too, so we offered little wind resistance and presented a low target profile. If all he had was a handgun—and that seemed to be the case—we had a big advantage with a scoped, high-powered rifle. And an expert professional soldier handling it.

Then I noticed something else: we were gaining. Slowly and steadily, we were drawing closer to them. I could now clearly see the man at the motor, steering with one hand and covering Larry, who was handcuffed in the bow, with the gun in his free hand.

Then I heard the rifle crack and saw the man flung forward, trying to grab at his back. Also, I thought I saw something fall into the water.

"You see that? He dropped his gun! Ha! We got him now!" Roantis was ecstatic, working the bolt fast, spinning out the hot empty brass casing and jacking in a new round. The rifle cracked again. I heard a distant thump come from the boat. A miss, but the man had been hit high on the shoulder: there was a growing patch of crimson on his yellow windbreaker.

With the second shot, the thug realized he was in deep trouble. He lurched to the bow, grabbed Larry, and made him take the stern seat and steer. This was awkward, but Larry managed it. Did the kidnapper have the revolver, or not? We couldn't see it. Laitis looked through the nine-power scope.

"Shit! I can't see him anymore, Doc, he's hiding behind Larry."

"Well, don't shoot then."

"I wish Larry would make a sharp turn—then I could get him—"

As if reading our thoughts, Larry, who always had a brain to match his body, swung the tiller over, and the boat made a sharp, leaning turn to port. Now we could see them both clearly. Roantis fired, and I saw bright shreds of aluminum fly up near the boat's bow. The man did not return fire. He knew now he'd had it.

And we were still gaining.

But then he showed that he had some brains, too. Even if it meant killing.

I saw him rise awkwardly and approach Larry. He bent down for an instant—I thought he had lost his balance and fallen. But he came up holding a fish billy in his hand. Larry tried to kick out with his feet, but the man, though wounded, was desperate now, and fast. He swung the club, hitting Larry on the head. Larry went limp, but before he could collapse into the boat, the man had him around the middle and heaved him over the side.

What happened in the next couple of minutes is still fuzzy in my memory, partly because I was in shock during a lot of it. At least that's what Roantis told me later. I remember screaming when I saw Larry go into the water. Unconscious, hands shackled behind him, and the water maybe fifty degrees, I knew he was a dead man.

And no matter what I had been through the past few weeks, and no matter what my suspicions were concerning him and Mary, I didn't want to see my friend Larry die.

39

ROANTIS SAID NOTHING AS THE BOAT, NOW LIGHTER, SPED away. I couldn't see him; I was watching the spot in the water where Larry had gone under. Out of the corner of my eye I saw him raise the rifle. My eyes stayed fixed on the spot in the water. Even as the speeding boat's wake covered the spot in a white filigree of foam and waves, my eyes never left it. As we approached it I took three of the deepest breaths I could, then dove in headfirst, kicking hard toward the bottom.

I was pumping a lot of adrenaline, but still was unprepared for the massive shock of the frigid water. It made me want to catch my breath, but I fought it. I swam down, cursing myself for not removing my boots first. I was dressed in wool for fall, and it soaked up water like a sponge. I went down, down. All I could see was cold, black dark.

Death . . .

I was on the point of turning back—my lungs were bursting, and I could feel my pulse in my neck and head. My ears rang with it.

Then I saw a silvery glint. A fish, I thought at first. But then, as I came nearer, recognized the handcuffs, and the big form attached, gliding downward with a stream of small bubbles coming from its mouth.

I put my hands on his hips and began frantically pumping my legs, trying to kick my way to the surface.

It wasn't working. My legs were heavy with shoes and thick pants, but the real reason was Larry, as I discovered afterward. For one thing, his lungs were almost empty by the time I reached him, so he had lost his natural buoyancy. But Larry Carpenter was much heavier in the water than an average man; he was all muscle.

I got him almost to the top; I saw the silvery sheet of the surface a few feet above, but I couldn't keep it up, I let him go and went up for air. Several big breaths, and shouting for Laitis, who was nowhere around. Then I realized he hadn't seen me go over.

I dove under again, chasing that heavy, descending hulk in clothes. I grabbed onto him once more, and again tried to kick to the top. I was on the verge of giving up for the second time when I saw something that gave me hope, and strength: a boat above, with a pole sticking down into the water at me: an oar. It was only a few feet up . . . I kicked and kicked, praying just for the strength for those last three feet. Then the oar came much lower, and I saw the wobbly shape of a man leaning over, thrusting the oar still farther down. I grabbed it in one hand. And then the man straightened up, carrying us to the top.

I grabbed the transom of the boat, gasping and spitting, the world going dim—loud pounding sounds in my head. . . .

Roantis took hold of Larry's shirt and hoisted him half out of the water, then grabbed his belt and pulled him in. It took a while, and we almost capsized. Then it was my turn. I pumped my arms and legs, but they were spastic and feeble as an infant's.

The last thing I remember was lying in the bottom of the boat, with poor Cassie McNally, while Laitis was holding

Larry halfway upside down, squeezing him in a bear hug to get the water out of him.

I woke up at Spooner's boat dock. Cassie was helping me out of the boat. I was shaking so much from the cold I could hardly stand. Roantis was holding Larry under the armpits. He was awake now and breathing roughly, sometimes still coughing and spitting. They dragged us up the dock and put us in front of the fireplace, which was blazing hot. I fell asleep for a while again. When I woke up, Mary was there, sitting on the braided rug next to me. Larry was waking up, still woozy and sick. But we recovered fast, and each had a cup of clam chowder.

Then the police came and talked with us. They had Sally with them; she appeared calm now. Mary and I went with her when she got into the cruiser. I noticed another cruiser nearby, with Steingretz and O'Mara in the backseat.

I leaned over to Mary and whispered, "What have they done with Bill?"

"He's on his way to the county morgue. Sally's holding up well, don't you think?"

"I guess so."

"I promised her we'd stay up here and be with her for the next several days. That okay?"

"I guess."

"Charlie, you saved Larry's life. You almost died doing it."

"I guess so."

She hugged me. "You're still tired, aren't you? Let's go back inside to your room; we can put you in bed with an electric blanket."

"Sounds good to me. What will happen to Cassie?"

"Not much, they tell me."

Then we heard Roantis calling. We went back to the lodge building, where he dragged us through the hallway to the back door, then led us out to the dock. He pointed at a motorboat making a wide circle in the middle of the lake. We could hear the faint drone of the outboard in low revs. The boat had nobody in it. Then Larry came out on the dock to join us. He looked pale and weak, for once in his life.

"What is it?" he asked.

Roantis pointed again. "Your friend who tried to kidnap you. He's still in the boat. Look—it's coming our way."

The boat, as all boats do when not steered, had gone into a wide, circular course. It had been doing slow loops in the lake for the past forty minutes. But each loop brought it closer to shore. Finally it ran aground on a low, gravelly point a few hundred yards north of the lodge. We walked down the road and through the woods, coming down to the shore to have a look.

The boat groaned in the shallows, oozing blue exhaust. The man lay crumpled in the bow, big red spots all over the yellow windbreaker.

40

"I JUST WANT TO TELL YOU AGAIN, DOC; I JUST WANT YOU TO understand—nothing intimate transpired between us."

I nodded, biting into my English muffin. "Good. But let's not dwell on it, okay? I think it all turned out for the best. It's a good thing neither of you was killed. I'm still pissed at Brad Taylor and company."

"Also, I want to thank you again for saving me up there. It's hard to thank someone for that. Nothing is ever enough."

I waved him off. "It wasn't a decision, Larry. It was just instinct. The only mistakes I made were not taking off my shoes first, and forgetting how damn cold the water was."

He almost laughed. "So, if you'd known the water was freezing, you wouldn't have dived in after me?"

"Who the hell knows? Let's just let it ride. By the way, have you had any ... fallout from the person-on-high who sent the thug after you?"

He shook his head. "He knows I could reveal him. I've talked to Margaret; she sneaked away and called me. She says he's scared to death, especially with the elections coming up."

"Ah! So he's a public figure, eh?"

"I shouldn't have said anything," he said, waving his hands sideways and grabbing his coffee mug. "But I told her I wouldn't do anything if he didn't. So I think that ends it."

"The police will investigate."

"I'll just tell them I don't have any idea who the guy was, or who sent him. Let them figure it out."

We were sitting in the breakfast nook of our kitchen in Concord. Mary and Joe had gone out to shop. It was a week after the incident at the lake in Maine. I thought at first, when we got back to Concord, that there were all kinds of questions I wanted to ask Larry—not just about his time with Mary, but about the stuff Joe uncovered about his supposed criminal activity in New York. But why? What would all that prove? It was just good that we were all back, safe and sound.

Sally Bedford was out on bail, trial pending. The smart money—as in Detective Lieutenant Joe Brindelli—was saying she would get off light, maybe even walk, with probation. They let poor little Cassie McNally off the hook, as we figured they would. All sources confirmed she didn't know a thing about the pirate trade. Matter of fact, they said, she didn't seem to know much about anything except those slinky baby-doll nighties.

The main source was Jason Steingretz. After first vehemently denying any connection with Bedford, Sam Ho, Johnny Ridge, the Sea Feast warehouse, and the others, he found himself in a tight corner and spilled everything. Shortly after this debriefing, the Coast Guard intercepted the *Nokuma Maru,* a Japanese long-liner, off Portsmouth, New Hampshire, near the Isles of Shoals, and found a big cargo of elephant and walrus ivory. This helped Steingretz in the eyes of the law, but he was still going away for a few years. "Or at least a month or two, which is hard time nowadays," Joe remarked cynically.

Pete O'Mara got off light, and all parties agreed that it wouldn't be long before he was soiling his mitts in crime again. A true repeater was Peter O'Mara.

And speaking of the Irish, it was Joe who told Larry, Mary, and me the news about Johnny Ridge. He came into the kitchen with his sister, my wife, who was looking sparkly again.

"What are you two guys doing?" Mary asked. She seemed almost afraid of the answer.

"Just reminiscing," Larry said. "I was thanking him for saving my life."

"We were wondering about the notorious Johnny Ridge," I said.

"Funny," Joe said, "we just can't find a trace of him. I mean, not a trace. We interviewed some of the people in the neighborhood. They claimed that a big white limo pulled up to the Steingretz warehouse and a bunch of men left with Johnny. The limo had New York plates—"

"Ah, the Mob got him," said Larry.

"Apparently not," Joe corrected. "Several people remember seeing the flag of Ireland on the limo's rear window. I think the Westies, the Irish gang from the Big Apple, finally caught up with him." He dipped his cigarette ash and continued. "It's my personal guess that we'll never see Johnny Ridge again."

"Hey," I said, shrugging and holding up my palms, "these things happen—"

"Yes, they do," Joe said. "I, for one, wish they would happen more often."

"Amen," I said.

"What's wrong, partner, don't you feel good?" Mary asked, patting Larry on the shoulder. He was leaning over the table, rubbing the side of his head.

"My head's been hurting all morning. Guess maybe I need some air. . . ."

"Well, getting smacked on the head will do that," Joe said.

"Thing is, I got smacked on the other side."

"Why don't you go up to one of the guest rooms and lie down?" she said.

"Good idea," he said. But his voice didn't sound right. He rose from the table like a drunken man. He went into the dining room, dragging his left foot. I didn't like what I saw. Neither did Joe or Mary. Joe caught him and turned him around. I went up close and saw that the left side of his face had fallen. His left eye was unfocused and drooping.

"Let's sit him down in the living room, Joe," I said softly.

"I'm fwine, Dog. Fwine . . ." he mumbled. His chin was wet with drool, which was oozing from his drooped lip on the left side, just like a patient shot full of Novocain.

I could tell that Larry Carpenter, for one of those rare times in his life, was embarrassed. He shook us off and lurched into the living room, where he tried to point at the ceiling. Then he muttered something. He turned, and tried to call my name.

But he could not. He did a slow pirouette, and crumpled to the floor.

Mary and Joe and I were in the hallway of Concord's Emerson Hospital. Mary and I spend a lot of time there since we're both in medicine. Still, nothing prepares you for times like these. Sid Abelmann, neurologist, came over to the couch where we were sitting.

"No, it wasn't the blow to the head that caused it," he said. "It was a classic, massive CVA."

Mary dropped her head, wiping her eyes.

"Could you tell me what that stands for?" Joe asked.

"Cerebral vascular accident," said Sid. "A bursting of a major artery in the head caused by an aneurysm. You familiar with aneurysms?"

"Yeah. A weakening of the arterial wall, right?"

Abelmann nodded. "The wall weakens and swells out, like a balloon being inflated. As it swells out the wall becomes thin, fragile. Sometimes it bursts, causing massive stroke or, as in the case of your friend, sudden death."

We stared at the shiny linoleum for a while, unable to speak.

Larry Carpenter, the big, strong, handsome jock from Marshalltown, Iowa, with the mind of a genius and the healthiest, strongest body I had ever, ever seen, was dead.

"But he was so . . . healthy," I murmured. "So goddamned *healthy*."

"Doc, when I did the autopsy I was amazed. He had the body of a thirty-year-old man. Maybe twenty-five. Absolutely amazing specimen. But . . . nothing's perfect. He had a genetic flaw. In his otherwise excellent circulatory system, there was a major vessel with a weak wall. He had a ticking time bomb in his head, waiting to go off."

We left the hospital and walked through the big, chilly parking lot to the car. We were to meet Larry's parents at Logan Airport later in the day. They would fly back with his body for burial in the family plot on the farm. We got into the car. Joe was driving; Mary and I sat together in the back.

"He told me," Mary said, through her tears, "that he decided to go back to the farm and work there with his family. He—he's got all kinds of nieces and nephews now . . . and there was his mom and dad, and his grandfather even. . . ."

She broke down, couldn't continue.

"Did you love him?" I hadn't meant to ask the question; it just came out. Mary nodded her head, which was buried in her arms. "Of course I loved him, Charlie. The same way you and everybody else loved him. How could you not love Larry Carpenter?"

There were other questions I had been dying to ask her. I though about telling her the dirt on Larry from his New York hotshot days, but I recognized this as simply a disguised attempt at some kind of revenge. I suddenly came to know that none of the jealousy or proprietary love interest mattered anymore.

It just wasn't important. What was important was that Mary was back, and we would go on together.

I hugged her, and realized we were both crying.

Rick ⚓ Boyer